CLOWN TOWN

Books by Mick Herron

Slough House Thrillers

Slow Horses
Dead Lions
Real Tigers
Spook Street
London Rules
Joe Country
Slough House
Bad Actors

Slough House Standalones

Reconstruction
Nobody Walks
The List
The Drop
The Catch
Standing By The Wall
The Secret Hours

Zoë Boehm Thrillers

Down Cemetery Road
The Last Voice You Hear
Why We Die
Smoke And Whispers

Standalone Books

This Is What Happened
Dolphin Junction

MICK HERRON
CLOWN TOWN

BASKERVILLE
An imprint of JOHN MURRAY

First published in Great Britain in 2025 by Baskerville
An imprint of John Murray (Publishers)

1

Copyright © Mick Herron 2025

The right of Mick Herron to be identified as the Author of the Work has been asserted by him in accordance with the Copyright, Designs and Patents Act 1988.

Epigraph quotation from John le Carré, *A Private Spy: The Letters of John le Carré*, edited by Tim Cornwell (Viking, 2022), reprinted courtesy of John le Carré Ltd.

All rights reserved. No part of this publication may be reproduced, stored in a retrieval system, or transmitted, in any form or by any means without the prior written permission of the publisher, nor be otherwise circulated in any form of binding or cover other than that in which it is published and without a similar condition being imposed on the subsequent purchaser.

All characters in this publication are fictitious and any resemblance to real persons, living or dead, is purely coincidental.

A CIP catalogue record for this title is available from the British Library

Hardback ISBN 9781399800433
Exclusive Hardback ISBN 9781399823869
Trade Paperback ISBN 9781399800457
ebook ISBN 9781399800464

Typeset in Bembo Std by Palimpsest Book Production Ltd, Falkirk, Stirlingshire

Printed and bound in Great Britain by Clays Ltd, Elcograf S.p.A.

John Murray policy is to use papers that are natural, renewable and recyclable products and made from wood grown in sustainable forests. The logging and manufacturing processes are expected to conform to the environmental regulations of the country of origin.

Carmelite House
50 Victoria Embankment
London EC4Y 0DZ

www.johnmurraypress.co.uk

John Murray Press, part of Hodder & Stoughton Limited
An Hachette UK company

The authorised representative in the EEA is Hachette Ireland, 8 Castlecourt Centre, Dublin 15, D15 XTP3, Ireland (email: info@hbgi.ie)

For Jo

In a healthy democracy it is probably not desirable that the intelligence services be wholly efficient, or wholly admired.

John le Carré, *A Private Spy: The Letters of John le Carré*, edited by Tim Cornwell

So many things can break a head, it's quicker to list the things that can't. A banana. A cuttlefish. One of those balloons party entertainers twist into sausage dogs.

Front offside wheel of a Land Rover Defender, though. Definitely top half-dozen.

He had pictured this many times, witnessed it twice. It was a swift end with a slow build-up; the seemingly never-ending moments while the subject lay there, head between concrete and rubber. Bound, but not gagged – denying a man his last valedictions would be cruel. Also, there was the possibility of funny shit being said. But it was best to keep the arms and legs wrapped, and to hold the subject down, which meant allowing someone else to control the car . . . Which was fine. Up close and personal was how he liked to witness this: the full melon effect.

Ker-runkk.

Which didn't come near the reality, of course. Just letters and syllables.

Putting things into words was always a disappointment.

Being there, though. Getting so close to the subject, you were sharing his final moment. The concrete petrol-patched and gritty; the tyre smelling of – well, tyres, but also of everything else: of dog shit, blood and feathers; of the rain on the streets, and stinking tar; of beer and chemicals and fist fights after closing time, and the wrong sort of music choking up the jukebox. Everything cascading at once, round and round. And your eyes on the subject's, and his on the tyre, so close he'd be breathing in the tread, which was where evidence would be left, because no hose was going to clean that wheel. All that panic; the rat-trapped memories scuttling about; the fine detail stored in the brain's grey matter – it would all be crushed like salt, crammed into the criss-cross pattern of the rubber, and left there so everyone would know what traitors get: the revving of an engine after midnight, and a close-up of their own misdeeds. They get that last second where they're thinking this can't be happening, and they keep right on thinking that until it happens. And then they get whatever comes next, hellfire or radiance, or just the endless silence on the wrong side of a closed door.

Take your man Stephen Regan. Little gobshite, due a nutting if anyone was: dobbing in names, scratching the wrong backs. Never buying his round. Acted like a big man but he squealed like a kitten at the last, crying for Jesus and shitting himself on the damp concrete. It had been a duty to turn that sack into landfill. Also, there'd been the matter of seeing what it looked like, this manner of dying, and what's life about if not satisfying the itch? Though every itch came differently, which meant soon you were craving the next. Which was Bernard Docherty. If Stephen had been a crybaby, Bernard had been all balls and no forgiveness; a roaring boy who'd gone to his maker with both fists clenched. Aye, Bernard had been special, which was why they'd been friends once, back in their youth, stealing cars together the way they might have scrumped apples if they'd been different people, somewhere else. But it was all history now, either way.

It hadn't felt like it at the time. At the time he just did what needed doing, and when it was over he carried on with life, which wasn't the life those around him thought he lived. This was the nature of covert operations. He walked a road no one had the slightest wee notion was there, and everyone was scared of him – of course they were – but they hadn't a baldy who he really was; didn't know the secret of how to be him. Which was this simple – listen – it was this simple: all he needed was to know he had no limits. That was all. It wasn't the killing, it was the not caring afterwards. It was going home and sleeping dreamlessly and letting nothing put him off breakfast. And then heading out into the world, knowing men would do anything to avoid his eye, and women leave the room rather than be alone with him. Though that happened too, of course. The more they didn't want it to, the more he made sure it did.

For years he'd lived this way, and now it was over – the secret hours done and dusted – he lived a charmed life, because once you were part of the covert world it had to keep you safe. That was the sacred bargain he'd made. *Betray everything, and we'll take care of you.* The joke was, he'd never betrayed a thing – for that, you had to feel loyalty. But they'd kept him safe, because that was their job; hid him away in the north of England with all the leeway in the world. There was food and drink on the table, and money for girls when the urge overtook him; there were distant trains to mark the passing hours, and owls at night he could hear doing his job, snatching up the weak and frightened. There was a rhythm to it that would go on forever; round and round, round and round, and nothing goes round like a wheel; the night-time noises the same as always – the pitch and yaw of the gathering dark. Tonight, like most nights, he'd fallen asleep drunk in his favourite chair. Tonight, like no other, he'd come round to the smell of the tyre: rubber, dog shit, blood and feathers.

You always think this can't be happening, and you keep right on thinking that until it does.

'Any final observations?'

The last words Stephen Regan and Bernard Docherty had heard.

He'd tried to move his head, but couldn't; it was wedged between the rubber and the road. His arms and legs were bound, and there was someone sitting on him, holding him in place, the one exact person that could never be doing this, and that was the clue, the get-out clause, because that was the detail that proved this a dream. He was asleep in his chair, and when he woke he'd wipe sweat from his eyes and pour another drink. He could taste it now, its smoky absolution. He'd light another cigarette, and let the match burn down to his thumb, and the bright sharp pain would prove him awake, and this would be over.

It was the same old story: round and round.

He kept right on thinking it wasn't happening, and then it did.

Part One

Hands On

Part One

What you see when you see a blank page is much what you hear when you hear white noise; it's the early shifting into gear of something not ready to happen – an echo of what you feel when you walk past sights the eyes are blind to: bus queues, whitewashed shopfronts, adverts pasted to lamp posts, or a four-storey block on Aldersgate Street in the London borough of Finsbury, where the premises gracing the pavement include a Chinese restaurant with ever-lowered shutters and a faded menu taped to its window; a down-at-heel newsagent's where paletts of off-brand cola cans block the aisle; and, between the two, a weathered black door with a dusty milk bottle welded to its step, and an air of neglect suggesting that it never opens, never closes. Should anyone look up, they'd see the legend W. W. HENDERSON, SOLICITOR AND COMMISSIONER FOR OATHS lettered in gilt on a window; might notice, too, the way the establishments comprising this block are distinguished by the varying discoloration of their facades, like the spines of books on disregarded shelves. But books, unlike spies, can't be judged by their covers, and there's no call for the busy pedestrian to pass sentence on this cluster of properties, which sits in one of those marginal spaces cities collect, then dump on disregarded streets or in corners never seen in daylight. London teems with them. In each of its boroughs you'll pass such buildings, resisting examination; squat – windowless – drab – and walking by them is like remembering a rainy Sunday from the seventies, triggering something that's almost boredom, almost pain, but never quite either.

It's a momentary sensation, quickly shrugged off. Pedestrians shake their heads as if reminded of a minor chore they've been avoiding – unwashed laundry, an unread novel – and shuffle by, unaware that the anonymous structures in their wake are identified on maps, if at all, as 'Government building', or that they house the secret servants of the state; that behind their walls the sharpest minds available are gathering intel, fabricating data, forecasting outcomes and analysing threats, when they're not playing Candy Crush and watching the clock like the rest of us. There are armed guards behind unmarked doors; there are cameras scrutinising pavements, sentries studying screens. It's thrillingly like a thriller. Sometimes – rarely – it might only have happened once – there'll be action: a car will scream to a halt, a door will burst open. Figures in black with holstered weaponry will pour from the building and be whipped away. Later that same day you'll see nothing about this on the news, and will struggle to remember precisely where it happened; being certain only that, wherever it was, it wasn't Aldersgate Street, where little disrupts the daily round of not much going on. The Chinese restaurant remains closed for long stretches; the newsagent's enjoys limited custom. Meanwhile, the black front door between them remains shut, and anyone foolish enough to seek entry must do so via a back alley, where a yard in which wheelie bins lurk like corpulent hoodlums also reveals, like an admission of guilt, a door which sticks in all weathers, and once forced open betrays nothing more high-tech than a staircase, lined with wallpaper peeling in some places and already peeled in others. A single dim light bulb casts half-hearted shadows, and should you ascend the stairs you would find on each landing a pair of offices, neither inviting. The carpeting is scuffed; the skirting boards warp from the walls. There is evidence of murine activity, but even this seems ancient, as if the mice responsible packed their bags for pastures new years ago. If there were a lift, it would have long stopped working. If there were hope, it would have left. For if the murkiest of London's depths are where its spooks congregate, Slough House – this being the name of the Aldersgate Street residence – is the lowest of the low; an administrative oubliette where the benighted moulder in misery. Their careers are behind them, though not all have admitted it; their triumphs are black laughter in the dark. Their duties involve the kind of paperwork designed to drive those undertaking it mad; paperwork with no clear objective and no end in sight, designed by someone who abandoned a course in labyrinth design in favour of something more uplifting, like illustrating suicide notes. The light in the building leaks away through cracks and fissures, and the air is heavy with regret. To arrive here for work every morning is its own punishment, one made harsher by the awareness that it's self-inflicted – because all the inmates need do to win freedom is claim it. No one will stop them walking away. Indeed, there's every reason to suppose that such a move would meet with admiration, or at any rate, a sigh of relief. Some employees are more trouble than they're worth, and after various adventures involving poor choices, idiot politics, appalling weather and violent death, it's fair to say that the slow horses fall into this category. It's not that they wouldn't be missed, more that they'd happily be forgotten. Whatever space they occupy on the map might more usefully be rendered a blank white nothing.

Though of course, blank spaces on maps are an invitation to the curious, just as empty white pages are a temptation to those with nothing better to do. In the drabbest of buildings, home to the dullest of spooks, stories wait to be told. And in Slough House – on Aldersgate Street – in the London borough of Finsbury – this happens the way it has always happened. One syllable at a time.

'A *letter*?'

'Or an email.'

'That's twice as fucking bad. You want me to write an *email*?'

'Don't think of it as a punishment, Shirley. Think of it as smoothing things over.'

'Yeah, right. Have you met me?'

Catherine blinked, pursed her lips, and decided to leave it there.

'Just think about it. Please. That's all I'm asking.'

She turned and went up two flights of stairs, a Manila folder clutched to her chest: protective colouring. Not that she required this – in some moods, on some days, she could walk past anyone in Slough House bar Jackson Lamb, and they wouldn't know she was there – but it was an ingrained habit, having a visible alibi in case of interrogation: *Where are you going? What will you do when you get there?* It was the recovering addict's companion, Jiminy Cricket with powers of arrest.

These days Catherine Standish listened when her conscience twittered, even if the bad decisions it informed her of were being made by others. In Slough House, it was Shirley Dander picking up the slack. Shirley's weapons of self-destruction might not be those Catherine had chosen – a traditionalist, it had been alcohol all the way for her – but that was a detail, and Shirley was impressively single-minded when it came to creating havoc. Her recent attempt at detoxification, for instance, had resulted in mass casualties at the Service-run facility she'd been sent to, an episode Catherine had been hoping to resolve with her suggestion that Shirley write to the manager offering words of regret. Shirley, though, had other ideas, predominant among them being that everyone should fuck off and leave her alone. Detoxification, in Catherine's experience, had been about facing her demons. Sooner than wrestle with those, Shirley would prefer a televised cage-fighting event with everyone else's.

A simple letter. It couldn't have hurt.

Probably never know, though. She had enough experience of Shirley to be sure that, having drawn her line in the sand, she'd not let the sea itself wash it away without a fight.

Not for the first time, Catherine wondered what life might be like in a less obstreperous workplace; somewhere whose occupants were prepared to leaven their take with a little give. Pointless fretting about what-ifs, though. Here was where she was, and – Jiminy Cricket be damned – she had to let others work through their own issues. Shirley would do that or not; she'd make it or she wouldn't. Entering her office, the one space of tidy calm in the noisy mess that was Slough House, Catherine allowed herself to shrug off her self-appointed role as mother hen, and accept a reality she spent too much time avoiding: that it didn't matter whether Shirley made it, because there'd always be someone ready to crash and burn. The best Catherine could do was deal with the damage, not attempt its avoidance. Because damage was inevitable – her colleagues' impulsive behaviours made sure of that.

Though it had always been true, of course, that some of them were more aware of this than others.

Three little words.

Hot. Girl. Summer.

Roddy Ho was having one of those.

And don't talk to him about best-laid plans, dude, because all he'd hear was 'laid'. So mark your calendars: the next few months would play like self-replicating code – you knew what was coming but watched it happen anyway, because, shit, well, *because*. What more reason did you need?

Of course, you also helped the process along, because that was the difference between being a doer and being did.

So yesterday, Roddy had got himself inked.

Truth was, he'd been meaning to get a tat for ages. It was today's art form, and with a gallery like Roddy, it'd be criminal to leave the walls bare. Besides, it was a means of communication, and Roddy was all about the comms. Give a dude a tat, it saved you having to get to know him. One look gave you the lowdown, which in the Rodster's case came to three little words again: simple, classical, beautiful.

Put it another way, a hummingbird.

Which was the stuff of poetry, you didn't have to read poetry to know that. Hummingbirds were the Roddy Hos of the avian world: compact, powerful, super-intelligent, and capable of lifting many times their own weight. Some of these facts he'd already known, but the guy with the needle had told him the rest. Put all that together and you basically had Roddy's spiritual equal. Chicks were going to crap themselves, in a good way. Like he said, hot girl summer.

(True, he hadn't actually seen it yet – it was still under a bandage – but the needle guy had told him, 'That's the best damn art I've made in years', before binding it up and saying not to let air hit it for twenty-four hours.)

So Roddy was just awaiting the moment of reveal, which it was tempting to put on TikTok – grab himself some viral attention – but the squares at Regent's Park kept circulating memos about social media, and Roddy didn't need The Man on his back. Dude: he followed Kanye on X.

But tomorrow, or day after at the latest, he'd be open for viewing: roll up, take a seat, marvel.

He patted his arm, yelped, then looked round to make sure no one had heard, but he was alone in the office because Lech Wicinski had taken to squatting elsewhere, on account of *Ho's room smells of pizza*, and *I can hear Ho's music through his earphones*, and *Ho ran me over in his car*, which had been totes accidental. Anyway, it hadn't been a yelp, more an . . . involuntary spasm.

Outdone by his own reflexes. Some days, being Roddy was a struggle.

More gently he stroked his bandaged arm again. Hot girl summer or not, there were moments you had to be your own wingman, but that was okay.

If there was one thing Roddy was used to, it was being his own best friend.

Sentence me to life, thought Lech Wicinski. Or sentence me to death. But not to this halfway state, neither one thing nor the other . . .

Sunshine was falling on Aldersgate Street, and London was boasting its version of summer, with traffic noises for birdsong and brickwork for grassy meadow, though at least the digging up of nearby pavements to no discernible purpose was over. Inside, however, Slough House remained the dark side of Narnia: always winter, never Christmas. There was nothing to celebrate in Lech's workload, either. The task to which he was currently assigned — and 'currently' had a swirling momentum to it, an actual tidal force; 'currently' meant he'd been doing it for as long as he could remember — was one he'd inherited from River Cartwright, when River had been Novichoked just this side of death. The safe house folder. What Lech was doing was cross-checking electoral rolls and census results against council tax bills and utility usage, in an attempt to determine whether supposedly occupied properties were in fact standing empty, potential hideaways for bad actors. A task to which River had applied himself with all the vigour he'd displayed while lying in a coma.

Which — lying in a coma — was about the only thing that hadn't happened to Lech lately. Two years' bad luck had snatched away the life he'd planned and left his face looking like someone had played noughts and crosses on the same grid, repeatedly. Instead of living with his fiancée and looking forward to tomorrow, he was alone in a rented flat that swallowed most of his salary, and setting off each morning to Slough House. So maybe he should quit before he was any more behind, and find a new life to pursue. But his face might as well have gone ten rounds with a sewing machine, and the only reference he could expect from the Service would be one hinting at dodgy online activities – lies, but they struck deep, and no employer would look at him twice. There was a way out of all of this. He simply hadn't found it yet. Meanwhile, he'd been staring at the same screen for thirteen minutes, and when he tried to scroll down discovered it had frozen, and wouldn't let him leave. This might have been some kind of metaphor, but was more likely just fucked-up IT. Welcome to Slough House, he thought, and left Louisa's office, which he'd colonised to avoid Roddy Ho, and went to boil the kettle instead.

Second paragraph in, the story turned nasty.

> *Derek Flint, who but for the grace of God and the good sense of the electorate might have been sitting in the London Mayor's office today, is rumoured to be under investigation by the Met. The Diary understands that irregularities in Flint's election funding are the cause of this inconvenience.*
>
> *Flint's mentor, guru and eminence noir is, of course, Peter Judd, for whom accounting irregularities are hardly a novelty. Since the failure of his pet pol at the polls, Judd has been keeping a low profile. Long may it continue.*

Okay, not as nasty as Judd deserved, but still.

Diana Taverner binned the newspaper. Whoever was doing her lackeying – turnover was high – would retrieve it for recycling in due course; meanwhile, she'd enjoy Judd's failure for a moment, even if the bigger picture, the one in which he had her in a stranglehold, remained undimmed. Judd might no longer occupy a great office of state, and even he had presumably come to accept that he never would again, but his unwavering belief in his innate superiority would doubtless be unstymied by this latest setback. Despite – or perhaps because of – his lack of moral compass, he always found another direction to head in. As for Flint, Judd would already have consigned him to the swing bin of politics. Loyalty was a marketing ploy: if it didn't get you your tenth cup of coffee free, it was wasted effort.

And she had to admit a certain attraction to Judd's attitude, particularly when it came to glazing over reversals. She could do with a little of that herself. A career spent running Regent's Park was inevitably more stained by failure than garlanded by success, because when a threat to the nation was stubbed out few got to hear about it, but when a bomb went off on a weekday bus, the whole world held its breath. Besides, success could shade into its opposite. The victory that had meant most to her – an under-the-bridge act of vengeance, funded with Judd's help – had long since curdled, her triumph ruined by the discovery that Judd's PR firm was bankrolled by Chinese money, meaning that Taverner herself was left holding one end of a chain of firecrackers which, if lit, would not only burn down her career but leave the Park a charred smoky ruin. In some circumstances, the knowledge that applying a match would destroy both parties might be a source of comfort, but the concept of mutually assured destruction didn't apply when one of the two considered himself fireproof. The time would come when Judd would act. He didn't even have to see advantage for himself in the prospect. He simply had to be bored.

That knowledge buzzed in Taverner's background day and night. Like having a neighbour with a floorboard sander and no boundaries.

Intermittently, though, since a recent email, the buzzing had faltered, as if she were either learning to live with it or starting to glimpse a way of pulling its plug.

The email – delivered to her personal address, known by few – had been anonymous, but not for long: while the principal reason for her being its recipient was that she was First Desk, its sender had evidently overlooked the fact that this gave her certain resources, and his attempts to cover his tracks gave little bother to Taverner's IT crew. The attachment that came with it, though, she had kept to herself, and listening repeatedly to its scratchy recording of mostly forgotten voices, she had reflected on how often the past could blow a hole through a squeaky-clean future. The new government had set out its stall in what it claimed was a bright fresh marketplace, but the same sad song was on the jukebox. *Meet the new gang. Same as the old gang.*

On the desk in front of her lay a thin sheaf of papers: personnel files, printed from an unused workstation, using a temporary password that expired at midnight, its usage report deleted. It wouldn't be impossible to determine that Taverner herself had accessed the material, but it would take active investigation, and it would be a foolhardy underling that attempted anything of that sort. Four of the files were labelled INACTIVE, but the fifth, though not the slenderest, was relatively recent: River Cartwright, one of Jackson Lamb's slow horses. Already she was having doubts about this choice, but a new detail, appended since Cartwright's medical misadventure, offered hope. A lesson of leadership she'd long since absorbed: always read between the lines. Having done that, she dealt with the paperwork in the time-honoured way. There was constant chatter, in all lines of business, about what was truly the key to success: integrity, foresight, the ability to improvise. What nobody mentioned was a shredder.

Her phone chirruped with upcoming appointments: a meeting with the Limitations Committee, and an afternoon session with the Home Secretary – the daily round continued; she was calm, she was in control. It wasn't so long since she'd contrived to have her bodyguard carry out an assassination, and she'd maintained that same air then, too. No one could know about the buzzing in her background, or guess the lengths she would go to silence it. And whatever way she found to do so, no trail would lead back to her.

'Paging River Cartwright.'

'. . . Huh?'

'Hate to disturb you. But I was wondering what planet you're on.'

River blinked. Earth. He was on earth.

Not something he took for granted lately. When he'd put his hand on that toxic-swabbed door handle – how long ago was that? – he'd nearly crossed a graver threshold too, and joined his grandfather in the afterlife; not the one where you sat bathed in heavenly light while a choir hummed ecstasies in the background, but the one where you were buried in cold hard ground and that was that. In earth, rather than on it. A future that had brushed him on its way past, and would one day make good on its promise. This time, though, River's death had been temporary: an induced coma lasting nine days, during which, he'd been told, his body had been a battleground on which medical science had slugged it out with the mad bastard variety, and thankfully won, though not without cost. He had a lost winter behind him; months off work, and an uphill struggle regaining his strength, not to mention his powers of concentration.

He was here, in the kitchen of the flat he shared with Sid Baker. They were eating breakfast, or that was the theory. An unfinished slice of toast sat on his plate. Some mornings, he had no appetite.

'. . . Sorry.'

'Interesting email?'

His phone was in his hands, true, and that was what had started his spiralling descent. But it took a moment to gather himself. 'From that researcher. The one in Oxford?'

'Who's sorting out your grandfather's library.' Sid knew all about the O.B.'s library; she'd spent weeks living there, hiding from her own close encounter with death, nesting on cushions like a child in a storybook.

'She's been looking at that video I made—'

'The one of me sleeping.'

'The one of my grandfather's study, yeah—'

'Which was mostly me sleeping.'

'Which makes it sound way creepier than it was, which was just me filming my grandfather's bookshelves, and happening to include a moment of you sleeping. And she's been using it as a . . . catalogue, to make sure none of the books got lost in transit. And so she can shelve them in the same order he did.'

'That matters?'

'Does to her. Or that's what she's doing anyway, in case it mattered to him.'

Which it might have done. True, it was a fantastical notion, straight out of Dan Brown or *Scooby-Doo*, but on the other hand, the O.B. – who, with his late wife, Rose, had raised River – had been Regent's Park's strategist par excellence, and had spent his adult life steering the ship of state security through historically choppy waters. He'd never been First Desk, but he'd stood at the elbow of several who had been, pointing out changes in the weather. Something of a teddy bear, those who didn't know him had liked to think; a reliable sounding board, but lacking the edge that might have taken him to the highest office. Others, more mathematically inclined, counted instead the years he'd spent as trusted adviser, coming up with a figure far higher than most First Desks managed, First Desks being notoriously vulnerable to the workings of events, not to mention the machinations of their subordinates. Besides, teddy bears weren't the companionable pushovers they were taken to be. It wasn't fun and games they planned at their picnics; it was long-term strategies for consolidating positions of influence. Nor were their objectives achieved wearing furry mittens. In recent years River had come to understand that his grandfather's hands, which he'd first seen tending his flower beds, had been soiled by more than garden waste.

Meanwhile, River was still looking at the email from Oxford. 'Anyway, apparently there's a book missing.'

'Stop the bloody clocks! A missing book? Shall I call the Park?'

'You can laugh—'

'Am doing.'

'And I'd join in, if that's all it was, a missing book. Could have been lost when the study was packed up, or been put in the wrong box and sent into storage with the furniture, or, I dunno, a hundred other things. It was a bit chaotic, I imagine.'

Imagination being all he had to go on, having been comatose at the time.

'So it's not just missing,' said Sid. 'That's what you're saying.'

'Yeah,' said River. 'Apparently this book, which is there on the film I took?'

'It's a rare and valuable volume?'

'No,' said River. 'It doesn't exist.'

A chapter of accidents, that was the phrase. A series of unfortunate events.

If Shirley were a TV show – which obviously she was not – but if she were, now would be a good moment for a *Previously on Shirley Dander* segment.

Decking a harasser at Regent's Park; exile to Slough House; Marcus. Running up the stairs at the Needle – that had been a killer. The gunfight out west, at the underground complex, and Marcus again, this time dead. The penguin assassins' UK tour, and that moment in the church when she thought she'd be crushed to death (didn't happen). Wales in the snow, and J. K. Coe lying under a tree like a discarded Christmas decoration. Hunting stalkers at Old Street roundabout; thumping a bus on Wimbledon Common. A week in the San, supposed to be a time of calm reflection, ending with a battle royale, a road trip with a former First Desk and a showdown in a car wash with a helmeted hooligan. It would be fair to say there were both ups and downs in that lot. Though ups were getting harder to locate, and more expensive to maintain. And the downs – best not to dwell on the downs.

All of which left her here, in her office, having just been read, yeah, chapter again: chapter and verse by St Catherine of Standish, patron saint of addicts. Who had herself graduated from the San with full honours, and obviously regarded Shirley's truncated experience of its rehabilitative wonders as some kind of moral failure, so fuck that. What she really needed, leaving aside all the bollocks inherent in what others thought she needed, was to be left alone for a while; a little solitude (the odd pick-up apart) and some clean living, with maybe the odd toot for variety's sake – it was relaxation, not canonisation, she wanted. A few weeks of that and she'd be ready for anything Slough House could throw at her, even including her current task, which involved an online trawl for youths exhibiting antisocial tendencies in specific postcodes, these centring on mosques identified by Regent's Park as being 'of special interest' . . . *Well,* she could imagine Lamb saying. *You have to start somewhere.* He had the notion, or pretended to, that it ought to be possible to identify those undergoing radicalisation not so much by their youthful careers of hooliganism as by those same careers being abruptly curtailed. Redemption, in Lamb's world, was less likely than the chances of being recruited by the forces of evil, forces which would prefer you kept your nose clean for the moment.

None of which had any relevance to her own situation, obviously.

She leaned forward and tapped at her keyboard to dispel the screensaver, but her computer had switched itself off, its usual response to being ignored for more than five minutes. She could boot up again, but on the other hand it was less than two hours to lunchtime, so she might as well just sit it out. *Coming up next on Shirley Dander:* fuck all. She leaned back in her chair, closed her eyes, and wondered if she were the only one in the building who had no real plans at all. Maybe. Maybe not. Time would tell. It usually did.

Book restaurant.

The memo was fixed to her monitor's upper corner, but she'd avoided acting on it yet.

Things Louisa had accomplished so far this morning included, pretty much exclusively, opening her window, through which now drifted the sounds of ordinary things, all of which had happened a million times before. Buses wheezed, traffic snorted, an airliner bulldozed its way through a temporarily cloudless sky. White noise, leaving no trace behind. On her windowsill lay two dead bluebottles, half a moth, and the scattered debris of city dirt, the kind that accumulates unseen, until it's suddenly a landfill site. Underfoot was threadbare carpeting; on the walls a dull shade of paint that had long given up its proprietorial singularity – November Frost? Autumn Lawn? – in favour of a universal beige. The space between felt like it was held prisoner by the 1970s. The shelving on the walls remained there largely through inertia, and the mismatched desks – her own kept level thanks to a folded piece of cardboard, the other with a surface scarred by the penknife lacerations of a previous bored resident, and both with drawers that didn't open easily, or wouldn't shut – might have started life in a more salubrious corner of the civil service, but were now a decade or more past their useful working life. Not unlike – but she held off completing the thought.

That other desk, the scarred and battle-worn one, had been commandeered by Lech Wicinski lately, but had belonged to Min Harper once, what felt like fifteen years ago, and she still imagined him there occasionally, balanced on its edge or standing by the window, like an overgrown schoolboy gazing at the playing fields. Min Min Min. Oddly, he spoke to her now.

You going to make that reservation?

She hadn't decided yet.

What's to decide? An old friend seeking your company? Not even a date, as such. Just . . . friendship.

Maybe. Maybe not.

Min wasn't there, of course, and even if he had been was unlikely to offer useful commentary on her options. He'd not been the most reliable source of advice while alive. It was unlikely he'd improved in that area since his death.

Still, he wasn't shutting up.

And it's not as if you're doing anything else this evening.

Yeah, thanks for that.

She made a pistol of her fingers, shot Min's ghost dead, and felt bad.

But he was right, she had nothing else on. And it shouldn't be a big decision, an evening out with an old . . . friend? Barely. They'd had someone in common, no more, and she wasn't sure there was a word for that. For him to reach out after all this time suggested he was after more than a nostalgic evening. *Choose wherever. My treat.* His words, so he'd obviously come up in the world. Whereas she remained on the same page.

Perhaps that was why she was havering. An evening spent basking in someone else's progress: did that sound like fun? Hearing about professional success, worldly advancement, while she looked forward to turning up here tomorrow, to an unswept windowsill? Except none of that sounded like Devon Welles, whom she'd known when he was one of the Park's Dogs; a friend to Emma Flyte – a good character reference – who'd left the Park after she'd been fired, another indicator of decency. Not the type to spend an evening boasting to a former colleague. No: he was after something else. And it was possible this might turn out to her advantage.

He's your ticket out of here.

Which wasn't Min speaking, but might as well have been, being about as grounded in reality as he ever got. What did Welles have to offer her? And why was she overthinking this, anyway? Pick up the phone, book a restaurant. It wasn't rocket science.

The Post-it note on which she'd scribbled the reminder fluttered for no obvious reason, and she thought *goose on my grave*. From overhead came a wheezing sound, which might be Slough House expressing its weariness, or Lamb expressing himself. Either way, it was not a reminder of how delightful these precincts were. The days were stacking up like dirty dishes, and each had been packed with moments like this, the kind where you look round and wonder how you got here, and why you haven't left yet. For the longest time, she'd thought – like every slow horse before her – that this was a temporary glitch; that Regent's Park would take her back once she'd proved herself. She no longer believed that. So why was she still here? It wasn't the decor. It certainly wasn't the company. And no, she wasn't doing anything tonight. She plucked the Post-it from her monitor, screwed it up and tossed it into the wastebasket, nearly.

Then took her phone out and began googling restaurants.

'On the shelf, Ashley. On. The. Shelf. You want to spend your whole life there?'

'Yes, Mum.'

'Because you're going about it the right way.'

'I said— Never mind.'

Because it didn't matter what she said: once The Lecture began, it would keep right on happening until it was over. Estimates varied, but Ashley Khan figured she could write off the next ten minutes. Just keep her phone jammed to her ear, and if anyone appeared, pretend she was busy. In Slough House, pretending to be working was so much part of the agenda, it counted as working.

None of which she could interrupt her mother to explain, because apart from not knowing Ash had been booted out of Regent's Park and exiled to this shitheap, she also didn't know Ash had been at Regent's Park in the first place, and if she had would have assumed it was the offices of the security firm Ash claimed to be employed by, rather than the headquarters of the UK's intelligence service. All of which would require more than a ten-minute call to set right. Simpler all round to keep listening to The Lecture, with its familiar arc in which her mother went grandchildless to the grave while she – Ash – wasted the best years of her life. Meanwhile, in front of her, was her ongoing project. *This will keep you out of mischief.* A pile of paper eight inches thick, and yes, don't even bother: *paper?* It was out of some old Harry Potter book. When Catherine had carried it in, Ash had just stared, not sure whether she was supposed to laugh or cry. I mean, this is *data?* It needed someone walking in front of it waving a red flag. You could literally have an accident moving it from one place to another. What was saddest was, Catherine spent all day every day doing precisely that. The woman had no idea. Ash should introduce her to her mother.

Who was now telling her, 'I know it's not fashionable to say so, but you do have to give some thought to what boys are interested in.'

Actually, thought Ash – speaking from experience, plus a lifetime spent online – what boys were interested in, what *men* were after, was the same two things, one being blow jobs and the other an audience, to fill the time between blow jobs. If she really wanted to send her mother grandchildless to the grave, delivering that information would get the job done without Ash leaving her chair. She'd as soon learn that Ash never went on a first date without packing a three-inch screwdriver, just in case.

Leaving her chair wouldn't be happening soon, either. The paper wasn't just to make the office look like a medieval crime scene, it was research material, the top half-inch being a list of night schools, a phrase used here in its loosest possible sense. From colleges of further education through private tutorial services to voluntarily run classes in rooms over garages, what these places had in common was that all offered courses – some leading to certificates recognised by national education bodies; others just providing a grounding in practical knowledge – in basic electronics, or chemistry, or – and here we were back in Slough House, and one of those team meetings in which Jackson Lamb dispensed his earthly wisdom – 'Your general basic lesson in how to build a bomb.'

'Seriously?'

'What, you think people make bombs without learning how first? Like it's bungee jumping, or writing a novel?'

She didn't think that. She just didn't suppose bomb-making was a night-school course.

After the half-inch of alternative educational outlets came seven and a half further inches: more lists, often incomplete, of pupils attending these courses, along with basic identifiers – addresses, NI numbers; where pertinent, criminal records.

'And I'm supposed to what, find you some trainee terrorists?'

'Best-case scenario, yeah. But worst-case, you'll bore your tits off and go find some other line of work. So that's a win-win.'

She had looked around. Louisa was nearest. 'Did he just objectify me?'

'Wasn't listening. But probably, yeah.'

The pile of paper had grown no thinner since that conversation. Ash still wasn't sure how many names it contained, but had a shrewd idea of how long it would take to verify the intentions of all concerned. A nillion years, this being her childhood quantification of, basically, eternity.

Meanwhile, her mother was reaching her showstopper – the part where she told Ash she didn't want to interfere, and Ash responded, as she mostly did, by refraining from asking her, if she ever *did* want to interfere, to make sure she let Ash know in advance, because short of her turning up in a tank, it was unlikely Ash would notice a difference.

'I only hope this has been of some use to you, Ashley.'

'So do I, Mum.'

'You'll thank me one day.'

Roll on, thought Ash.

She put her phone down. The task in front of her hadn't gone anywhere; the office still smelled beige. Nominally she shared with River Cartwright, but he had yet to return from his long-distance skive, as Shirley put it, so it had been Ash's alone since her arrival. A small mercy buried within the bigger punishment. But it meant the smell, the damp, the creaking noises in the corners were also hers alone. For a while she sat with her face buried in her hands, her mind playing out various alternative futures. Then she sat up straight, brushed her hair from her eyes, checked her phone, and carried on doing nothing.

Works have recently been completed on Aldersgate Street. The digging up of pavements is done, the re-laying of slabs complete, and if the end result is that the walkways are a little more crooked – a little less safe – this is one more argument for leaving things as they are for fear of making them worse. But while this is a lesson the slow horses might be wise to heed, if they were wise they would not be slow horses, and even those whose windows look down on the recently patched pavements – and who have spent hours moaning about the workers' noise – now gaze down at the sight of pedestrians tripping on unaligned edges without reaching that conclusion. And this, perhaps, is another lesson: that those very things which ought to be plain and obvious are often among those most difficult to read. But perhaps this depends on the reader.

For now, though, the only reading being done is the slow, excruciatingly dull assessment of columns of figures and lists of names, of spreadsheets teeming with cells and sparklines, of ancient files in prehistoric formats, whose previous readers – long since dust themselves – have amended and footnoted with marginal squiggles in ink that time has turned purple. If there are stories here, they're crying out not to be told; would much rather go the way of lost myths, and be allowed to perish silently on pages that remain uncut. But things leak out regardless. Old legends are exhumed, to test their durability against the modern world. This does not always result in a happy ending.

Endings of any kind, though, remain distant for the moment. Behind their doors, behind their windows, the slow horses plough on with their tasks, and if the world wanders past them regardless, this can be counted as success. For spies, unlike books, can be judged by their covers, and this outward show of ordinary boredom is their saving grace; as long as it is maintained, these grunts of the intelligence service are ignorable and unlikely to come to serious harm. But any attempt to shake off anonymity will leave them at the mercy of those lurking on Spook Street's borders – its scarecrows and hangmen – its hawks and its hoods – and such mercy is frequently withheld. This has happened before. There are only so many times it can happen again, but this is one of them.

It starts like this.

THE SKY WAS as blue as an egg, provided the egg was blue. The fields were as yellow as cars. The escarpment whose exit revealed the county spread out like, like, like – he wanted to say *a dartboard* – had felt, as he'd driven through it, part of a child's game; a cavern crafted from cardboard, say, through which a small vehicle could be pushed, and from which its emergence would always be a surprise and a delight.

It would be fair to say that River Cartwright was in an uplift mood.

He was heading to Oxford the same day the Brains Trust was convening there in the safe house, though he couldn't know that at the time. Of more interest to him was the simple state of being alive, and taking in the associated pleasures. Breathing, for example. Breathing was not something he'd take for granted again, or that was how it felt most mornings, when he woke and found himself doing just that: drawing in air, expelling it, his lungs doing their job unassisted, in a room empty of equipment designed to cope with the possibility that they might not. Waking up next to Sid, too. His new life was full of good things; moments he'd never call miracles, because once you did that you were hostage to a belief system, but still: pretty good. He'd been dead, or next worst thing; had spent nine days in a coma. Sid had also been dead; dead to him, and to everyone else, for longer than seemed feasible – and now they were back, and sharing this new chapter together. It shouldn't surprise anyone, least of all himself, that he had these passages of joy to contend with. Just so long as he kept them quiet.

Good things weren't the whole story, of course. There was still the occasional convulsion to deal with, meaning make sure nobody noticed – as far as the world was concerned, he was one hundred per cent fit. 'The world' meant Regent's Park. It was just a matter of time, then, before the powers above – before Doctor Desk, the Park's chief medical officer – passed him ready for the workplace. Whether anyone was ever really ready for Slough House was one for philosophers rather than medics, but even so, what mattered was his physical condition, and occasional convulsion aside, he was fit, he was ready. The rest was paperwork. And having done all he could to chivvy that along, he was just killing time until the documents were signed and stamped.

Which was why he was in the car this morning: because movement beat staying still; it whisked up time, sent it spinning faster. River was heading to Oxford, to discuss the matter of his grandfather's library, and the book it had contained which had gone missing before turning out not to exist; a puzzle which would either yield to straightforward explanation or wouldn't. It didn't much matter either way. But addressing it would keep him busy, and deposit him that much nearer his own actual life, which this time round he would handle with wisdom and finesse, as befitted someone who'd been given a second chance. Slough House was for keeps: the slow horses had heard that so often they'd been beaten hopeless by the knowledge, and barely questioned it any more. But River knew what he was capable of, and while it was true he'd had troubles with Diana Taverner, she was far too canny an operator to deprive herself of a talented agent out of what, pique? They could have a sit-down, or a stand-up. A face-to-face. However it came about, he'd make it work. The sky was still blue; the fields shading to green. As he drove towards Oxford, still uplit, he might not have a song in his heart but he had a radio that worked, and was playing 'Solsbury Hill'. That would do for now.

A low-slung waddling creature in a cherry-coloured waistcoat was leading a middle-aged couple along the Barbican terrace, pausing every few yards to catalogue recent canine activity, but there was no one else in sight. Way overhead, a sliding noise was a window opening, too high to be a worry, but she glanced upwards anyway because this was the world Diana Taverner moved in, requiring alertness to the possibility of someone watching, of records being kept. Never was the only right moment to drop your guard.

The bricks – this was the Barbican; there were bricks everywhere, except where there was concrete or glass – were shining in the noonday sun, and weeds were flowering in crevices, adding yellow and purple notes to faded greys and reds. The sky was largely blue, barring a contrail growing puffier by the moment, like cotton wool dropped in water. The hands on her watch overlapped, precisely. The bulky shape approaching was her appointment. Late.

He was wheezing, and overdressed for the weather; his familiar greasy overcoat flapping around his thighs. Hardly out of character, but still: she found herself arching her eyebrows, shaking her head. 'My god, Jackson. Do you never think about losing weight?'

'Yeah, once a week I take an extra big dump.' He patted his stomach. 'Keeps me in trim.'

'It keeps you in heart attack territory.'

'Potato potahto. What do you want?'

'Never been one for small talk, have you?'

'Nice weather, seen the news, up the Arsenal,' said Lamb. 'Small talk's just bullshit leaving the body.'

There was a bench next to one of the concrete flower beds that were there to add insult to injury. Whether by design or good fortune, it sat permanently in shade cast by one or other of the overhead towers, whose continuing existence arguably amounted to a victory for terrorism. When Lamb lowered himself onto one side Diana half expected it to tilt, but hadn't taken into account that it was bolted to the ground. She sat, placing her tote bag between them, and when she looked up he was holding a lit cigarette, which he hadn't a moment ago. Lamb could peel an orange one-handed in his pocket, if doing so would save him having to offer you a segment.

She said, 'There's a rumour those things are bad for you.'

'And there's statistics prove healthy people die. What's your point?'

'Forget I spoke.'

'Already done.' He inhaled, exhaled, admired his own prowess, then said, 'You look like you found a condom in your cornflakes, Diana. You going to tell me about it or just piss off back to the Park?'

Taverner was a great believer in what mediators call 'deep listening', whereby the person she was talking to, regardless of how violently they disapproved of what she was saying, would shut up and agree with her. Lamb was never likely to fill this role, but here and now – as regrettably so often – there was no one else to unload on. Or at least, no one she'd not have to fire afterwards. 'It's the Park that's the problem.'

'You're looking for somewhere new to bunk up, you can share with Ho. Though I warn you, he's not the most refined of characters.' Lamb shook his head sadly, then farted.

'Finished?'

'Floor's yours.'

'So I get a call from HR notifying me of a grievance being taken out. This is one of my favourite things, obviously, what with my being not very busy keeping the nation safe from terror attacks and stuff like that.'

'Someone's made a complaint about you?' Lamb shrugged. 'Find out who and either slap them silly or buy them a box of Smarties. You really need me to tell you that?'

'Except the grievance process allows for anonymity, so no one making their whines heard has to worry about getting wedgied in the changing rooms.'

'You'll have to forgive me,' he said, dropping into his plummiest voice. 'Not having attended public school, I've no idea how these rituals work.'

'Yes, you were too busy having knife fights, I'm sure. Anyway – *anyway*. The nub of the matter is, it seems I have caused offence, owing to a, ah, *threatening* turn of phrase I habitually employ. The poor darling "doesn't feel *safe*", apparently. Is worried I might be planning some kind of genocidal onslaught on the gender-fluid, on account of my tendency to refer to the boys and girls on the hub as precisely that, the boys and girls, instead of adopting some less heteronormative terminology more respectful of the range of sex-based identities that a diverse cohort might be expected to embrace.' She paused for breath. 'Or something.'

Lamb said, 'Intolerable.'

'Isn't it?'

'I meant you.'

'Of course you did.' She held a hand out, palm flat, and with a sigh suggesting he'd just been informed of the death of a loved one, Lamb fished a cigarette from somewhere, presented it to her, and lit it. 'Boys and girls,' she said. 'That's what they've always been called, they have always been called the boys and girls, regardless of their age, their gender identity or their sexual leanings. I don't care about any of those things, why would I? So long as they do their job, that's all I ask. Do their job, and not bother me with their millennial whimpering.'

'It's touching, the bond you share with them,' said Lamb. 'I hardly know whether to cry or tug myself off.'

'And the thanks I get, the respect they should be showing, instead of that I'm accused of acting like some . . . heartless bitch.'

'Imagine.' Lamb dropped his smoked-out cigarette, and performed his social duty by grinding it underfoot and leaving it where it lay. 'Well, I'm glad you've got that off your chest. Anything else bothering you, you can always reach my voice-mail, which I make a point of deleting unlistened to.' He stood. 'Saves us both time.'

'Sit down and shut up. I'm not finished.'

He sat. 'Are you really coming to me for advice on this, Diana? Because joking aside, your next move's obvious. Admit nothing, deny everything, and make counter-accusations. Sound familiar? It's the Number Ten playbook.'

'It's the schoolyard playbook, to be fair. And while I appreciate the input, no, I don't need your advice. I'm not dumb enough to think you give a flying dog-dump about grievance procedures, but there's an important difference between us, which is that I'm not you. But the way things have been lately I'm under siege, which means any threat to my position, no matter how trivial, might have consequences. And while I'm famously tolerant of all manner of outrageous impositions, if there's one thing I will not do, it's suffer fucking consequences.'

'You want this whiner found.'

'Your boy Ho should be able to do it in his sleep.'

'Might interfere with his sex life. Which also only happens in his—'

'You'll do this for me?'

'Provided it doesn't inconvenience me in the slightest, sure. What are friends for?'

'Thank you.'

'Oh, please, you'll set me off again. Can I go now?'

'There's something else. You're not going to like it.'

'That's a broad spectrum.'

'Cartwright won't be coming back.'

Lamb didn't so much as twitch. 'And this upsets me how?'

'Because much as you like to pretend otherwise, you enjoy having him around.'

'Well, I'm not saying he won't leave a gap. He goes, I might have to hire a living statue, or an influencer. You know, someone with no discernible talent beyond a misplaced sense of importance.' He was holding another cigarette now, and put it in his mouth unlit. 'But it's hardly a surprise. The way I remember it, the whole point of Slough House was to get the idiots off the books.'

'And the way it turned out, we dispatch them to you and they take root.'

'I can think of a few got weeded out.'

'Yes, your mortality rate's distressing, given your remit's paperwork-based. Most offices in the country, you could expect raised eyebrows about that. You're lucky we're still a secret service. There was such a thing as OfSpook, you'd be in special measures.'

'Always been special,' said Lamb. 'So what's Cartwright's problem, anyway? Apart from being Cartwright, I mean.'

'He won't pass the medical.'

'They've introduced an IQ test?'

'He suffered a toxic shock, Jackson. From a nerve agent whose long-term effects remain unknown. We keep him in employment, we could be looking at God-knows-what liability in the future, so the sensible route is to get shot of him now. With all due sensitivity, obviously.'

'Well, yeah. Kid fucking gloves.'

'But he might need reminding that when he found himself rattling death's doorknob, he was on what the lawyers call a frolic of his own. So if he's expecting a disability pay-off, he's in for a disappointment.'

'He's a slow horse. Disappointment's his factory setting.'

'You're taking this suspiciously well.'

'Cartwright's just part of the furniture,' said Lamb. 'And I hate furniture. Losing him won't keep me up at night.'

'Does anything?'

'Viagra.'

'Sorry I asked.' She stood. 'Well. Back to civilisation.'

'Just so I've got this straight,' said Lamb. 'You want my boy Ho to work out who made this complaint against you so you can piss on their chips while saving your career. And at the same time you're crapping on one of my crew just to save the Park some workman's comp down the line. Pardon me if I'm being obtuse, but what's in it for me?'

She reached into her tote bag and pulled out a bottle wrapped in green tissue paper.

'Deal.'

'Something else you should know,' she said.

'For fuck's sake, what is this, *Columbo*? What now?'

'An enquiry came into my office. About another one of yours.'

'Let me guess. Standish has been swiped on Tinder, and someone's checking her sex tree.' Lamb made a vague hand gesture, as if offering Taverner the keys to his kingdom. 'Just hand over the employee list for the 1990s, that should cover it.'

'Not Standish. Louisa.'

'Guy? I imagine she's been through Tinder twice by now. Surprised she has time to show up in the office, to be honest.'

'Well, that might not be on the cards much longer either. She's being headhunted.'

'Really?' Lamb looked doubtful. 'If someone's collecting heads, I'd have thought Dander's was a better bet. Make a good bowling ball.'

'Maybe you could add that to her employee profile. That aside, remember Devon Welles? He was Flyte's second.'

Emma Flyte: former Head Dog. Resting now in peace.

'I remember someone called Dorset. Or was it Rutland?'

'That's him. He's in the private sector now, doing very happily for himself. And recruiting former comrades, it would seem.'

'Fairly indiscriminately, too.'

'Harsh. I've often thought she's the best of your lot.'

'It's comparative, isn't it? Like, you're the best First Desk since Charles Partner. And he was working for the fucking Russians.'

'I nearly had her brought back last year.'

'To the Park?'

'It felt like she'd done her time.'

'No one ever goes back to the Park.'

'I know. Imagine how much it would have pissed the rest of your crew off.'

'You do realise, if I tell her that now, it'll fuck with her head.'

'Of course.'

'All this and Talisker too,' said Lamb. 'Must be my birthday.'

And he shambled off in the opposite direction to that from which he'd arrived, which might have been spook instinct kicking in – the one that tells you never to take the same route twice – or might have been because this was the Barbican, and remembering how you got anywhere was an upstairs struggle at the best of times.

Diana, meanwhile, headed for street level and the nearest cab, replaying the encounter as she did so. Lamb distrusted most stratagems: throw him a bone, he'd have been asking where it came from before it hit the ground. Throw three bones, though, and even he might just accept you'd been to the butcher's and leave it at that. No guarantees, but you did what you could. Having done that much, she headed back to the Park.

The college was on the Woodstock Road, one of the two main thoroughfares leading northwards out of the city. Finding it was simple, thanks to Google Maps – which gave River pause; a spooks' nursery should surely be, what, cloaked? – but parking was a challenge. Welcome to Oxford. After circling his target a while, he wound up on a side street five minutes' walk away, then, as long as he had the app open, he checked on Slough House, and Jesus: that was there too! He looked forward to mentioning this to Lamb. He'd have to explain what Google Maps was, and possibly also the existence of social media, but some punchlines take longer to drop than others. He was whistling as he headed for the college, crossed the main road and called at the porters' lodge. There, waiting for Erin Grey to be summoned, he gazed at buildings old and new, and reflected that this route he'd never taken had its charms, even if those who emerged at the other end frequently lacked them. Or maybe he was exaggerating. Sid, after all, was an Oxford graduate, and look at her. Not that she'd attended the Spooks' College.

'Mr Cartwright.'

Erin Grey had arrived while he'd been gathering wool.

Until now, their conversations had taken place on the phone, and this was his first chance to see what she looked like, or would have been, if Sid hadn't cyberstalked her. 'I'm not sending you on a blind date without knowing what the enemy looks like,' she'd said.

'This is not a blind date. And not with an enemy.'

'I'll be the judge of that.'

To be fair, she had a point.

Grey was a redhead, somewhere around thirty, somewhere around five eight, and there were doubtless other numbers he could have called upon had he been inclined. The hair, evidently abundant when unleashed, was held in check by a cream-coloured Tilley hat, a brand River's grandmother, Rose, had favoured for protection from the sun. Erin also had pale blue eyes and wore jeans and a white blouse, which as far as it went was pretty much a match for what he was wearing himself. In other circumstances this might have been a starting pistol for entry-level flirtation, but River still had that conversation with Sid replaying in his mind.

'Not my type,' he'd said, carefully not looking at the picture she'd unearthed. Did you 'unearth' things online? Probably not the moment to set that hare running.

'You don't have a type,' she told him. 'Up till now, you've barely had a look-in.'

'Well, all I'm going to look at in Oxford is the old man's book collection. And find out about this non-existent volume Ms Grey has identified.'

'Ms Grey!' This delighted Sid, for some reason.

It could still be, after all these months, utterly discombobulating how quickly a conversation could metastasize. It was like trying to catch soap in a Jacuzzi while drunk, and also maybe handcuffed to something.

'Sid? I don't care what she looks like, which incidentally isn't as hot as you seem to think. I have no interest in her other than as the, what, the curator of Grandad's library. Okay?'

'Said the spy.'

'Well what's that got to do with—?'

'Spies lie. They betray. It's what they do.'

He knew that. He just wouldn't have set it out quite so uncompromisingly, in this particular context.

Meanwhile, Erin was waiting for him to respond, so he said, 'River, please.'

They shook hands and she spoke some more, introductory stuff about the college, and had he been here before, and the library was this way. He had already told her this would be his first visit, but sometimes you had to say things twice – it was normal human interaction. They walked round a corner into a small courtyard, if that wasn't too grand a word, bustling with summer foliage.

'We're a centre for Russian studies,' she was saying. 'A lot of analysts, a lot of historians, a lot of experts. And yes, before you ask, that includes Moscow watchers.' The phrase they used at the Park, back in the O.B.'s day. 'But if you were expecting a basement where they test exploding sandwiches and invisible cars, you're in for a disappointment.'

'Shame. I've often wondered what an exploding sandwich tastes like.'

'It's the last thing I'd eat.' She delivered this so deadpan, he wasn't sure a joke was intended.

She led him into a vestibule equipped with coat hooks and noticeboards and a set of pigeonholes. A poster for an evening of Ukrainian folk music, and another for a lecture series, also on a Ukrainian theme. A corridor stretched ahead; the floor tiled in a soft brown colour, the various doors on either side new-looking. It was cool, bordering on chill, and there was no obvious noise until he moved, to discover his shoes percussive on the tiles.

'You're not the actual librarian, are you?' he asked.

'God, no. I'm doing a master's, but I was roped in to help with your grandfather's collection. Maybe because I was at the Park not long ago.'

'Yeah, you said. I remember. Sorry.'

'No, I've enjoyed it. It felt like a huge jigsaw puzzle. Also, there are free meals involved.'

He'd been apologising for forgetting her backstory, but it didn't seem worth picking up on. Too often, lately, he'd found himself on the wrong side of a social miscue. Hard to tell if this was a symptom of his brush with a destabilising nerve agent or just who he was, his occasional gaucherie writ larger post pandemic, in common with most everyone else.

'We're in here.'

They'd come to the end of the corridor, having passed a set of doors to what looked like the main library: a tall room, book-lined, with carrels round the edge, though none of this as leather-bound or oak-lined as his imagination had expected. Instead, it was all glass and blond wood, with high windows through which the upper limbs of trees could be seen, lazily weaving patterns out of sunshine. He hadn't noticed any readers, though it had been a quick glance. Calm, though. Peaceful. That behind him, he was shown through another door into a room that was smaller but nevertheless punched him when he entered. He had to hide an intake of breath and hope Erin hadn't noticed.

It wasn't the O.B.'s study – no *Night Watch*, no armchairs, no fireplace – but the books on the shelves, arranged as he'd always known them, triggered something he hadn't realised was there. Like entering a strange room to find the view from his childhood window. It wasn't as if he'd memorised the shelves' contents, more that they'd imprinted themselves; it was the wallpaper he'd grown up with, and long stopped noticing. Now, something between grief and undirected longing welled inside him. Here were the shelves no one was allowed to dust. Here were the patterns that had always been there. The feeling crawled up his spine, not for the first time, that there was a cipher lurking beneath the surface of these texts, its meaning all but ready to surrender, if you held the key.

He pulled himself back. 'Blimey . . . I mean, I knew what you'd done. I just hadn't thought it'd be so . . .'

He hadn't thought it would be so like time travel.

The room, yes, was smaller than the O.B.'s study, the rows of shelves packed more closely together. Not the exact configuration, then, but unnervingly similar, and as he stepped towards the books, he found himself remembering their titles, or at least, finding the touchstones when he looked for them – there was Churchill, there was Beevor; there, among newer volumes, were Macintyre, Andrew and Aldrich. Biographies and histories and analytical studies, with the occasional frivolity thrown in, in the shape of a smattering of paperbacks kept low down, where the casual gaze wouldn't encounter them — not an embarrassment, but a private pleasure: Deighton, Ambler, Price, Littell. The le Carrés in hardback on a shelf above, next to Dickens.

That was it for fiction, though. More prominent was the shelf of almost spineless pamphlets; samizdat material, and fugitive releases from the presses of long-defunct academic institutes, or Roneo'd in garages by bearded dissidents — impossible to escape that detail: they all had beards, in River's experience. He couldn't swear to this particular ragtag, dog-eared collection being in the identical order it had been back home, but he couldn't discern a difference. Perhaps they'd been jammed together so long they'd moulded into place, each pamphlet squeezed against the next so snugly it was all but glued there, the whole shelf-load demanding to be viewed always in the same order, one way and one way only.

She said, 'We made good use of your film, as you can see.'

His film, the six-second video he'd shot the night his hand had touched that nearly fatal doorknob. This had been a punctuation mark on a dreamlike passage of time, during which he'd discovered that Sid had come back from the dead — the memory of a bullet still embedded in her brain — and holed up in the O.B.'s house, which had been emptied of belongings, except for his study. She'd made herself a nest, hiding from a homicidal pair of Moscow-centred thugs who planned to kill her a second time, and had been curled up asleep there when River scanned the room with his phone: the O.B.'s shelves, his books and mementoes, the print of *The Night Watch* above the fire, Sid herself. He'd hacked the last second off the copy he'd sent Erin.

'It's just a pity the room isn't more of a match for your grandfather's.'

'No. No, it looks great. You've gone . . . above and beyond.'

Erin looked pleased. She was, he guessed, someone for whom

a task wasn't worth doing if it wasn't done in such a way that casual bystanders were impressed. She said, 'It's a shame we don't have any of your grandfather's *objets*. They'd have added a touch of authenticity.'

It had been an odd collection of trophies to be sure: a glass globe, a hunk of concrete from the Berlin Wall, a twisted lump of metal that had once been a Luger, and a letter opener which in a previous life had been a stiletto belonging to Beria, and in a more recent one had been used by Sid to terminate one of those thugs she'd been hiding from. Unlike Erin, he was more relieved than otherwise that these items remained out of the picture. Books could form a personal collection, but were not, in themselves, personal. Books belonged to everyone. Blood-stressed knives and furnace-blasted handguns, though, spoke of a more intimate history, and River couldn't imagine his grandfather being happy about their being placed on show. Or Sid, for that matter.

Anyway, that was moot. In his medically unavoidable absence, his mother had wrested control of the house and what remained of its contents, and allowed her lack of sentimentality about her father to take the reins. It was a wonder she'd deigned to preserve the books, though this might have had to do with her fear of being thought a philistine. Her late-onset respectability came with some advantages.

Because Erin seemed to be awaiting a response, he said, 'They mostly wound up in a skip.'

'Oh. Shame.'

That was after the house's façade had been stripped away, along with every last trace of poison, or so everyone hoped. You couldn't help but wonder, though. It wasn't like the nerve agent in question was a known quantity. Its very name meant 'the new guy', making it sound like a stranger in a western: riding into town, looking for trouble. Hard to deny it had found it.

And River was now dragging his sorry arse from the saloon and getting back on his horse.

'Tell me about this missing book,' he said.

If you were designing a set for a small theatre group – something you could throw in the back of a van, then build in a village hall – you'd arrive at something like this: walls close enough together that two people holding hands could span the room's width; a window with lace curtains nicotined with age; a two-seater sofa with floral design; and something that might be a drinks cabinet, from the days before anyone noticed that drinks taste better from a fridge. On those too close walls, actual wallpaper, one strip peeling upwards where it met the skirting board; hanging from the ceiling, a paper globe of a lampshade, its underwire poking through the ruffled surface. And pervading it all, the way a bad smell might, the sense that what you saw was all you'd get; that beyond the room's only door would lie a cramped hallway, off which lay a mean kitchen; that overhead would be two bedrooms, one small, one tiny, and a bathroom barely big enough to drown a dog, with a shower curtain decorated with Disney characters wielding umbrellas. Sometimes the unseen is contained by the seen; one small corner offering up the whole. But that's a desirable characteristic in a safe house, its easily assimilated limits part of the security it offers.

Al Hawke, who had already toured the house – big verb, small effort – assumed that the couple he was opening the door to would gauge its dimensions with a single glance. 'I know what you're thinking,' he said. 'But we've stayed in worse.'

But Avril just said, 'Al.'

'Avril. Daisy.'

They hugged, all three, once the door was closed and the occupants of passing traffic couldn't bear witness. Then they trooped into the sitting room, where Daisy sat on the sofa and Avril stationed herself by the window, which was barred. Al was left hovering by the door, his status as first arrival elevating him to the role of host. CC had texted him the code for deactivating the alarm. 'There's coffee. But no milk.'

'CC has always been better about remembering his own needs than others'.'

'Not entirely fair.'

'I'm not saying he's mean, just . . . unimaginative. Have you seen him?'

Al shook his head.

'Since when?'

'Last year. October, I think. How about you?'

'About the same.'

Daisy, from the sofa, said, 'He calls.'

Al, who had once been in CC's company when he made such a call, could guess how that would have gone. A lot of talking on CC's side – mostly gentle descriptions of what he'd been up to, places he'd been – and a lot of silence on Daisy's. Al thought those phone calls were like playing the radio for a cat: they calmed her, but the flow of information went one way.

Like a cat, too, Daisy had taken to the sofa partly for the comfort it offered, partly as a defendable redoubt. Not that she had anything to worry about in present company, but habit digs deep roots.

Avril Potts said, 'Is this the best the Park runs to these days? Or is the decor born of nostalgia?' She pursed her lips, as if in genuine thought. 'I mean, short of a few secret policemen, we could be in the GDR.'

But she said it in a way that sounded like she was okay with it. Anyway, they'd not be here long.

Still, he had to ask. 'When were you in the GDR?'

'Don't get literal with me, Hawke. I've toasted bigger pedants for breakfast.'

'Fair enough.' He winked at Daisy, who was watching them as if they were engaged in a tennis rally. 'You can take your pick of the bedrooms. Back one's smaller, but there's less noise and you won't get the street lights.'

'The back one,' said Avril, 'will be barely big enough to contain the bed. And there'll be less traffic at night, so that's not an issue.' Al held up his hands in surrender, but she was already continuing: 'But you need more space. Daisy and I will manage, I'm sure.'

Meaning, he guessed, that the more contained Daisy was, the safer she'd feel, and that Avril would gladly offer up her own comfort for that result.

Traffic might not be an issue later, but there was no shortage of it now. A main road wasn't the obvious location for a safe house, but if obviousness was the criterion, the houses would be less secure. Besides, along this particular stretch there was little other residential property; on this side, the row of strangely out of place cottages, of which the furthest left adjoined an empty space that had once been a car park attached to what had once been a pub. A little beyond that, before the road curved, a lane led to public tennis courts. Opposite, behind a fence, lay school playing fields, where the sons and daughters of the obscenely rich, the frighteningly wealthy and the merely well-to-do could begin to absorb the lessons their lives would hold, chief among these being that money helped. The school itself was along the road to the right, its stout frontage dominating a hundred yards or so of pavement. Obviously most pupil drop-offs and pick-ups involved SUVs, so there was little pedestrian hustle. No, Al concluded; the site had been well chosen. This was a stretch of road on which nobody lingered.

As for why CC had summoned them, they'd have to wait to find out.

To Avril, he said, 'Well, up to you. If you change your mind.'

'It's not a mini-break, Al. We can cope with a little discomfort.'

Daisy herself either agreed with all of this, or didn't disagree strongly enough to voice her opinion. She was gazing through the window's yellowed lace. From outside, she would be a vague shadow. There were times when she was much the same if you were in the room with her.

And whose fault was that?

The women had been carrying one small holdall between them. Al knew better than to offer to carry it upstairs.

'About that coffee,' he said.

'Let me,' said Avril. 'I remember your coffee only too well.'

She found the kitchen. Sounds of tap turning and kettle filling followed, while Al watched Daisy. Watching Daisy in the past had sometimes been a duty, sometimes a joy, but had never been undertaken without a rearrangement occurring in his heart. This time round, it was the increasingly familiar sensation of recognising time's footwork, the marks it leaves as it stamps all over you. She was a little more worn, a little more lined, and while carrying nothing like the damage his own battered frame had weathered, was through her middle years now, everything speeding up. Which did not alter the fundamental truth of her: she was, always would be, beautiful. He, meanwhile, would always be a bruiser. It took all sorts.

He said, 'How've you been?'

She took her time replying, and could only manage, 'Same old.'

'CC drop any hints what this is about?'

Daisy shook her head as Avril came back in. 'I swear, sometimes I'd swap a safe house for a convenient one. There's no plunger for the cafetière.'

Al laughed, and even Daisy smiled.

Outside, traffic rumbled as the afternoon got into gear.

'Tell me about this missing book,' River said.

'Yeah, no, better than that. I'll show you.' Her laptop was on a table in the corner, and he hovered while she called up the footage.

When they'd first spoken, some weeks previously, she'd asked for his memories of the room; whether he had clues to offer about the books' arrangement. 'You don't have a photograph, by any chance?'

'I might. I'd need to poke around in my phone. Or, tell you what, we could hire a hypnotist? See if he could prod me into recalling what went where?'

'Maybe as a last resort,' she'd said, her tone suggesting she was used to humouring oddballs. Well, an Oxford college.

'Or I could send you this short video which pans the whole room, bookshelves included.'

'. . . Yeah, that might work.'

He had rewatched the clip several times since. The shelves were captured, but the books remained largely anonymous: so fleetingly observed, you'd need to be a speed-reader to catch a title. His grandfather, he'd sometimes thought, had absorbed printed material; cloistered in his study, he'd been party to their dialogue. All those words, dancing in the air. With a little effort he could see the O.B. before dementia carried him off; leaning back, eyes closed, glasses on a chain. His hands conducting the melodies the books were making; his mind translating it into information. But it was too easy for the image to corrupt. Stare for long and you'd see David Cartwright alone and frightened in his ruined memory palace, its beams and rafters collapsing around him. River shook his head. Let the old man be.

Erin had the clip running on her laptop. He leaned forward, suddenly conscious of the soap she used. The shot panned as he remembered, ending just short of the sleeping Sid.

'The book's on the bottom shelf of the second stack. A white spine with red lettering. Block caps. Let's get a little more focus and a little less speed.' She magnified the screen so only the bottom shelves showed and ran the clip again in slo-mo, making River dizzy. When she hit the space bar the scene froze, and the writing on the spines – already enlarged beyond decipherability – became a ghostly buzz, as if the lettering had suffered an electric shock. What had been blurred furry letters were now ornate but inscrutable patterns; the clawprints of wading birds awaiting the tide's erasure.

'I'm not sure I can read that,' River admitted. Not sure: he was damn sure. All he could make out was a calligraphic soup. He knew this was writing, but he'd have been hard-pressed to determine which alphabet.

'No, we had to run it through a motion-capture program to read the titles. But you just need to see it's there.'

'It's there.'

'And trust me, it says *The Secret Voices: A Hidden History of Deep Cover Lives*. By M. H. Leggaty.'

'Okay.'

'And there's no record that a book with that title exists. And the author's untraceable.'

'So you said on the phone. And the book's now missing.'

'If it was included in the boxes that arrived, it's disappeared since. It's the only book I can identify onscreen which isn't here.'

River looked again at the frozen image on her laptop. It had been there when he shot the video; was part of his grandfather's library, so he must have seen it countless times. But he couldn't pretend that, even in its vague and fuzzy form, it was ringing any bell.

He said, 'I don't remember it. I mean, obviously, yes, it's there. But the title means nothing to me.'

'He never mentioned it?'

River gestured around the room. 'He had a few books. As you've discovered.'

'But this one wasn't real. So maybe it weighed on his mind more than others.'

A nerve was pulsing in his neck and he pressed a palm to it. Then took a step back so Erin wouldn't notice. She might think he was hiding something: guilty knowledge? All he wanted was to keep presenting as healthy and untroubled. *Any physical tremors, spasms, uncontrollable shakes or shivers?* he'd been asked at his last check-up. No. None. But a nerve was pulsing in his neck.

He said, 'A fake book. You're thinking it was a box.'

'One he made himself, it would seem.'

'Or borrowed from stores.'

'Which would make it antique. The Park stopped making cute little hidey places about the time they gave up equipping agents with jetpacks.'

'And it doesn't read like an antique title.'

'My thoughts too. No, this wasn't a work souvenir. I think Cartwright — I mean, your grandfather — I think he was using it. And now it's gone.'

'Along with whatever was inside.'

Erin pushed her chair back and stood. 'Yes.' She'd removed her hat and her hair was making a statement of sorts, possibly a declaration of independence. 'Which is why I thought you ought to know about it.'

'Thanks. Have you told the Park?'

'I used to work for First Desk, did you know that?'

'For Taverner?'

'Well, it was hardly going to be Ingrid Tearney, was it? How old do you think I am?'

River wasn't going anywhere near that. 'And was it a joyous experience?'

'I'm guessing you don't really need to be told. But no, I've said nothing to the Park. On account of having had enough to do with them to see me through the rest of my life.'

'Okay. Well, thanks for putting me in the picture.' He realised this sounded ungracious, but it was said now. Words were slippery beasts. 'I suppose we'd better think about how and when the book might have gone astray.' Even to his own ears, he sounded like a third-rate Sherlock. 'Or who might have—'

'Way ahead of you,' said Erin.

'You have a suspect.'

'Well, I know it wasn't me. So that only leaves one candidate,' she said.

Like a blue tit tapping on a milk bottle top, some things only have to happen once, somewhere, before they're happening everywhere, all the time. In Slough House, this morning's milk bottle was Roddy Ho, unless he was the tit – either way, it was in his office that the slow horses congregated, eager to investigate a rumour that had circulated with the usual speed of rumours in offices: no one knew how it started, but everyone was in sudden possession of the same facts.

'Roddy, hi!' said Ash.

'Roddy, ha!' said Shirley.

'Roddy, hey!' said Louisa.

'Roddy,' said Lech. 'Huh.'

Roddy did something that switched all his monitors to screensaver mode. 'What do you want?'

'We can't go on together,' said Shirley, 'with suspicious minds.'

'Yeah, lighten up,' said Louisa. 'We just want to know about your wound.'

'My money's on some kind of street hassle,' said Lech. 'You know, like you were facing down a horde of angry squaddies.'

It was true that this was the kind of action Roddy was likely to find himself elbows-deep in come a Friday night, but that was due to his movie choices.

'Either that,' Lech continued, 'or a Girl Guide gave you a dead leg.'

'To match your head,' said Shirley.

Ash had wandered to the window and leaned against the wall, arms folded. 'But I reckon you've got yourself some body art. That's what I reckon.'

So she'd been giving him some thought. Figured. As a reward,

Roddy gave her a look he'd been practising lately, involving one half-closed eye and a slight curl of the lip. Half amused approval, half invitation, basically.

'You about to throw up? Because I am not watching that.'

'Is she right?' said Shirley. 'You've had a tat done?'

'Joined the brotherhood,' Roddy admitted.

'You're in a boy band now?' Louisa asked.

'The brotherhood of . . . wrestlers.' Which is what his ink slinger had called Roddy, meaning he was like The Rock or someone. 'You wouldn't understand.'

'So what is it?' Ash said. 'My guess is a motorbike in flames.'

'Or a unicorn jumping over a rainbow.'

'Or some kind of heraldic thing,' said Lech. 'Like a dickhead, rampant.'

'It's none of those,' said Roddy.

'Let's see it,' Shirley demanded.

'It's not ready yet.'

'What, the transfer's still wet?'

'It's not a transfer.'

'I think it probably is,' said Lech. 'On account of tattoos hurt. And you've got the pain threshold of a marshmallow.'

'Yeah, well, you've got the pain threshold of . . . *two* marshmallows.'

'Come on, Rodster,' said Louisa. 'No point going under the gun if you're not gonna show it off.'

'"The gun"?' said Lech.

'What they call the tattoo machine,' she explained. 'The way they call crybabies "wrestlers". Because of all the wriggling.'

Ash said, 'There's a thought. We could just wrestle him to the ground and strip his bandage off.'

'It would take all three of you,' Roddy said.

'It would seriously not,' said Shirley.

'I'm supposed to keep it covered another twenty-four hours.'

'But we can't wait that long,' explained Ash.

'Clinching argument,' said Lech. 'Shirley, do the honours?'

Roddy sighed, and held up a palm. It had been bound to come to this — there was always speculation about the RodBod behind his back. Murmurs about his six-pack, mutterings about his butt. Just this morning, entering Costa, he'd heard his usual barista whisper 'Massive cock' to her colleague. He rolled his sleeve up and peeled the bandage away carefully, not because he was worried about it hurting, but because he didn't want anything to smudge.

Everyone went quiet.

'What are we looking at?' asked Louisa at last.

'It's a hummingbird,' said Roddy. 'Duh.'

'Yeah, that's never a hummingbird,' said Lech. 'Maybe a platypus?'

'Or a sheep,' said Shirley. 'Is it a sheep?'

'Do sheep have five legs?' Ash asked.

'That's not a leg.'

'. . . Ew!'

'It's a dung beetle, I think,' said Louisa. 'An upside-down dung beetle.'

Shirley tilted her head. 'Actually, yeah, a beetle. But why dung specifically?'

'Because it's shit.'

'It's a hummingbird,' Roddy repeated, arranging his bandage back into place. 'Philadelphians.'

There was a moment's baffled silence. Then Louisa said, 'Philistines!', and Shirley high-fived her.

'This tattoo artist,' asked Lech. 'How much did you pay him for making your arm look like a duck crapped on it?'

'And where'd he learn his trade, prison?'

'Everyone having fun?'

And this was Catherine, who was standing in the doorway regarding the pack of them like a secondary school teacher who'd just tracked down vapers.

'Because as I'm sure you're aware, there's nothing he likes more than you enjoying yourselves.'

'I thought he was out,' Lech said.

'And that makes you feel safe? That's nice. Monthly reports up to date? He wants to see them this morning.'

'Even though he never reads them,' said Louisa.

'Yes, well, the perks of leadership.'

'Yeah, right,' said Shirley. 'The . . . schmerks of schmeadership, more like.'

'Needs work,' said Lech.

'And you need plastic surgery. But you don't hear me going on about it.'

'Upstairs in ten minutes,' Catherine warned, leaving them to it. She had work to do, there was always work to do, even if it consisted of the pointless rearrangement of unnecessary information. Lamb insisted on seeing paperwork, because if he ignored everything she gave him onscreen she wouldn't know about it, whereas when she found a meticulously formatted report she'd printed out at 4:45 tipped into his bin at 4:50, he was clearly making a point. As he no doubt was now, in a different way, by turning up early: when she walked into his office, intending to empty the inevitable ashtrays – an umbrella term which covered anything with an interior space – he was already in occupation, slouching in his chair like a sleeping bag someone had stuffed with potatoes. There'd not been a squeak while he'd climbed the stairs, not even from the back door, which screamed like a startled goose most days.

Hiding her surprise, she asked, 'How did the meeting with Taverner go?'

'She implied I look fat,' said Lamb. 'This caused me to feel unsafe.'

'I'm sure you'll get over it. Anything else of importance?'

'Nah, not really.' He put a cigarette in his mouth, but didn't light it. For Lamb, this was on a par with giving up. 'Just chucking her weight around. There are days when I wonder if they shouldn't bring witch trials back.' He rolled pious eyes heavenwards. 'But of course, you're not allowed to say that any more.'

'Political correctness gone mad,' Catherine agreed. 'What's this morning's meeting in aid of?'

'Just general morale boosting.'

Oh God. She headed back to her own office and collected printouts – progress reports on the various projects Lamb had instigated – and returned to his room with them.

'More recycling?' he said. He was holding a disposable plastic lighter now, as if fighting a rearguard action against her eco-activism, but hadn't yet put it to use. 'What's the matter?'

'What makes you think anything's the matter?'

'I can read you like a . . .'

'Book?'

'Newspaper. They get thrown away afterwards.'

'Silly me. Nothing's the matter. Barring the usual, that is.'

'Ah,' he said wisely. 'You'd be referring to what I'm supposed to call my "team". The silly custards.'

'Coming from you, that's suspiciously benign.'

'Well, "bastunts" doesn't really work. And here they come.'

They trooped in, Lech leading the way, then Shirley, Roddy, Ash. Louisa hung back on the landing, muttering into her phone. Lamb raised an eyebrow, but all avoided his gaze, preferring to concentrate on the surroundings – the corkboard with its display of tattered clippings; the dismal picture of some dismal bridge some dismal where; the desk lamp teetering on a calcified pile of telephone directories, a concept which Ashley, for one, had difficulty getting her head around; the blinds pulled over the skylight, muting the daylight to a drab shroud. Stuffing her phone into her pocket, Louisa attempted to enter the room without being noticed. She did not succeed.

'I'm sure that must have been a nuisance call, from someone

who just wouldn't let you go,' Lamb said. 'Because otherwise, you'd have been deliberately wasting your colleagues' time. And that would be really fucking rude.'

And you hate fucking rudeness, she silently offered. 'Sorry, yes,' she lied. 'Cold caller.'

'You know how I get rid of them?' Lamb said.

'Pretty sure we don't want to,' said Lech.

'I pretend to come.'

'Not sure that would work for me,' said Louisa.

'Or me,' said Ash.

'Or me,' said Shirley.

'Or me,' said Roddy. '. . . What?'

'Valuable as this no doubt is,' said Catherine, 'perhaps we could skip the preliminaries? I'm sure there are things we could more usefully be doing.'

Shirley snorted; Ash rolled her eyes. Lech said, 'Like what, throwing ourselves out of a window?'

Lamb tutted. 'Let's not lose hope. Remember, you're only ever one spiked drink away from a happy ending.'

'Is there an agenda for this meeting?' Ash asked. 'Because I've got, like, an office full of boring stuff I could be boring myself to death with.'

'There, see?' Lamb's beaming face included them all in its benediction. 'Our newest recruit, and already she's as welcome as a banjo on a soundtrack. Now, group huddle. No, not literally, it's not an excuse for a wank. Let's just take a moment to be grateful for what we've got here.'

The shared incomprehension of everyone else in the room might have powered the whole of Aldersgate Street, had the appropriate technology been available.

'If my years on this planet have taught me anything, it's that we're in it together. All for one, one for all. So, a few small things. First, I don't want anyone hassling Louisa, because she has a big decision to make. She jumps the right way, the rest of you are going to be feeling even more fucking sorry for yourselves than usual, so give her some breathing space. And second, leave Ho alone too. He's going to be doing an important job for me while the rest of you are busy with the usual crap, because that's all you're good for. Everything clear? Grand.' He clapped his hands, then rubbed them together like a vicar. 'And they say I don't know how to inspire the troops. Now, I've been told to make sure to use inclusive language when addressing staff. So fuck off, all of you. Not you.'

This meant Ho.

The rest of them fucked off, Ash asking, 'We went upstairs for that?'

'Yep. Today's been a good day,' said Lech. He glanced at Louisa. 'Mysterious phone calls, cryptic comments. What's your big decision about?'

'He's yanking your chain,' Louisa said, disappearing into her office and kicking the door shut.

'One for all, all for one,' Lech muttered.

'Don't you start,' Shirley said, and clumped off down the stairs.

First visit or not, River knew an interesting fact about the college, and specifically the centre of Russian studies it housed. This had come, of course, from his grandfather.

'The centre's first director was the man who recruited Guy Burgess.'

'For which side?' River had asked.

'A good question, but do be careful in whose company you ask it. Skins are still thin in some areas. Burgess and his pals left scars that will never heal.'

Spies lie. They betray. It's what they do.

Now, to Erin, River said, 'So Stan—'

'Sta*m*. With an M.'

'. . . Okay. This Stam, he's a fellow of the college?'

'Well, he's a fixture. He has dining rights and uses the library, though whether that's because he has official status or because the librarian doesn't want to bar the door to him, I've no idea. He's writing a book, I expect. And he was very interested in this project, your grandfather's library. They worked together, back in the day.'

'So he was in the Service.'

'Yes. That is, he's never actually come out and said so. They don't, do they? But he worked with David, he made that clear. Not as a contemporary – I mean, he's old, but . . .'

But not that old. Fair enough. 'Was anyone else helping?'

'If there were, I'd not have been so quick to point the finger. I mean James, the librarian, he has oversight, obviously. But all the work, the organisation, has been left to me, and Stam's been my only help. Sorting through books, finding the right place on the shelves. Believe it or not, it wasn't all straightforward.'

'No, I didn't—'

'There was the crew who delivered the boxes, of course, but they arrived sealed up. And nobody could have known what was in each box. Even if they knew what they were looking for.'

River said, 'Yes, but. Presumably they were the same crew who packed the boxes at the other end. It's possible that the missing book—'

'*The Secret Voices.*'

' – never got as far as your library in the first place.'

'That would be my preferred outcome,' Erin said.

'Don't worry. Nobody's going to be blaming you.'

'You've probably forgotten I mentioned this,' she said. 'But I used to work at the Park. Trust me, if anything happened, someone's going to get blamed.'

An interesting thought occurred to River: that the person who had supervised the packing of the books in the first place was his mother. 'What kind of name is Stam, anyway?'

'Short for Stamoran. Charles Stamoran. But nobody calls him Charles.'

'I'd better meet him,' he said.

'Which is why we're heading to the dining hall.'

For lunch, which sounded like a treat – lunch at an Oxford college – but turned out not that different from lunch at a department store. John Lewis, say. A spacious dining area, modern, with long tables and matching chairs. The walls boasted big windows, offering views of the rest of the college: buildings arranged around a small area which, because this was Oxford, was a quadrangle, though anywhere else would be a lawn, some flower beds, a few trees, a litter bin. The buildings weren't terribly old, but then the college wasn't one of the ancient institutions; a latecomer, it had the tact not to try too hard, and not to pretend to hallowed customs, or traditions steeped in time. As for the food, you helped yourself from a buffet: lasagna, vegetarian moussaka, baked potatoes, roast meats, salads. Individual trifles in plastic pots. Water, fruit juices, Coke. Then you processed past a till, collecting cutlery from plastic troughs. He offered to pay, but Erin was already proffering a card to the woman totting up their choices. 'He's here,' she said, as she hoisted her tray. 'Far end of the room. Sitting by himself.'

'Let's join him.'

'Do you want me to stay?'

'It'll look weird if you don't. But maybe leave before I do?'

He liked her. Because she'd worked at the Park, they shared common ground he'd never find with civilians. Not that he'd be mentioning this to Sid. She led him past tables occupied by serious-looking young folk and towards a window under which a man sat alone, tucking into the moussaka.

'Stam? Have you met River Cartwright?'

He looked up. 'Grandson of?'

'That's right.'

'A pleasure.'

They shook hands, and Stam invited both to sit, sit.

He was a bullish man. River couldn't gauge his height while he was seated, but he was still broad-shouldered, still muscular, into his seventies. Bald on top with a white trim of hair around the ears, meeting in a well-tended beard and moustache, and a nose that begged for classical adjectives: Roman, aquiline, something like that. His colour was high, suggesting blood pressure issues. He wore a blue shirt under a light brown corduroy jacket, and spectacles hung on a chain around his neck. As if he were the host, and a duty fell upon him, he began to talk, first asking River if he'd visited the college before, and then embarking on a potted history. River ate his lasagna, not so much absorbing the information as studying the man delivering it, who had worked with his grandfather.

This was a broad church. Cartwright senior had worked in elevated circles but he'd reached low too, claiming the allegiance of joes and handlers alike – of course he had. Holmes had his irregulars; Smiley had his people. Naturally the O.B. had had a crew. *Spying is networks*, the young River had learned that at his grandfather's knee. You didn't run an intelligence service without calling on local talent. *Spying is other people*. Hell, the clue was in the vocabulary. They called it Spook Street, and a street without inhabitants wasn't worth the name. Besides, any time you found yourself alone, you'd know you were the one being watched . . . Watching Charles Stamoran, River wondered how close he'd been to the O.B., and whether they'd shared secrets. And whether Stam had stolen some the O.B. had tried to keep.

'Great to see you, Stam, but would you mind excusing me? I've emails I need to get round to.'

'Of course. See you later.'

Both men watched Erin leave, neither speaking, both recognising that the conversation had just shifted onto another playing field. River had finished his lunch, or finished eating it, anyway.

He was toying with the rest, pushing it around his plate with his fork. Stam was watching him do so. He laid his cutlery down and dabbed his lips with a napkin. 'I like to walk a circuit after lunch. Helps with the digestion. Care to join me?'

Couldn't be better.

They left the dining room, Stam collecting a scarf from a hook by the door and knotting it round his neck. The weather hardly called for it, but River was well short of seventy, so made no comment. Others were leaving the hall at the same time but had places to go, and the quad soon emptied. Stam walked briskly, whether a further aid to digestion or his natural habit wasn't clear.

'I knew your grandfather,' he said, halfway round their first circuit.

He had one of those *I, Claudius* voices: not especially loud, but you could make out every syllable. 'I know,' River answered.

'In fact, we met once. I doubt you'll remember.'

'Really?'

'You'd have been eight or nine. I was delivering a file to your house. I knocked at the door and you answered. I asked if your grandfather was in, and you said, "I don't know. I'll have to ask him." I found that funny, though I was careful not to let you see.'

'Did he take you into his study?'

'He did. So yes, I saw his books in their, what would you call it, original habitat. Didn't help when it came to arranging them.' He delivered a sly sideways glance. 'Live long enough, and you stop believing in coincidence. Things happen, that's all. Naturally there are echoes.'

'Grandfather used to say everything happens in one of two kinds of pattern. The kind you see straight away, and the kind you have to work at.'

'Well, that's how you get a reputation for being wise. By issuing cryptic little jewels like that.' He tugged at his scarf.

'That came out wrong. I admired David Cartwright. He was far higher up the tree than I was, but that didn't matter to me. I was never Desk material.'

'What did you do?' River had never met a spook whose life story he didn't want to hear, or one who'd been happy to share it, his grandfather being the notable exception to that latter point.

'Field work. Mostly field work.'

Which evidently included delivering files, a task some might have thought entry-level. But there were files and files; there were people you trusted to deliver them, and people you didn't.

River said, 'There's a book missing.'

'Yes.'

'Erin's mentioned it?'

'She didn't need to. And yes, before you ask, it wasn't actually a book. I know that too.'

'A box of some sort.'

'We used to call them safes.'

River had known that: of course he had. But the word had got lost, or at any rate, hadn't sprung to mind when he and Erin had been discussing it. This fazed him: what else had he forgotten lately? Was there a whole page of vocabulary torn from his mind, scattering in his wake? Like the O.B. in his final days; that bright shining intelligence grown rusty, and its owner barely aware of the fact. Except for occasional moments, the memory of which River suppressed; moments in which his grandfather's eyes had turned black with horror in the knowledge of what was happening to him.

'How did you know?'

'Well.' Stam came to a halt, the better to fix his eyes on River. 'I could say it was obvious. That I've studied the film you sent us, and it became apparent something was missing. That that was always likely to happen, don't you think? Items going missing in the . . . kerfuffle of books being transported?'

Kerfuffle was one way of putting it. The facade of the O.B.'s house had been removed, to ensure that any lingering toxicity had been dealt with. This wasn't a state secret. There'd been a photograph in the *Times*.

'But this wasn't a book, it was a safe,' said River. 'So what are the chances this particular volume would be the one to vanish?'

'I'm not a statistician. But that would be unlikely.'

'And isn't what happened.'

'No, of course not. I took it, as you've guessed. Erin too, probably.'

'Yes.'

'And you want to know why.'

In fact, the why seemed obvious to River: because it was there. You were unloading a spook's library, and came across a treasure chest. Why wouldn't you steal it? But what he said was, 'As long as we're here.'

Stam started walking again. They were on their second circuit, and a light breeze was blowing. It chased sunbeams around, or that was the effect beneath the quad's largest tree, its branches' shadows rearranging themselves as they passed. Stam said, 'I wish I could tell you the box contained state secrets. We might both feel better about that. Well, you might.'

River felt the ground shift beneath his feet. 'What do you mean?' As soon as the words were out of his mouth, he wanted them recalled; wanted nothing more to do with this conversation. He could walk away, unpark his car, perform the morning in reverse. Fold the landscape behind him as he tootled back to London, to Sid, pretending nothing had happened; that the book was a book, that it had turned up again. But it was too late for any of that, even the parts of it that were possible.

'He was a good man, your grandfather, even a great one. He achieved a lot. That the Park is still standing, that we have an intelligence service esteemed the world over – that's down to him. Don't forget that.'

'What was in the box?'

'But he was still just a man.'

'What was in the box?'

'The safe,' Stam corrected. And then repeated himself: 'Just a man, with a man's ordinary wants. I found nothing that would make you think better of him, but that doesn't mean you should think him any the worse.'

He thought: I could hold this old man down on the ground and pound the truth out of him until it bleeds. I need to know everything. I need to know now. But the breeze was still pushing its way round the quad, ruffling the grass and setting leaves to trembling, and the day was just too ordinary – too civilised – to shatter.

Instead, he took refuge in the obvious. 'You found pornography,' he said.

'Yes.'

'You found pornography.' It didn't sound any better, second time round. 'Was it illegal?'

'It wasn't – it wasn't *desperate*.'

The very hedging, the prevarication, made it all so much, so much worse.

'River,' said Stam, and his voice was gentle. 'I destroyed it. All right? I destroyed what I found, the safe too.'

'Why the safe?' Irrelevance is a shelter; stops you thinking about anything else. 'Why not just put it back?'

'I should have done. I'm sorry. You need never have known about any of this. But I wasn't thinking. I burned what it contained, and I threw the safe, the box, in the fire too. It's all gone. You don't ever need to think about it.'

'Easy to say. I mean—'

But he didn't know what he meant. His grandfather had raised him, he and Rose. When he thought about being an adult, living a proper life, it was David and Rose he was thinking about. That his grandfather had a secret life was a given. That the secrets it held might be so banal: this threatened to unmoor him.

'We all have things we'd like to hide in boxes,' Stam was saying. 'That we wouldn't want exposed. It doesn't undo all the good in our lives.'

Or augment it, either. The uplift mood he'd been in earlier, the tunes waiting to be whistled, were all gone. They walked another circuit in silence, Stam evidently knowing he'd said enough, that River didn't want to hear words of comfort. All spies' lives end in failure: that was something else the O.B. had once said. And this was what failure looked like; the last of your secrets taken out of their box and exposed to the daylight. And what shabby, paltry things they were after all.

IN THE SAFE HOUSE, the trio were playing cards.
. . . There should be rain lashing windows, power cuts and candles; a bottle of vodka and a hunk of bread. Instead they were drinking tea, sharing a plate of special biscuits from a deli three minutes' walk away, and – so far successfully – making a collective effort not to use the words 'Do you remember?' But remembering, anyway, the days of cold passes and brush-bys, of synchronised watches and dead letter drops – methods already antiquated when the three of them were operational, but in joe country you clung to the old ways, because the new ways gave themselves away: a phone you weren't supposed to have, a bugging device that might as well have been Mickey Mouse ears. Things you weren't supposed to have became the treasures you'd be buried with: when you were dug up, you'd still be clutching – or have been made to swallow – the emblems of your trade; the toys Regent's Park had supplied you with, to keep you safe. That this had not happened to any of them did not require saying; that it had happened to others was unforgettable. Even here, in this throwback of a safe house, eating special biscuits, drinking tea.

'Two aces.'
'Cheat.'
'Sure?'
'Yes.'

'Because you can change your—'
'*Cheat.*'
Al displayed two aces. Avril sighed, and collected the pile.
Daisy said, 'Is there anything to drink?'
'You want some more tea, love?'
'To drink.'
'Best not,' said Al. 'Safe house rules.'

Daisy pursed her lips. Picked up her empty cup and studied its lack of contents: the tea had been made with bags. There was no future to be read. And the past was not to be discussed.

Avril watched her replace the cup in the exact spot she'd raised it from, thinking *Daisy, Daisy*. Of them all, Daisy was the one who had suffered most, the one who'd picked up the tab. And still paying it, all these years on.

Some debts you never settled. The interest crippled you; you never got close.

One of the things Avril had learned in the Park was that your joes were yours forever. This wasn't in the handbook, but it was what your mentors taught you, what CC had told her. *Love them or hate them, they're yours for good. You're bound to them by barbed wire, and no point trying to escape it.* He'd said all this more than once. *Their sins are yours, because you mould them. Give them their first communion. Confirm them in their saint's name. Sometimes you bury them too. But you never let go of them, on the ground or in it. Best you know that from the start.*

But CC was old school, and the new school was being built before he'd vacated the premises.

Avril was old school too, of course, recruited in this city, between Bodleian stack and lecture theatre. The fabled tap on the shoulder . . . And CC had been her mentor; his lamp had lit her way, and in his company she was always the acolyte. *Come to Oxford. I've a plan.* Which, from anyone else, might have meant a night serenading past triumphs. *It'll put you back on track.* If there was one thing CC was sure of, it was that they'd all been thrown off track, but he didn't know the half of it. They'd kept the worst hidden from him. And where was he, anyway?

Daisy picked up on her thoughts, or drew them from the air in the room. 'When'll CC get here?'

Which was the moment in the fairy tale when a name summons its owner, because here was his key in the door.

The restaurant was off Brewer Street, and thankfully wasn't trying too hard. Devon Welles was there before her, which Louisa had expected, and had done her best to guarantee by being precisely seven minutes late: there might not be actual rules, but there were tried and tested guidelines. He was wearing an immaculately tended goatee these days, which like all goatees was a bit of a shame, and also a suit, which fitted well enough that she was probably supposed to recognise the designer. The best she could manage was clocking the price range: four figures. Whatever Devon was doing for money, he'd either climbed a ladder or crossed a line. What she remembered of him – specifically, that he'd been close to Emma Flyte – probably ruled the latter out, but like everyone else, she'd been fooled before.

She wondered if he'd opt for the hug or the kiss on the cheek, but it was a surprisingly formal handshake he offered. 'Louisa. Thanks for coming.'

'It's good to see you, Devon.'

She meant it, too. They hadn't known each other well but she'd been impressed by him, and – style upgrade and facial hair apart – he was the same man; black skin still unlined, eyes still clear. It occurred to her that this was the first time she'd seen him since Emma's funeral, and they hadn't spoken then beyond brief condolences. The death of a common friend could be a barrier as much as a bridge, the more so when guilt was involved. Slough House was the reason Emma wasn't around any more. Slough House was the book of Louisa's dead. Inside its pages love and friendship were buried, alongside others who had mattered less to her, but who were no less gone.

Because there was wine on the table already, and Devon was pouring her a glass as she sat, she made her opening remarks to it. 'I miss Emma. I didn't know her well, though we were getting there. But I respected her and I liked her and I wish she were still around. I know you were close. I'm sorry you lost your friend.'

He said, 'She said something similar about you. That you were getting to know each other, I mean. Not the stuff about respecting or liking you.'

'Thanks.'

'Yeah, Emma didn't go in for that. But if she hadn't liked you, you'd have known about it.' He raised his glass. 'Absences.'

She tapped it with hers. 'Emma.'

They drank, and Louisa said, 'You left the Park on your own two legs, I heard.'

'I walked before they made me run,' he said. 'When Emma quit, the writing was on the wall. They weren't going to promote her BFF to take her place, and I didn't want to work under whoever that turned out to be. Also, I was ready for a change. It turns out I bore quite easily.'

I'm made of sterner stuff, thought Louisa. 'And your new line?'

'Personal protection services.'

'That sounds . . .'

Tact draped itself in an ellipsis.

He said, 'Don't be afraid to use the phrase "well dodgy".'

'Well dodgy.'

'I can see how you'd think that. But it's not all babysitting rich bastards. Much of the time, we're analysts. You know, offering advice on how to manage home life when you're in a public position. Kids' schooling, family holidays and so on.'

'To rich bastards.'

'Well, yes, I was trying to skate that past you. Obviously rich bastards, or they'd neither need nor afford the service. Though in fact we also do some, well, not exactly pro bono, but we give reduced rates to deserving causes. As for the rest, bastards or not, none of them are scumbags. I'm sure you appreciate the distinction.'

'No guns, drugs or rabble-rousers.'

'We vet our client list. Anyone likely to end up in The Hague or the Old Bailey, we nix. Nepo brats are an occupational hazard, as are former politicos living with death threats. But no one I've worked with has seen the inside of a cell.'

'That's noble. It's like you're the Lone Ranger or something.'

'It's pragmatism. Anyone with a chance of winding up behind bars is less likely to pay their bill. But not only that. If Emma – I mean, she'd have skinned me alive.'

That much was true.

'But I won't pretend it's a charity. It's a well-paying gig. Ever flown in a private jet?'

'I've driven in a private car. And ridden on a private bike. But no, never.'

'It's an experience.' Being in the presence of someone else's wealth didn't strike Louisa as the kind of experience she wanted, but Devon was clearly on a mission to impress. 'And the pay's good, like I said. And also, I'm going to cut to the chase, every so often you get to beat the crap out of a lowlife.'

'Seriously?'

'Well, no, but you get to act as if you might. And I mentioned the pay, didn't I?'

'Often enough that tonight is on you. What's up, Devon? I'm glad you've found a soft landing, but—'

'We're recruiting.'

'Ah.'

'And your name came up.'

Which gave her something to think about while the waiter appeared and took their order. She opted for the fish; Devon for the mushroom risotto. They had enough wine for the moment, though the waiter did his best to remedy that by refilling their glasses uninvited. When he'd gone again, she picked up where they'd left off. 'Came up? How did that happen?'

Welles dipped his head modestly.

'Well, thanks. I guess. But I'm not sure it's for me.'

'Can't know until you try. You'd be a shoo-in – there's marksmanship as well as fitness, and you're savvy enough to ace the paperwork. All of which is to say, it's a serious business. We don't just hoover up Service and forces dropouts. And I'd like to have you on my team.'

'Your team?'

'Did I skip that bit? Yeah, my team. You'd get to call me Guv, or possibly Sir. There'd be a certain amount of forelock tugging, some small acts of abasement. You know the drill.'

'That's a big selling point. But seriously—'

'Want to know how much I earn?'

'Not really.'

'Low six figures. Plus a car and other perks. Want to know how much my crew earn?'

'Not really.'

'High five figures. They don't get cars though, the sad fuckers. How much are you on, Louisa?' She added ten. He shook his head. 'I was on more than that at the Park, and one of the reasons I left was finding it hard to get by. And that was before the economy tanked.'

'I have a modest lifestyle.'

'Time you could afford better. And Louisa – Slough House? Seriously? You've been there too long, for all the wrong reasons. You're never going back to the Park, because they'll never let you, and more fool them. Why spend the rest of your life paying for one mistake you made years ago? Walk away now and make some money. Close the book on Slough House. It's a shithole, you know it is. How is Lamb, anyway?'

'You really care?'

'Nope. Round the Park, they called him Prospero, you know that?'

'Because . . . ?'

'He breaks his staff.'

'No they didn't.'

'Yeah, okay. Would've been good, though. And he is a dinosaur.'

'If you mean he's a thick-skinned bastard it'll probably take a meteor to kill, then I'd have to agree.'

Their food arrived, in portions small enough that Louisa hoped the bill was a stinker. So maybe this was the life she was missing: being overcharged for undersized meals, while the waitstaff filled your glass before you were ready . . . And not spending the rest of the week living out of tins. A high-five figure would dull the pain all right.

There were other pains, though. When Emma died, she'd been wearing Louisa's coat, and Louisa had never quite rid herself of the notion that the two facts were connected.

For the rest of the evening, they spoke of other things, Welles apparently satisfied that he'd planted the seed. He admired her sunflower brooch. She teased him about the suit, and he told her how much it cost. He was living in Peckham, he told her; a duplex. Next year's holiday: Machu Picchu. That they weren't in fact talking of other things landed slowly, so maybe she wasn't cut out for intelligence work after all. But she was enjoying his company, and he ordered a second bottle.

Later, when they were parting, he said, 'Don't think about it too long, Louisa. For your sake, not mine. Stay where you are much longer, you'll lose the will to leave. No pun intended.'

'I appreciate the offer. Thank you.'

But don't pass judgement on my life.

It was the last thing she needed, she thought, waiting for her Uber. But only because not a day went by that she didn't do that for herself.

After the hugs and the handshakes, after the unshed tears, Al got down to business. 'It's good to see you, CC,' he said.

'Yes—'

'But a safe house? Seriously?'

'This is Oxford. You want to guess how many Chinese students the city hosts?' CC unwrapped himself from his scarf, and – a habit Avril recalled – swaddled his fist in it, as if he were about to punch through a window. 'So why not take advantage, save ourselves a few quid?'

'But it's not scheduled for use tonight?' Avril asked.

'Yes, I thought we could sit quietly in a corner while a debriefing occurs. No, Avvy, it's not scheduled for use tonight. And before you ask, I know this because someone has to make sure there are custard creams and spare light bulbs and all the rest. So I'm informed when guests are expected.'

Al said, 'You're a housekeeper now?'

'Little errands is all. A far cry from running joes in the badlands, but there's a small sum turns up once a month, and we've all got ends need meeting.' He looked at Daisy. 'I wouldn't have brought you here if there was a chance we'd be disturbed.'

Daisy was gazing at his hand, as if awaiting broken glass. CC pulled the scarf free and draped it over the armchair. He'd arrived carrying a weighted bag-for-life; its contents, Avril gauged, comprising their supper and a bottle of something, she was guessing Irish whiskey. CC was never one for avoiding the obvious.

'You've been giving this some thought, then,' Avril said.

'You're never far from my thoughts. None of you. You know that.'

'Fuck off, you old ponce,' Daisy told him, and that was that: they were together again.

The cards were tidied away, and a fresh pot of tea made. CC's bag held a big fish pie from a nearby supermarket, bags of prepared greens, and a bottle of Bushmills. That was for later. First was talk. CC was on his feet, his posture tutorish, his back to the door. Daisy remained on the sofa, and Avril joined her. Al leaned on its arm, every atom of his aura declaring, *This had better be good.*

Charles Cornell Stamoran – 'Stam' to most; CC to his inner circle – held the floor.

'You'll know David Cartwright passed a while ago.'

'And good riddance,' said Al.

'Hush now,' Avril said. 'He was one of the good ones.'

'Was he, though? Was he?'

'By his own lights.'

'We're all good by our own lights, Avvy. There's no effort involved in being good on those terms.'

'Good or bad, he's just as dead,' CC reminded them. 'And we're not here to argue about his merits, though I think it's fair to say, Al, that the man well knew he'd stained his hands often enough.'

'Well, maybe he made a deathbed confession and that smoothed his path to eternal light. But I heard he came apart like a jigsaw in the end. The man had no more sense of things he'd done than he knew what day of the week it was. Which is not a state for making confessions in, wouldn't you say? No, I think David Cartwright took his past to the grave unshriven.'

CC raised an eyebrow.

Al said, 'What, I don't get to use a vocabulary?'

Daisy said, 'Pitchfork,' and they all looked at her.

'That's what we're talking about, isn't it? Pitchfork.'

'Yes, Daisy,' CC said. 'It's Pitchfork.'

★

'So glad you could make it, Diana.'

'Well, family.'

Not hers, obviously, but Peter Judd's.

The occasion was his youngest official daughter's eighteenth; the location Nob-Nobs, a club on the far edge of Shoreditch which, if it survived its name, would only have its decor, acoustics and bar staff to weather if it hoped to see its anniversary. Diana assumed the choice of venue was the daughter's, though a good half of the guest list, comprising former MPs, was clearly of Judd's devising. So many recently unseated players, she might have been backstage at a rodeo. The pasted-on expressions of merriment would have been over the top for a pantomime, but then the election wipeout wasn't so much a memory as an ongoing trauma.

Judd seemed to be enjoying their distress enormously – it had been some time since he'd sat in the House himself, and his resignation gave him licence to proclaim, loudly and often, that he'd never been ousted by the electorate. His air of dishevelled bonhomie was as cultivated as ever, and he could, when he wanted, make for a diverting companion. But accepting his invitation had been responding to a tug on the leash. This state of affairs couldn't be allowed to continue.

'She's looking very . . . robust,' she continued.

'Xanthippe? Yes, she takes after her mother.' As with so many of his statements, there was no telling whether Judd believed his own words or merely expected others to. In this instance, Diana compared Judd's dad-bellied figure to his wife's elegant form, and reached her own conclusion as to whom their daughter was taking after. Judd, meanwhile, was leaning sideways to accost a passing former cabinet minister, the joke he whispered provoking huge mirth. 'Just think,' he said to Diana in the man's wake. 'When he has someone explain that to him, he'll laugh even harder.'

'Always an education, PJ. But do you mind if I slip away? I'm sure the young won't notice, and I've a busy day tomorrow.'

'No, you hang on. I need a word.'

There was no pretence that this was a request.

She weighed her options, but it didn't take long — releasing herself from Judd's web wasn't going to be achieved by making small stands. So she smiled, sipped her wine, and sidled into a corner where she could watch the young dance and the middle-aged ogle. The music was vaguely familiar and specifically unpleasant. When a short, bespectacled one-time holder of several great offices of state unknotted his tie, wrapped it round his forehead and joined the throng on the dance floor, she wondered if Judd's personal protection team might escort him from the premises, but had to settle for hoping the excitement would see him off.

When Judd had finished making her wait, he led her down to the cloakrooms, where there was a lobby with a two-seater sofa, a giant plastic rubber plant and a mirror in which she looked old. Passing straight through that, he led her into the disabled toilet and locked the door behind them.

'For God's sake—'

'Oh, don't be a schoolgirl. Anyone clocks us, they'll think we're screwing or doing a line. Perfect alibi.'

'One of these days, your lack of decorum'll get you into trouble. Meanwhile, it's just the rest of us need worry. What do you want?'

'So abrupt. Maybe we *should* do a line. It might relax you.'

'Peter—'

'All right, hair on. Little favour to ask, that's all. A few words need whispering, and you're the perfect woman for the job, what with your access to the corridors of power. And also, of course, you being a force of nature, wit and beauty any red-blooded man, and no few women, would happily lend an ear to.'

'You missed a bit,' she said.

'With tremendous dress sense.' Turning his back, he examined his reflection in the mirror, winked, then smoothed his eyebrows. 'You'll have noticed a certain jaded quality about the guest list?'

'What, the yesterday's men? I imagined you felt more comfortable among your own kind.'

'As cruel as she is beautiful. Puts me in mind of those cards you find in phone booths. It's true, my cohort of late has been a little on the wilted side. But then my *persona*'s not exactly *grata* round Westminster right now.'

Which was up there with Tuesday following Monday. While Judd's history was a teeming catwalk of strange bedfellows – he would fuck a dalek, if it was draped in scarlet ribbons – politically speaking he was now firmly among the coyote ugly, and only the desperately unshaggable would want to be seen with him in public.

'Well, feed the bloody birds,' Diana said. 'You've been the new lot's panto villain so long, the only surprise is they haven't nailed you to a beanstalk.'

'Picturesquely put. You're aware that it's temporary?'

'We're a democracy. All governments are temporary.'

'That would be the undergraduate answer. But what I meant was, give it a little time and the new lot, as you put it, will embrace certain realities.' Satisfied with his eyebrows, Judd turned, shot his cuffs, and leaned against the sink. 'One of which is me. Electoral power is all very well, but it does tie one down to accountability and appearances and all that nonsense. After a while, you come to appreciate the quiet efficiency of influence.'

'I'm not sure that *quiet efficiency* is a phrase people associate with you.'

'But you're as aware as I am that more gets done outside the public gaze than ever passes before it. And that the bedrock of our system doesn't shift whatever colour flag we're flying. Like it or not, Diana, you're walking proof that we're all subject to forces above and beyond our nationally accepted pieties. I am – well, modesty forbids. But if not one of those actual forces, I am one of those through whom it flows.'

'You mean, you've whored yourself out for so long and so thoroughly, you've lost all sense of nationhood. I think we all know that. But do you really think a new government will revert to type quite so quickly?'

'I think they'll swiftly appreciate that their new-found allies in the shires and the suburbs might have made a difference on election day, but they're bugger-all use when it comes to the heavy lifting of global intercourse. For that, you need experience, a willingness to accept a certain latitude when it comes to human rights, and the mother of all address books.' If he was attempting to suppress a smirk here, he wasn't successful. 'I appreciate that those qualities aren't necessarily trumpeted from the front bench, but they're warmly welcomed where deals are actually done. Whether that's a London club, a Hong Kong casino or a Dubai brothel.'

'In other words, some things never change.'

'Not even the personnel, Diana. Not in any meaningful way. A few token sink estate brats aside, the paths to power are where they always were, and lead through the same school gates. And it's difficult to maintain a stony silence when you're side by side at a fundraiser for the alma mater. No, I'm confident that, in time, relationships will flourish, friendships blossom, and my worth as a power broker come to be valued for what it is. An indispensable national asset. But until that happy day, I find myself a little short of . . . warm welcomes. Which throws me back onto your company.'

'And that's why we're sharing a toilet? It's nice to be wanted, but you'd be better off strengthening bonds with your former colleagues upstairs. At least they're not embarrassed to be seen in your company.'

'Come come. It takes more than my presence to embarrass

you. No, the only thing I can think of that would manage that would be if it became common knowledge quite how close our relationship has been. And I'm not talking about our early-days dalliance, you understand.'

She understood.

'Which brings me to my point. Excuse me while I multitask.' He stepped to the toilet, unzipped himself, and with his back to her kept on talking. 'Been following the news lately?'

'No, I generally change channel and watch *Friends*. Of course I follow the fucking news. I'm First Desk.'

'Then you'll know there's dissatisfaction in certain quarters regarding the proposed UN resolution about ownership of territories in the South China Sea.'

And here it was: the second boot hitting the floor. The moment she'd known would arrive, ever since he'd told her that the money she'd spent wreaking justice on a Russian assassin had been converted from Chinese yuan.

'Now, if the UK were to indicate that it won't be supporting such a proposition . . . that would be really, *really* useful.'

To his Beijing backers, he meant.

It wouldn't be impossible to kill him here and now. Hold his head down in the bowl. The satisfaction of the moment would see her through much of what followed: arrest, trial, imprisonment. But he was still talking:

'And given my current lack of access to the places that matter, my, ah, silent partners – you remember, I told you about them – my silent partners were wondering whether you might lend your own influence to their cause. Ah, here we go.' His stream hit the bowl, and he gave a little sigh before continuing. 'It would make them very happy, and you know what they say. A happy silent partner is a . . . *silent* silent partner.'

Diana said, 'This is dangerous territory. It could easily be interpreted as treasonous.'

'Lucky for me, then, I'm simply having a private conversation with an old friend.' This was accompanied by a hefty shake. 'A friend, I might say, who is herself compromised beyond her ability to report our conversation without revealing her indebtedness to those partners we're discussing.' He flushed, then tucked himself away and zipped up. When he turned around Diana stepped aside, allowing him access to the sink.

'So if we follow this train to its station, what we're left with is quite straightforward. Should you find it within yourself to drop the appropriate word in the appropriate pairs of ears, then any possibility of an embarrassing indiscretion or two ups and disappears. Whoof!'

She said, 'Tell me you're joking.' From the lobby came the sound of footsteps and a cackle of laughter. The door handle rattled. 'Fuck. *Off.*' Someone fucked off. Judd, meanwhile, was smiling the beatific smile of one for whom joking was a foreign language. In this case, probably Mandarin. 'I'm a civil servant. I don't steer the government, I abide by its rule of law. The idea that I might dictate policy is ludicrous.'

'We both know you're more than that. Your word carries weight. And you've more experience than the Cabinet put together. These people are all at sea and desperately need a navigator. The few sensible minds among them are aware of this. You'll be listened to. And it won't be difficult to construct a sound, real-world reason why Britain should want to ally itself with the next great global power, instead of the United Fading States.'

Diana shook her head. 'They may turn out to be another coalition of gonks, but they've been itching for power for a decade and a half. Whereas I've been First Desk for the last sixteen prime ministers, or whatever it is, all of them from the other side. They don't look on me as an ally. It's a wonder I still have a job.'

'Well, why don't you just do your best?' Judd was working the mirror again, straightening his tie. 'All I ask.'

'All you ask, in its bare bones, is treason.'

'That's a very narrow-minded way of looking at a business proposition. I'm a patriot, Diana. I would die for this country, should the need arise. But until it does, I have a family to feed and a career to pursue. And this is currently the course of action that satisfies those needs. I trust you won't make things difficult for me.'

Again, the image seized her of his head down that toilet bowl. An Eton education: it wouldn't be his first time . . . The last feeble thrashings of his limbs. A curtain pulled down.

'What's your timetable on this . . . fantasy?'

'It's oh-so tempting to say twenty-four hours. But you've a little longer than that. Shall we say the end of the week? Less dramatic, but we can't have everything.'

There was a knock at the door. 'Are you all right in there?'

'Oh, we most surely are,' Judd called. 'Vacating now.' He looked at Diana. 'Unless you need to . . . ?'

She shook her head, not trusting herself to speak.

'Righty-ho then. Back to the fray.'

As if he'd choreographed it in advance, 'Simply the Best' was powering the dance floor as they walked back up the stairs.

Pitchfork was what they were talking about, because Pitchfork was what they were, or had been. No: *were*. A hard lesson Avril had learned, that you didn't stop being part of something just because it was over. However much you'd changed in the years between.

And the years had made their mark on this quartet. Al Hawke least of them, outwardly; there remained something of his near namesake in his bearing, in his nose too. He was tall, and age hadn't bent him yet; there was still strength in those arms, power in those legs, and his eyes were as clear and cold as a frozen lake. In his grey chinos, white shirt and dark jacket – tonsured like a monk – he looked, and still moved, like a man with purpose, someone in whose way you'd not want to be standing. But an element of doubt had moved in with the passing years. If Al was still the man she'd want watching her back, should such a need return, he was no longer capable of the feats of stamina that had once been his trademark. And while this was hardly a surprise, or shouldn't have been, the fact that he too had grown aware of this pained her. The Als of this world should remain convinced of their strength. It was one of the things that made them Als.

As for Daisy, even her lost years hadn't stolen her beauty, though it lay below the surface now, hidden from casual glances. Hair that had been long and dark was short and grey, framing a pinched face that once had been softly rounded; her eyes, too, no longer glittered. The Irish lilt was gone. It had never been pure affectation — Daisy's grandmother had been from Cork, and the accent was hers for the taking — but had been discarded now, as if she had shed anything that might anchor her to the past. Indeed, she might easily have shed her whole life, leaving an empty skin on the pavement. As ever, that memory provoked anger: that here was someone who had given the best part of herself to her country, and in the giving had ensured that lives were saved and buildings stayed standing; that there were bombs that had never gone off. And in return, here she was; a damaged person allowed to become lost. If they hadn't reached her in time, she'd have ended her life in that dismal no man's land below the overpass, as much a discard as the broken cars surrounding her. *If not for us*, Avril thought, and then thought: *but who put her there to begin with?*

Avril herself had grown old in her own way; not so much a diminishment, more a concentration. Or so she hoped. Certainly there had been no dilution of feeling. Emotions coursed through her the way they always had done, and there were days she opened her eyes in the morning and thought herself sixteen again. But this never lasted more than a second or two. And those days were growing rarer.

Whether CC still found within himself the remnants of his younger being, it was hard to say. Right now, he had the air of a tutor addressing a seminar group. They might have been young adults, wary of disappointing him.

'Pitchfork was the beginning of the end for us. All talk of Avvy being a Second Desk, of Al moving into security—'

'I never wanted that—'

' – but it would have been a promotion, Al, and it went away. As for me, it was the last op I was given. Nobody said anything, but everyone knew, and the sooner I accepted it gracefully, the less embarrassment there was all round. And Daisy, well, I'm sorry, my love. It was a bad time, and none of us want to rehash it. But we were made pariahs, and why? Because we had a nasty job to do, and we did it well. Dougie Malone was a psychopath, but the gods in their glory decreed that we use him, and use him we did. And for that, we paid with our careers.'

'CC,' Avril said softly. 'We know all this.'

'You'll allow me my tendencies, love. One of them being a fondness for clarity.'

Al said, 'Much more of this, and I'll be opening that bottle before we've warmed the microwave up.'

'We'll be drinking soon enough. But fine, let's hurry along. Like all operations good and bad, Pitchfork came to an end of its useful life, we all know why.'

'Good Friday.'

'Yes, thank you, Good Friday came and went, and in its aftermath the powers that be heaved a sigh of relief and put Pitchfork out of our misery. It did so With full honours. Charles Partner was First Desk, and signed off on it himself. David Cartwright was there, as were the minister, the Cabinet Secretary, a lawyer or two. The meeting was Mozart level, the highest classification at the time, which meant no minutes were kept. The recordings were wiped, no transcript made. Not even a record of who was present. This nasty slice of history was buried deep as it would go, and curses muttered over its remains. In a better arranged world, Pitchfork would never have been mentioned again. The very word would have dropped from the dictionaries. But that's not what happened, was it?'

He gazed round: the expectant tutor. His students refused to cooperate.

'I'm to do all the work, eh? All right. What happened was, the rumour factory got into business. Mutterings on Fleet Street. The *Sunday Times* investigation. *Panorama*. All of it accompanied by absolute rebuttals in the House and complete stonewalling outside of it. As for the Park, well, the Park did what the Park does and denied Pitchfork absolutely, dismissing the rumours that the Service had aided and abetted a psychotic murderer as sectarian venom designed to undermine the Agreement. While we were cast out into the cold, because nobody, and especially not the Park, likes having reminders of its guilt hung round its neck like a four-headed albatross.' He paused. The other three heads of the burdensome bird remained fixed as they were: Daisy's staring into space, Al's looking straight at him and Avril's concentrating on the floor, though likely seeing something that wasn't carpet. 'Then time's winged whirligig brung in its changes, and one sacred day Dougie Malone was killed, thanks be to God, and in the ten years since the whole topic's dropped off the agenda, which hasn't improved our situation any. And what I'm wondering now is – what I'm wondering now is, have the three of you been listening to a word I've said?'

It was Al who answered. 'That we have.'

'And?'

There was more mutinous silence.

'I said—'

'We heard you,' said Al. He glanced at Avril.

Avril said, '"Not even a record of who was present."'

'I'm glad you were paying attention.'

'And yet you told us who was there.'

From outside came the noise of a wailing child, carried past their window at the speed of a trundling pram.

Al said, 'How, exactly?'

CC, no longer the rambling tutor but the professional fact deliverer, said, 'The late David Cartwright, presumably unknown to anyone but himself, recorded the proceedings. He kept the tape hidden in a box-safe among the books in his library. It turned up at college a few weeks ago when his library was delivered there.'

'And you're the only one who knows about it?' Avril said.

'About the contents, yes.'

'But not the box?'

CC said, 'His grandson knows. There's a smart girl working in the library, she put him onto it. But as far as they're concerned, the box has been destroyed, and all it held was dirty pictures.'

'That's weak,' said Avril.

'It only has to hold a little while.'

'. . . Why so?'

'I'm not a great believer in things happening for a reason. But in this instance, it seems quite clear we've been given an opportunity to achieve redress.'

Only Daisy was unbothered by this, and remained staring into space.

Al and Avril shared a look.

Al said, 'What are you saying, CC? You want to make this stuff public? Because I'm not sure you've thought through the implications.'

'I think I have.'

'If there was wrongdoing — Christ, what am I saying? We know there was wrongdoing, we were part of it. We were Operation Pitchfork. Malone might be dead, but his deeds live on, yes? If we make this public, force the Park to admit its complicity in murder and torture and all the rest of it, where does that leave us? Because I don't want to be making headlines my time of life.'

Avril said, 'Have you found religion, Charles? Or a black spot on your lung? Because whatever it is, this urge to make a clean breast, bear in mind you're not the only one this involves. If you go to the wall, we all go.'

'No one's going to the wall. Can I make that clear? I have no plans to go down in flames, and if I had, I wouldn't take you with me.' CC raised a palm, as if inviting a high five, then let it fall. It was an oddly theatrical gesture. 'But we're in possession of proof of something the Park has long denied, that it was responsible for an operation which gave a madman free rein to indulge in carnage. They need to know we have it. And we need to know what they're prepared to offer to keep it in its box.'

'So. Just so we're on the same page. You want to blackmail the Park about the details of an operation we were part of.'

'Who better?'

'To threaten we'll go public—'

'With proof.'

'Go public with the details of an operation we helped implement.'

'That involved at least thirteen murders. That we know of.'

'And rape,' said Daisy. 'Let's not forget rape.'

Avril said, 'No, CC. It's madness.'

'We'll be waving a stick, that's all. All they need to know is, we have a stick. And they'll back down.'

'And what does backing down look like? You expect an apology? "We're sorry we made you work with a piece of human detritus like Dougie Malone?" We agreed to do it, CC. We might not have liked it, but that was never in the job description, and it's late to complain about it now. We knew what we were getting into.'

'Did we? Did we really? Because nobody spelt out the consequences, or I don't remember them doing so. I remember David Cartwright polishing his glasses while he lectured us on the greater good. About making sacrifices for the men and women in the street. For the good of the country. And he's dead now, and I'm sure he gave the country his best, but he died in a five-star nursing home between clean sheets, and as long as he had his marbles, he lived in a house with a wrap-around garden.' CC was tiring of being on his feet; at any rate he reached out a hand and steadied himself against the wall. 'But maybe it's not the job we'd be complaining about, Avvy. Maybe it's the way we were treated afterwards. I don't know about the rest of you, but old age — which I'm a little further into than you are, so you'll bow to my greater experience — is an absolute fucker. Absolute. Fucker. I never expected to end my days in luxury, but I didn't expect to be worried about turning the heating on in the dead of winter. Or making a single-serving meal last two nights. I gave my best years, same as you did, and didn't ask for a lot in return. But I didn't expect to be given so little. And don't tell me the three of you are faring better, because I'll know that for a story.'

They let this settle before Al said, 'I had to sell my fishing gear. Didn't get half what it was worth, but I needed a winter coat. And they're not cheap.'

Avril said, 'I took in a lodger. It didn't work out.'

Daisy said, 'I lived in a gutter for eighteen months.'

They fell quiet for a while until Avril said, 'Okay, you win.'

Only Daisy laughed.

Avril looked at CC and said, 'I'm not disagreeing with your analysis. But we can't do this. We'd be opening a can of snakes.'

'A can that needs opening.'

'We could end up in prison.'

'I'm not going to pretend there's no risk involved.'

'I don't want to die in a cell.'

'And I don't want to live on baked beans and a two-bar fire.'

'It doesn't have to be one or the other.'

'Glad you see it that way. But I've ten years on you, and frankly, I'm running out of alternatives.'

'Are you dying?'

'No. This isn't about going out with a bang. It's about . . . avoiding a whimper. They owe us, Avril. You, me and Al. And especially Daisy.'

Al said, 'We've mentioned prison. But that's the least of it, if the Park decides not to play ball.'

'If it was just one of us,' CC said, 'a lone wolf, yes, they might try to bury their mess. But four of us? Our ages? They'd be mad to try. It would make a worse stink than what they're trying to keep under wraps. Besides, we didn't survive Northern Ireland without knowing how to make a brush-past.'

'A brush-past? What were you planning on doing, dropping a note through First Desk's front door? We'll be on seven kinds of CCTV before we're in her postcode.'

Avril said, 'Why are you even talking like that? It's not going to happen.'

'I have her email address,' said CC.

'Her *personal* email?'

'The young woman in the library I mentioned, she used to be Taverner's PA. And she doesn't always keep an eye on her phone.'

Avril said, 'You looted her mobile? That's a serious violation of her privacy.'

'Wasn't it, though? On the other hand, we have, collectively, abetted numerous murders. Scrolling through someone's contact list doesn't make me feel I've plumbed the depths of misbehaviour.'

Daisy made a noise which might have been a giggle. When

Avril threw her a glance the sound was history; the face that issued it blank.

'Anyway,' CC said. 'That's it. Why we're here. I'm not suggesting we shake them down for millions, just a fair sum. Al?'

'No. I'm sorry, CC. But no.'

'Avvy?'

'You know we can't. It's madness.'

'Daisy?'

All three turned to her, as she broke off her study of nothing much.

'I think we should do it,' she said.

CC breathed something. It might have been 'Tied vote'.

'Daisy, love,' Avril said gently. 'We can't. You know why.'

'But they owe us.'

'That they do,' said CC.

'They owe *me*.'

'We did our jobs,' said Avril. 'We did our *duty*. We can't throw that away now.'

'Like they threw us away? Why not?'

Because because because, thought Avvy. You know why not.

CC was reaching for the Bushmills, breaking its seal. 'I think we need this now, don't you? There's no ice, you'll be relieved to hear.'

'We haven't made a decision,' said Al. 'There's nothing to toast.'

'I love you all,' CC said. No one had been expecting that. 'And this will be fine. Trust me.'

He began to pour: good big healthy measures.

'Please don't say what you're going to say,' Avril said.

'I'm sorry, Avvy.'

'You've already done it, haven't you? You've set it all in motion.'

'It's what Daisy wants. And she, more than any of us, deserves recompense.'

'This will destroy us. You've destroyed us.'
'No,' said CC. 'I'm making us whole again.'

Slough House, coming on midnight, and flickering screens were strobing Roddy Ho's form and throwing shapes – he looked like a disco king, if only there were an audience to admire him. But the way of the data warrior is a lonely one, and his keyboard his only companion. Still, it was a comfort to know there were others like him, out in the darkened city – men on their own, hunched over laptops, putting the world to rights – and it was hard not to believe that they sensed his presence as they went about their duty; that as they spread their virtual seed hither and yon, they were following his path, if not so stylishly.

Were less tasked, too, with vital missions. Earlier in the day, Lamb had pleaded with Roddy to attempt the impossible – as per – and then, secure in the knowledge that the RodJob was on the case, had told him, bantz, to fuck off till it was done. You had to hand it to the old man, he could do a straight face like no one else. But anyway, here was Roddy, monitors alight with life, an orange Post-it affixed to the nearest – he'd always enjoyed digital dancing in the dark. The hummingbird flies by night, he told himself, rubbing his arm. He knew this for a fact. He'd googled it.

But nightbird or not, cracking the Service's online traffic was no task for lightweights. It took your Stan Lees, your George Lucases, your Roddy Hos to achieve this level of creative brilliance, and careful pacing was required. So on the clock ticked, and on the RodMeister laboured, weaving a passage through a maze of encrypted corridors, many littered with the virtual equivalent of IEDs, triggering which would set floodlights converging on him . . . A mental image formed of Roddy scaling a high-wired fence, caught in the crossbeams of conning towers . . . A blaze of bullets; a torn tattered body; a beautiful corpse hanging by the ankles. It would take a heart of granite not to weep.

'The fuck you still here for?'

Roddy gave a note-perfect imitation of a man squeaking in fright.

'I . . . What are *you* still here for? I mean, the fuck still here for?'

Shirley was chewing gum with her hands in her pockets, like a cartoon rendition of a ten-year-old. She must have been up in her office, because she hadn't come through the back door: no one did that without a ruckus save Lamb, and even he sounded like a walrus attacking a lobster pot most times. Her hair, what there was of it, was tufted into spikes, which had provoked Lamb into asking *Is that fashion or chemo?* Roddy was on the verge of echoing him, but luckily Shirley spoke first. 'No law against staying late. Besides, *I* wasn't working. Creep.'

In fact, she'd been asleep, though the end result was the same: pushing midnight, still at work. She should be on overtime.

Ho had been eating pizza, so she helped herself to a slice from the box on his desk, nearly but not quite tipping it to the floor, and leaned against the wall to eat, choosing a spot where she could see his monitors and attempt to work out what he was doing. This, she accepted, was unlikely. It was akin to watching performance art, which in theory Shirley approved of – it allowed the talentless to call themselves artists, which appealed to her anarchic streak – but in practice was appalling shit that no one understood. But at least Roddy, if he didn't volunteer explanation, could be coerced into divulging one. Besides: pizza.

He said, 'Yeah, this is classified?'

'We, like, literally do the same job? Duh-brain.'

Roddy looked at his screens. There was nothing on them

that would mean anything to Dander. Put him in front of them and he was looking at trapdoors and trolleys, tracks and tramlines; he was Indiana Jones on a subterranean railway, avoiding poison darts. But all Shirley would see was streams of glowing numbers. For a moment he hovered between two worlds, the one he mostly lived in and the one he suspected Shirley and everyone else inhabited. Perhaps if they understood more about his world he'd feel more at home in theirs. But the moment passed, and they were on opposite sides of a chasm again. He said, 'If I was allowed to tell you about it . . .'

'Yeah?'

'I still wouldn't.'

'Asshat.'

The pizza box chose that moment to topple to the floor, landing contents-side down as the laws of physics dictated. Both stared at this for a second, then resumed their glare-off.

Shirley said, 'This was Lamb's little job?'

'Yeah. I mean no. And it's not little.'

'Breaking and entering, right?'

'Like I said. Classified.'

'Into some place or person's records.'

'Above your pay grade. Loser.'

'Which means you must've written it down. Because no way do you remember details. *Loser.*'

She stuffed the last piece of crust into her mouth without taking eyes off Roddy, who stared back unflinchingly, almost, until a slight tremble gave him away. Then he grabbed for the Post-it, almost managing to cram it into his mouth before Shirley had him by the wrist, twisting his hand and unwrapping his fingers, forcing him to relinquish it.

'Munchkin!'

'Watch your language. Or I'll twat you.'

She unwrapped the orange paper square while Roddy stared in murderous hatred. 'I'm doing this for your own benefit,' she explained. 'Secrets between colleagues is not a good idea. I mean, okay, we're spies, but . . .'

Unscrunched, the Post-it turned out to carry two words. A name.

'Next question,' Shirley said. 'Who the fuck is Julian Tanner?'

When Avril woke in the early hours, it was only partly because of Daisy's bad dream: she had known putting head to pillow that if sleep came, it would come briefly. Pitchfork had sunk its prongs into her mind, where Pitchfork did what a pitchfork does: it shifted, lifted and sieved. Daisy's whimperings might have had the same source but she had no coherent report to make, so Avril held her until she grew quiet again, and then lay while darkness skulked outside the window, slowly surrendering its ghosts.

Pitchfork was the operation, and also the codename of its subject. Dougal – Dougie – Malone, long-time IRA enforcer, and the owner of a well-earned reputation for brutality, fostered not simply by his keenness for punishment beatings, but by the methods he chose to implement them: the hammer, the car jack, the crowbar. A short, narrow man, he carried himself like an unpulled punch, and to look into his eyes was to set your darkness echoing, as if his presence dared you unleash the devil in yourself. For two decades he was the Provos' iron fist in its studded glove, seeking out dissent in its ranks and pounding it flat. He had raped at least seven women. And for half the time he enjoyed such power he had been an informer for the British intelligence service, an asset so highly valued that he had a team of four assigned to his care and security: herself, CC, Al and Daisy. If he was Pitchfork, so were they.

All spies together, then, though it hurt Avril to admit Malone into their company. She would rather focus on their difference: Malone had become a spy not to uphold a cause, nor even only for the money, but to gratify evil urges. The dark was where they all worked, she could acknowledge that. But it was where Malone lived, and where he found his joys, chief among these being the death of his enemies, or some of them, because it would have taxed even his endless hatred to murder everyone. He did his best, though, directing his IRA death squad at those whom he named as informers, partly to protect his own position, but mostly because that was who he was, a man who delighted in torture and murder and rape; and who, when it was over, was removed from the Province and settled in Cumbria under a false identity, with a rumoured £80,000 a year in a Gibraltar bank account. Fifteen years later, he was found dead in his own garage, murdered by a method he'd pioneered himself on two luckless colleagues, Stephen Regan and Bernard Docherty; Provos both, and in need of jail time, but who ended up stains on a concrete floor for looking sideways at Dougal Malone.

Last night, three drinks down, CC had offered a toast: that its subject roast in hell.

'Dougie Malone, the nastiest bastard who ever walked the earth. Who helped bring about the arrest of thirty-four terrorists bent on wreaking carnage both sides of the Irish Sea, thereby saving the lives of innocent civilians – and when he wasn't doing that, damn his hide, was running his own little nutting squad with our help and protection, whose victims we could have forewarned, or offered escape routes.'

His glass trembled.

'So here's to the numbers game, played for the greater good. And here's to the nameless heroes who put Malone down. But most of all, here's to Dougie dead. May our Pitchfork even now be tossed on a bigger one, and the devil himself be giggling at the sight.'

He downed his whiskey. Daisy had started working on hers before he was halfway through. Avril and Al, though, held their hands.

It was Al that CC focused on. 'Come on, Alastair. Empty your glass.'

'I'll not drink to another man's death.'

'Not even Malone's? Can you think of a man deserved it more?'

'Leave him be,' said Avril.

'What is this, a mutiny? An uprising?'

'No more than you deserve. Jesus, what were you thinking? What have you done? We'll wind up in a pit of sorrows.'

'Not if we're careful.'

'And I'll not see Daisy back in a dark place.'

'I can speak for myself,' Daisy said.

'Of course. I didn't mean to—'

'And I've said we should do it.'

'But Avvy's right,' Al said. 'Sorry, love. But this is a door better left closed. There's no knowing what'll come crawling through it.'

Our own past lives, thought Avril. Our own misdeeds.

'I don't care,' said Daisy. 'CC's right. They owe us.'

She glanced around, causing Avril to do likewise. At that moment the safe house stood for all of their dwellings; its doors too near their opposite walls, its ceilings too near the floors. When you walked up its stairs, you had to tuck your elbows in. This was what they'd been left with; any greater ambitions they might have had had been packed into storage long ago. It was true – the Park owed them. But collecting on that debt could bring all their roofs crashing down.

CC said, 'I was careful. I used a newly created email address on a public, anonymous computer. The Service can track it to source, but all they'll find is "guest user". We're secure.'

'You sent a copy of the tape?'

'An extract. Enough that First Desk will know what it is.' He had recorded several minutes' worth on his phone and attached the file to his email, he told them, proud of his expertise.

In the absence of other comfort, they'd drunk to that.

Light was busy in the room now, and traffic amassing its battalions. Daisy was sleeping, or pretending well enough. Avril slipped out of bed and shuffled her feet into unlaced trainers. The morning might be packed with more than the usual amount of regret, but it had to be got through, same as always.

'Guess what?' Shirley asked.

'No,' said Louisa, and carried on past the kitchen, up the stairs, into her office. Everything there reminded her of yesterday, and foreshadowed tomorrow. Hanging her bag on her chair, she booted her desktop up – how many people in London, slow horses not included, still used desktops? Maybe eight. Shirley entered without knocking. 'I said no.'

Shirley closed the door. 'Lamb's got Roddy hacking Doctor Desk's emails.'

'I don't do cryptic crosswords and I haven't had coffee yet. Bugger off and annoy someone else.'

'Julian Tanner, that's his real name.'

'Is whose real name? No, forget it. Bugger off.'

'Doctor Desk's.'

Doctor Desk was the *ex officio* nickname of whoever was holding Regent's Park's stethoscope.

Louisa had more than enough to be getting on with. First and least was her actual job: Lamb's latest attempt to see if the human head might explode when subjected to too much useless information. Prison was known to radicalise younger inmates; no one was holding the headlines over that insight. What interested Lamb was the number of anti-radicalisation groups that had consequently sprung into being, their attentions focused on incarcerated youth, offering support, alternatives, help upon release – anything to divert them from the path to extremism.

'Sounds a good idea,' she'd said.

'Yeah, the thing about good ideas? There's always some fucker'll bend them out of shape.'

Because – his view – if you had an interest in recruiting halfway-radicalised hotheads, getting the prison system to identify them for you sounded like a shortcut. *Or maybe that's just your twisted outlook*, she'd wanted to say, but why bother? You'd have more luck talking Lamb into changing his shirt than his opinion. Especially when clinging to it meant him keeping on doing nothing, and someone else pulling a whole new wagonload of mind-currying paperwork.

So that was the job in hand – due diligence checks on almost certainly legitimate social enterprises – while a more pressing concern was running through last night's conversation with Devon Welles. *The door's open.* Good to know.

Meanwhile her actual door was closed, and Shirley leaning against it. 'You think there's something wrong with him?'

'With Lamb?'

'Yeah.'

'How long have you got?'

There was a muffled knock, and Shirley edged aside. 'Okay if I come in?' Lech said, coming in, then noticed Shirley. 'Or am I interrupting?'

'No it isn't. But no, you're not.'

'That's actually ruder to me than it is to you,' Shirley explained to Lech, 'because I was already here.'

'Would you both get lost? I have work to do.'

'Lamb's got Roddy hacking Doctor Desk's emails,' Shirley said.

'You think there's something wrong with him?' Lech asked, hanging his bag on the nearest chair.

Louisa closed her eyes and counted to three. Nothing

changed. 'Why would Lamb wanting Doctor Desk's emails mean there's anything wrong with him?' she asked wearily.

'Because that's how he operates,' said Shirley.

'It is how he operates,' Lech confirmed.

'If you want to crash in my room, the least you can do is not agree with Shirley.'

Ash appeared. 'Is this a meeting?'

'No.'

'Then how come you're . . . meeting?'

'It happened by accident,' Louisa said. 'And it's over. All of you, out. I've a phone call to make.'

There was grumbling but also exodus, an Old Testament coupling. She'd thought she was about to call Devon, but it turned out she was wrong. River answered on the third ring.

'Louisa.'

'How's the patient?'

'I'm . . . okay. Thanks.'

'Had your all-clear yet?'

Which would come from Doctor Desk. If Lamb was hijacking the medic's email traffic, the verdict on River was the probable cause. Not that Lamb would care, but he'd want to be first to know.

'Not yet. But it'll be okay. I'm fine.'

The flatness of his tone suggested otherwise.

It occurred to Louisa, not for the first time, that River might be her oldest friend. Partly this was due to the emotional downsizing Slough House required – if you didn't shutter your horizons, the view would drive you mad – but not only that. There might have been something there, once, and its ghost lingered. 'No,' she said. 'You're bothered. Want to talk about it?'

Which would at least distract her from her own impending decision.

'. . . That's okay. Thanks.'

She said, 'Cool. Offer's open,' and wondered how soon she could disconnect; a question whose answer came from above, in the shape of pounding on the ceiling, accompanied by a strangled version of what might have been her name. 'But it seems I'm needed upstairs.'

'Yeah, good luck with that.'

The last time River opened his heart to her, he'd been worried about his grandfather. But that train had left the station: Louisa had been there when they'd buried the old man, and while she'd attended less dramatic funerals, it was clear that David Cartwright was beyond causing problems. Lamb, on the other hand, was still among the quick, and when she arrived at his door was bowed over his desk like a Francis Bacon study in onanism. It took a second for her to realise he was engaged in the act of darning his socks while still wearing them, except for 'darning' read 'applying duct tape'.

'Adds years,' he said. 'You wouldn't believe the savings.'

'I've often wondered how you fund your wardrobe.'

Though it was accepted office lore that he raided charity bins.

Lamb hauled himself upright with the effort another man might have used to land a marlin. 'Spoken to Cartwright lately?'

'We're in touch.'

'More than he is with me.' Lamb sighed and shook his head: you raise them, you send them into the world, and do they phone, do they write? 'Too busy playing doctors and nurses with young Baker. Been meaning to offer condolences on that score, by the way. Always thought you were in with a chance, especially since Sid's, you know, "accident".' He waggled an index finger at his right temple. 'Head wounds, best-case scenario, if you're not left a vegetable, you're borderline mental. Not judging. But I wouldn't share a bed with one.'

'That's not likely to come up, is it?' said Louisa.

'Bit hurtful, but I'll let it pass. Anyway, thought you'd like to be the . . .' He paused, and counted on his fingers. '. . . Fifth to know. If Cartwright's left anything of value in his drawers, you get first pick.'

'He's not coming back?'

'Turns out his warranty's lapsed. And the Park's not picking up the tab if that toxic doorknob does for him.'

She said, 'You've seen his medical report.'

'Better than that. I've seen the instruction his medical officer received, from Taverner, to bin him. Taverner already told me he was for the chop, but let me think it was Doctor Desk's decision, which is an interesting lie, don't you think?'

'Interesting?'

'Because it wasn't necessary. I mean, the fuck do I care who pulls Cartwright's plug? And why's she doing it anyway? If she hates his guts, why turn him loose? It torments him more being here. Even if he doesn't realise it himself.'

Louisa was aware that her role was to supply prompts while Lamb thought out loud. This was usually Catherine's destiny, but no doubt it would become clear why she'd been chosen instead. Unless it didn't. 'Anything else?'

'Yeah, she bought me a bottle. I mean, talk about uncharacteristic behaviour. This is a woman who smokes more of my fags than I do.' This triggered a deep response: his hand disappeared between two of his shirt buttons, scratched vigorously, then reappeared holding a cigarette. Tucking it between his lips he went on, 'She drops three lit matches in my lap. Says she's got a grievance pending, which is about as likely to give a cat a sleepless night as make her worry, and she tells me about Cartwright, and she mentions that you're out shopping for a new job, which so what? So no, it was specifically Cartwright she wanted me to know about, which means she wants me to tell him he's surplus to requirements so he'll be looking for a way back in. Open to persuasion.' His eyes sparked. 'And that's it. She needs him to do something for her. Something off-book, so probably dodgy. The sly monkey.'

Louisa said, 'She said what now? About me?'

'Don't change the subject. Which is, what's she got lined up for Cartwright? Bearing in mind he'd have trouble setting fire to a petrol pump.'

There was little point pursuing any topic other than the one that gripped Lamb. 'Are you sure you're not seeing a conspiracy where there isn't one?'

'What, the way a hammer thinks everything looks like a thumb? Yeah. Except we're talking about Taverner, who if she tells you the time means she's faking an alibi.'

'So . . . She wants River junked regardless of his medical just to leave him open to some other scheme she has in mind?'

'Yeah, which part of that doesn't make sense?'

She'd been in Slough House too long, because none of it didn't. 'Okay. So what are you planning?'

'Me? I plan to light this thing, and maybe do some more tailoring.' He tapped the cigarette still hanging from his lip, then picked up the reel of tape. 'My collar could do with reinforcing.'

'So I'm here because . . . ?'

He rolled his eyes. 'Can you lot never keep up? You're here, learning this from me, so you can find out what Taverner's got in mind for Cartwright.'

Which explained why it was her, not Catherine, in the room. 'Is that with a view to helping or hindering him?'

'Whichever causes me least aggravation.'

'But you want her to reverse her decision? About River not coming back?'

He had found a lighter, and answered her by clicking it to no effect.

Louisa said, 'Why should I? Like you said, he'll be better off in the wild. So why would I help you keep him here?'

'Because that's what he wants, poor sod. Closest he'll get to living his dream. Back at his desk, imagining he's protecting the nation. Happy as Lazarus.'

'Larry.'

'He came back from the dead, didn't he? Mind you, one place he's never going is the Park, not while Taverner's in charge, but that penny hasn't dropped yet and probably never will. Whereas you – your penny's in the well, isn't it? Made your wish yet?'

She had, even if she only knew it this moment. 'I'm leaving.'

'So this can be your farewell present.'

'To him or you?'

His lighter flared, and he applied it to his cigarette before tossing it over his shoulder.

'I'll get started, shall I?'

'Soon as you like,' said Lamb.

It doesn't matter how you wind your clock, time comes out different lengths. The night River had just endured was one of his longest, and as it approached its end he couldn't decide which had been worse; the hours spent awake, staring into nothingness, or the minutes he'd been asleep, dreaming furtive versions of his grandfather. Stam's words had spiralled through both states – *We all have things we'd like to hide in boxes. It doesn't undo all the good in our lives.* But he'd already known that, hadn't he? Over the past few years, River had come to understand that the grandfather he'd adored had harboured a dark side. Had made ruthless decisions, reached brutal conclusions. Neither his favourite gardening gloves nor his moth-butchered cardigan could cover up a life lived on Spook Street. But this was not new information: River had known it was there, awaiting acceptance.

But it was the banality of this new item, that the O.B. had used pornography, that River found hard to take in. He was neither innocent nor a prude – the internet had inured his generation to degrees of porn that even a Victorian might have found shocking – but something rang false, and as he rose from the bed Sid had vacated earlier, as he showered and brushed his teeth and chose clothes, it became clear what this was, an epiphany that would have arrived sooner if he'd been on his game. It was that the old man had hidden his stash among his books. That was what was unfathomable; that his grandfather had – here was the word – *sullied* his library with porn. Because he wouldn't have done that. There were nooks and corners, angles and crannies, a hundred places where he might have filed this lesser secret. He would not have chosen to include it among the shelves so dear to his heart – no, if he'd hidden something among his books, it was because he wanted it found. That was the spook's code; everything you did should be read backwards. David Cartwright would have known his bookcases would be assessed and pored over, if not by River himself then by a Service archivist, or a book dealer. His box-safe would come to light, its contents be unpacked. There was no version of his grandfather that would have allowed his pornography to be revealed in such a way.

Stam had lied to him.

When he arrived downstairs there was a note on the kitchen table from Sid, whose phone he'd heard ringing an hour ago. *See you later.* Which gave him the opportunity to head out without explaining where and why. Living with Sid was everything he'd hoped for, but that didn't mean he wanted life to be an open book. Jacket on, car keys in hand, he left. His own phone started ringing before he reached his car.

London is London, every last inch of it, but some parts more than others. Crossing the Thames, Sid Baker found herself gazing down at the rolling water, none of which would be in the city for more than – what – twelve hours? A day? And yet it was the essence of the capital; always London, but always passing through. As if the whole could be captured by a single moving part, the entire story held within a verb.

She was not sure she had entertained such transports before her accident, but it didn't much matter either way. She was who she was now, and that was all there was to it.

Diana Taverner was waiting on the south bank, not far from the Globe. Legend had it there was a streak of pigeon shit, a plastic transfer, affixed to the bench she occupied, effectively reserving it for her own use. Given that the bench sat on a small patch unmonitored by CCTV, and was thus one of the few places in the city where you could kiss your lover, adjust your underwear or pick your nose without someone making notes, this was a valuable resource, but Sid found she was no longer sure about such facts; whether they were rumours in the service of a myth Taverner spread about herself, or part of the Park's carefully maintained reality, with props supplied by the Tricks and Toys department. In the end, you could never be sure where a story originated, only where it ended up: trapped between the pages of a book, like a pressed flower or ancient bus ticket. Moving carefully, the way you might approach an uncaged tiger, Sid reached the bench and sat.

Behind them, the usual parade unfurled: visitors and residents, heroes and trolls.

After a second or two Taverner turned and assessed Sid in a way that might easily seem rude — actually, there was no 'seem' about it — but also contained something of ownership, as if Taverner were checking an item of personal property, recently loaned to someone unreliable. Sid had to resist the impulse to stick her tongue out, or at least, she hoped she'd resisted that impulse. There were occasions when she wasn't sure whether she was having a thought or acting upon it, as if her injury had left her with blurred borders. River could be studiously non-reactive at such moments, when she might have said out loud something she'd meant just to think, but then again, he'd presumably not react if she hadn't actually spoken. These were the rabbit holes she navigated daily.

Taverner said, 'You're looking . . . well.'

'For someone who's been shot in the head, you mean.'

'You should learn how to accept a compliment. Trust me, there'll come a time they'll stop being offered.'

When Taverner invited you to trust her, count your spoons. And if you didn't bring spoons, check she hasn't planted one on you, to have you arrested for theft later.

Sid looked about. The sky was clear and blue, and summer added glint and sparkle to multiple surfaces: car windscreens on the opposite bank, the railings on bridges, and the many small corners the river wears from moment to moment. She said, 'This is where you bring people when you don't want anyone to know you're meeting them. Which, by the way, calls into question the security of the location. If even I know about it, I mean.'

'Oh, if I'm meeting anyone here they're by definition unimportant, don't worry your damaged little head about that. Now, small talk. You and Cartwright are an item, I gather.'

'By "gather", you mean it's on file.'

'And how is he? We were dreadfully worried.'

'Yes, my turn to offer advice? When you use that phrase, that you're "dreadfully worried", if you could match it with a show of concern? Tone of voice, facial expression, whatever. Something suggesting sincerity.'

'Quite the spitfire, aren't we? I seem to remember you as being more . . . pliable. Or is this a side effect?'

'Of being shot in the head? It's too small a test group to say. But if you're volunteering to swell the ranks, I'll hold your jacket.'

'Let's get back on track before we both say something you'll regret. You were telling me about Cartwright.'

'He's fine. Better than fine. We're just waiting for the all-clear.'

'Yes. Good. That's not happening.'

This with an equal stress on every word, the way she might

address an infant or a shop assistant, the better to ensure no ambiguity slipped through her net.

Sid waited a beat, then said, 'He's fully recovered.'

'If you say so. But he's not fit for active duty. Never will be.'

'He's not a field agent—'

'It's a technical term, and it covers Slough House. Let's not beat about the bush. Cartwright isn't coming back. His next medical report will draw a line under his career. After that, he'll need another path to tread.'

The scene still glittered in the summer sun, but its dazzle was all hollow now, bright with empty promise.

'Also, to be clear, his injury was not incurred in the line of duty. Just because you're poisoned by a pair of Moscow hoods doesn't mean you were doing your job at the time. Cartwright was out of hours and off the books. If he's hoping for an active service payout, he's barking up someone else's tree.'

'If you think River joined the Service for the benefits, you don't know him one bit.'

'Still,' Taverner went on, as if Sid hadn't spoken, 'he can always share yours. Though of course, given how well you're looking, it's possible you won't remain signed-off yourself much longer. How do you think that'll go down at home? You heading back to the Service, Cartwright sloping off to the job centre?' She tilted her head to one side. 'I can see him as a PE teacher, actually. He'd look good in a tracksuit, and he'll relate to teenage boys just fine. On the right wavelength.'

'And you're telling me this why? To save you the trouble of having somebody type a letter?'

'Oh, this is a call I'll be making myself. Why should the underlings have all the fun?'

Sid stood. 'It's been a total pleasure. Let's not stay in touch.'

The bridge was waiting for her. She'd use it to put as much of London as possible between herself and Diana Taverner.

Who said, 'I thought you were the smart one.'

Sid paused.

'But you're going to walk away without hearing the rest.'

'No, I just want you to get on with it. I can do without the gloating.'

'Sit down.'

'Talk first.'

'It's not complicated. You do something for me, and I clear young River's path back. Which might not be what you want, and it's nothing I give two damns about, but it's what he's desperate for and we both know it.'

'Back to Regent's Park?'

'Christ, no. To Slough House. Where he belongs.'

'Like I say. A total pleasure.'

This time, she got a few yards.

'Wait.'

She waited.

'You're very sure of yourself.'

'You're the one wanted to meet.'

'That doesn't mean I'm offering blank cheques.'

'Suit yourself.'

Another yard. Then Taverner said:

'He'll have to have training wheels fitted. And unlearn everything Lamb's taught him.'

This time, Sid turned. Her smile as she approached the bench might have looked sweet, to anyone but Taverner.

'Keep talking,' she said.

'This is fucked.'

Which was Al speaking. Avril didn't necessarily approve of the phrasing, but she couldn't argue with his assessment.

'It is what it is,' she said. 'Isn't that what we're supposed to say these days?'

'Yes,' he said. 'But what it is is, it's fucked.'

Having risen late, they were showered, dressed, hungover. CC had spent the night but was up and out now, gathering provisions; even so, the pair were huddled in the backyard, a tiny breathing space for potted plants and a bin, so they could formulate a plan, or lament its absence, without Daisy overhearing. If the muffled conversation of the pipes scaling the wall was a guide, she was currently in the bathroom.

Avril's head was clanging too – her body regretting the Bushmills. She said, 'Maybe the Park will do the right thing. There's always a first time. And we could all do with some extra income. CC's not wrong about that.'

'I'm not a charity case,' Al said.

None of them were. That wasn't her point. Poverty came in different sizes, and it wasn't like they were using food banks, but she, at least, was browsing the reduced-to-clear shelf when there was no one around to notice. They weren't poor the way poor people were poor, but they were poor the way middle-class people were, and that felt poor enough – four former agents, a fistful of medals between them, none of which could be displayed in public, and their joint assets wouldn't pay a deposit on a flat in central London. With their degrees they could have gone into banking, politics, industry, and it was bolted on they'd be looking at a twilight spent in second homes on the coast, the odd cruise, instead of shivering each time inflation took a bite from their pensions. None of which made CC's plan more sensible. But it gave her – gave all of them – a vested interest in its outcome.

Besides, it was happening. If she retained anything of her training, it was to bend to the inevitable rather than break herself against it.

Al said, 'We all love the old idiot, but this is dangerous, not the quirky caper he seems to think. From what I've heard, Diana Taverner's ruthless. You think she'll stand for a half-arsed blackmail attempt?'

'But there are four of us, as he pointed out. Safety in numbers.'

'Or a buy-one-get-three-free tragedy. If we're all in the same car that goes off the same cliff . . .'

Then it's not a string of coincidental deaths. Just one sorry accident.

She said, 'First Desk won't sanction mass wet work just to avoid headlines. It's not the seventies any more.'

'Doesn't have to be. CC thinks he's running an op, that he's got his old crew back together, but we don't work like that any more. Christ, I need a piss break on a supermarket shop. Can you see the four of us scamming the Park? And then there's Daisy.'

Yes, there was Daisy. Who had suffered most in the aftermath of Pitchfork; who had quit the Park within a year, an extended leave of absence – medical reasons – becoming permanent. She'd then dropped off the map, and to Avril's eternal shame it had been months before she noticed, so weighed down had she been by her own baggage. Coming to terms with the human cost behind a supposedly successful operation; learning to live with the nights during which Dougie Malone's face, words, acts, hovered like a mobile over her sleepless head. Ever since, the knowledge that Daisy had spent that time lost inside the ever-diminishing circles of her despair had added to the baggage: all those unanswered calls she had allowed herself to forget about, the ignored emails put down to Daisy being in *one of her moods*. It had taken Al to bring her to her senses. *She's moved out of her flat,* he'd told her. *I don't know where she is.* And all the reasons she'd given herself for Daisy's silence had melted.

Her first port of call had been the Park. We have a duty of care, she had said. Daisy's one of ours.

Not any more she isn't, came the reply.

'. . . Avvy?'

'I'm thinking.'

A noise from the front door was CC returning from the shops. Lack of noise from the pipes was Daisy, no longer in the bathroom.

She said, 'Remember what they used to tell us before we headed into joe country? Nine times out of ten, nothing happens. Odds are, this will be one of those times. The Park'll think CC's a crank and ignore him. We wait it out a few days, then go home. Everything back to normal.'

'I can only admire your optimism.'

'And Al? Two words. Incontinence pants.'

'Not living that down, am I?'

'Not while I draw breath.'

They went back inside, leaving the plants to plot amongst themselves.

Taverner said, 'Someone's trying to extort money from the Park.'

It took Sid a moment to catch on to this, as if a lifeline had been thrown which went wide, and her arms were still flailing about. 'What?'

'Extortion. You know, give us all your money or we'll hoist dirty washing up your flagpole.'

'You can't be serious.'

'I certainly can. You think it's the first time this has happened?'

'Hardly. But why tell me? What are the Dogs for, if not to sic on trespassers?'

The Dogs: the Service's police force, ostensibly to keep personnel on the straight and narrow, but all too often used to nip their ankles to remind them who was boss.

Taverner said, 'That thing about using a sledgehammer on a nutcase? I wouldn't want to be accused of going in heavy on a pensioner. No, this can be defused with tact and sensitivity.'

Which suggested that Taverner wouldn't be doing it herself. 'And you want me as your go-between?'

'It wouldn't be the first time.'

'But the last time ended well.' She couldn't stop herself rubbing her head, feeling the groove, like a dancer who can't resist the beat.

'Don't underestimate yourself. Just because you screwed up once doesn't mean you'll do it again.'

'I didn't screw up, I got shot. There's a difference.'

'If you say so. Doesn't look a huge one from the gallery.' Taverner raised fingers to her lips, as if expecting a cigarette to materialise, then seemed to realise what she was doing. She lowered her hand. 'But that's by the by. You're empathetic, you get on well with people. I know this. It's in your file.'

'I'm touched.'

'So in the absence of any other candidate, you'll do.'

Sid said, 'You said pensioner. You know who's doing this?'

'I know who he is.'

'He *told* you?'

'That would be lax, wouldn't it? No, the demand came through anonymously on an email account set up for the purpose. On a public access computer in a public library.'

'Which was traceable.'

'And libraries have CCTV, yes, or some do, which sometimes work. He was unlucky, I'll give him that. But not as careful as he should have been. He's fortunate he picked a gentle soul like me to play with. Else he'd be waking up in Rwanda, with a barcode where his head used to be.'

'So you caught him on camera typing out this email?'

'Near enough. I have footage of a former agent leaving the public library in question within five minutes of the email being dispatched. Do the mathematics.'

Sid said, 'You found all that yourself?'

'That's right, while drinking a cup of coffee made from beans I roasted with my own fair hands. Of course I didn't do it myself. I'm First Desk, I have staff. Who follow instructions and then forget they received them. To all intents and purposes, what I've just told you is strictly between us.'

Sid doubted that. Being ordered to forget something was on a par with being told to stop feeling itchy. But Taverner had been in charge so long, she'd forgotten her word wasn't natural law. This was how empires fell, and also TV presenters.

There was activity on the Thames, one of those polka-dotted tourist boats that either undermined or underlined the franchised nature of contemporary art, depending on how ironic you were feeling. Sid's eyes were drawn to it as it reorganised the surface of the water, causing what looked like widespread turbulence but which soon settled back into the same old patterns. 'What does he want?'

'The clown in question is threatening to go public with one of the messier stories from our recent history. Unless we make his life a little more comfortable.'

'And you think he's a nutcase.'

'Trying to blackmail me, that's a medically recognised symptom.' She turned to face Sid, giving her a full hundred watts of well-meaning. 'But I don't plan to trample him into the dirt. The truth is, he wasn't treated as well as he might have been. And it's possible I'll find a way to augment a pension somewhere down the line, or at least make sure he's not actually destitute. But it won't be in response to threats.'

'You can't tell him that yourself?'

'What, turn up in person? Don't be ridiculous.' She dipped into her bag and produced an envelope. 'This is a be-good payment, not a fuck-you fund. Enough to pay his way around the big city for a few days, where he'll be coming to deliver his proof into my hands. Details to follow.'

'And where exactly do I find this mystery man?'

'Oxford. His name's Stamoran. Address and so on in the envelope. I'll trust you not to siphon off any of the cash.'

'I'm flattered.'

'But let's understand the ground rules. Do the job, and Romeo gets his heart's desire. Scribble outside the lines, and I'll make it my business to upset both of you. A lot. Are we clear?'

They were clear.

And also done.

Taverner watched the younger woman walk away. Sid Baker evidently hadn't known that Cartwright's future had been wrapped in black ribbons, which meant either Lamb hadn't passed that news on to Cartwright, or Cartwright hadn't shared it with his lady love. Just as well Taverner had taken the belt and braces approach; just as well, too, that Baker hadn't questioned why the reward on offer was so large, given the low-level nature of the task. But then, few of us argue ourselves out of a wage hike; and besides, if it was clear that Baker would sooner put her Spook Street days behind her, it was equally apparent that she'd bite any bullet to keep Cartwright happy. Taverner understood Baker better than the young woman suspected. Besides, she'd been on Spook Street long enough to know that our first betrayal is always of ourselves.

As for Charles Cornell Stamoran – who had once led a crew known as the Brains Trust – whether this was his first betrayal was moot; that it was going to be his last, all but certain. It would, though, be in a good cause. Old he might be, but Taverner didn't believe in writing people off because they were old. She believed in writing them off because they were no longer useful, and that shit could happen at any age. And given her current needs, Stamoran was demonstrably useful.

The polka-dotted boat had gone. The Thames had erased its passage. Tossing her imaginary cigarette and gathering her bag, Taverner similarly vanished into the ebb and flow of London life.

Erin said, 'I've not seen him since yesterday lunchtime. I mean, he's a volunteer, it's not like he has to clock in.'

Traffic was light on the westbound A40, the weather perhaps persuading people to stay where they were, for fear of jinxing it. River had come through London with his temper no more frayed than the average city driver, about ten degrees short of psychic meltdown, and was now in the countryside, or its urban edge, where the cows and sheep were so used to cars they probably had provisional driving licences, and continued grazing for anything short of a seven-vehicle pile-up.

'Do you have his address?'

'No.'

'Does anyone?'

'Well, *some*one will . . . Look, I'll call you back. Is this to do with the missing book?'

'I just want to talk to him. Thanks.'

He ended the call overtaking a coach and his phone rang again immediately. Louisa. He'd ignored her earlier, fearing another sensitive assessment of his physical and/or emotional well-being, but couldn't avoid her forever. They'd shot bad actors together, and this formed a bond, the way – if they'd been in different jobs – navigating a tricky spreadsheet might, or unjamming a photocopier. Besides, a friendly voice. He could do with a boost.

She said, 'Lamb says Taverner's kicked you off the pitch, probably as a way of applying pressure. So I'm wondering if she's got you doing something dodgy in the hope of getting reinstated.'

'. . . Lamb said what?'

'River, you're not doing anything stupid, are you? We know Lady Di can't be trusted.'

The coach was in his rear-view. If he slammed on his brakes it would plough right into him, finishing off the job those Russian berks had screwed up. Instead, he accelerated, finding space on the inside lane while rescrambling Louisa's words into something he could make sense of. 'Lamb told you Taverner's fired me?'

'You're not coming back, she says. No clean bill of health. I'm sorry.'

He carried out a mini-medical on himself: brain, internal organs, limbs. He was fine; he was fucking brilliant. More to the point, Taverner wasn't trying to squeeze him, so what was going on? 'And you got this from Lamb?'

'Who got it from Taverner. Shit, you didn't know? I thought . . . Ah, fuck it. I could have been more tactful.'

A drunk monkey with a water pistol could have been more tactful. River wondered if this was what working for Lamb did to you: wore away your gentler instincts, leaving you pumice rough when breaking bad news. 'He might have been . . . Shit.'

He might have been anything: lying his eyes out, having a laugh. Laying the first breadcrumb in a trail that would lead off a cliff. With Lamb, you never knew. And even when you did, it didn't help.

'River?'

'I'm fine. Driving.'

'Look, I'm sorry, I—'

'Talk later.'

The coach was history.

The sun was still climbing the sky, which was still blue. Yesterday, driving this way, all had been fine and all had been dandy. He'd been planning his comeback, the degree to which he'd impress Taverner and have her waxing the tiled floors at Regent's Park, the better to host his reflection on his triumphant re-entry. By the time he'd been heading home his mind had been full of the O.B., and the dirty pictures hidden on his bookshelves. And now, third time of passage, he'd just learned that his career had flatlined; was so dead his best friend assumed he already knew about it. Maybe he should find another route home, in case bad shit started happening.

His phone rang again, Erin, with Stamoran's address and phone number. He fed the former into his satnav while Erin not so subtly probed for an explanation. When she rang off, clearly not thrilled, he dialled Stam, but got no reply. Then he contemplated calling Lamb, seeing if he could find out precisely what Taverner had said, but concluded he'd sooner French kiss a wet dog. If Taverner planned to squeeze him, so be it: he'd suffer being squeezed – squoze? – if it would settle his future. Talking to Lamb would hardly help, 'Cry me a you' being his standard consolation for River's woes. And meanwhile, River had his grandfather to worry about: what crap Stamoran was pulling that required the O.B.'s name to be tarnished, and what it was that had really been hidden in the box-safe. Enough to be getting on with.

Not going back – his career over – the Park a fantasy – that could wait.

Meanwhile, the satnav took him what felt like all the way round Oxford, largely because that's what it was, then dumped him in a tailback heading towards the centre, along a road lined with hoardings advertising mattresses, warehouse-sized electrical stores, and too many traffic lights. Somewhere in the distance, a train was crossing a bridge. He called Sid but it went to voicemail so he fiddled with his radio instead, and finding nothing he wanted to listen to sat and fumed, the traffic nudging forward, his temperature rising, the morning crawling by.

It was the train before the one River noticed, or even the one before that, that Sid had arrived on. An otherwise admirable TV series had recently suggested that London–Oxford rail travel was a complicated business, but Sid simply caught the Tube to Paddington and hopped on a direct service. While the train did its job, she read the notes Taverner had included in the envelope: Charles Cornell Stamoran's home address, which was off the Botley Road – a short walk from the station – plus a reminder of where the Spooks' College was, where he mostly spent his days, and the safe house on Woodstock Road he had nominal care of, tidying up between periods of usage, replenishing stocks, binning junk mail. If she hadn't been on medical leave she could have accessed Park files and found out more, but the list of places he might be had to suffice. The envelope also held a thousand pounds in box-fresh twenties and a burner phone. She resealed it, and spent the rest of the journey gazing through the window at the sun-flattened landscape, noting the absence where Didcot power station's chimneys once stood. The train carrying her forward was also taking her back: she'd studied at Oxford, and this scenery was familiar. The cows were probably different, though.

At the station she cut under the railway bridge and within five minutes was at Stamoran's address: a terraced house that backed onto the river, and had three doorbells replacing a knocker. Stamoran was on the top floor, or was when he was in, but Sid rang twice, and then a third time, to no avail. She thought about ringing one of the other bells, but if he wasn't there, he wasn't there. The college was her next best bet; on the other hand – the city's geography returning to her – she could reach the safe house by walking up the canal, and the weather made that an attractive prospect. Besides, Stamoran was old school, she was guessing – a pensioner, Taverner had noted – and safe houses were where the old school hid themselves when sins had been committed. And also, maybe she should give herself time to wonder whether she was doing the right thing.

Cash was cash, and presumably wouldn't be unwelcome. It also suggested that manacles weren't awaiting him, but Stamoran had attempted to extort money from the Park, so any amount of fucking him about was within the acceptable range of responses. And now she was part of that, her own agenda weighted by self-interest, or River-interest at any rate. Did she want River back at the Park? Not as much as he wanted to be there. All of this, though, was after the event. She was hopping to Taverner's beat. There was no point leaving the dance floor now, even assuming the choice was hers to make.

Up the canal, across the meadow, over the railway line once more. A northwards stroll through suburbs where the houses were large, the pavements leafy. The safe house itself was on a busy thoroughfare heading out of the city, and was small – a cottage – and out of place, though might be cosy inside. Walking past on the opposite pavement she saw no signs of life, though all that meant was, there was nobody hanging out of a window or sitting on the roof. A wheelie bin had the next door's number painted on it. A hundred yards up the road, whose curvature meant the manoeuvre couldn't be spotted from the house's window, Sid crossed the road and headed back.

Charles Cornell Stamoran. She was composing a mental picture: greying, benign, a corduroy jacket. Spectacles on a chain. He'd ride a bike – a black step-through with a basket up front – and tuck his trouser turn-ups into thick woollen socks. Would open the door when she rang the bell and pretend to be someone else, but the elbow patches would give him away. His home address: Spook Street. Here's a grand and here's a phone. *Someone wants a word.* That's if he was even here in the first place. One way of finding out was ringing the bell, though even as she did so she was thinking *And this is what you do in a safe house, right? When someone rings the bell, you answer it.* The days she'd spent in David Cartwright's study flashed through her mind, in the snug nest she'd made, surrounded by his books. When anyone approached the house, she'd made herself invisible. Answering the door was not on the agenda.

But this one opened. 'Yes?'

It was a woman of sixty or so, Sid's height, with grey hair, wearing jeans and a thin lilac sweater, and whose eyes glittered in a way Sid found disturbing, not least because she recognised their sparkle. It was the same look she caught in her reflection, on mornings when her wound felt recent. The phantom bullet lodged in her head pulsed. 'I'm sorry, I might have rung the wrong—'

'Daisy!'

A man appeared at her shoulder: an apologetic figure was Sid's first thought, a little raggy of sleeve, a little threadbare at the hem. Bullish of frame, reddish of face, whitish of hair. And also, to her stifled satisfaction, wearing a pair of spectacles on a chain around his neck. But his gaze was piercing. He placed a hand on Daisy's forearm, adding irritation to the sparkle in those eyes. 'You are?'

Good question. She hadn't thought to prepare an alternative identity, though why would she want one? If what Taverner had said was true, it was this man who needed a cover: he was the one shaking down the Park. She said, 'My name's Sidonie Baker. If you're Charles Stamoran I've something for you.'

'How did you know to find me here? No, don't answer. It's obvious.' Something went out of him: air. As if he'd been keeping himself aloft on hope, and had just seen that blow away down the road.

'May I come in?'

He thought for a moment then stepped back, drawing Daisy

with him. It was a narrow hallway, barely worth the name. Turn right, you were in the front room. Daisy released herself from Stamoran's grasp and slid away to give Sid space, and as Sid entered she became aware – nothing extra-sensory; it was too small a house to keep secrets – that they weren't the only ones within, and this required a quick rethink. Stamoran wasn't alone. Was Taverner aware of this? The window's view of the front road was shrouded by a net curtain; there was a two-seater sofa, and a hint of last night's alcohol in the air. Maybe Stamoran was guilty of other crimes, like running a Service safe house as an Airbnb, but that was another rabbit hole she'd best not tumble down. She turned to ask a question, and it was on her tongue, all but spoken, when her legs were whipped away from her and for one turbulent moment she was unconnected to the floor. And then she was on it and Daisy was on top of her and there was a blade at her throat, and that was it; that was all there was.

Roddy would have been the first to admit he had an excellent singing voice, though a long-established difficulty in finding the second meant he generally refrained from breaking into harmony when the slackers were about. Their loss. His gift for leaving even the roughest melody glazed in honey deserved its own label: a pity R & B was taken – Rodz Beatz – but there was still room for Roddy-pop. *R-Pop*. Hard not to see queues forming outside stadiums. Slough House, obviously, was never going to make it onto his touring schedule, but a combination of headphones, sheer joy in his own talent, and the fact that Wicinski was a sneaky bastard meant Roddy was in full song – had his Hojo working – when Lech returned from lunch.

'Losers and boozers,' he was crooning. 'Something something fingernails.'

'Working on your theme song?'

Ho's attempt to look like he was simultaneously upright, working and not singing resulted in his headphones and his mobile hitting the floor at not quite the same time, as if an experiment in gravity had just failed.

'Yeah, and you've found your . . . cheese grater.'

'Nice one.'

'Because that's what you shave with.'

Lech rubbed his cheek: funny, he could go for hours not being reminded about the mess his face had become – Londoners were unfazeable, by and large, when they weren't online – but seconds into Ho's company and he was contemplating bandaging himself up like the invisible man. 'Did you ever think about a vow of silence? Or maybe having your vocal cords pruned?'

'Jealous. I went pro I'd have groupies. You've just got rubberneckers.'

'Ho, your voice sounds like you're feeding an arthritic seal, very slowly, into a cider press. The only way you'll draw groupies is if you sign up for assisted dying.'

'You need your ears plunged. My voice puts the Ho in "hot".'

Lech, who would have quite liked to put the Ho in hospital, said, 'You should leave your brain to science. They could do with one that's not been used.'

'Yeah, and you should leave yours to . . . the Tiny Brain Museum.'

'Good comeback.'

'They could do with one that's really small,' Ho called after him as he left the office and trudged up to Louisa's, where he begged her to reconsider the no squatters policy. Otherwise he might kill Ho.

'Sounds a plan. No, I meant killing Ho.' Too late: Lech was already booting up the PC on the spare desk, which Louisa hated anyone calling 'the spare desk'. 'It makes it sound like people can plonk themselves there whenever they feel like it,' she'd said more than once, usually to Lech, which proved her point. And just to underline how his presence was disturbing her, his phone rang.

'Yeah, what?'

'You working on the safe house register?'

'Is that what we're calling it? A register?'

River, who'd spent the past two hours watching the house where Stamoran lived, said, 'Shit, I don't know, call it what you like. But are you at your desk? Can you look at the list?'

'Yes. Or no. But okay. Hang on a minute.' He pulled the spare chair from under the spare desk with his foot and crashed onto it while waiting for the spare screen to stop grinding grey and ask for his password. Meanwhile, Louisa had guessed it was River he was talking to: this probably had as much to do with the rarity of Lech's receiving a call as it did with River being on her mind. 'Ask him where he is,' she said.

'Where are you?' Lech asked. Then said, 'Oxford.'

'What's he doing in Oxford?'

'What are you doing in – you know what, hold tight.' He tossed the phone to Louisa, and used his newly free hand to slap the PC, a verified method of making it feel like you were speeding things up.

'What you doing in Oxford?' Louisa said.

'Not much. What you doing in Slough House?'

'Same. Why d'you need to know where the local safe house is?'

'Seen all the tourist stuff. Did you know they have an underground train here, taking books from one library to another?'

'Sounds like a lot of effort to avoid a bit of work. Who's in the safe house?'

'Until I know where it is, hard to say.'

'What you up to, River?'

'Just tracking down someone who knew my grandfather.'

'Is this for Taverner?'

'No.' There was a moment's interest when a passer-by paused at Stamoran's door, but whoever it was was posting junk mail, and moved on swiftly. 'I'm on medical leave, remember? From which, according to you, I'm not coming back. So I'm hardly doing anything for Taverner. Has Lech accessed that file yet?'

Lech had not done so.

'Have him call me back,' River said, and disconnected.

Rude bastard.

River, in his car, stiff from lack of movement, wouldn't have disagreed. He knew he was blaming Louisa for delivering bad news earlier, even if it were bad news he hadn't wasted a moment disbelieving – had he known all along he was kidding himself; that his nine-day time-out wasn't something to be shaken off after a few months' convalescence? It was hard now to see such wishful thinking as anything else. But that was what life could do: turn you upside down, shake your pockets empty, in the time it took to bite your tongue. One moment everything's fine. The next, your mouth's full of blood.

Stamoran's door opened.

He turned his head lazily, careful to avoid sudden movement, but the young woman emerging from the house couldn't have cared less, pulling the door shut behind her and setting off without a glance in River's direction. There were three doorbells, and nothing about Stam suggested he might be playing house with a young woman, so this must be one of the other tenants. He turned back to his phone. Try Sid again? And say what? He didn't want to tell her where he was; there was too much backstory involved. He hadn't told her about the box-safe, about Stam's saying it held porn, and would have to explain why he hadn't mentioned that before going on to mention why he'd decided Stam was lying. Simpler to leave it until they were together again. There was a lot about being in a relationship that was easier to control when you weren't actually having a conversation. It was possible that this attitude needed work, but he was busy. His phone chirruped but it was a text – spam. Did he want to change energy supplier? No, he wanted Lech to call back with the safe house address. Lech, though, was still having trouble with his PC, and had pretty clearly pissed on his picnic when it came to seeking help from Ho. He looked at Louisa, who pretended not to notice, but he didn't dare call her on it because she was annoyed about something. Then Catherine came in, distributing worksheets, and noticed the atmosphere.

She said, 'Please don't say you need mother-henning too. It's bad enough dealing with Ashley's protracted adolescence and Shirley's . . . being Shirley.'

'Relax,' Louisa said. 'No one's asking you to interfere.'

Catherine might have responded – should have done – but settled for giving Louisa a look which Louisa, on a roll now, also pretended not to notice. Lech thanked Catherine for the worksheet with his eyebrows, then thanked God or whoever when the PC accepted his password and blinked back into blankness, a possible precursor of emerging into life. Catherine, meanwhile, crossed into Ash's room and laid the paperwork on her desk with a quiet, 'Here's your worksheet,' ignoring Ash's muttered 'What is a fucking worksheet, anyway?', but failing to quash a mental response as she carried on up the stairs: It's a record of tasks completed in hourly time slots, *as you very well know*, these last five words rendered in italics. Frankly, she did not understand how she managed not to drink. Sometimes it beggared belief that she managed not to scream.

Lamb was in his office, unshod feet on his desk, his socks looking like someone had glued the contents of a puncture repair kit onto a dishrag. One of his eyes was closed, but the other tracked her movements as she entered the room, giving her the feeling of having wandered into a reptile enclosure.

The smell, too, was perhaps not dissimilar. He didn't speak as she laid several days' worth of emails in his in-tray — he preferred them printed out: you can't rip up a screen — but before she was safely through the door again he said, 'What's pissing you off now?'

'I'm fine. Thanks for asking.'

'Yeah, stroll on. I can read you like a . . .'

'Book?'

'Election flyer.'

'Nobody reads election flyers.'

'My point exactly. So save me the bother and say what's drunk your lunch.'

She said, 'This place is a war zone. They're all at one another's throats. And I'm sick of trying to keep the peace.'

'So let 'em tear each other apart. Slough House, it's pretty much our mission statement.'

'They're people, not lab mice. Damaged people. We can't just let them bite chunks out of each other.'

Lamb rolled his eyes, both open now, heavenwards. 'Are you there, God? It's me, Jackson. Got one of your do-gooder types here, meaning well and causing trouble.'

'I'm not the one—'

'You've been here long enough, you should know what brings this lot together. Grief, pain and shit-the-bed clusterfucks. You want them putting on a united front? Be careful what you wish for.'

'I'll go, shall I?'

'Thought you already had. Oh Christ, what now?'

What now was Louisa, coming in as Catherine exited. 'You asked what Taverner had River doing.'

'I know I did. Your job's to provide answers, not restate questions.'

'He's in Oxford. And he's asked Lech where the local safe house is.'

'So maybe he's after a freebie dirty weekend. Show young Baker round the ivory spires, then take her up the Woodstock Road.' He adopted a pious expression. 'Not that I approve of either fornication or freeloading, but really, Guy, if this is jealousy-driven cockblocking, I hoped for better from you. Cartwright's made his choice. Deal with it.'

'There's never been anything between me and River.'

'If you say so.'

'And what business is it of yours anyway?'

'It's an admin thing. Any staff fraternisation, which is like workplace incest with added frotting, I have to write it up for the Park.' He adopted his muggins here expression. 'I don't get paid extra for that. It's one of the burdens of rank.'

'You write it up?'

'Well, Standish does. Amounts to the same thing.' He reached inside his shirt to palpate his belly for a satisfying few seconds, and when he withdrew his hand it was holding a cigarette. 'Not that I'm opposed in principle, you understand. I mean Cartwright, I'm pretty sure that ship's sunk, but if you're planning on resurrecting your love life, go for it. I'm a great believer in getting back on the bike.' He studied his cigarette for a moment, then put it in his mouth. 'In this scenario, you'd be the bike. I hope that was clear.'

'I'd appreciate a little less commentary on my private life,' Louisa said, after a long pause.

In his plumpest tones, Lamb said, 'I do apologise. If I have a failing, it's that I care too much. Always been my Achilles tendon.' He frowned. 'Unless I mean elbow.'

'Can we get back on track? River's in Oxford, he's up to something and he won't say what. You wanted me to step into whatever it is he's doing. So I'm going to Oxford to help him. Okay?'

'I'm all for the hands-on approach, but I can't help wondering if he's not beyond help. We already know he's for the chop, plus there's the whole post-traumatic stress bollocks.' He was rummaging around his desk, looking for a lighter. 'You ask me, the best you'll be able to do for him is pat him on the head a little.' He mimed the action, to be sure she got it. 'If you can reach his head, that is, with him curled up in the faecal position.'

'Foetal.'

'As I just explained, he's probably shitting himself.' A lighter came to hand, and he clicked at it vigorously. 'But sure, yeah, why not. Take a day's leave.'

'It would count as work,' Louisa said. 'It would actually be work.'

'Get Standish to sign you off.' The lighter flared into flame and he torched the end of his cigarette. Then tossed the lighter over his shoulder, where it hit the wall with a bump and dropped into shadow. 'And send me a postcard. No, write me a postcard, saying exactly what's going on, then call me up and read it out to me.'

'Woodstock Road.'

'Wicinski can find you the number.'

He could and did, and had already phoned River, while attempting to extract some basic information, like: what are you up to? But River wouldn't say, though he did at least remember to offer thanks. Then programmed the address into his satnav: it wasn't far from the college, or at any rate was on the same road. The program promised roadworks if he attempted the direct route so he headed out to the ring road, mentally repeating Lech's question as he did so – what was he up to? Chasing down Stam, to find out why he'd lied about what was in the box-safe. And also, to discover what had actually been in the box-safe; his grandfather's final secret, which was River's own legacy.

In his last days, the O.B. might have thought a plastic toy from a cornflakes carton a secret worth preserving. He had lost his grip on his former realities. When River visited him at Skylarks, the home he'd been moved to when home itself grew strange, his talk had been of boys' own derring-do, the details dredged from a mishmash of school-day stories and gung-ho war films. All his life, River had listened to the old man talk. Never before had he wanted the flow of words to dry up. Now, skirting Oxford with the post-lunch traffic, he remembered something his grandfather had said years back, when he still controlled the narrative; words that seemed freighted with hindsight, a warning that hadn't been heeded because there were no precautions you could take against growing old, no tradecraft that would keep you out of senility's clutches. *Old spies can grow ridiculous, River.*

He'd meant if they hung on too long. Old spies outgrow their covers; their sleeves become tattered and worn. They forget which lies they're meant to tell, which truths they ought to conceal, and that was without the added pain of dementia, of cells fraying and losing their connections, of neural networks decaying into leaderless chaos. Once, his grandfather had haunted Molly Doran's archive, secretly adding conclusions to the unfinished stories collected there. In the end, conclusions were beyond him . . . Best to tune out gracefully, and accept retirement's package of slip-ons and slacks and slow movements. Better the boredom of the afternoon nap than to stay on the road too long and end up a laughing stock. Old spies can grow ridiculous. Old spies aren't much better than clowns.

River wondered what the O.B. had hidden in his box-safe; wondered what Stam, another superannuated spook, might be up to, and wondered what Sid was doing, and this time called her, but after three rings went to voicemail again. Then he thought about trying Louisa, and apologising for being a bastard, which brought to mind what she'd asked earlier, about whether he was on a job for Taverner. What had that been about? If old spies grow ridiculous it was because young spies wove their lives into knots, forever making cat's cradles out of straightforward lengths of string. No wonder there was so much pent-up rage in Slough House, an observation which summoned images of Shirley, who right then was rousing herself from a post-lunch torpor and pondering a raid on the kettle. Given her long-standing and devout refusal to contribute to the kitty, out of which teabags, milk and coffee were purchased, such expeditions were fraught with the possibility of conflict. Good. She paused for a moment, wondering how a worksheet had appeared on her desk, then headed for the kitchen, hoping for an unattended teabag, and found Ash boiling water in her usual manner of addressing such tasks: as if it were below her pay grade, and God only knew how it had fallen to her.

On seeing Shirley, she said, 'What do you think Louisa's up to?'

'What makes you think she's up to anything?'

'Duh, because Lamb said she was? That she's a big decision to make?'

'Lamb,' said Shirley, 'likes to fuck with our heads. It's what gets him out of bed in the mornings.'

'Yeah, I don't want to think about Lamb in bed. But do you know what I do think? I think she's leaving.'

Shirley had paid little attention to what Lamb had said, feeling only the usual relief that a meeting was over. Meetings were not among the things she was best at, and there were some things she'd never done – skateboarding came to mind – that she'd probably be better at than meetings if she did try them. But Ash had a point: maybe Lamb hadn't simply been sowing discontent. Maybe Louisa had something going on.

Ash said, 'And if she's leaving, it's because she's got somewhere to go. And I don't mean some bank or estate agents' or shoe shop. I mean a proper job.'

Shirley couldn't see Louisa working in a shoe shop. 'You

reckon she's going back to the Park? Because I hate to break it to you—'

'That wouldn't be a big decision, would it? She'd do that in a heartbeat. We all would.'

Shirley said, 'But none of us are going to. And Louisa won't get a reference from the Service that'll get her into security work.'

'Yeah, but really, she'll need one? I mean think about it. This might not be what we signed up for, but it's still intelligence work, isn't it? We're still – you know – spies. For anyone working the nightshift on an industrial estate, watching the vans don't get nicked, this'd be a career highlight.'

('Career highlights are for other people,' had been a recent Lamb observation. 'You lot have career landfills. And not the sort some idiot's buried an old laptop in, with a fortune in bitcoin, but the stinking horrible kind, swarming with gulls.')

'More fool them,' said Shirley.

The kettle boiled and Ash poured water into a mug, saying, 'You're hundy missing the point. Your average security company'd shit themselves to get a real-life former spy on the books. Reference or no reference.'

'Except the Park'd deny we ever worked for the Service. If we claimed we had, I mean. And . . .'

And who's going to believe us? was what she didn't say. *Who's going to believe you and me, that we're spies?* Even Shirley didn't believe it half the time. She reached for the teabag tin.

'Uh, not yours,' said Ash.

'Yeah, I gave Catherine a fiver this morning?' She fished out a bag, dropped it into the cleanest mug within eyeshot, and reached for the kettle. 'So if Louisa's actually been offered a job worth having . . .'

'It's with someone who knows her. Probably ex-Service themselves, but not Slough House. And anyway, a fiver? I gave her a tenner last week. We all did.'

'That what she told you?' Shirley shook her head sadly. 'I knew she was skimming, but I didn't think she'd be so blatant. You might be right, though. About Louisa being recruited by someone she knows.'

'And what I was thinking is, if they'll take her, they'll take us. Why not? I mean, I'm younger, and I didn't fuck up the way she did. And you're . . .'

Shirley waited.

'You've got bags of personality. Is she really stealing from us?'

'Catherine? Yeah, but we're not supposed to talk about it. Lamb covers for her. He'll pay you back. Just speak to him when no one's around.'

'Yeah, okay. So, shall we ask Louisa, then?'

'. . . Sorry, what?'

'About who's approached her.'

'. . . You mean . . . What, just *ask* her?'

'There's a better way?'

'Well, we could follow her. Or get Ho to bug her phone or sack her emails. Or . . . yeah, no, you might be right. We could ask her.'

Weird, though.

'Shall we go together?' Ash asked, and Shirley had the sensation, strange to her, of being the adult in the room.

'Well, first I'm going to drink this,' she said. 'Then I'll probably have a wee. But yeah, okay, let's do that.'

Though the odds of Louisa telling them anything were on a par with Lamb refunding Ash's kitty money. Besides, Louisa had left; was on her way to Oxford to find out what River had got himself into, and was currently barrelling down the M40, enjoying not being at work, the day's tasks postponed. And also finding space to think about her words to Lamb earlier: *I'm leaving*. That, it seemed, was how decisions were made; you opened your mouth and heard them happen. She should speak to HR, make it official. Talk to Devon again, and sort details out: holiday entitlement, pension arrangements — company car? That provoked a giggle. Company car . . . This from a woman who'd financed the deposit on her flat by stealing a diamond following a shootout with Russian gangsters. She was on a slippery slope. She'd have a savings account next, an investment portfolio. Start inviting friends around for dinner parties. Start having friends.

Mostly, though, what loomed large was not what was waiting but what would be left behind. At first, Slough House had felt like a temporary punishment, a proving ground where she'd redeem the desperate error that had seen her exiled from the Park. And then there'd been Min, of course, and a period during which the future had been something waiting with open arms rather than with its hands behind its back, concealing weapons. After Min died — after that, life had been a blank page on which she'd written nothing, but which she hadn't been able to turn. Paralysed — affectless — she might as well have been at Slough House as anywhere else, and the future became something to be postponed, which she did by existing only in the present. Things were different now. Things always became different if you left them long enough. That sounded too basic a lesson to have taken her so long to learn, but you live your life in the order it happens, and here she was now; heading to Oxford, her last outing as a slow horse. Who would she miss? River, maybe Lech. She'd think about Catherine, but doubted she'd see her again. As for Lamb — well, she'd think about him, too. But in time all of this would be fragments; the years patchworked by memory until she could no longer fit actions to places, faces to words. When she looked back on this, it would be like reassembling broken crockery. Even if the bits fitted, the cracks would remain.

But she'd keep in touch with River, if only to piss him off, a process that would almost certainly be brewing again this afternoon – whatever he was up to, he didn't want Louisa to be part of it, that was clear. And while this was true, what was mostly pissing River off right then was the traffic snarling up the road in front of him, caused by another set of temporary lights. Cars harrumphed and spluttered like retired colonels. River had a headache coming on: not a symptom – he was fine – just a reaction to road hassle. Satnav showed the safe house on the left, a few hundred yards away; before he reached it there was a turn-off where there might be somewhere to park, so as soon as the traffic allowed, he pulled into it. It turned out to be a lane running past a children's playground towards tennis courts, and had bollards in place and stern warnings posted. He parked, thought about leaving a note under his wiper – *Spy on call* – and headed round the corner on foot. The safe house was one of a row of cottages weirdly placed on this main road; cars were crawling past it like a rolling surveillance mission. Little point doing a walk-by, he'd only draw attention to himself, so River ignored the drivers, stopped at the door, and rang the bell. For the moments that followed he had the strange sensation of everything coming to a halt – that he'd been part of a busy flow and was now outside it; that something had happened before he'd arrived – but whatever that was about, it dissolved inside a greater frustration: that nobody came to answer the door. He rang again, then knocked loudly. Same response. He dropped to a knee and peered through the letterbox, but all he could see was a small empty hallway, and a half-open door leading to the front room. He caught no sense of movement, no trace of sound. The house felt vacant.

River stood, turned, and faced the traffic. Faces stared back: of course they did. Where else were people going to look, stuck in a queue of cars? He pulled his phone out, called Stamoran, then held the phone away from his ear, straining to catch a telltale ringing inside the house but there was nothing, and when he put the phone to his ear the silence was dead and echoey, as if he'd stuck his head inside a dustbin. He had the feeling he was running out of options, with a long drive home ahead, and no answers found. Automatically — his fingers doing the work by themselves — he called Sid again. Now might not be the time to explain where he was, but now was definitely the time to hear her voice. The numbers did what numbers do; they reached out and rang bells in someone else's life. In between one breath and the next a connection was made, and Sid's phone rang. Soon it would go to voicemail again. But until it did, he could hear it twice; once in his ear, and once behind the door he was standing by. And because this made no sense at all, he disconnected, then did it again, and then did it again, each time expecting a different result.

But the ringing didn't stop.

Part Two

Gloves Off

Louisa, on the phone, behind the wheel, said, 'Can we get in the back?'

'We'd have to go through three gardens, all with high walls. We'd be spotted.'

'And we can't wait for dark.'

'And it's on a main road. Did I mention the traffic lights?'

'You're right, we're fucked. Shall we go for a drink instead?'

River didn't laugh. 'Are you with me?'

'You know it.'

His next question – did she have a crowbar? – indicated both that he had a plan and that it wasn't subtle.

There were hardware places off Oxford's ringroad. She swung into one, made the purchase, and swung out again inside eight minutes, River still on the line, his voice cold as bricks. He had gone to Oxford looking for a former colleague of his grandfather's and had found Sid's phone instead, behind a safe house door. She'd left a note that morning, *See you later*. Now he'd thought about it, this left a lot unsaid.

Louisa tried for reassuring. 'Look, so her phone's in there but that's all we know. She's probably fine. Trust me.'

'There are so many things wrong with that, I'm not even going to start. How far away are you?'

Not very.

When she pulled up he was leaning against his car, his face taut. 'Did you get the crowbar?'

'I already told you. Do you want to slow down a second?'

'No.'

There were cars at the lights, but not many: it was outside rush hour, outside school set-down. At a rough estimate – and not counting the three adults supervising children in the play area, the old man walking his dog and the two couples playing tennis – only eight or ten people saw River carry a crowbar to the mild-looking house midway down the row, apply it to the door at lock height, and put his whole body weight into leverage. The lock gave way with a splintering noise and a small cloud of dust, and he was inside, shouting Sid's name; Louisa, in his wake, pointlessly trying to shield him from view, but conscious of being the object of stunned attention. River dropped the crowbar in the hallway. Someone sounded their horn, but that didn't matter. What mattered was all the sounds Louisa couldn't hear; the alarm that had been triggered when the crowbar's edge slipped into place and was now bellowing their presence; the clatter of boots hitting the ground. River shouted Sid's name again, but no one replied.

Nice plan, thought Louisa.

We've got three minutes.

In his days of spads and lackeys – political appointments made by party bosses to ensure he didn't get into trouble, or no more than could be kept from public view – there would have been smoke signals going up: *PJ is bored.* Never a good sign. PJ is bored, meaning he'd be seeking adventure. The best that could happen was he'd disappear for an afternoon with his best friend's wife, 'PJ's best friend' being a temporary post, candidates assessed largely on the condition of their wives. The worst-case scenario was that he'd start creating policy, and nobody wanted that. But those days were behind him, and the only brakes on his behaviour were those imposed by his own self-restraint, so it was pure chance he wasn't snorting coke off a teenage hooker's breasts when his phone rang, early afternoon. His screen read 'Number withheld'.

'Diana. Lovely to hear from you.'

'I've set up a meeting.'

'How splendid.' Judd was looking through his study window onto the garden, where Xanthippe and some friends were recovering from the previous evening's excesses, the four of them sprawled across three sunbeds like an exercise in fractions. 'But I'm pretty sure the, ah, whispering of sweet nothings into receptive ears was your function.'

'Peter, we can do this two ways. You can insist on being a pompous prick, and we'll get nowhere. Or you can listen to what I've arranged, agree that it meets your requirements, and put your happy face on. Shall we continue?'

'Since you put it like that, I'll choose door two. Who's my lucky confidante?'

'Dominic Belwether.'

He allowed silence to gather. Belwether, the new security minister, was a rarity among the current intake of MPs inasmuch as he had a hinterland, having done several tours of duty with the armed forces, and generally kept quiet about it. Because of this, he was one of the political faces of the moment, and if the face was somewhat round and a bit shiny, that did him no harm with the electorate, particularly that large and growing sector which didn't give a fuck about politics. And if the Whitehall rumour tree was still reliable – its rustlings reached Judd through his erstwhile party colleagues, the way sound travels through dead leaves in autumn – Belwether was being groomed for higher things.

Judd said, 'Interesting choice.'

'Because?'

'Because you're not famous for cosying up to rising stars. And nor, unlike every career pol ever, do you grow moist in the company of graduates who've seen active service. But then . . . Do you know, I heard a rumour about Belwether. From a friend of a friend.' He paused, allowing Diana time to draw up a mental family tree: what kind of friends friends of Judd might have, given that Judd didn't have any friends, not really. She was doubtless picturing trolls. 'That in his army days, he worked on . . . special assignments.'

'Peter—'

'Waterproof.'

'Oh, not that canard. Again. Waterproof didn't happen, Peter. And I was nowhere near it when it wasn't happening.'

'So you've said. But if it did happen, someone had to be in the vicinity. Those black sites didn't take out ads in *The Lady*. And Belwether was well placed, wasn't he, in his eastern European postings, to make the kinds of contacts Waterproof might need?'

Which weren't the kind of contacts you'd put on your CV afterwards. The Waterproof protocol had been a form of anonymised rendition, whereby bad actors were removed from the stage without benefit of curtain calls; their destination, prison blocks in former Soviet states, whose regimes were prepared to exchange hard time for hard currency. Those rumoured to have been on the receiving end had, understandably, been unavailable to appear at the eventual inquiry, and would no doubt have been disappointed by its final ruling.

'So I do hope,' Judd went on, 'that in choosing him as a cut-out, you're not issuing a veiled threat.'

'He's now a politician, Peter. And available and willing. Let's not overthink this.'

He laughed. Diana Taverner telling him not to overthink was like Liz Truss suggesting someone apologise. She probably dreamed in crossword clues. Not that this was strange to Judd.

The political life was all about decrypting hidden messages – the ministerial code was broken so regularly, cabinet meetings resembled a Bletchley Park re-enactment event – and the daily discourse was riddled with secret meanings; thus 'information management' meant lying, 'message discipline' meant lying, 'manifesto deliverance' meant lying, and so on. These were the waters Taverner swam in. In conversation with her, overthinking wasn't possible.

For his own part, he didn't expect people to believe every word he said. He simply expected them to act as if they did.

Down on the lawn, the young women had abandoned the loungers and were tossing a frisbee about. Xanthippe's mother wouldn't approve – the lawn would take a battering – but Judd was relaxed. *Of course, darling. As many friends as you like. Hang out. Chill out. Sunbathe.*

'I'll try not to,' he assured Diana. 'So, will you be at this meeting?'

'I'll be on hand. In case I'm needed.'

'Manual assistance, eh? I'd have thought that below your pay grade. Whereabouts will it take place?'

'I'll leave time and place to you, Peter. Wherever you feel most secure.'

The frisbee overshot its intended recipient, and bounced off a downstairs window. The young women shrieked in unison.

Judd smiled. 'I'll think of somewhere,' he said.

Three minutes, because it was a safe house. Not a high-security, fend-off-marauders fortress, but somewhere meetings happened, debriefings took place. So there'd be a high-priority alarm system, with a response time in low single digits. She didn't know whether the Park had a local station or whether the police would take up the slack, but either way they'd soon have company, and it wouldn't be taking the softly approach. Bang heads first and worry about appearances later. Details she didn't bother raising now because there was a phone on the floor, half underneath the sofa, and River had found it.

'Sid's.'

'But she's not here.' The stupid words were out of her mouth before she could stop them, but River was already up the stairs.

The other downstairs room was the kitchen, which was clean and tidy. In the bin Louisa found ready-meal packaging and grubby napkins; in a bucket-sized food bin, vegetable ends. On the drying rack sat four plates, four glasses, four cups, cutlery. By the sink, a rinsed-out Bushmills bottle, set aside for recycling.

Overhead, River was making noisy work of establishing that the house was empty.

The front door was hanging open; probably wouldn't close now anyway, being splintered at the lock. Louisa had the sense there were people gathering outside, wondering, in a very English way, whether they ought to do anything.

A minute passed.

Hurry up, River.

The service station was bustling, as such places always were. Overpriced energy bars, American doughnuts, soft toys and slot machines. There was a motel next door, in case you wanted to stay.

Which they could have done, using the money that had been in the envelope the young woman had been carrying, though CC hadn't mentioned this to the others yet. Nor the phone, now switched on, which hadn't yet rung; it weighed heavily in his pocket as he washed his hands, trying to avoid the mirror. There was an old man who followed him around these days, and that was the sort of place he popped up.

Next to him, Al was saying, 'We need to get Daisy somewhere quiet. Somewhere safe.'

'We will.'

'Without involving her in any more—'

'We will.'

Al said, 'She's fine, really. She can keep a lid on it. But put her in a pressure situation, or throw a dangerous surprise her way—'

'Al. It was my fault. There'll be no comebacks, I promise. Not on Daisy.'

'There'd better not be.' He glared at his reflection, perhaps as a way of avoiding glaring at CC. 'I won't let there be.'

CC said, 'I thought I was doing the right thing.' He spoke softly, the bluff all-pulling-together tone laid aside.

'I know you did,' Al told him. 'And the girls know it too.'

'But?'

'But it's not working out that way, is it?'

He led the way to the concourse, and they waited by a bubblegum dispenser for the others.

'She was here.'

'We have to go, River. There's a response team coming.'

He'd found nothing upstairs but abandoned toiletries, a tube of haemorrhoid cream, a sliver of soap and an empty blister pack of ramipril. Back in the sitting room he looked wildly round, as if there might be hidden doors, secret passageways, from one of which Sid might bounce. *Surprise!*

'There was a crew here.'

'Four of them. Can we discuss this later? We need to go.'

And quickly. Their cars were not best placed for a getaway; the whole strategy might have been better thought through. Or even just thought through.

The front door was pushed open. Someone called, 'Hello? Everything all right in here?'

'River . . . '

He had dropped to his knees and was peering under the sofa again. Sid still wasn't there.

'I've called the police,' the voice said.

Send in the clowns, Louisa thought. 'It's all good,' she said. 'Nothing to see.'

'You broke in! We were watching!'

Jesus, didn't anyone mind their own business any more?

River was on his feet, still clutching Sid's phone. 'They cleaned the place out. So how come they left this?'

'It was under the sofa. Maybe they didn't see it. Can we leave?'

'I saw it. First thing.'

'You were looking. You knew it was here. River—'

A distant siren. But not distant enough.

She said, 'Being arrested is not going to help. We need to go. Now.'

A man appeared in the doorway, holding a phone like a light-sabre, filming. 'This is evidence,' he said. 'This is evidence you're breaking in.'

'For fuck's sake,' said River. The siren was growing loopier as it bounced against walls and tumbled round houses. The man shrank back but kept his phone trained on them, or did until River snatched it in passing; he made an attempt to retrieve it, but Louisa pressed a palm against his chest, briefly pinning him to the wall.

'Please,' she said, meaning it, then caught up with River who was out of the door now, a phone in each hand, robbery added to the charge sheet. She'd paid good money for that abandoned crowbar. Unlikely she could claim it on expenses.

The traffic was moving, the lights green, but two cars remained stationary, their occupants watching the show. She was sprinting now, on River's heels, and as they turned into the lane where they were parked, blue lights spiralled into her peripheral vision, bouncing off the trees that lined the opposite side of the road. River's car was winking at him; he'd tossed the stolen phone aside and his keys were in his hand. She fumbled in her pocket for her own. What were they going to do, take off in two separate vehicles? The fast and the futile.

That seemed to be River's plan. Throwing open his driver's door he said, 'Different directions. They can't chase us both.'

'Of course they can chase us both! They're the fucking police!'

And were here already. Two cars pulled into the lane, the second so close behind the first they might have been humps on the same camel; both were unmarked but with flashers on their dashboards, and their blue genies pounded against the squat building to their left, somersaulted River's and Louisa's cars, then bounced across the children's playground before regrouping and doing it all over again. River was shaking his head, anger and frustration boiling off him, and gripping his keys so tightly he might have been making impressions. Police officers emerged from their vehicles. Louisa was wondering just how much trouble they were in when her phone rang.

'Put that down!'

'Put down your phone!'

'Put it down!'

But she answered it anyway.

'What?'

Lech said, 'You still want to visit that safe house? Because I can let you have the alarm code, if it's any help.'

Nepo brats are an occupational hazard.

This was plainly true in other professions also: acting, singing, modelling, anything involving lounging round a pool, monarchy.

As are former pols living with death threats.

This one more specific, but definitely a growth area in the UK.

What Devon Welles hadn't mentioned to Louisa was the overlap between the two – last night, while they'd been having dinner, his team had been babysitting a nepo brat's birthday bash thrown by a former pol living with a death threat, a duty Devon had been glad to avoid. He was professional enough to keep personal feelings wrapped while on the job, but Peter Judd tested boundaries. Before he had fielded security for the one-time Home Secretary, the most challenging of Devon's employers had been Diana Taverner, who was equally persuaded of her general rightness, though less inclined towards narcissism and mendacity. That aside, the main difference between watching Judd's back and working Taverner's home security was having to suffer the former's self-satisfaction, which oozed from him like slime from a slug.

Actually, no. The main difference was the amount he was getting paid.

Which was not something that bothered him, he thought – checking his kit, preparing for his afternoon shift – though he sometimes wondered what Emma Flyte would have made of it. He missed her, and still heeded her judgement on important questions, though would admit to resting a thumb on the scales now and again. Emma had understood the need to make a living, but she'd have drawn the line at working for Judd.

Maybe, he admitted, tempting Louisa Guy into working alongside him was a way of spreading the guilt. Which might also explain why he had neglected to mention Judd when doing the tempting. Some death threats, he could imagine Louisa saying, you'd as soon took their course. Words you didn't want to hear spoken by someone you were offering a job.

Another difference was, he usually wore a tie to work these days. He was knotting this, checking his technique in the mirror, when his mobile rang . . . Judd.

Abandoning his task, he answered, thinking: What now?

So now they were both in River's car, but going nowhere; their exit blocked by police vehicles; the officers themselves stalking around like geese. River had already tried to shoo them away, using nothing more than his technically invalid Service card.

'Sir, I'm going to have to ask you to remain in your vehicle.'

'You mean, stay in my car?'

'As I said, sir.'

'How long are we supposed to—'

'Until you're instructed otherwise, sir. If you wouldn't mind.'

'They've been told it's a Service house and to wait for the grown-ups,' Louisa explained to him. Again.

'I haven't got time for this.'

'She's probably fine.'

'So how come—'

'I don't *know*. All right?'

River looked at the phone in his hand and began pressing buttons.

'You know her password?'

'Of course.'

'She *told* you her password?'

River didn't answer, too busy accessing Sid's phone.

'Jesus . . .'

On the main road, traffic rolled past. She wondered if the door they'd broken was police-taped, festooned with yellow-and-black bunting. Never a good look on a safe house.

River said, 'Withheld number.'

'What?'

'Why's Sid been called by a withheld number?'

'I don't know. Because heavy breathers like their privacy?'

'This morning. Not long before she left the house.'

See you later.

Trying to keep River calm was a way of keeping her own fears in check. Louisa had too many dead already, and Sid wasn't even part of this world any more. Damage had no business reaching for her. Damage should keep its distance.

River had his own phone out, and was maybe about to start

juggling. But it was Lech's number he was after, and when he got an answer said, 'Charles Cornell Stamoran.'

'Is that supposed to ring a bell?' Lech asked.

'He does the cupboards at the Oxford safe house.'

Does the cupboards, meaning kept the place tidy and stocked with the basics: toothpaste, coffee, toilet roll.

'Right. I haven't actually memorised—'

'Which means he'll be on the list of contacts appendixed to the register.'

'Yeah, okay. So what?'

'So you can access his file,' said River.

'Yeah, I'm really not sure I can do that. I mean the only reason I can view the safe house lists is so—'

'So you don't identify as a terrorist property somewhere that actually belongs to the Service. I was doing this first, remember? And I know the register's hyperlinked to the personnel records, so all you need do is click on a link.'

'This is Slough House,' Lech muttered, though it sounded like he was rattling a keyboard. 'I click on a link, a trapdoor might – oh. No, actually, that seems to have worked.'

'I'm putting you on speaker. Louisa's here.'

'Hi, Lou. Yeah, Stamoran was active late eighties, nineties. Was on the semi-detached list after that. And he's been . . . doing the cupboards the last few years.'

'Tell me about his active service.'

Lech said, 'A lot of it's redacted. Or at least it says, refer to Annex B. That's sensitive material. So he wasn't a desk jockey.'

'But no hint what that was?'

'Probably Ireland. He was cleared for work in Ulster in '89.'

'Contacts,' River said.

Lech said, 'I'm kind of worried about hanging around in the—'

'Just do it, okay? His contacts.'

'You owe me a serious drink,' Lech muttered. There was

more clicking. 'Okay. Yeah, he was part of a crew, they called themselves the Brains Trust. Or someone called them that. You want their names?'

'That would really, really help.'

Lech read them out, River jotted them on the palm of his hand, and Louisa watched another car arriving, this one as unmarked as the cop cars, but more so.

'Any chance you're going to tell me what's going on?' said Lech.

'Not really,' River said.

'But stay out of my room,' Louisa said. 'Oh, and Lech? Don't ever call me Lou again.'

'It's been wonderful talking to you both.'

River stared at the jottings on his palm, committing them to memory in case he washed his hands by accident. Louisa was watching a pair of familiar types emerge from their black SUV.

'Oh, great,' she said. 'Who let the Dogs out?'

A club was a different place during daylight: the bar shuttered, the tables wiped. The balloons had all been burst. But this, in fact, was business as usual, because Nob-Nobs was mostly closed; had only opened the previous evening as a private hire. Its owner, a trust-fund wannabe mover and shaker learning the hard way that post-uni event management was a different story, was happy to do Judd a favour, or even two; the first, a knock-down price for the party booking; the second, allowing him access this evening, in the absence of other custom. No doubt he imagined he was greasing his way into Judd's good books with his largesse. But Judd didn't have good books, and for him, giving discounts betrayed uncertainty about your value. Give him a freebie, you were lunch. Still, learning that lesson would stand the pup in good stead. When the club folded at a heartbreaking loss, it wouldn't come as a total surprise.

I'll leave time and place to you, Peter. Wherever you feel most secure.

Though as far as actual security went, he'd be on his own.

'I've used up credit I don't have persuading Belwether to speak to you,' Taverner had said. 'And it's got to be somewhere private. Somewhere you won't be seen. Last thing he needs is to be written up on a Westminster blog, having a tryst with one of his party's sworn monsters. You're lucky he's intrigued.'

Judd had said, 'And you can't simply pass on my message yourself?'

'You asked for access, Peter. This is access. What more do you want?'

An honest answer would have been a single word. Seb.

His current personal protection team – discreet, well dressed, expensive – did its job, but the truth was he missed his one-time factotum, a word chosen to piss people off. Seb himself had never cared what Judd called him so long as the terms of his employment remained elastic. Thus he had performed the usual duties of a gentleman's gentleman – driving, dry-cleaning, dealing with tradesmen – while also, on occasion, fucking up people's shit. Jeeves with a sockful of ball bearings. He could be very persuasive when the situation demanded. Even when it didn't, you paid attention.

One evening, though, Seb had gone out on a job requiring maximum deniability and had never showed up again. Judd had monitored body-recovered-from-river stories for months following, but no joy. In other circumstances – any that had not involved him instructing Seb to commit murder, for example – he would have pointed the police in the direction of one Jackson Lamb, but as things were, that might have proved unproductive. Lamb remained an unresolved item on Judd's agenda, but in the ongoing absence of Seb was likely to remain so. This new crew fulfilled its remit with dedication and intelligence, but when it came to fucking up people's shit, he needed freelance talent.

Still, this was business as usual. While personal security was a must-have for someone with Judd's history, a meeting with an up-and-coming pol, even one from the party he'd spent his career alternately mocking and vilifying, was unlikely to end in violence.

So he'd simply said, 'All right, then. Eight p.m.,' and given her the address.

Phone once more in hand, he stood now in the centre of Nob-Nobs's dance floor. The previous evening the room had been awash with sound and light; coloured rays chasing each other, glancing off the young and the shop-soiled alike. Tonight, it felt like a cavern, the floor damp where cleaners had mopped up spillages, and the air refreshed by artificial means rather than anything as retro as an open window. Noises off included a transistor echoing tinnily on a staircase and the wheeze and suck of a Hoover. There was probably an equation you could apply, the time and effort it took to clean up after a party versus the time and effort it took to make the mess; or, more fundamentally, how much you paid those doing the cleaning compared to how much the partygoers spent. But that was how the market worked. You went to the party or you mopped up afterwards. Secure in his status as one of life's partygoers, he called one of its mopper-uppers. 'You're off the hook.'

'. . . Excuse me?' said Devon Welles.

'I said you can stand down. The evening's your own.' A woman roughly the same shape as the vacuum cleaner she was pushing appeared from behind the bar, and Judd's eyes followed her while he spoke. 'Kick back, hang loose.' His precise enunciation was the oral equivalent of using tweezers. 'Or whatever it is you do when you're not at work.' Welles was one-time Met and former Service; now private sector, and unlike Seb, not someone you'd ask to break a journalist's legs, though the task clearly wasn't beyond him should he have a hankering. Having him as a shadow added a touch of class, reminding Judd how important he was, in the unlikely event it slipped his mind. But Christ, he was boring.

'Where are you?'

'You're off duty. That's not your business.'

'Sounds like you're in a big empty room. Except someone's cleaning it.'

'Welles, I won't need your services this evening, and I don't need your Sherlock Holmes tribute act now. I'll see you tomorrow.'

'Yes, the thing is—'

There's always a thing, isn't there? thought Judd, breaking the call. There's always a *thing*. What this one was, he didn't care.

The woman was banging her Hoover against the legs of the tables that circled the dance floor, and the out-of-sight transistor was still emitting Tinnitus Pan Alley pop, but Judd had been assured the cleaners finished at five, and that he'd have the place to himself thereafter. Not a standard venue for a chinwag, but left-field thinking had its advantages. For a start, Belwether wouldn't be expecting it, and Belwether's role tonight was to be knocked off guard before being helped up, dusted down, and told what was what. The new world order was putting its boots on, polishing its shield and preparing for the long march west, and Britain could either accept the new reality and pledge support, or stand cap in hand by the roadside, choking on dust. Judd was clear on where he wanted to be, which was somewhere in the vanguard, an accepted ambassador from the old order showered with appropriate gratitude, and if it took an off-piste assignation to smooth his path, he was fine with that.

Also, he liked a fucking nightclub. Sue him.

'Missed a bit,' he told the cleaner in passing, and the look she gave him was a perfect mask. You needed to be an expert, someone like Judd, to appreciate the hatred beneath.

The Dogs were little and large, old and young. *I used to knock about with your former boss*, River thought. *He kneed me in the balls; I laid him out with a length of lead piping. Good times.* But discretion being the better part of getting your head kicked in, he remained in the car with Louisa while the new arrivals chatted to the police officers, flashed their ID, then watched the uniforms reluctantly climb into their cars and depart.

'That is not a welcome development,' Louisa said.

'It means we can leave. I need to find Sid.'

'We broke into a safe house. They're not going to just let us go.'

'If my career is as . . .'

'Finished.'

'As finished as you say, you know what? These guys have no jurisdiction over me.'

'No, but there are two of them.'

'I'll explain I'm a civilian.'

'They'll find out anyway. Once they run your card.'

'Louisa, Sid's missing. If you think I'm going to sit here while those clowns fiddle with their buttons, you're on the wrong channel.' He opened his door.

'Just don't hit anyone.'

'I hardly ever—'

'Just don't.'

She watched him get out of the car and walk towards the Dogs, one of whom was on his phone, the other awaiting instructions. Both regarded River with the amused contempt of tourists approached by a juggler. Louisa shook her head and looked at her own phone. She had a text from Devon: *I don't mean to hassle. But had any thoughts yet?* Yes, so why hadn't she let him know them? She keyed *Okay. I'm in*, deleted it, thought some more, then rekeyed the exact same words. Then deleted them. When she looked up, River was punching the young Dog in the face.

'Of course you did that,' she said.

The other Dog was reaching into his jacket for something, far more quickly than those words suggest, when River leaned into him, hooked a foot behind his ankle, and then the Dog was on the ground and River was running to the car. 'Change of plan,' he said, climbing in, starting the engine.

'This is a *plan*?'

The Dog jumped aside as River swerved past, loose stones scattering. He lost a wing mirror to the no parking sign and hit the main road to a fusillade of complaint. Louisa, seat belt secured, nevertheless had a hand on the dashboard to inhibit her departure through the windscreen and suppressed a yelp as he turned right, avoiding collision with a Deliveroo scooter by a weasel's whisker. She caught a glimpse of a face turning white, and then they were up the road, the playing fields to their left giving way to houses, driveways, a succession of sculpted hedges and pebbled drives. She said, 'Drop me anywhere. I can walk from here.'

'He was basically asking for it,' River said, meaning the Dog he'd punched.

Her phone rang, and when she answered Lamb said, 'On a scale of one to ten, how fucked up is your afternoon? Asking for a friend.'

'Yeah, turns out River's not on a job for Taverner after all.'

'I worked that out. Ask me how I worked that out.'

'How did you—'

'Because I am a senior officer of His Majesty's Intelligence Services, with responsibility for a department manned, sorry, *personned*, by wetbrains. And when a pair of half-arsed fuckwits from said department crash a safe house, attract the attention of the local woodentops and bring the wrath of the Service's trained poodles down upon their heads, I get woken up and told all about it. Is Cartwright behind the wheel?'

'Yes.'

'Tell him to undo his seat belt and head for the nearest concrete wall at eighty-five.'

'Is that Lamb?' asked River, who wasn't doing eighty-five, but only because the bus in front wasn't either. 'Does he know where Sid is?'

Louisa blanked him out, because she hated having two conversations at once. 'We've had a little difficulty, but nothing that can't be worked out.' Admittedly, working it out might involve scrubbing the internet. They were probably on footage shot by fifteen different mobiles. 'Normal harmony will soon be resumed.'

'Yeah, I can hear the horn section from here. Could you dicksplain to young Vin Petrolhead that the reviews of his latest misadventures ruined my nap? He'd better hope he's killed attempting a wheelie, because what I have in mind for him will be more protracted.'

'I'll let him know. Yellow car.'

'What now?'

'Nothing. Where's Sid Baker?'

There was a moment's silence. 'What's she got to do with it?'

'I'd explain, but I have no bloody clue.' River was on the wrong side of the road, causing the driver of an oncoming car to veer into the bus lane, while blasting a terrified *Fuck you!* on her horn. Somewhere behind them was the Dogmobile, its big black tinted presence a demonic avatar. She hoped River cooled down or wised up soon. She didn't want her last thought to decorate this particular windscreen.

She said, 'We don't know where Sid is. Her phone was in that house.'

Lamb hung up.

River queue-jumped four cars by climbing the luckily unoccupied pavement and joined the big roundabout just in time to miss ending both their stories under sixteen wheels of Norwegian logistics.

Catherine was on one of her periodical search-and-swoops, excavating paperwork placed on Lamb's desk for his signature that had migrated — unsigned — to unexpected places: beneath his desk, behind the hatstand, into a carrier bag containing stray items of laundry that hung on the back of his door. Whether he arranged this to amuse himself or irritate her wasn't worth dwelling on. The two outcomes were so nearly synonymous, any difference had long ceased to matter.

Lamb, meanwhile, was at his desk, having just come off a call, and was staring at his ceiling, his expression suggesting either deep thought or indigestion. He had recently both farted and removed his shoes, which put Catherine in the uncharacteristic position of being eager for him to light the cigarette he was playing with, instead of rolling it between the fingers of his right hand: a slow, stately process that threatened to mesmerise her. So much so, it was with a start that she noticed he was no longer focused on the ceiling but watching her, his upper lip curled. 'You're getting warmer,' he said.

'It would make my life less difficult if you didn't play games with official documentation.'

'Make it less entertaining, you mean.'

'You think I enjoy this?'

'Course you do. I can read you like a . . .'

'Book?'

'Parish newsletter.'

'They're used for kindling.'

'Now you get it. Of course you enjoy this, because otherwise what'll you do? Sit in your room and not drink? I tried that once. Longest ten minutes of my life.' He tucked the cigarette behind his ear and reached for his phone. 'Plus, it gives you the opportunity to do what you do best. Which is stick your neb where it's not invited. I'll put this on speaker, shall I? Save you bursting an eardrum.'

She made to leave, but he extended a shoeless foot to impede her passage. Whoever he'd called had answered. He said, 'Did I thank you for the Talisker?'

'You grunted. I assumed that was as good as I'd get.'

Catherine recognised Diana Taverner's voice.

Lamb said, 'I was speechless. Not every day someone gives me Talisker. Which in retrospect should have got me thinking harder. I'd have been just as happy if you'd refrained from poncing fags off me. So why a bottle of Talisker?'

'Do you have to keep saying "Talisker"?'

'Products don't place themselves.'

She sighed. 'Did you call just to play games? I gave you the *Talisker* in return for the favour I asked. That you'd find out who made the complaint about my so-called threatening terminology. Which you still haven't done, by the way. Though I'm guessing you've drunk your fee.'

'We both know you don't give a donkey's arse who's grassed you up to HR. More to the point, HR don't either. If they wanted to pull you up on your managerial style they'd have found a hundred reasons by now, starting with the way you wipe your feet on your PA every morning. No, that was the excuse you made to get me to come running so I'd hear all about Cartwright getting canned, in the expectation I'd pass the happy news on to Cartwright myself.'

'Getting you running anywhere would take more than an excuse. I'd need death threats and an angry dog.'

Lamb removed his cigarette from its nest and eyed it quizzically, as if hoping to find printed instructions. 'Now, canning Cartwright's not a bad idea. He'll last longer. But what you were after was putting him in a position where he'd be inclined to prick his ears up when you threw a task his way, because we both know he's still stupid enough to think that if he does you a favour you'll do him one in return.'

'Instead of telling me what you think we both know, why don't you tell me something I already don't? Anything to make me feel this isn't a colossal waste of my time.'

'How's this? I've just heard Sid Baker's missing. Which reminded me of something I shouldn't have forgotten in the first place.'

'And what's that?'

'That you're a world class mindfucker.' He opened a drawer and scrabbled around in it with his free hand, which emerged with one of those pincer-like gadgets that remove staples. He clicked it a few times between finger and thumb, then, when it failed to produce a flame, tossed it over his shoulder. It missed Catherine by a good eighteen inches.

'How kind,' Taverner said. 'You're going to have to elucidate.'

'It's Baker you had doing whatever it is you wanted doing. Putting the screws to Cartwright was your way of making sure she'd dance to your drum.' His hand was rummaging again. It found a pencil sharpener, of all things, which followed the staple remover. 'And whatever that was, it's gone banana-shaped, because I've just had your kennel boss on the dog and bone. See what I did there? Seems those angry dogs you mentioned are off the leash in Oxford.'

'Funnily enough, the world is full of people who report to me before they report to you. So if that was your idea of telling me something I don't know, try harder.'

'No, that was me filling in the background. Now you tell me something I don't know. What Baker's been doing and where she is now.'

'And why should I tell you that?'

Lamb said, 'Because she was working out of Slough House

when she got shot in the head, and at no time since has she been reassigned. Which means she's one of mine, Diana. You want me to go into detail?'

After a pause, Taverner said, 'She was running an errand. Nothing complicated. If any harm's come to her, it's because she's tripped over her own laces or walked into a door. You don't really expect me to check an agent's apron strings every time she leaves the premises, do you?'

'That depends what you've tied the other end to. It wouldn't be the first time you used a tiger as a tethering post.' His hand was back in the drawer, and this time came out with a matchbox. He opened it one-handed, his thumb pushing the cardboard tray free. 'And I'm— what the fuck is this?'

'What's what?'

'A tooth. Why is there a tooth in a matchbox? In my own desk drawer? I'm going to sack somebody one of these days.' He tossed the matchbox over his shoulder. 'Call the Dogs off, Diana. And whatever your errand is, wrap it up.'

Taverner said, 'I'll call mine off if you call yours home. I'm trying to keep the nation safe, Jackson. That's my job. Yours is keeping your bunch of retreads off the streets and out of sight, where the rest of us can be reasonably sure they're not pissing in the well.'

She disconnected.

Lamb looked at Catherine, who was collecting something from the floor in the far corner. 'I'm sorry you had to hear that. People can be so rude.'

'I'll survive.' She straightened up. 'Is Sid really missing?'

'Well, our finest minds seem to think so. So she's likely at home reading the paper. On the other hand, Cartwright and Guy breaking into that safe house has flown a kite.' He regarded his unlit cigarette bitterly. 'Mind you, they've probably trodden shit into the carpet. I should really just let them take a kicking.'

Back by his side, Catherine held her hand out and he extended a palm. She dropped four lighters into it. 'Did you really just threaten First Desk?' she said.

'Me? Course not, I'm house-trained. Everyone knows that.'

'Who was it made the complaint about her?'

'Her PA.'

'Roddy found that out?'

'Nah, but it's obvious. I was her PA, I'd dob her in just as a change from spitting in her coffee.' He lit his cigarette at last, coughed madly, stubbed it out, stood, stretched, and farted again almost inaudibly. 'I'm off for a dump. You were so close, by the way.' He nodded towards the free-standing bookcase under which a tattered rug had rucked, before inserting a hand into the waistband of his trousers and scratching vigorously as he left the room.

Catherine found her final missing document under the rug.

'I've got this under control,' River said, cutting across both lanes, much to the anguish of his tyres, other road users and local wildlife. Louisa was busy watching her life unspool on her eyelids, and had just reached the part where the Spice Girls split when she was aware of a sharp turn as they departed the A40, a softer exit than departing this life would have been had River made his manoeuvre half a second earlier or later, courtesy of, respectively, a Tesco delivery lorry and an airport coach. The car took another steep curve and hit a straight River maintained for about seven heartbeats before peeling right then left with barely a pause between. There was a bump from beneath the car Louisa hoped was nothing organic, and the road surface became a rough crustiness.

Then everything stopped.

She opened her eyes to find they'd ploughed through an open gate into a field, the car now obscured from the road by a hedge, the way cartoon mobsters might evade pursuing police.

She looked at River, who interpreted this as admiration. 'That went well.'

The world outside had gone quiet. Possibly it was faking its own death. Louisa loosened her grip on the door handle, surprised it didn't come off in her hand. 'Where are we?'

'Oxford's that way.' He indicated the rear of the car, though Louisa was sure they'd come through a hundred and eighty degrees since leaving the main road. 'Anyway, we've lost them. The Dogs.'

'Great. If they didn't know who we are, and didn't currently have possession of my car, you could argue we've got away.'

'Okay, fine. We'll have explaining to do. But we can get on with finding Sid.'

Rattled, she wound her window down, and was struck by the feeling city dwellers get when they're somewhere apparently remote: that she was supposed to like this kind of thing, the smell of grass and the buzz of insects. Even the background motorway hum had a country feel to it, traffic unaccompanied by drum or bass.

River said, 'Sorry about your car. We'll collect it tomorrow. After I've found out who sent Sid to that safe house. Though I can guess.'

'Taverner.'

'Who else? Last time Sid got caught up in one of her webs – yeah, we both know what happened.' He started the engine. 'She'd better not be up to fun and games again, that's all. Let's go.' A large black SUV pulled into the field, blocking their exit. 'Fuck.'

The Dogs emerged from their vehicle with a macho swagger they'd spent hours perfecting back at the Park. Both wore dark jeans, dark jackets; both, Louisa thought, would have pullstrings in their backs. *Let's see some ID. Keep your hands where I can see them.* They kicked up dust approaching the car, from ground that was clodded and clumped.

To River, she said, 'Let's take this as gently as possible, yeah?'

'They've got no authority here.'

'They don't need authority, River. They're pissed off.'

'So am—'

'Stay in the car.'

She got out, wishing she had more than the trainers on her feet. A couple of hand grenades, for instance, would have been nice. 'Good afternoon,' she said.

'Tell that fucker to get out here.'

'Yes, my friend — who's a civilian, by the way — he's sorry about what happened back there. He's just had some bad news. He's still processing it. So you can't blame him for overreacting.'

'Nobody's blaming anyone for anything,' said the older Dog. 'It's just that some of us are going to put the rest of us on the ground.'

'I can tell you're upset. But before this gets out of hand, could you please call the Park? They'll tell you, this is all a misunderstanding.'

'Can't get a signal,' the younger Dog said.

His phone rang.

'Can't hear a fucking thing, either. Being punched in the face does that to you.'

River was getting out of the car now too. One day she'd suggest a course of action, he'd take her advice, and then they'd both sprout wings or something. Meanwhile they were in a field with a couple of trained thugs he'd recently sucker-punched, and she doubted they'd remember she'd been otherwise occupied at the time. Or it wouldn't matter. Men didn't like women seeing them bested in a fight.

The younger one tucked his phone away. 'You want to try that again?' he said to River. 'This time while I'm ready?'

River looked at the older Dog. 'Fair warning. If he starts singing "I'm just Ken", this'll get ugly.'

'You're very funny. Let me guess what you do for an encore. Spit teeth?'

'Jesus Christ!' said Louisa. She looked at River. 'This is a good use of your time? I thought you were worried about Sid.' And then at the Dogs. 'And you two, what the actual fuck? You're supposed to be upholding, I dunno, law and order? Maintaining standards of conduct among Park operatives? Because you're not exactly an advert for the Service, are you? Getting ready to beat up a civilian because he got a lucky punch in.'

'She wasn't paying attention,' said River. 'Or she'd know that was a class uppercut.'

The older one was shaking his head. 'No it wasn't,' he said. 'This is an uppercut.' He demonstrated with his right fist. 'What you did, you just flailed about, basically.' He did this too, making it look like he was shaking out a duster. 'She's right. It was a lucky punch.'

'Seriously, does he look like someone I'd need to be lucky to punch? He's actively—'

'Fuck you!'

' – begging for it.'

The young Dog advanced on River, who dropped, scooped up a clod of earth and tossed it at him. He caught it neatly, then froze to the spot.

'See?' River said to the older Dog. 'He's standing there like a crash test dummy. I could ring for an Uber before hitting him. Or organise a mortgage. He'd just wait for me to finish.'

The older Dog was shaking his head. 'I don't train them,' he said. 'There's a rota. We're partnered randomly.'

'I feel your pain.'

'I still plan to kick your head in.'

'In case it matters,' Louisa said, 'I haven't gone anywhere. Also, I'm cammed up.' She tapped her sunflower brooch. 'So smile. Everyone's up in the cloud, and how delighted are your bosses gonna be when they take a look at this?'

The two men exchanged a glance.

'And you know where bad Dogs go, don't you?' River said.

'That's the difference between you and me,' the younger Dog said. 'I was offered the choice between Slough House and cleaning shit off blankets, I'd take the blanket any day.'

'Well, we all find our level.'

The Dog took a step forward, but his companion put a restraining hand on his arm. At the same time, his phone rang. He answered without taking his eyes off River. 'Yeah. Okay. Okay. Understood.' He finished the call with his hand still on the other man's sleeve, but it was to River he spoke. 'To be continued.'

'Definitely,' the other Dog said.

'Let's make an appointment,' River said. 'Put it in your calendar, ring it in red. It'll still come as a surprise when I punch your lights out.'

'Get in the car, you,' Louisa told him. To the Dogs, she said, 'Let's write this off to experience, yeah? Trust me, he'll have walked into a lamp post before the day's out. Save you slapping him.'

Neither man replied. Both returned to their car.

River said, 'How many Dogs does it take to change a light bulb? Answer, no one asks a Dog to change a light bulb.'

'Are you finished?'

'Because they're too fucking stupid. I'm finished now.' He pointed to her sunflower brooch. 'Is that really a camera?'

'Now who's fucking stupid? And what was that about? You're Jack Reacher suddenly? Jesus. You're lucky you're not being scraped off a shovel.'

'Yeah, well, they decided not to mess with me, didn't they? Us, I mean.'

'Because they were called off. Lamb's work, probably. And

not because he hates the thought of you getting hurt. It's because I told him Sid was missing. You know what he's like when a joe's in trouble.'

His face crumpled.

'She is in trouble, isn't she?' Louisa said.

'She might be dead,' said River.

I'M DEAD, THOUGHT SID.

Brand new iPhone, not a scratch. Cherry-red cover, because why not? A present from River, and for some while now – up to and including yesterday – any time River saw Sid on her phone, he'd make indirect, or sometimes direct, reference to that fact. And now she'd lost it . . . I'm dead.

Then again: been there, done that. At least this time she wasn't bleeding from a head wound on a pavement in the rain.

When Daisy had attacked her, the sweet old lady had been holding a blade, and knew how to work it. The sharp end had been pressed to Sid's throat, and the sweet old lady was saying words. Sid had been too shocked to hear them. *This is it. This is all there is.* And then the blade was gone and she was being helped to her feet, and other, more intelligible words were on offer, like 'Sorry' and 'Are you hurt?' and 'Can you stand?'

She could and did, but was almost immediately swept off her feet again, this time by a wave of anger large enough that she might find herself in a tree later, miles inland. But first she locked sights on Daisy, who was no longer holding a blade and appeared unperturbed by her actions. 'Try that again and I will slap the snot out of you.'

The bigger man stepped forward. 'That's enough.'

'You too.' Sid was blazing. The night the Russians took her she had thrust a stiletto upwards through a man's jaw, so the question of what she would do in such circumstances had forever been resolved. If this sweet old lady attacked her again, Sid would turn her lights out.

Maybe something of this was written on her face, because the big man said, 'Lay a hand on Daisy, I'll shoot you.'

'Al!' This had been the other woman, who turned out to be called Avril.

Charles Cornell Stamoran was checking Sid's tote bag, possibly for weapons. He removed the envelope Taverner had given her. 'This is for me?'

She nodded.

He unsealed it and looked inside, without revealing its contents to the others. No one seemed surprised. A moment passed. Then he said to Sid, 'Sit down. Avvy, you drove here?'

'We came by train.'

'Good. Now we clean house. Al, keep an eye on her. And no one's shooting anyone.'

'Like no one'll trace your email, right?'

'We'll do post-mortems later.'

So there Sid had sat, while the team cleaned house — obviously a team, used to such removals. The way they split tasks without conferring. The way they didn't talk while doing them.

Al had watched her without seeming to, a skill honed in a million pubs, a hundred market squares. River would love this guy. He'd want to hear his life story, then recount it all to Sid afterwards. *I'll shoot you dead.* That's been tried, she wanted to tell him, but to make it effective she'd have to remind him what he'd said, and that would remove its punch.

Cleaning up took three minutes. Sid had days it took her longer than that to rinse a coffee mug.

When they were done, CC sent them out to his car — blue Peugeot — bags in hand; still clearly the boss, despite what she read as a hairline fracture in his command. He said, 'A thousand pounds isn't what I had in mind.'

'My day isn't going to plan either. I'd intended to return a library book.'

'What's Taverner going to do?'

'Teach you the error of your ways,' Sid said. 'I imagine.'

'But if she was planning a hard stop, she'd not have sent you.' He tapped his breast pocket, where he'd tucked the envelope. 'Or this.'

'No.' Don't get involved. You had a job to do; you've done it. But it couldn't be helped; she was who she was. 'Look — CC?'

'What they call me.'

'Okay. Whatever you think you're holding over Diana Taverner, she clearly doesn't care. She told me she wasn't going to do you harm, but she lies just for practice. If you want my best guess, by trying to blackmail her, you've given her leverage.'

'So no happy ever after.'

'I don't know how this'll end. But you've money in your pocket. If I were you, I'd give some thought to dropping out of sight.'

'This isn't 1963. With a thousand pounds I could barely drink myself to death. And there are four of us.'

'Not if you walk away.'

'You think I'd do that? What do they teach you at the Park these days?'

She assumed he wasn't anxious for an answer to that.

He said, 'You'll have to come with us.'

'Am I expecting a bullet in the neck in a lay-by?'

'Al is fond of Daisy. It's not a good idea to threaten her in his presence.'

She walked in front of him, out of the house, down the road, round the corner. The others were already in his car, and Avril got out at their approach, making space for Sid in the middle of the back seat.

'I'm next to her?'

'Just don't make eye contact,' Avril said.

Between the other two women, Sid put her head back as CC started the engine. She imagined it raining, imagined it night. Wondered how a day that had started the same as most others had come to this, and decided that the blame lay with herself, for believing that any task devised by Taverner would turn out other than a mantrap.

She did not think, though, that these people were about to kill her. Even Daisy, whose thigh she could feel against her own, wasn't a danger; just someone who'd miscalculated a threat and responded accordingly. Not so different from her own history, or that small part of it that involved being bundled into a car by strangers. The anger that had drained from her now had left her feeling worn out, like a story told too often. In the front seat, the big man – Al – was asking CC, 'How long has it been since you handled an op?'

Fifty minutes later they pulled into the services at Beaconsfield, and Sid found herself being escorted into the loos by Avril and Daisy. Before slipping into a cubicle, she said, 'You think I couldn't escape?'

'You're not a captive, dear. Just a bit of a nuisance.'

CC and Al were waiting by a bubblegum dispenser when they'd finished. CC ushered the others back to the car with a hand gesture, then handed Sid her tote bag, which held her purse, her sunglasses and her emergency make-up kit. 'Where's my phone?'

'I haven't touched it.'

Which, if true, meant it was back in the safe house, having scattered when she went sprawling. Shit. A cherry-red cover, a present from River. She was dead.

'I'm sorry about this.' He looked it too, and a penny dropped. She wasn't about to be left in a lay-by with another bullet in her head. She was about to be abandoned in a service station twenty miles from London, muzak blaring from hidden speakers, and no phone to call an Uber.

She said, 'Whatever Taverner wants you to do, run a mile.'

'I appreciate the advice. But I've the others to think about.'

She tried to come up with something else to say, anything that might put a brake on what she feared would turn out a runaway train, but he was gone already, so she stood a while longer, weighing her tote bag in her hand. Taverner would be expecting her to report back, but that was an irrelevance. She'd delivered a burner phone: Taverner would be hearing from CC himself before long. Sid was a surplus detail. It would have been handy to have had this insight earlier that morning, but she could berate herself at her leisure. She was also going to have to find a phone and summon up some numbers, but before she brought any more grief down on herself, she might as well have a cup of coffee.

The others were in the car, like a family gathering gone wrong; Avril and Daisy now with the back to themselves, Al up front, scanning the surrounding vehicles for threat. CC didn't doubt he actually had a gun – *I'll shoot you dead* – but the only immediate threat was CC himself. He had put them all in the crosshairs, though the nature of the approaching bullet had yet to be determined. Who would be pulling the trigger was less of a mystery.

Raising a finger in his friends' direction – one minute – he retrieved the burner from his pocket, found its contacts and selected the single number listed. It rang twice before he heard four high-pitched beeps and the call ended. When he attempted a redial, the number had vanished from the list, and didn't appear on the numbers dialled screen either. Spook tech. He allowed himself a moment's frustration then dropped the phone back in his pocket. Immediately, it rang.

Diana Taverner said, 'So you'd be the chancer who thought blackmailing the Service was a smart idea.'

'Not one of my better days.'

'No, those are behind you. Charles Stamoran, formerly of the Brains Trust. Was that a name you gave yourselves, by the way? It smacks of those lumbering giants you meet called Tiny.'

This didn't need answering. 'Thanks for the money. I'll admit I had a larger sum in mind, but that was when I thought I was anonymous. You won't be hearing from me again.'

That got a laugh, if not one CC hoped to hear again. 'Where are you? Still in Oxford?'

If in doubt, lie. 'Yes.'

'And Baker?'

Phoneless, thought CC. So won't have reported back yet. 'Gone for her train.'

'You're alone?'

'Yes.'

'Good. You can find Calthorpe Street?'

'. . . In London?'

'Obviously.' She gave him a street number. 'Five p.m. Don't be late.'

And then he was listening to dead air. When he checked the calls received folder, nothing was listed.

Putting the phone away, he returned to the car, where he found, you might call it, an atmosphere.

'All done?' Avril asked. 'Or are more mysterious phone calls required? You need us to carry on sitting here like children?'

'I liked Sid,' said Daisy. 'Are we leaving her here?'

'We're all done. There'll be no more calls. And yes, we're leaving her here.' He was standing by the car, his door open. Al was in the passenger seat, his bag between his feet. 'Here, I'll put that in the boot.'

'I'm fine.'

'Don't be ridiculous. You'll get thrombosis or something. Do you girls need anything putting away?'

'Call us that again, and you'll find out.'

CC took Al's bag from his reluctant grasp and went round the back.

Avril said, 'Do you think he's okay?'

Daisy said, 'He's CC. He'll always be okay.'

Al turned to face them. 'He trod on a nest of snakes when he tried to lean on First Desk. Do you really think sending a messenger with an envelope is the worst she'll do in response?'

Then CC was climbing back into the car, handing out wads of banknotes.

'What's this?'

'Three hundred quid.' Each, he meant. 'Your share. I'm sorry it's not more.'

'What's going on, CC?'

'That envelope. There was twelve hundred quid and a phone. I've just spoken to First Desk. More sorrowful than angry, it turns out. No, blackmailing the Park is not a good idea. But yes, we have a point. Badly treated, wouldn't happen now, all that kind of thing. She can't give us more than petty cash, but on the other hand, we'll not be facing a firing squad. Provided our mouths remain forever shut.'

There was silence for a short while. Then Avril said, 'And that's it?'

'That's it.'

'Not even a visit from the Dogs?'

'She's already put the fear of God into us,' said CC. 'Or me. It was a stupid thing to do, it put us all at risk. I'm sorry. I should have thought harder. Talked to you all first.'

'Yes. You should have done.'

Al said, 'But we get three hundred quid each.'

'Like I said. I'm sorry it's not more.'

'So you'll have another three hundred in your pocket right now?'

'Al . . .'

'I'm not suggesting he's skimming. I'm wondering if he kept any for himself.'

CC said, 'We'd better get moving. I'll drop you at King's Cross. That's good for everyone, yes?'

Grunts were the best he was getting for that.

He started the car and pulled away, thinking: a burner phone, a brown envelope and an address. Join those dots and you drew a stark picture. Whatever Taverner was up to – whatever task she had in mind – it wasn't official. The upside of which was, there'd be no surveillance, no eavesdropping, no satellite tracking. No drones. The downside being, he was likely in more trouble than would fit in the average day.

How the seesaw would tilt, up or down, remained to be seen. But he supposed he'd find out before long.

Lamb was back from his mini-break in the lavatory, and Catherine shuddered at the thought of the state he'd have left it in – she'd once put up a sign reading PLEASE LEAVE THIS TOILET AS YOU WOULD LIKE TO FIND IT, and by the following morning he'd installed a stack of pornographic magazines and a dartboard. Now she watched from her desk – their offices faced each other, and both doors were open – as he slumped behind his own and rummaged in a drawer, eventually producing half a cigarette, its end trumpet-shaped where he'd squashed it out. Catherine could already smell it: dead tobacco, an acrid tang she associated with long nights, empty bottles and suppressed memories. It was awful to ponder, but there were whole spheres of experience she held in common with Lamb. There might be another world somewhere in which they'd exchanged roles. Pray God it never crashed into this one.

Instead, the crashing sound was someone slamming a door and coming up the stairs. Ashley.

Lamb greeted her with a beaming smile. 'What, is it come-to-work-in-a-huff day already?'

'My phone just rang.'

'And? You're Generation Text, I know, but phones do ring occasionally. It's what they're for.'

'The one on the desk, I mean.'

Lamb's free hand paused on its way to scratching his arse.

'She said – let me get this right – she said she'd had to buy a burner, and it was the only number she knew off by heart. On account of my desk used to be hers.'

Lamb called to Catherine, 'Sounds like our lost sheep's turned up. Hang out some flags. Where you going?' This to Ash, who'd put a scrap of paper with a number scrawled on it on his desk, and had turned to leave.

'Back to my office?'

'Yeah, pop next door first, and fetch an order of whatever they're calling "firecracker" this week. Chicken, pork, prawn, whatever. And special rice.'

Her face was mutinous. 'What did your last slave die of?'

'I want to say Novichok poisoning,' said Lamb, 'but he recovered. Must've been the Welsh knife fight, then. Before your time. Off you fuck.'

'He runs a tab,' Catherine said, coming in as Ash left. And then to Lamb, 'Sid's okay?'

'Probably just taking a brief holiday from Cartwright. Must be like being stuck in a *Carry On* film after a while.' He was already dialling the number Ash had left. It was answered immediately. 'I'm touched we were the first place you thought of,' he said. 'I mean, clearly you've got no friends or self-respect, but still.'

'It was the only number I could remember,' Sid told him.

'Yeah,' Lamb said kindly. 'That'll be the brain damage. Your boyfriend found your phone, if you were wondering. He's now busy racking up a new record for pissing people off. Dogs, traffic cops, other road users. Do they have street cleaners in Oxford? Them too if so.'

'He found my phone? In the safe house? He must be going out of his mind!'

'There's no obvious way of telling. You're on Taverner's shilling, aren't you? Presumably because she promised she'd give young Uh-Oh Seven his Park privileges back if you did. Want to hear the bad news about that? Or have you worked it out for yourself yet?'

There was a pause before Sid said, 'You're still very smart, aren't you, sir?'

'I shine by comparison. That's the advantage of hanging round with a bunch of special needs yo-yos who couldn't find their crotches with a sniffer dog. So – what were you doing in Oxford? And who with? Spare no details, but if it's anything frisky give me five minutes to warm up.'

Catherine watched while Lamb listened, his right hand toying with the half-smoked cigarette he'd found. She could read nothing in his face. Sid might have been telling him he'd won the Lottery or lost his pension. When he hung up he considered the ruined cigarette for a while.

'Well?' she said at last.

'She called me sir. Maybe I should shoot the rest of them in the head, if that's what it takes.' He scratched his nose. 'On the other hand, how come even the smart ones are stupid? If Baker doesn't know what a cut-out is, she's about to find out.'

Catherine said, 'Taverner?'

'I mean, it's not like I expect them to learn from experience or anything. But you'd think they'd know not to stick their dicks in a live socket by now.'

Ash was coming back up the stairs, preceded by the smell of warm food. Placing a tinfoil container in front of Lamb, she said, 'I went for the steamed cauliflower option. Because I'm vegetarian.'

'Yeah? Me too.'

'. . . Really?'

'Well, no. But I never eat anything cleverer than myself. So we've got the same boundaries.' He peeled back the lid and peered at the contents. 'Say what you like about the Chinese.'

She waited. 'But what?'

'Nah, I was finished.' He wrinkled his nose. 'You sure he didn't scrape this out of the bin?'

'Would I spoil the surprise if he had? He wants his bill paying, by the way.'

'He can go take a runny dump.'

'. . . Running jump.'

Lamb resealed the lid. 'I was reading my future. Oh God, who now?'

Who now was Lech. 'Louisa rang. She and River just had some kind of run-in with the Dogs at—'

'I know.'

'Okay, good, but they're on their way back now. And apparently Sid Baker—'

'I know.'

Lech said, 'It's like talking to an oracle. Or a teenager.'

'Or your boss. You know, according to yesterday's business section, a good team should predict its leader's needs and act accordingly. So why haven't you both fucked off yet?'

When they'd done so, Catherine said, 'So Taverner's playing games again.'

'Games are where no one gets hurt. The way Taverner plays, you wouldn't want to be sitting in the front three rows.' The lighters she'd given him earlier were in a pile next to the takeaway, and he reached for one.

'You're not really going to smoke that?'

'Well I'm going to need something to anaesthetise my taste buds.' He looked at the tinfoil container sourly.

Catherine said, 'What are you going to do about River?'

'It's a bit late to have him neutered. Baker'll have to take her chances.'

'Would you be serious for one minute? If Taverner's putting pressure on him and Sid, then whatever she's up to is off the books. River's barely back to health as it is, and you know what he's like. If his career's at stake, he'll do anything to save it. Things could get nasty.'

'They usually do. But Cartwright's not the issue. Nor is Baker. Taverner was using her to get to someone else, name of Charles Cornell Stamoran. Heard of him?'

'Rings a vague bell.'

'Me too. But he's ancient history, and that's a worry.'

'That Taverner's looking at ancient history?'

'That Taverner's looking for someone expendable.'

Catherine said, 'That's what you meant by a cut-out.'

Lamb was still toying with the lighter. With the squashed-end butt in his mouth, he looked like some clown had just fed him an exploding cigarette. He said, 'Uh-huh. Baker's still on medical leave after a bullet bounced off her brain. What you'd call a deniable asset. I'm guessing Taverner's scrubbed any record of their having had a recent conversation.'

'And Stamoran's expendable.'

'Find out what you can.'

'I'll talk to Molly.' She hesitated. 'You don't think . . .'

'What?'

'If Taverner's looking for someone for an under-the-bridge assignment, well. Who's the likeliest target, would you say?'

'You're asking me who's the biggest thorn in Taverner's side?' He shook his head. 'Nah. She wouldn't dare. Besides. I haven't done anything lately.'

'Strange as it might seem,' Catherine said, 'it wasn't you I was thinking about.'

At King's Cross traffic flowed in all directions, while on the concourse in front of the station crowds milled busily: there were coffee stands, street-food stalls and souvenir merchants peddling junk, and pedestrians who weren't heading into the station wheeling luggage were wandering with coffee cups in hand or perched on available seating, forking food from cardboard containers. The station served the north, and Al, Avril and Daisy could all catch trains from here. CC parked illegally and they got out and fetched the bags from the boot.

Daisy said, 'So you're dumping us. What will you do now?'

'Lie low for a few days. Do quiet penance. Then head back to Oxford with my tail between my legs and pick up where I left off.'

'Eating your single-serving meals in front of a two-bar fire,' Avril said.

'Yes, well, I might have exaggerated a touch. Besides, no need for heating yet. It's set to be a glorious summer.'

'We should talk more about the weather,' Al agreed. 'You're full of shit, CC. And if we're not doing anything about it, that reflects how pissed off we are, not that we've been taken in.'

'I'm sorry.'

'So you should be. I mean, involving Daisy—'

'I never meant to—'

'It's okay,' said Daisy. 'She pulled my triggers, that's all. Turning up like that. At a safe house.'

'It was over long before you jumped on her. The fact that she was there at all meant we were finished.'

'Well, I know that. I might lose my shit now and again, but I'm not stupid.'

CC said, 'Well, Taverner's granted absolution. I mean, I'm not her favourite bunny, and I can probably kiss the housekeeping job goodbye, but she won't be unleashing the Dogs, and I'm not expecting a knock on the door. So, you know. Compared to some places we've found ourselves, we're on Sunny Street.'

Avril, Al and Daisy shared a look. It was Avril who spoke. 'You're a hundred per cent on that?'

He put a hand to his heart, noticed what he was doing, and let it drop. But said, 'Sincerely. It's all fine. You're unsullied and I'm forgiven.'

'Okay, then.'

'Fly, my little ones. Fly.' He made an ushering motion with both hands. There were people nearby, total strangers, who thought they were watching a rep company go its separate ways.

Daisy gave CC a hug, and Avril did the same, and then Al, and the fact that he muttered 'You mad bastard' while doing so didn't make it less genuine. Then the three of them watched while CC got back in the car, sounded the horn twice, and pulled out into traffic. To stand watching until he was gone from sight would have swallowed what was left of the afternoon, so they turned and walked towards the station entrance, bags in hand.

'And that's that,' said Al.

Avril gave him a look.

'Yes, I know. Of course it bloody isn't. What did you use?'

'My watch.'

'And that has a tracker on it?'

She rolled her eyes. 'No, Al. Every five minutes it launches a barrage balloon. Yes it has a tracker on it. Like everyone else who ever worked at the Park, I pinched a few toys before they showed me the door.'

'Wish I had.'

'At least you have your gun.'

'Bought that with my own money.' He was flexing his arm as he spoke, raising his bag, gauging its weight. 'And I'll tell you what. CC's taken it. When he put this in the boot.'

'Figures.' Avril had put her own case down and was checking her phone. 'Wouldn't have minded hearing that chat he had with First Desk.'

Daisy said, 'You think he plans to shoot her?' She might have been asking about CC's dining plans.

'That'd be extreme,' said Al. 'It's never a good idea to jump straight to the endgame before considering all possibilities.'

'You think?' said Avril. 'And here's me imagining that's been our signature move all these years.'

They stood in a huddle while she began tracking the watch she'd left in CC's car.

Molly Doran said: 'Name a weed and you find it growing everywhere.'

'I'm not sure I follow.'

'Charles Cornell Stamoran. You asking about him, that's not the first time his name's come up this week. Can't tell you how often that happens.'

About as often as any other coincidence, Catherine thought.

Calling the Park's archivist had required mental prep. Catherine's relationship with Molly was not uncomplicated. She knew – suspected – no, *knew* – that the woman had shared secret hours with Jackson Lamb, a history neither would speak of. But that there was a bond was clear, and if its existence meant that they couldn't quite be friends, it also meant that when Catherine needed a favour, Molly was prepared to supply it.

At a price.

'He was the handler on Pitchfork. That was the IRA operation, remember?'

Catherine did. Every so often the story cropped up in the Sundays, only for the Service to deny it had made an asset of a murdering sadist.

She said, 'Pitchfork, that's surely in the digital archive.'

Which covered anything that had happened in the last several decades. Molly's domain stretched back further, and there were those who'd like to see it reactivated. Its digital counterpart was available to anyone with Service ID and the sign-in code, which didn't always limit access to Park operatives in good standing. Molly's archive, on the other hand, was the real thing: shelves of paperwork, vulnerable to any number of threats – fire and water damage, termites, mould – but to steal from it, you had to make an effort. Slackers with laptops from Moscow to Miami might troll the world's virtual corridors at will, but Molly Doran's fortress was outside their reach.

'Yes, but there's a hard copy file overlap,' she told Catherine. 'The personnel records of the operatives involved predate the birth of the Beast.' Which was her designation for the Service database, possibly because she regarded it as one of the signs of approaching Armageddon. 'So the source records are down here with me, even if updates aren't.'

'And that would include Stamoran's crew.'

'The Brains Trust,' Molly said. 'There were three of them. Avril Potts was a bright spark. Probably still is. Al Hawke, too. And Daisy Wessex.' Molly paused. 'They're long off-book now. But what happened to Daisy still gets talked about.'

'She's the one who dropped off the map,' Catherine said, the detail swimming up out of nowhere. Some had a way of clinging on; the ones that said *There but for the grace.*

'Eighteen months or more. Until her crew found her and brought her back.'

Her crew, thought Catherine. Not the Park. The Park had washed its hands.

Molly said, 'I doubt there's an official record of that, but everything else, you'll find on the Beast.' She paused. 'I realise you're not in good standing over there, but I presume Roderick Ho doesn't let a detail like that get in the way.'

'Roddy does wander where he will,' Catherine agreed, 'when it comes to digital footpaths. On the other hand . . .'

One of the prices Molly demanded was that things be spelt out. No trailing away into ellipses allowed.

'On the other hand,' she finished, 'Jackson was wondering what you might have that never found its way upstairs.'

'Was he now?'

'Apparently you've suggested in the past that such things happen.'

'It's always disappointing to be reminded of one's indiscretions,' Molly said, though what Catherine traced in her tone was not so much disappointment as satisfaction; perhaps that she was in a position to be indiscreet about such matters, or perhaps that it was Lamb who had remembered it. 'But yes, such things do. Or did, back in David Cartwright's day. It was something the old man took to doing, adding notes to old case files.'

'What kind of notes?'

'Endings.' Catherine could picture Molly, shuttered in her archive with its carefully modulated lighting, its temperature-controlled stillness, that felt like a crypt. She famously allowed no Dogs in her chambers – there was a rumour she'd once run one down in her wheelchair – but was happy to have her archive used, its pastures grazed, and Catherine could understand that she might tolerate the pencilled intrusions of a David Cartwright. For Molly had never believed that history should be preserved as it was. She believed history was still happening, and with careful tending might produce new shoots. To Catherine, that was what made it dangerous. 'He liked to . . . tidy up. To seek completion where there never was any, where there'd been only the messy fog you get when operations collapse. Which they mostly do. Something an archivist appreciates, that tidy endings are for storybooks.'

'And Cartwright was a storyteller? That's what you're saying?'

'Perhaps I am. You know how he was in the end.'

'He had full-on dementia.'

'Yes. I don't know how the condition develops. But I do know that during his last days at the Park, he indulged this compulsion to embellish, to speculate. Especially about operations that had ended . . . unsatisfactorily.'

'And he did that with the Pitchfork file?'

'That's not here, remember? It's part of the digital archive. No one can add material without authorisation.'

'But the files of those involved. The personnel files. He might have added notes to those.'

Silence fell. Here's where the bill arrives. From Lamb's office came the sounds of his occupation; rustlings from an urban undergrowth. The slow horses ducked when he bellowed, but for Catherine, his furtive creakings were worse. They indicated that he was up to something, but that even he didn't know what it was yet.

Molly said, 'When you're there late at night. When he pours you a drink. Are you tempted?'

'How do you know he does that?'

'Because some habits never change.'

'I see.' It was a strange question to ask, because the answer was obvious. 'Yes. Of course I am.'

'And if you gave in, what would he do? Watch you drink? Or slap it out of your hand?'

She said, 'I think it would depend on what mood he was in.'

'Really? Perhaps you don't know him as well as you think you do.'

And perhaps I didn't tell you what I really think, thought Catherine. 'Maybe you're right.'

Molly said, in a brisker tone, 'Cartwright might have added material to those files, but if he did, it's not there now. Like I said, you're not the first person to be taking backbearings on Charles Stamoran this week.'

Catherine didn't need to ask the follow-up question. Molly answered it anyway.

'Taverner was here late the other night. Supposedly researching some of our Cold War warriors, for a memorial service next year. But I know she had Stamoran's file down, and his team's, because she didn't reshelve them as carefully as she thought she had.'

And anything that might have been added by David Cartwright – whether fantastic speculation or considered conclusion – had been removed or erased by then.

So we'll probably never know, thought Catherine, which might be as well. When Taverner was slotting pieces together, you didn't really want to see the completed jigsaw.

'Thank you, Molly.'

'I'd ask to be kept in the picture' Molly replied. 'But we both know that'll only happen if Jackson so decrees.'

Because this was so clearly true, Catherine had nothing to add. Disconnecting, she went to brief Lamb before the shouting began.

Taverner said, 'I had a meeting here not long ago.' She was looking out of the window at the building across the street, as if calculating a trajectory. 'It went well.'

The flat was on Calthorpe Street, on an upstairs floor. A Service property, its furniture sourced from a catalogue. CC said, 'Are we alone?'

'If I'd planned on having you bagged, I'd have arranged that without getting out of bed. So yes, we're alone.'

No Dogs; no hard exits. He supposed he should be relieved. When he'd taken Al's gun from his bag it had been with such a prospect in mind, but seriously, who was he kidding? The time it took him to unpocket the gun, they'd have read him his last rites and put a notice in the paper.

He said, 'I've brought the recording.' On a disk: he put it on the table. 'That's it. No copies. I don't plan to cause more trouble.'

Taverner glanced at her watch.

'Nor will I apologise. We got the shitty end of the stick, handling Pitchfork. We kept him in check best we could, but afterwards we were treated like dirt. We didn't deserve that. We were his handlers, not his accomplices. Even if it's true what they've said since, that he ended more lives than he saved.'

'There are always those who'll pick holes after the event,' Taverner said. 'And it's easy to show the Service in a bad light. But we're not monsters. No, let me rephrase. We're sometimes monsters, but we have to be. To kill the bigger monsters. And we make mistakes, but who doesn't? The royal family? The Post Office?' Her words were clipped, precise, delivered without passion. Just another debate in the office. 'And we don't own up to those mistakes for the same reason nobody else does. That once we did, we'd lose all credibility.'

'And that's your main concern.'

'Yes. Besides, those whose deaths he caused were enemies of the state, remember? We're not talking about the slaughter of the innocents. And in case you need reminding, you didn't come to me demanding a light be shone on the truth. You came for money.' She picked up the disk and examined it briefly. 'This belongs in a museum. The tech, I mean, not the contents.' She dropped it into her bag.

CC said, 'You could say the same about me.'

'The thought had occurred. Where are your friends?'

'They had nothing to do with this.'

'Of course not. Where are they?'

'On various trains. Heading home. Forgetting this happened.'

'It was all you, wasn't it? Your hat, your rabbit.' She shook her head. 'Supposing I'd told you to screw yourself and publish? Where'd that have got you?'

'I knew you wouldn't.'

'Because you'd have wound up in court. Or been tried by the press. Public enemies numbers one through four. And yes, the Park would have had headlines too, but we've weathered worse.'

'If we were going to be part of the cover-up, we deserved to be compensated. And since we weren't, why help cover it up?'

'And what about the murder charge?'

'We never committed murder.'

'A good lawyer might agree that Pitchfork's crimes were his alone. That you were bound by the rules of the Service not to warn his victims, that doing so might have been treason. But it's Malone I'm talking about.'

In the street a horn sounded, then another. Two cars having a row. CC said, 'Malone was found by his old comrades. The identity you gave him fell apart, and the Provos found him. Executed him.'

'That's certainly the official rumour. I mean, the coroner delivered an open verdict, but we all knew what she meant. But it doesn't really fly. Because if his old colleagues had come for him, we'd have been aware of it. It's not like we weren't keeping an eye on them.'

'What are you trying to say?'

'Well, I was hoping you'd join the dots and save me the bother. But if you need it spelling out, what I'm trying to say is that your friends Avril, Al and Daisy murdered Dougie Malone. Are you sure you won't sit down? You look fit to drop.'

'I was thinking,' Daisy said, 'there's probably a party shop round here. There's always one somewhere, have you noticed?'

Al and Avril shared a look.

'Only then we could buy some big red noses, and maybe clown shoes or something. In case we're not conspicuous enough.'

Though in fact they were just three people, none of them youngsters, who'd emerged from a taxi, which had made a significant dent in the bounty CC had dispensed. CC's car was nearby, on a meter. Avril's watch, meanwhile, was still tucked down its back seat cushion. And CC himself was presumably close at hand, answering a summons from Diana Taverner . . .

Not for the first time, Avril wondered what CC had thought he was doing, trying to put one over the Wicked Witch of the Park. Except the answer was obvious; he had thought, like any hero, that his guile was a match for anyone's. Same old story. But in the real world Hansel and Gretel were eaten, and hungry bears watched Goldilocks dance herself to death. 'Cover the area,' Avril said, and they separated. If Taverner had a place round here for covert meetings, it might be possible to recognise it from the exterior. Service properties came in different varieties. Intelligence factories were notable for a lack of windows, while upstairs rooms commandeered for surveillance purposes would have theirs propped open, to allow for unimpeded lines of sight and sound. A safe apartment would have thicker windows than its neighbours, light hitting them in a different way. It was all about glass; reflective surfaces. *Mirror mirror on the wall.* But maybe she was out of date.

Her phone pinged, and a moment later did so again. Al and Daisy, checking in. She pinged back, the single letter K. For the busy spy, the time it would take to key the preceding vowel was an unaffordable luxury.

Having ironic little thoughts was a self-indulgence too. Whatever CC had become entangled in, he had Al's gun in his pocket. With a prop like that to hand, the chances of things getting messy skyrocketed. But then, things had become messy long ago, when they'd decided to kill Malone.

A figure up ahead who might be CC morphed into someone else: wrong age, wrong shape. Keep looking. She turned a corner, crossed the road, reversed direction.

At the time it had felt like unfinished business; something that should have happened sooner. Leaving CC out of it, though, had required deliberation — CC would have balked at wreaking revenge. *It's not revenge, it's housekeeping. Where there are germs, you bring bleach.* Though the bleach had stung their own fingers in the end.

Her phone pinged again: Al, this time with a full sentence. *CC would never have tried to blackmail the Park if he'd known what we did.* She had to smile: synchronicity. In a different life, they'd have made a reasonable couple. In this one Al loved Daisy, and always had done.

She didn't reply. Looking skywards, as if checking the weather, she scanned upstairs windows, trying to gauge the depths each concealed. Maybe behind one of them Di Taverner, a woman whose very thoughts were gilded splinters, was talking to CC. She'd be explaining, first, why his blackmail attempt had failed, and then why he had no choice but to fall in with whatever she was about to outline.

Which would doubtless be ugly and dangerous, Avril thought. But he wouldn't be facing it alone.

Shirley had done as much staring out of the window as she could tolerate, and given that the alternative was to work she took to brooding instead about Louisa's future plans, and how she might – well, maybe not fuck them up, but that was the backup plan. They were colleagues, and she had the greatest respect, but Jesus: if Louisa was in line for some high-profile security job, she – Shirley – would be failing in her duty to herself if she didn't point out to whoever was in charge that she was the better candidate. The most basic review of their respective CVs underlined that. Louisa was in Slough House because she'd botched an op that put a bunch of hooky guns on the street, whereas Shirley's so-called crime was decking a handsy colleague, which wasn't so much misdemeanour as social duty. Anyway, long story short, she, Ash and Lech were now in Roddy's room, brainshowering – which she wasn't a hundred per cent was an actual word – how to get the lowdown on Louisa's new job, supposing it actually existed. Or some of them were.

'Not really our business, is it?' said Lech.

'Not really our business, is it?' Ash mimicked.

'Fuck off. I mean, if she's decided to move on, who can blame her? She's been here longer than any of us.'

'Except me,' said Roddy.

'I wasn't counting you.'

'Why not?'

'Because you don't count.'

'It's not that she's leaving, it's where she's going,' Shirley said. 'If they've got openings, we should know about them.'

Lech shook his head. 'What, she's found a new job, so we should all go with her? What world are you living in?'

Ash said, 'Same one as you. That's our problem.'

'You can quit. No one's asking you to stay.'

'Just because your face looks like an emoji for despair doesn't make you wise and all-knowing.'

'Yeah,' said Shirley. 'It just makes you basically unemployable.'

She was starting to think Ash might not be as annoying as first and also second through twentieth impressions had suggested. Maybe she'd let her know that talking to Lamb about her kitty money might not be a happy chat.

'So ask her,' Lech said.

'She probably won't tell us.'

'I can find out,' said Ho.

'Yeah, right. The tattooed wonderboy.'

'I'd rather have a tattoo than a face like a . . .'

'Pissed-on bin-fire?' Shirley suggested.

'You're very free with the insults, for someone the shape of a pedal bin. Anyway, how can he find out?'

'Simps,' said Ash. 'He can check her email.'

Lech looked at Roddy.

Roddy said, 'Who do you think raided Doctor Desk's inbox?'

'If you've ever even *thought* about—'

'Yeah, yeah, no one wants to read your emails,' Shirley said. 'You have no life.'

From downstairs came the unmistakable sound of Slough House's back door opening, the aural equivalent of a purple-inked letter of complaint. Then feet on the stairs: a purposeful clatter, someone in a hurry. Two someones.

The door burst open and River was there, Louisa close behind him.

'Oh, hi,' said Lech. 'Did Sid reach you? She called earlier, I think she's lost her phone.'

River stared.

'I said—'

River stepped forward, grabbed Lech's head in both hands and kissed his forehead. 'Thank you,' he said. Then released him. 'It didn't fucking occur to you to let me know?'

'It wasn't me took the call.'

'Where is she?' Louisa asked.

'I'm not your out-of-office bot,' Ash said. 'She called, I told Lamb. End of.'

Shirley said, 'So what's this new job you've got?'

'How was she? What state was she in?'

'What am I, her therapist? I've never even met her.'

'Did she sound hurt? What was she doing in Oxford?'

'Had some ink done.'

'I know. I was here. Remember?'

"Cause I'd consider a move too, if the money's right.'

'And where is she now? Anyone?'

'Have you tried texting her?'

'Well, since I'm carrying her actual fucking phone—'

Lamb said, 'Boil a bloody frog.'

Sometimes you heard something for the first time and realised you'd always known it, had been waiting for the words to be said. Or, in CC's case, waiting for them never to be said, because they didn't need to be made real. They needed to be nailed down out of sight, so you could pretend they'd never happened.

'Don't get me wrong. Pitchfork was a murderous bastard, and while we've spent decades denying we'd have touched him with a railway sleeper, we also wondered whether it wouldn't be simpler to have him wiped. Only we didn't need to, because your friends took matters into their own hands.'

Diana Taverner had spoken to him as if he were a remedial class. Probably that's how she spoke to most people.

'They turned up at his farmhouse one February night, took him out to his barn, and squashed his head with a Land Rover. Probably wanted us to think what you suggested, that his former colleagues had found him and used his own party trick to dispatch him. Either way . . .' She had put her hands together, then brought them apart suddenly. *Pyow!* 'His head burst like a melon.'

'And you hushed it up.'

'Well, not personally. Before my time. And "hushing it up", that smacks of conspiracy. No, as far as I'm aware only one person knew who killed Pitchfork, apart from the killers, and that was your old friend David Cartwright. Nobody else cared. The investigating police force knew he was living under a fake identity, rumours about who he really was got around, and that was that. Case closed. He'd been found by his old mates in the IRA. Good riddance.'

Amen to that.

He wondered where he'd parked his car.

While he walked around looking, trusting that his earlier self, the man he'd been forty minutes earlier, would recognise a landmark – a skateboard decal fixed to a street lamp; a bollarded section where the ground had shrugged off the pavement – Taverner's voice ding-donged round his head.

How had Cartwright known?

'Because that's who he was. A man who thought up endings to stories, and scribbled them in the margins of old files. But don't worry. I've made sure his jottings won't see the light again. Unless . . .'

She'd had a meeting in that same room not long ago, CC recalled. *It went well*. This was her territory, not his; a bounded space in which negotiations happened.

Negotiations were like threats. Many began with the word 'unless'.

Unless what?

'There's a new spirit abroad. New government, new broom. And before too many people notice that they've scaled the moral high ground wearing designer freebies, they need to prove themselves, show they're not like the old crowd. By way of a public handwashing, perhaps — early enough in their life cycle to be forgiven by the public, or at least be forgotten by the next election, which amounts to the same thing. And if that means acknowledging one of the dirtier little secrets of Britain's recent past, well, that'll show what a straight-shooting bunch they are. Besides, it won't cost the earth. We're not talking infected blood or nuclear test victims. We're not talking Post Office. This is limited liability stuff, only a dozen or so dead. No, the more I think about it, the more it might be in everyone's interest — and when I say "everyone", I'm using the technical sense, meaning the party currently in power — in everyone's interest if we let the whole story into the open. Including that fascinating little addendum about your chums being murderers.'

Instead of replying, he had found himself wondering whether speeches like that trotted from her lips box-fresh, or whether she'd arrived before him to rehearse. Whether the room had heard earlier drafts, their words now curling in its corners like dropped petals.

'Funny how it goes. Only this morning, you were planning on holding exposure over the Park, playing your tape to the mob. And suddenly you're back on the inside, hoping Pitchfork never gets public, because if it does, your colleagues won't emerge looking like victims, forced to compromise their principles for the good of the state. They'll be charged with murdering the man they helped commit those crimes. A good prosecutor could make it look like they were covering up their own sins, which would be an entertainment, don't you think? Nothing tickles the masses like a public crucifixion.'

'What is it you want from me?'

'The same thing you want, CC. I want you to be useful.'

He could feel a pendulum swinging overhead. Time getting ready to crush him. 'I've been retired for over a decade. And I was out to grass long before then. How could I be of use to you?'

So she had explained.

And here was his car, third time of looking, exactly where he'd parked it.

The keys were in his pocket. While he fumbled around, fishing them out, the gun he'd taken from Al's case banged against his ribs like an extra heartbeat, arrhythmical and heavy.

'Well, boil a bloody frog,' Lamb said. 'Here's me thinking you're beavering away like centrefolds, and instead there's a party in full swing. My invitation's in the post, I presume?'

He had appeared in the doorway with his customary stealth, which is to say, the stealth he adopted when he wasn't lumbering like a rheumatic armadillo. Catherine, behind him, raised an eyebrow in River's direction: welcome, apology, warning, resignation.

'So who's going to give me a rundown of the playlist?'

Louisa said, 'Taverner's had Sid recruit an old network.'

'CC Stamoran,' River said. 'Who found something in my grandfather's library.'

'And his crew.'

'The Brains Trust.' River read their names from the palm of his hand.

Lech said, 'They probably worked in Ulster with CC. So they're not desk drones.'

'Ulster's in Ireland,' said Roddy.

'And that was a brainstorm, was it? If brains were actual weather, none of you'd get wet.'

'Just bringing you up to speed,' River said.

'Yeah, right. You realise I have to decelerate when you do that?' Lamb looked round sourly. 'Yes, Taverner, or this Stamoran creature, or both, found something somewhere that David Cartwright squirrelled away, possibly before but maybe after he developed runny brain, as a result of which a bunch of past-their-sell-by spooks may well be doing cartwheels at Taverner's bidding. Just another day at the spy factory. And yes, we're maybe early doors for another monumental balls-in-a-mousetrap situation courtesy of First Desk's never-ending desire to prove herself queen of fucking everywhere, but you know what? I don't care. Which means, in case you're all too hopped up, dumbed down or just plain thick to notice, that you don't care either. So back to work. Except you.' He pointed at River. 'You can fuck off home. Your plug's been pulled.'

River said, 'Taverner used Sid as a sock puppet. Me too.'

'Well that's better than using you as a toilet brush, which would have been my choice. And guess what? Baker's fine and you're – I don't care what you are. But nobody got hurt, which means I don't have to listen to Standish moaning about staff shortages or stay late while she finds forms for me to sign. That's a positive outcome, which, if you'd ever had managerial experience, you'd know is like a wet dream after a free beer. Doesn't happen often, but when it does, you don't spend time worrying who's doing the laundry.'

'Taverner's up to something,' Louisa said.

'Have recent years taught you nothing? She's always up to something.'

'Right,' said River, 'and whatever she's found to use as a weapon, who do you think she's aiming it at?'

'Taylor Swift?'

'You've been a thorn in her side forever.'

Lamb looked sideways at Ash. 'It's young Baker I feel sorry for. This one doesn't know foreplay when he sees it.'

'You know what?' River said. 'I'm not bothered either. If Lady Di's primed a geriatric hit squad to clean your clock, I think I'll just buy a big bag of popcorn and find a comfortable chair.'

Catherine said, 'Let's everyone cool down, shall we?'

'Don't look at me,' said Shirley. 'I lost track five minutes ago.'

'We just wanted to know about Louisa's new job,' Ash explained.

'Since when did my life become everyone's business?'

'They wanted me to crash your inbox,' Roddy said. 'I told them private's private, ya feel me?'

'. . . Thank you.'

'Also, I blocked that randomer who's sending you dick pics.'

'Taverner isn't coming after me,' Lamb said. 'If she wanted to do that, she'd make damn sure not to involve you lot. Even tangentially.'

'You're pretty sure we'd have your back,' muttered Lech.

'No, I'm pretty sure you'd fuck things up,' said Lamb. 'She'd use someone efficient. Is Ronnie Corbett still alive?'

'So who's her target?' River asked.

'Christ,' said Lamb, turning to leave. 'It's days like this I miss that psycho we used to have. At least he could think straight.'

'Shoot straight too,' Shirley said, remembering.

Lamb had gone. River shook his head. 'I've had enough of this. I'm going to find Sid.'

'Not sure you'll have to,' Catherine said, as the door downstairs groaned another welcome.

After Stamoran's departure Diana Taverner studied the disk he'd brought her. Dynamite came all shapes and sizes, and Stamoran had obviously thought this had the potential to blow a big enough hole in her desk that she'd dig into the reptile fund to defuse it. But then, he'd been a handler, not a weasel. A good handler thought in straight lines, at the end of which a joe came safely home. The weasels were the Service's planners and strategists; they could take a scenario and bend it in any direction, at the end of which a joe might be strung out in pieces by the side of a road, and the op still branded a success. If not by handlers, obviously. This particular scenario had more curves than Stamoran could see round. It was possible it had more than she'd yet identified herself.

It was true what she'd told him, that a brave government might decide that the mess in question was best dragged into daylight. But it was more true that brave governments were rare, and for most, no time was better than the one that occurred on another party's watch. To have the contents of the tape made public would involve fallout, even if it did no more than confirm what had long been rumoured. The prime minister at the time was beyond damage, true, his reputation long since soiled by his brokering of an illegal war, and his self-esteem bomb-proof, but still, this dirt would not easily be swept away. A psychopath had been used and protected, paid and pensioned off, despite possibly being responsible for ending more lives than he'd saved. Owning up to the state's sanctioning of such crimes might ultimately be a step towards national redemption, but it was a step most politicians would prefer someone else take, lest in the process they tangle their feet and smash their teeth on an unforgiving pavement.

For her own part, she thought seeking forgiveness unnecessary, but then, she was First Desk. The luxury of a conscience was for those without the responsibilities she bore.

And she'd imagined David Cartwright had felt the same way, until she'd discovered his habit of annotating the files he consulted in Molly Doran's archive; obsessively juggling the secret histories he'd helped write, tracing endings never part of the official record. Jottings among which she'd found an oddity:

a copied-out sentence from that classified meeting that had discussed Pitchfork's pay-off, words included in the extract Stamoran had sent her; anodyne in themselves, but with the power to come bouncing down the years as wildly as a rubber ball hurled into a concrete cell.

There's one further matter we need to cover, I think, sir. The question of inflation-proofing the pension arrangement.

As carefully as that sentence had been written, Diana had torn it from its margin and destroyed it. The fact that Stamoran had made no reference to it was proof he hadn't understood what he'd had. He might have recognised that it was dynamite, but had failed to appreciate that dynamite wasn't designed to be a cause of indiscriminate havoc. Handled correctly, it was a precision instrument.

There's one further matter we need to cover.

There always was.

Locking the door behind her, Taverner walked down the stairs and emerged into sunshine, satisfied she'd primed her own explosive charge.

The nearest pub was a heartless space, catering for those who wanted to drink but were disinclined to put effort into it. For Catherine, being here was like stepping back inside one of her own blackouts. This is where the magic happens, she thought, but even within the confines of her head the joke fell flat: nothing here offered welcome, or whispered sweet come-ons. The magical place – like a children's playground, its edges smoothed with soft-impact material – lay on the far side of her next drink, and she'd have to be alone to turn that key. If she ever did.

'Are you okay?' Lech asked.

'I'll have a mineral water. Thank you.'

There was hubbub, though they were the only group there. Sid was with them. She'd been abandoned by the Brains Trust in a motorway service station, without her phone – the contemporary equivalent of sensory deprivation – but she was resourceful, and a functioning adult, so it shouldn't be that surprising she'd found her way home. Her reunion with River had been brief and low-key, and Catherine had found herself having to turn away, though none of the others did.

It had gone five thirty. They were on their own time, which didn't mean Lamb wouldn't find a way to make them suffer. But anyway: there was hubbub as Sid went over details of the story she'd already told.

'You sure you're okay?'

'I'm fine. I lost my phone, that's all.'

'You should have seen wonderboy. Crowbarred that door like it was a jam jar.'

'He usually has trouble with jam jars.'

'What was in the envelope?'

'Money. A burner.'

'Had some ink done.'

'That's nice.'

'What are they like? This Brains Trust crew?'

'Old. Not ancient. But sprung chickens.'

'I met Stam.'

'He's their boss. But actually, I think Avril's their leader.'

'This Daisy chick flattened you?'

'The way a startled animal might.'

'Do people come here for fun?'

'I expect only sad people.'

'"I'll shoot you dead"? Did he even have a gun?'

'It was a threat. He didn't have it notarised.'

'And you think Taverner's primed them for an op?'

'She's up to something. That's for sure.'

'Doesn't sound like they're dangerous.'

Catherine joined in. 'There's a story about them. Molly reminded me.'

'Share?'

'Daisy had a breakdown. She walked out on her life, didn't tell anyone where she went. The others spent a year looking for her. The Park didn't help because she'd quit the Service by then. Anyway, she was living in an encampment beneath a motorway flyover with a group of whatever the PC term is. Not the kind of people who call the police.'

'Why would they call the police?'

'Because when the Brains Trust fetched Daisy away, it was an enemy action.' Catherine sipped her mineral water. It tasted like exactly what it was. 'They might be old,' she said. 'But that doesn't mean they're safe.'

Everyone was quiet for a while. Then Lech said, 'Who is Taverner aiming them at?'

'Could be anyone,' Shirley said.

'Except Lamb seemed to think he knew.'

'Lamb thinks he knows everything.'

'Yes, but if Lamb thinks it's obvious, then it's someone we all know,' Louisa said. 'And not, I dunno, her postman or someone.'

'Why would First Desk set a hit crew on her postman?' Ash asked.

'You've not known her as long as we have.'

River said, 'Either way, she shouldn't have used us as her . . . Allen key.'

'"Us"?' said Ash.

'Sid and me.'

'Us,' said Shirley.

Sid said, 'Taverner's out of control. If she's using this crew as expendables, she should be stopped.'

'We don't know that's what she's doing.'

'We can take a fair guess.'

'They're pensioners.'

'They ran ops in Northern Ireland, during the Troubles. If

she's got a hold on them, it's because they know how to get things done.'

'Creepy things.'

'Peter Judd,' said Louisa.

'We're playing word association?'

'No.' She set her empty wine glass down. 'He's Taverner's bête noire, not Lamb. That whole firefight thing with the tiger team, remember? That was down to him. And more grubby stuff since. He's got something on her, or she'd have dealt with him by now. So maybe this is her way of sorting him out. Using a crew of deniables.'

'If so,' Lech said, 'she'll make sure the deniables are dealt with too. Afterwards.'

They all thought about that for a bit.

River said, 'CC worked with my grandfather.'

'Everyone worked with your—'

'They were friends. I don't want these guys hurt. Not as expendables in Taverner's war with Judd.'

'Might not be Judd she's setting them on,' Shirley said.

'Might not even be a hit.'

'It might not be Judd, and Taverner might be assembling a squad for a crack at Eurovision,' said River. 'But I don't plan to sit back and hope for the best. Taverner's never played nice, and I doubt she's starting now.'

'And we've been told to do nothing,' Shirley said, her tone suggesting this was a persuasive argument in favour of the opposite.

'Taverner should be stopped,' Sid said again.

'Should have been stopped long ago,' Louisa said.

'So we're going live on this?' River asked.

'On what exactly?'

'Preventing this crew from doing something dangerous. Which will result in their getting hurt.'

'I'm not a hundred per cent sure I want to protect Judd.'

Catherine said, 'Preventing harm is always a good move. But let's nobody get hurt, right? Including all of you.'

'We don't even know where Stamoran and his crew are.'

'But if it's Judd they're after,' Louisa said, 'I know someone who'll know his movements.'

'Can we agree first that that's a priority? None of you getting hurt?'

River said, 'This is about talking people down from doing something stupid. Nobody's going to be jumping in front of bullets.'

'Well, I'm in,' said Shirley.

'Me too.'

'And me.'

River looked at Ash and Roddy, neither of whom had spoken.

Roddy said to Sid, 'It's a hummingbird, by the way.'

'That's nice,' she said again.

He nodded importantly. 'I'm in.'

Ash said, 'Whatever.'

Avril watched from a distance as CC fumbled for his car keys, found them, slipped them into the lock on his fourth attempt. That he'd been with First Desk was apparent from his flustered state. It didn't take a genius to guess what she'd told him. Which meant a reckoning was due.

Overdue, even. Avril had no belief in a life after this one, but that didn't mean sins didn't need paying for, and that murdering Dougie Malone had been a sin brooked no argument. The act of killing him had been a minor infraction, on the level of stamping out a cockroach, but their method had been unforgivable – a necessary means of disguising their involvement, but unforgivable. And in the end, this was what had done for Daisy; its stain propelling her onto the streets, a punishment she'd had no right to endure on her own.

Being in London was a reminder of bad times. The streets

were full of homeless soldiers. We wind them up and point them, but we don't always bring them back afterwards – Christ, even Kipling recognised this. It's not a new problem, it's an old story. They had come home after Belfast, the four of them, accustoming themselves to a new existence; one in which danger was less overt, but car ignitions couldn't be fired without the engines being checked first. As for their memories – of what they'd done, whose evil they'd helped facilitate – these had seethed unchecked. Pitchfork had been a nightmare made flesh; raping, murdering, but protected from justice by virtue of being a Service asset. The Troubles might be over, and the operation put to bed, but that didn't mean sleep came easily. So in the end they'd made new vows, leaving CC out of it because he was too straight, too narrow, too *good*, to be included, and she and Al and Daisy had hunted down the beast in his Cumbrian fastness. As the previous evening's events had reminded her, this was not something she would ever raise a toast to. But nor was it something she'd regret, or if she did, that would only be on account of what Daisy went through as a result, years afterwards, when she dropped off all their maps.

It was Al who'd found her, after months of searching. Avril had done her part, ruling avenues out. Daisy wasn't using a credit card, wasn't on an electoral roll. Driving licence, medical records, council tax; none of the usual snags had checked her fall. The more she looked, the more Avril feared that one of two scenarios were in play; either Daisy had deliberately taken on a new identity, shedding her old existence like a peeled eggshell, or, more frighteningly, had no plan, no design; had simply lost her hold on the everyday. In which case she could be anywhere – lost in the gaps that appear between stable lives – and would be impossible to find, because every gaze would pass through her.

But not Al's. He found her in a settlement on London's western edge; a reservation erected in the liminal space under a flyover, between two slip roads. There were caravans, and a heartbreaking attempt at homesteading had been made, with wire fencing marking out territories. A pair of cars, looking like collateral damage from a hotrod movie, were parked nose to tail, and from the rear window of one a pole extruded, a flag tied to it, though it hung too limply to be identified. There were dogs, because there were always dogs, and the air tasted of metal and ancient barbecue.

That same night, they'd gone to fetch her home, CC too, because it would have been a crime not to include him. It had been a straightforward affair, complicated slightly by the dogs. The encampment numbered eleven hostiles, not counting children, because on enemy territory every warm body is a hostile. The men were in their thirties or forties, allowing for some rough journeys, and had made the fundamental error of assuming that CC and Al were what they appeared to be, and Avril herself their harmless accessory. That had been the last occasion on which she had used a handgun, and while she regretted shooting two dogs, she did not regret it very much, not after opening the caravan where Daisy had been kept. They had taken cash with them, all they could rustle together, in case that proved the simplest solution, and in the end Al had tucked a ton into the shirt pocket of the camp leader as he lay on the ground, nursing a leg that wouldn't ever work properly again. And then they had brought Daisy back into the world.

In the years since, the old Daisy had poked her head round the door, but she still had long stretches of silence. Her voice, like her frame, was frailer than before, like a dandelion being blown. But she had taken young Sid Baker down in a single fluid movement, and dandelions don't do that.

CC was in his car now, starting up the engine. And there was Al, watching from a different corner: *Oh you big hunk of man*. He would still put himself between them and the slightest danger, she knew. Danger, these days, was younger and faster than him, but that wouldn't stop him. Even if Daisy weren't here, he'd act the same.

The car pulled away. She checked her phone: the tracker was transmitting. That CC hadn't noticed them showed how distracted he was, which in turn suggested that whatever his meeting with Taverner had been about, it hadn't included a mindfulness break. Daisy had appeared now too, on the corner behind Al, and as the pair crossed the road towards her, Avril had the sense they say comes with your last moments; not so much that she saw her life flashing before her eyes, but more that she felt it behind her, all its pent-up force propelling her into whatever would happen next.

After the pub, Catherine alone returned to Slough House. It was approaching the violet hour, and traffic was dusty and boisterous: crossing the road she spent three minutes on the median strip while cars, vans, buses and a trio of wide, expensive motorbikes kicked up a northbound fuss. Looking at Slough House's windows, she thought them dark and wretched. Why did thoughts like that occur?

Over the road at last, and round the back, and up the stairs. Lamb was in his room, his door open, his feet malevolently planted on his desk, his attention fixed on the landing even if his gaze was aimed elsewhere. Lamb could look at a ceiling the way an artist studied a canvas. You knew that whatever he was seeing, it wasn't a blank empty space.

'All fucked up in bed, are they?'

'They've gone home, yes.'

'Yeah, right. But you can't keep away.'

Any more than he could. She entered his room, leaving the door standing wide; she brushed the visitor's chair on which ash had settled, and pulled it across to the desk so she could sit facing him. The smell of alcohol was in the air: it might have followed her across the road, except, of course, it hadn't;

it had been waiting here. A finger-smeared glass sat on the desktop, a healthy measure weighing it down. Healthy might not be the word. Lamb was holding a cigarette, which counted as one of his vital signs; a surer indication than a heartbeat that he was still among the living. It was unlit.

River had once described Lamb as a coiled sponge. That was his current mode. At any moment, without warning, he might not do anything.

She said, 'This isn't like you.'

'What isn't?'

'Not to care when Taverner's up to something.'

He shrugged. 'I don't care much when anyone's up to something. Or when they're not.' He'd found a match, and struck it expertly against his thumbnail. The head broke off and fizzed into the air like a model comet. 'I thought you'd have noticed that by now.'

'You care when a joe's in trouble.'

'These Brain Salad bedblockers are not my joes.'

'Why not give Taverner a call? Let her know whatever she's planning is no longer as secret as she thinks it is.'

'Sloth, apathy, lack of interest . . . A whole misogyny of reasons.'

She couldn't help herself. 'Miscellany.'

'Piss off, woman.'

She shook her head wearily. 'You're not as funny as you think you are.'

'Then I'm in good company. Even Graham Norton's not as funny as I think I am. And he's a regular fucking caution.'

She stood long enough to grind out the very small fire that had begun to take hold of the carpet, then resumed her chair. 'You think it's a good idea to let Taverner run another off-the-books op? Given that the last one nearly got River and Sid killed?'

'No, I think it's a good idea to notice that when Taverner

runs an off-the-books op, people nearly get killed.' He struck another match, off the desk this time, and successfully lit his cigarette. 'Except when they actually get killed. So no, what I think should happen is everyone should do what I told them to do in the first place, and fold their fucking arms. Then whatever goes tits up'll be someone else's grief.'

'You think they're useless.'

'And you think they can redeem themselves. But only because you've not been keeping score.'

'All they want is to keep some old spooks out of harm's way.'

'Yeah, what could go wrong?' He reached for his glass and drained about half its contents. It didn't seem that he found any pleasure in the action, or dismissed any pain.

She said, 'Just now, over the road. Discussing what to do. For once they were all on the same side. Do you know how good that felt? You rot in here all day long, drinking that and smoking those, and you don't care that they all feel like they're in purgatory. I swear, I worry Shirley will self-harm just to ease the boredom. At least just now, they looked like they were alive.'

'Get back to me when their game of cops and robbers has run its course. If they're all still looking the same, I'll owe you a drink.'

'That sounds like you, Jackson. Pick the one debt you'll never have to repay.'

She didn't even know why she said that. It wasn't true. Lamb looked every inch a man who'd been paying off a debt for longer than she'd known him. It was just that he'd never explained to her – to anyone – what that debt was, or how he'd acquired it.

He didn't reply. Standing to leave, she shunted her chair back into place. If she could have re-dusted it with ashes, she'd have done so. Sometimes it was best to leave no trace of your presence behind.

Before she was out of the office, he spoke. She could tell without turning that he wasn't looking at her; had assumed his default position, feet on desk, head pointed towards ceiling. His glass would be full again, and soon would be empty once more. There was no defining Lamb by how he viewed a glass and its contents. Whether half full or half empty, soon enough it would be its opposite.

He said, his voice devoid of apparent feeling, 'Here we fucking go again.'

'Yes.'

'Just stick your head round the door once it's over.'

She'd have done that anyway. Let him know things were okay, or that they weren't. This had been her job for as long as she could remember, but it was the first time she could recall that they'd exchanged places; that it was she who'd sent the slow horses out, he who was wishing them safe at home.

When she reached her room, she closed her door. There was work to do – she could always find work – but she wouldn't do it. Instead she sat and let the dark gather round her, wrapping her as tightly as a bandage.

Off the hook, because his Sherlock Holmes tribute act wasn't required – thank you, Peter Judd, whose own Honey-Monster-meets-Vlad-the-Impaler schtick wore thin on short acquaintance – Devon had nevertheless checked in with the office, because while the client was always right the client was also frequently a dick, liable to confuse his own best interests for something momentarily more attractive. Whether this involved a night on the lash or an interlude with a mistress, you couldn't – in Judd's case – rule out his needing a personal protection officer at some point, if not an exorcist or a vet.

The mothership was in Holborn, a suite of offices with customer-facing talent in the shape of a well-groomed pair who might have been brother and sister, or possibly sisters, and with whose blessing he borrowed the key to the Watchtower. This was the big brother room, tech heavy in the stylish way more common to TV shows than reality: there were no discarded bits of kit, no unattached cables; just a space station's worth of expensive hardware, all varying shades of white, and no surfaces disfigured by anything as harsh as a right angle. A room where you might happily drink bubble tea, Devon thought, as he settled in front of a screen and keyed in Judd's customer code.

Because here at POM – Peace of Mind – they watched people but they also *watched* them. They were there when the client needed backup, but they were also there when the client thought the client needed privacy because it was in the quietest moments that the loudest bangs occurred. So clients not only knowingly ceded backstage passes to their public events, they unknowingly surrendered their daily toings and nocturnal froings, the moments when they believed their watchers off the clock. There were privacy issues here, but the contracts POM's clients signed contained enough small print to give an owl a migraine, and encoded within that clusterbomb of subclauses was all the legal protection POM required to monitor its clients' bowel activity, let alone their more public movements. In Judd's case, this legal raincoat took the form of a tracking device Devon had tucked into his possession, a barcoded Gift Aid card, which Devon was confident Judd was unlikely to notice. On the monitor in front of him, this now flashed its location. Judd, it seemed, was over to the east; near Nob-Nobs, the club he'd hired last night for his daughter's birthday. Devon recalled their earlier conversation: *Sounds like you're in a big empty room. Except someone's cleaning it.* Yeah. He was at Nob-Nobs.

Probably a follow-up encounter. Nightclubs employed young people, Judd's natural prey. He remembered telling Louisa that *rich bastards or not, none of them are scumbags*, and suppressed a sigh. There was a reason he hadn't told Louisa that Judd was on their client list, and the reason was this: Judd was on their client list.

He wiped the screen, closed it down and left the building, looking for somewhere to eat. Judd was no longer on his agenda. Louisa, though: here was a coincidence. He'd been thinking about her not two minutes ago, and now, as he joined the early evening throng, her name was lighting up his phone.

'I'm assuming you keep tabs on where your clients are at any given moment?'

'It was good to see you too. And no, it was my pleasure.'

'In which case, it'd be handy to know where Peter Judd is right now. For your sake as well as mine. His too, come to think of it.'

'Judd?'

'Don't play games.'

'I don't remember mentioning—'

Not to mention remembering not mentioning.

Louisa said, 'Devon, did you really think I wouldn't do due diligence? Of course I found out he was on your client list. And what I need to know now is, where is he?'

'What's up?'

There was silence, or nearly; an aural scuffle came down the line, as if Louisa had her hand over her phone while a mini-conference took place.

When she came back, she said, 'It's a possibility, nothing more.'

'What is?'

'That he might be in danger.'

'What sort of danger?'

'How many kinds are there?'

He came to a halt. Louisa was one thing, but the slow horses? They weren't famous for jumping the right fences. If this was her own conclusion, he'd be prepared to back it. If it was something a Slough House cabal had come up with, it would be wise not to overcommit.

'That sounds vague.'

'Yeah, and there's a school of thought says we should just let the chips fall. Apart from anything else, if someone whacks Judd, we might all get a bank holiday.'

'I need details, Louisa.'

'Sure. Do you have a pen? I'll spell this out. S.O.D.O.F.F.'

'Louisa—'

'You're not the only one with skin in this game. You want details, I'll meet you wherever Judd is.'

He said, 'Is this what it's going to be like? I give an instruction, and you do whatever the fuck you want?'

'Believe it.'

She reminded him of Emma. Not that he'd ever been in a position to give Emma instructions. Starting to move again, he said, 'I'll take it that you're accepting the offer?' And then he told her about Nob-Nobs.

The royal family, apparently, never travel en masse in the same vehicle – this is to avoid the possibility of lineage-shattering accidents. That's what they tell Andrew, anyway. The slow horses didn't have the same protocol, and were madly crushed into River's car. Should a sinkhole open in front of it, Slough House would need restocking from the ground up.

'Where are we going again?'

'Place called Nob-Nobs, it's—'

'Did you get a postcode?'

' – in Shoreditch. No.'

'Would you shift your knee?'

River was driving mostly one-handed, his free hand seeking out Sid's when it wasn't required for more complex operations. Sid was squashed with Louisa in the shotgun seat, while, following negotiations that only Shirley and Ash had found satisfying, Roddy was on Lech's knee in between them, in the back.

'Is that where he'll be? Judd?'

'We don't even know for sure—'

'That's what Devon reckoned.'

' – he's being targeted.'

'We discussed this.'

'Just saying.'

'You can always get out.'

'And it's a nightclub?'

'Closed, apparently.'

Louisa looked out of the side window, at London's streets and London's pavements, wondering not so much whether this was sensible as to how much – curiously – she seemed to be enjoying herself. She was going to miss this.

'This CC guy—'

'Is this even safe?'

'You're supposed to be a spook—'

'Because it feels like there's *twelve* of us—'

' – not a fucking chicken crybaby.'

' – in a car built for like three.'

'This is a spacious car,' River said. 'It is roomy. Shut the fuck up.'

' – is he dangerous?'

Sid said, 'He looks like someone you'd not look at twice. Someone who used to be in marketing, or real estate.'

Roddy said, 'Sounds lame.'

'What, you think a tat of a baby squid makes you John Wick?'

Well, maybe not miss it. But she would think about it often, at least at first, when she was in her new job, enjoying her new salary, and sitting in an office she didn't share with any of these people.

Sid said in her ear, 'What are you thinking about?'

'Nothing. Why?'

'You're smiling.'

'Yeah, well. Life's an adventure.'

River made an illegal turn to avoid an upcoming set of lights, then another, faster one to avoid an oncoming vehicle. They weren't far from Nob-Nobs now. No: in fact they were here.

They weren't the only ones.

So. Louisa sometimes felt like she was forever getting out of cars at strange places, like this nightclub, which would be like all nightclubs everywhere, glittery with potential then drab and disappointed as an uncollected ashtray, not that she was here for the usual reasons – at the back of her throat was that catch familiar from previous occasions, ones in which danger was more immediately apparent, such as the time at the top of the Needle with a Russian shooting at her across a carpet of scattered diamonds, or facing that private militia beneath the streets of west London with River, or when she walked down a snow-covered road in Wales, hoping to find Min's boy before men with guns did, but it was best to put such thoughts aside and concentrate on the task in hand, which was piling out of this vehicle with the other slow horses, so many of them it must have looked like a clown car, and each with different ideas about what to do next . . .

Judd had arrived fifteen minutes earlier, after killing time in a downscale coffee bar, enjoying the sordid nature of his surroundings. The grubby could be attractive, as a memorable tryst in a cupboard after an all-night session in the Commons once proved. With that fond memory tickling his ivories he stepped into early evening to find the city not yet soft but getting there, the honking and squalling of its traffic like a toddler's last protest before bedtime. He had the keys to the night in his pocket, or the keys to the nightclub, which felt like the same thing.

He was meeting Belwether at eight. Had the club been successful, it would be starting to fizz: lights on, glasses sparkling, sound system thumping; all of it prelude to the serious business – in nightclubs, men bent others to their will. This was what they were for. Nob-Nobs might be on the skids, its very name a portent of abysmal marketing, but here, soon, Dominic Belwether would arrive, the coming man in his party's ranks, and hardly one of Judd's natural allies. The task of co-opting him would give a lesser being pause, but lesser beings were always pausing, the ones who hadn't come to a halt. Sharks kept moving. Wise men took note.

Which Judd had done long ago, a moral absorbed alongside other crucial lessons. A youthful ambition to enter the intelligence world, for example, had foundered on the rock of psychological assessment – apparently he was unsuitable for any undertaking which involved the sublimation of his ego. Okay. But spying wasn't only about concealing your true self any more than it was all gadgets and gizmos and dead letter drops – spying was persuading others to betray those whom they loved, a game Judd was properly good at. That House of Commons tryst, for example, had been with his opposite number on the shadow cabinet.

The club, a converted warehouse, occupied a corner space, with an alley running alongside and behind it, and two similar properties locking it in place: one a set of temporary offices for start-ups and wind-downs, the other a collection of rehearsal spaces for bands and drama companies. The stop/start wheeze and whine of uncoordinated instruments suggested that a junior orchestra, or a modern jazz outfit, was in residence.

Using the key he'd been given, Judd let himself in through

a side door, five yards down the alley, and was swallowed up by darkness.

Devon watched this from across the road. He'd been there ten minutes — most of his job involved waiting. In this instance he was occupying a table outside a bar, browsing his phone, drinking zero beer from the bottle; every inch the man with nothing better to do and enjoying doing it as the day deflated and warmth settled like a blanket. It was approaching the hour when the city grew calm, or pretended to; the evening's first drinks lending an amiable slant to everything. Give it time, though, and the picture would grow crooked, alcohol and heat combining to fan that rosy glow into a fire. Not everyone in the city drank. But those who did more than made up the slack.

For the moment, there was peace and city quiet, like actual quiet, but with the buzzing of traffic pasted on.

He had walked the alleyway bordering the club before sitting down. Beyond the door Judd had just disappeared through, at the corner of the building, a sash window above a larger pane was open a fraction; both were of fuzzy glass. Round the back, a pair of doors had their handles secured by padlock and chain. Beyond that, a rusty fire escape zigzagged roofwards. No signs of life within.

It was possible — probable — that nothing more serious than a carnal assignation was planned. It was also possible that Louisa was winding him up; payback for his not having told her Judd was on his client list.

Either way, he sipped his beer and waited.

CC had parked a short distance away. There was a garage with a forecourt on which car washing was taking place: three men with cloths and a hose, creating rainbows in the spray arcing from a windscreen. CC watched, Taverner's instructions ticking in his head. He could follow them or not. If he didn't, an old sin would rise from its grave and swallow those he loved. There wasn't really a choice, not if you were CC.

His phone rang. Avril. Whose soundtrack bubbled with ordinary noise but lacked the rattle and clatter of a track being pounded beneath her.

'Why aren't you on a train?'

'Because they're not like Ubers. They don't just go when you're ready.'

He conceded this point by leaving it unaddressed.

'Anyway, my watch. It's slipped off my wrist – it's always doing that. Please tell me it's in the back seat.'

'A minute.' He unclipped his seat belt and twisted round. 'Doesn't seem to be.'

'Maybe behind the cushion? I'm fond of it.'

He let himself out, opened the back door and ran his hand behind the cushions, all the while failing to make encouraging noises. *I am on my way to do something that shouldn't be done. To keep you from harm.* His hand encountered an object. He pulled it out. 'Got it.'

'I'm so glad. Could you stick it in the post when you get a free moment?'

Free morning, more like. Post offices. 'Of course.' He put it in his pocket. 'Got to move now, Avril. Safe journey.'

'We love you, CC.'

He was still fumbling for a reply when Avril ended the call.

Old Dog, young Dog. Big Dog, little Dog. The latter had a bruise blooming around his left eye: in days to come it would navigate the gloomier end of the spectrum, concentrating on purples, dark blues, blacks. His mood would roughly match it, his scowl deepening every time he caught someone throwing him a second look.

His partner had a more clinical attitude towards injuries

received. You didn't clench your fist, you marked a card. Then shuffled the deck and dealt yourself the hand you wanted.

Which, in this case, meant running a number plate through Service software and finding out where its vehicle was.

He glanced at the dashboard. 'We're off the clock.'

'Huh.'

'Want a drink?'

'Suppose.'

'Or would you rather sort out unfinished business?'

It took a moment for that penny to drop, as if it were finding its way through a slot machine. But when it did, lights pulsed and buzzers hummed: if he'd had a handle to pull, young Dog's eyes would have flashed bells and lemons.

'Skills,' he said.

Old Dog suppressed a sigh. Different language. On the other hand, the language they had in common – the kind most people could be made to understand – was the one they'd be relying on once they caught up with River Cartwright, so he simply nodded, and looked for the best place to turn around.

Avril said, 'He's moving. Slowly.'

'This is London. He might be in his car.'

Daisy said, 'Also. Also, he might be doing what he said he was doing. Finding somewhere to lay low.'

'With my gun.'

Daisy looked like she was about to argue a case for having a gun with you most times, just in case, but in the event didn't.

'How accurate is that thing?'

Al meant the tracker. 'It's Park tech. It works. Just don't rely on it for a moral compass.'

'We really think First Desk has sent CC to kill someone?'

Avril repeated his point: 'He took your gun. And if Taverner simply wanted someone threatened, leaned upon . . .'

She wouldn't have co-opted someone in their seventies.

They were on Farringdon Road. CC was in Shoreditch. 'We need another cab.'

'Well, if we don't stop someone dying,' Al said, 'at least we're breathing life into the economy.'

But he stepped off the kerb and raised an arm, and only four taxis went by before one stopped.

Judd texted Diana: *Side door unlocked.* She'd pass this on to Belwether, who would let himself in. This felt satisfyingly covert, and engorged him somewhat, as most things did. Later, he'd allow himself an indulgence. One of Xanthippe's sunbathing chums had asked about interning with his PR firm. *I feel I need more . . . experience before entering the job market.* Her number was on his phone, waiting to be unravelled.

He walked the steep incline of the shabby backstage corridor, which was harshly lit and uncarpeted, towards a bucket and mop standing sentry by a door, a reminder of how easily an evening of indulgence might tilt. Through that door, in the club proper, the only lights were a dim glow behind the bar, which stretched the full length of the furthest wall and was bordered by a row of tables currently burdened by upside-down stools. Beyond the bar, a pair of swing doors led to the lobby, through which, in the building's wildest dreams, young people would rush to buy overpriced drinks. On the other side was a staircase that went both directions, downstairs to the toilets; upstairs to the balcony. Another staircase, leading up, came to a halt by the door he'd just come through.

Right now, the building's emptiness felt like a long-nursed grievance. The dim light didn't reach the dance floor's corners, which squatted out of sight as if covering up some misfeasance requiring that mop and bucket. There was a smell of bleach, with undernotes of stale beer. Best to stay by the bar for his encounter with Belwether. Just the two of them – *I'll be on hand*, Diana had said, but she was unlikely to make an appearance. Not wanting to turn lights on, feeling shadow the better backdrop, he propped open the door to the corridor, allowing its single bulb to illuminate the space. Belwether would arrive soon. Propping himself on a stool, he settled in to wait.

. . . each with different ideas about what to do next, no wonder Slough House was a mess – anyway, yes, here Louisa was outside Nob-Nobs, and there was nothing doing with the front doors, which were locked, so River took charge, trying to impress Sid, because men always think the way to impress women is to be slightly more of a dick than they actually are, suggesting they pair off and circle the building, and after pointing out that seven didn't divide into pairs Louisa stepped off on her own before she could be partnered with Roddy, heading down an alley by the side of the club the same way you'd enter Slough House, wondering if this was how her story was doomed to play out, forever re-enacting spaces she was familiar with, and then stopped wondering that and wondered instead if this was another colossal waste of time, and if the slow horses, as usual, were just looking to fill the void where their jobs used to be, back when they felt useful . . .

CC's heart was beating irregularly, skipping, then banging hard. He told himself this was normal, then adjusted: normal for me. The gun in his pocket, swinging heavily against his ribs, was a more reliable measure. Age might be paddling in his wake, but he was rowing the boat.

But if he were his own handler, the instruction he'd give would be *Abort*. He was leaving a trail an infant could follow; his car on a meter, his reluctant steps passing, don't even count them, cameras. This was London. You could not move without becoming an extra – one of those stray characters exiting a Chinese restaurant, or leaving a hotel and hailing a taxi – until you became a star. And then the footage would be re-cut, and your movements tracked from where you ended to where you began – the only journey left to him after this.

'Afterwards . . .' he had said to her.

'No harm will come to your friends,' Taverner said.

There were lines you could read between, and others whose gap swallowed you whole.

'And it's not as if you're being robbed of years.'

He had thanked her for her certainty.

'Oh, I'm sure you've been told you might wobble on for another decade. But your medical history indicates otherwise. And this way, your comrades enjoy a happy ending. Or avoid an unhappy one. Hardly a win-win, but in the circumstances, the best you can expect.'

The irregular beat, then, needn't be a concern.

The nightclub, Nob-Nobs, was where he'd been told it would be, and even as he determined that, his new phone buzzed. *The side door has been left unlocked.* He deleted the message and dropped the phone in a bin. Then paused, removed the remaining notes from his wallet, and dropped them in too. A shame to deprive the needy, and the needy looked in bins. The fact that he was no longer among their number should have cheered him, but unaccountably failed to do so as he crossed the road.

They found Cartwright's car on a side street, where it was a toss-up as to whether it would be ticketed for a parking offence or towed away for being fly-tipped, and walked from there to the main road, where there was a garage on a corner, a nightclub on another, and a row of bars and retail premises on the facing pavement. Then Big Dog went one way and Little Dog the other. Seven times out of ten such uncoordinated canvassing got you nowhere, but the other three times you got lucky. That had been Big Dog's experience, and he'd been doing this longer than Little Dog. They'd give it ten minutes; after that, well, no way would Cartwright remain unfucked up for long. The odds on that went so far past maths, they became religion. Ten minutes. They went their separate ways.

. . . instead of, like now, finding some makeweight mission that had them feeling still in the game, but she could sit and bemoan her fate or find a way into this building, so she skipped down the alley, ignoring the first door because it would clearly be locked, turning the corner at the end, passing a double door secured by padlock and chain, and came to a fire escape, its metal struts and handrails a Meccano construction in the fading light, but presumably these things were assessed by Health & Safety so up she went, the structure creaking under her weight, which was a cheek – she wasn't a hippo – and debris on every landing suggesting the stairs were used as a breakout space, cigarette ends, empty vape tubes, the scraggy end of joints, plastic cups, a pair of boxer shorts, and a stray lyric swam into her mind, something about smoking cigarettes and staring at the moon, and then she was focused again, checking each door until she came to one that opened, that had had its tenon taped over to prevent it locking, which was maybe a clue as to why the club had folded, and she slipped through this door and was inside the building . . .

While Lech and the others went round the far side, River and Sid followed Louisa down the alley. She hurtled past the first door they reached, which, when Sid tried it, proved unlocked: it gave onto an upwards-inclined corridor. The lighting was harsh – an unshaded bulb – and a door at the far end was ajar, suggesting a large dark space beyond. Someone should have put up a sign reading *Trap*, River thought.

'Maybe going straight through isn't the best idea.'

'What, suddenly you're Mr Discretion?'

They spoke in whispers.

'Well, it's been a long day.'

'You mean, you're being cautious because I'm with you. You think CC's through there with a gun?'

'I'm still thinking of him as Stam, actually.'

'Because even if he is, he's not likely to shoot us.' She amended this. 'Or not me, anyway. I think he quite likes me.'

'Why were you in Oxford?'

'I had a good reason.'

'Like getting your job back?'

'Shall we focus on whether CC, Stam – whatever – is here to kill Judd? That's probably more urgent.'

'I thought you were dead.'

'I lost my phone, that's all. Are we going through that door?'

'Me first.'

'Fuck off you first. I'm smaller. Less of a target.'

'Thought you said he wouldn't shoot you.'

'It was a joke. Lighten up.'

She led the way through the half-open door into the club.

When walking a city, look up.

Something Big Dog's dad had said to him when he was a pup, meaning there were things you missed if you didn't: the skyline, clocks on corners, the unexpected niches in which statues sat. A bit of a poet, the old man, who'd spent his life advising people on the best kind of mortgage to take out, or at least, the best kind the building society he worked for offered. Big Dog didn't know whether his lyrical tendencies were a reaction against his day job or in some incomprehensible way an extension of it, but he did know that every time he remembered the old man saying this, he looked up. Which was how come he saw someone climbing the fire escape of the nightclub on the corner; someone who looked like a slow horse, the one who'd been with Cartwright in Oxford this morning.

Nursing a smile, he headed towards the alley.

Lech and Ash were by the padlocked doors. Louisa had disappeared up the fire escape. Shirley and Roddy had carried on round the corner, where Lech figured their next move would be for Shirley to hit some coke while Roddy mentioned his tattoo.

'It's a combination lock?' said Ash.

'I can see that.'

'With like four numbers. So how many possibilities is that? A million?'

'Well, nine thousand nine hundred and—'

'Which might as well be a million.'

Lech thought: Yes, but do they make everyone who works here learn a number? He had the feeling it was the sort of place, if you could do numbers, you'd get a job somewhere else. Though saying that in front of Ash would earn him a black mark.

'Except,' said Ash, 'they probably don't make the dorks who work here memorise numbers.'

'. . . Woke, much?'

'I'm woke.' She glanced around at takeaway cartons, vape cartridges, broken bottles. 'I'm not, like, insomniac.'

So they were on the same wavelength as far as combination padlocks went, which — short version — was: instead of being asked to remember a number, those with responsibility for locking or unlocking these doors would probably be expected to remember one other simple action instead, like moving the final dial up one (no) or down one (no) or just the first dial up one (no) or down one (no) or all the dials up one (no) or down one (no), or—

'Fuck's sake,' said Ash. 'Give it here.'

'Oh, you can pick locks?'

As it turned out, yes, if by picking locks you meant inserting a screwdriver and prising one apart. The padlock offered little resistance, being more of a disincentive to loiterers than an actual security device. Ash smirked as she pocketed her tool, unhooked the chain and pushed the doors open.

'You always carry a screwdriver?'

'Girl about town,' she said, slipping inside before him.

. . . where it was dark, so Louisa headed down the stairs to the next landing to find two more doors, one locked and the other revealing, by the light of her silvery phone, a jungle gym of stacked chairs and electrical equipment, and on she went, down a stairwell on which posters for expired events had been tacked in a spirit of triumph or nostalgia, or possibly neglect, and she couldn't rid herself of the feeling that this was displacement activity, another idiot's errand for the slow horses to pursue, this one River's fault, because River had never been one to sit quietly when he could be making a fool of himself instead, which was harsh but true, and maybe the harshness was because River and Sid were together now, but it was way too late to be having thoughts like that so she went down the next flight and this time found herself pushing through a swing door onto what appeared to be a balcony . . .

'That's open.'

'. . . So what?'

'So you could fit through it.'

Under discussion was a sash window: a metre wide, fifteen centimetres high, it was fuzzy glass and sat above a larger pane, similarly opaque. A toilet, obvs. Ideal for passing contraband through, the stuff bouncers confiscated at the door – bottles of vodka, more bottles of vodka – but also, it occurred to Shirley, Roddy Hos, if you bundled them small.

'There is no way I'm fitting through that. It's the size of a letterbox!'

'Your trouble is, you're all about the problems.'

Plus, if you were stuck with him as your partner, you were coming last. Louisa had disappeared, and Shirley could hear Lech and Ash round the corner, rattling a chain like Houdini shedding a skin. River and Sid had gone the other way, and had probably found an open door. So she and Roddy would be out here arguing about a window while the action, whatever that was, happened elsewhere. Grim fucking outcome. As usual.

And who was this?

Who not what, because Shirley could spot a Dog at the usual distance: a mile off. Everyone here was way outside their ground – with the notable exception of Shirley herself, because nowhere was off-beat to Shirley – and all of them scuffling about because River thought a black-bag op was going down, and if Shirley had her doubts about this at least some of them dispersed then and there, because why would a Dog be here unless bad shit was suspected?

Bad shit was Shirley's favourite kind.

Before he reached them, Shirley adopted what she thought of as her non-confrontational stance, and others recognised as her pre-confrontational stance: legs apart, hands on hips; cheerily welcoming, with a hint of fuck-with-me-at-your-peril. Which covered all the bases in most social encounters she was likely to be involved in, with the possible exception of a job interview.

'Brilliant,' she said. 'Just what we needed.'

'. . . You what?'

'My friend needs a bunk-up. Would you mind kneeling there for a minute?'

And she gave him her best smile, with the same care she might have shown applying a match to a fuse.

★

Once inside, Lech and Ash found themselves in a wide corridor where dim strip lighting hummed overhead, remembering better times. Open doors revealed an office so resembling Slough House someone might have been taking notes, another room in which boxes containing paper towels, plastic beakers and cleaning fluids had been stacked in a shape roughly approximating a bed, and a staff toilet whose narrow sash window above a larger fuzzy pane was propped open an inch, not enough to dispel the smell of mould. Muffled squabbling could be heard outside: Shirley and Roddy were discussing the window's potential as a means of ingress. Lech shook his head wearily.

Ash said, 'And we think Peter Judd's here somewhere?'

'That's what Louisa's mate reckoned.'

'This the guy who's offering her a job?'

'You'd have to ask her.'

Ash rolled her eyes.

The final door gave onto a staircase leading up. Lech led the way; he was on the third step when Ash said, 'Wait a minute.'

'What?'

She pointed back the way they'd come. 'Wee break?'

'Are you kidding?'

By way of answer, Ash slipped into the staff toilet, leaving Lech wondering at what point Slough House had become a nursery, and how come he was in charge?

When Sid's eyes adjusted to the gloom, she made out an open space, a bar, tables and stools. A human shape was visible, too big to be CC. Peter Judd – because you had to have lived the past decade in a cornflakes box not to know who this was – eased himself upright. 'If you're looking for somewhere to dance, remove yourselves. The club is shut.'

River whispered, for Sid's benefit, 'That, right there, is why they say never meet your heroes.'

'Shut up,' she said. Then, to Judd, 'We're not here to dance.'

'Who are you?' Judd came closer. 'Have we met?'

'We think someone's been sent to harm you.' Then: 'We're not them. We're the cavalry.'

'Well you don't bloody look like cavalry.'

'Thanks,' said River.

'You look more like stable hands, to be honest.'

'Yeah. Just out of interest, who did Taverner say was coming to meet you?'

'*Taverner's* sent someone to harm me?' For a moment, Judd's tone sat on a knife's edge; he might have been about to slip into scorn. But then he said, 'Oh. I see. Right. Yes. Fuck.'

'It's simply dealt with,' Sid said. 'Just leave.'

'I'm quite capable of planning my next move.' He was squinting at River now. 'I do know you. You're one of Jackson Lamb's squad.' Something passed across his face. 'Is that what this is about? Is this Lamb's doing?' He looked towards the door.

Which opened.

The taxi stop-started, stop-started, and each jerk scribbled a memo on Avril's bones: being old was a pain. She glanced at her phone. CC wasn't moving either. Had Taverner really wound him up and pointed him? It wasn't a comfort to know he'd stolen Al's gun.

Its owner, former owner, sat next to her; Daisy opposite, in a pull-down seat. She could sense tension in his rigid posture. Daisy, on the other hand, might have been on her way to a spa afternoon. This was a worry. When Daisy seemed calm, it was best to lock the doors.

When Avril flexed her hands, shaking stiffness away, her knuckles felt sore.

They were getting closer though. If they avoided more hold-ups, they'd reach CC's location in minutes.

★

CC could hear voices, which wasn't right. The whole point was, Judd would be on his own. Or what was he supposed to do, mow down a room full of strangers?

And Christ, look at him: a killer in elbow patches . . . You could take James Bond, turn him inside out, doodle silly features where his face used to be, and still be nowhere near how wrong CC was for the role. This wasn't who he'd always been – this shabby duffer who spent his days pottering in a library – but it was who he was now, and even in his quiet hours he couldn't recall the man who'd known horror and fear, who'd lived with the possibility of being turfed from his bed by balaclavaed strangers, keen to put a bullet in his head. That had been his life, but its only lasting value lay in the bonds he'd forged. He'd betray the Park in a heartbeat for his comrades: like flapping a duster in the wind. And if they'd sought justice for Pitchfork's victims by murdering the man himself, his only regret was that they hadn't allowed him to help. Slaying a monster was a forgivable thing; protecting one's loved ones a duty. Enough. His heart skipped a beat, and the gun slapped his hip. Laying a hand across his pocket to steady it, he walked through the door.

'I don't know what you're on about, but would you mind shifting out the way?' His eyes flickered upwards, then back at Shirley. 'I've somewhere to be.'

She nodded. 'That's what they say about old dogs, isn't it? Always in a hurry.'

'Ah.' He reappraised her. 'You're Park?'

'Service,' said Shirley.

'Slough House,' Roddy added. '. . . What?'

But the Dog was grinning widely. 'You're slow horses?'

For fuck's sake, thought Shirley. 'A little respect? We're Service. Why are you here?'

But any hope of respect had gone. 'Yeah, see, we had a report that a couple of Einsteins were eating yellow snow back here. So I came to take pictures for our WhatsApp group.'

'It's not snowing,' said Roddy.

'He means we're stupid.'

'Now we're clicking,' the Dog said. 'Let's see your cards, then. I mean, you do have cards, don't you? Or do they just stick labels round your neck?'

'Don't get me wrong, I could listen to you rubbing yourself off all day. But we're busy, so here.' Shirley fished in her pocket and produced a tube of hand cream. 'That'll speed you up.'

'Funny funny.' He took the tube from her hand. 'You comedians part of Cartwright's posse, are you?'

'He's part of ours, more like,' said Roddy.

'Shut up,' Shirley said. 'What's Cartwright got to do with anything?'

'Yeah, the other reason I'm here is to explain myself to you. So why don't the pair of you fuck off back to Slough House, where you can get on with your colouring books and sniffing plasticine, and leave me to do my job.'

'Except if you were doing your job you'd have pulled some weight by now,' said Shirley. 'Instead of just throwing it around.'

'You want me to throw things around? I can do that. Here.' He tossed the tube of hand cream in Shirley's face.

'Oh shit,' said Roddy.

. . . and when Louisa looked over the edge, to the dance floor below, there was Judd, and also River and Sid, and nothing worse than a conversation was happening, River saying, *Out of interest, who did Taverner say was coming to meet you?* and just like that it was over; all this charging about, and either nothing was happening or whatever was happening hadn't happened yet, they'd got here first, which was a new experience for the slow horses, who generally turned up after the cannons had fired and all that was left for them was to go round picking up litter like the sad lonely clowns they were, so yes, she was ready to leave all this behind her, because life was about forward motion, and next time she took stock — next time she sat by her little flat's window, gazing at the greenery — she'd be on a calmer plane, no longer weighed down by work, or at least, not for the same reasons; she'd have a job that didn't remind her she was a failure, where the next desk along wasn't occupied by a ghost, and she was just relaxing into that thought, and wondering whether HR would make her work out her notice, when an old man with a gun came through the door downstairs, and Louisa thought *Shit, no more ghosts, not now,* and headed for the stairwell as quickly as near silence would allow . . .

Devon, who'd watched the slow horses peeling away in pairs, thought: Okay, hard to know whether to sound an alarm or raise a white flag. Louisa was good, and Cartwright knew which way was up — even if he generally approached it from the wrong angle — but the others were an unknown quantity, and Slough House's rep suggested they might not be clear which planet they were on. Still, they were here because of an imagined threat to Judd, not to do him harm. And also, he'd just bought another zero beer. There was an old guy wandering down the alley, probably lost or looking for a place to piss, and Devon was watching him when someone said, 'Devon Welles?'

Not a face Devon recognised, but he placed the profession no problem. Cop.

Except not cop but Dog, as his next words indicated:

'There's a picture of you on the glory wall back in the Park.'

He was young for a Dog, who generally had miles on the clock, but young came cheap and Devon didn't need reminding about budget restrictions. He said, 'I'd have thought they'd replaced that by now.'

Young Dog said, 'Are you kidding? They still count it when doing diversity stats. You private now?'

He nodded. 'And having a beer. Are you working?'

'Nah. Off duty.' But his eyes glanced at the phone in his hand, then shifted towards the club over the road. One of those eyes was sporting a technicolour badge.

Devon thought: Oh-kayyy. Slow horses in the picture, and the Dogs are off the leash. He should collect Judd before things got tasty.

'You worked with Emma Flyte, yeah? Her picture's on the wall too.'

He nodded.

'Mate, I'd have given that a go.'

Devon was about to reply – there were a hundred options – when the sound of breaking glass tripped over the road: a heartfelt smash, not a dropped beer mug. 'To be continued,' he said, but young Dog was already history, or geography anyway: over the road, down that alleyway, seeking the source of the commotion.

Of course her phone rang then. Of course it did.

'I'm busy,' said Ash.

'Too busy to speak to your mother?'

Well, yes.

'Because it sounds like you're on the toilet. And—'

'Mu-um!'

'Well you can't pretend to be working, can you? Even if it wasn't already mid-evening.'

Which it only was if you went to bed at like nine.

'And the reason I'm calling, the weather is so nice, your father and I have decided—'

(You mean *you* have. Whatever it is, you've decided. Not Dad.)

' – to throw a garden party on Saturday, and I'm giving you plenty of notice so—'

(You are *so* not giving me plenty of notice!)

' – you can invite your colleagues. Especially your boss. Something you'll notice when you're older, the more responsibility they have, the more polite and considerate people are. They make nice guests.'

'I don't *think* that's—'

'Ashley, why must you always make difficulties? All I want is to meet your friends.'

There was scuffling outside, where Shirley and Roddy had been skulking. Someone had joined them, a voice Ash didn't recognise.

'I don't think you want my colleagues at your party, Mum.' Standing, Ash fastened her jeans with her free hand and opened the cubicle door. 'They can be a bit – raucous.'

'Raucous?' Her mother laughed. 'Oh, Ashley. Your father and I don't mind high spirits. When we were your age – well. Tomfoolery doesn't begin to cover it. Once, I remember—'

A body crashed through the window, the heavy slap of its landing accompanied by the tinselly laughter of breaking glass, as a thousand splinters showered down like audible confetti.

Through the jagged frame of the broken window, Shirley and Roddy stared in at the wreckage.

'Wasn't me,' said Roddy.

'Ashley?'

'I'll call you back,' said Ash.

When River saw CC coming through the door, his first thought was: I was right.

The second was: He's got a gun.

This dangled loosely in CC's hand, as if he hoped not to be associated with it.

Sid said, 'CC? We know what's going on.'

No we don't, thought River. We just know what the result's supposed to be.

'We know Taverner sent you, and what she wants you to do. Which means there's no point doing it now. You can't get away with it.'

CC said, 'Ms Baker. You've had a busy day.'

'We all have.'

'And River. I'm sorry I misled you about your grandfather. About what was in his box-safe. It was a necessary lie. I mean it felt necessary at the time.'

'I understand.' He was keeping both eyes on the gun while trying to make it look like he wasn't. 'Funny thing is, I still don't know what he was really hiding.'

'Something too important to be buried forever. He was hiding it because he knew it would be found.'

'He was a great one for thinking round corners.'

Someone made a noise like a walrus demanding attention. He'd almost forgotten Judd was there. Guns do that: they suck up all the scrutiny in the room.

Judd said, 'This? This ridiculous . . . figure is an assassin?'

'Not helping.'

'One of you take that from him. And then all of you get out of my way.'

It was a plan. River couldn't help noticing, though, that it depended on everyone else's actions rather than anything Judd might do.

Before it could be put into play came the sound of breaking glass.

Al Hawke said, 'That's where he is?'

The taxi had left them on a garage forecourt. Avril paid in cash. The traffic had grown sclerotic, and the pavements were busy; from office to home, to bar, to restaurant, wherever. Avril didn't actually know where people went any more. It didn't matter. Her tracker showed that CC — or Avril's watch — was in the building Al was pointing at, its italic, unlit sign reading

Nob-Nobs. Clearly Nob-Nobs wasn't somewhere the drifting public was heading.

'It looks empty. Locked up.'

'There'll be a back door.'

Daisy said, 'Perhaps CC is having an assignation.' She laid an unnatural stress on the final word, camping it up.

'To which he took my gun?' Al asked.

'He was never what you'd call a born romantic.'

Avril tucked her phone away. 'Stay here, Daisy.'

Daisy opened her mouth to reply, then closed it.

'I mean it. Safer that way. And we'll be back soon.'

Al put a hand on her shoulder briefly. 'Anyone follows us in, call.'

Daisy watched as they crossed the road, and was still standing there when they disappeared down the alley.

Devon was right behind the young Dog when they reached the scene: five people, two of them one side of a broken window and three the other, one having arrived there quite recently, judging by the way he was covered in glass. He looked posed for a photograph: *Don't Try This at Home*.

'You guys are so dead,' young Dog said.

Inside the toilet, the old Dog groaned.

'How is he?'

Lech knelt to check. 'It's just as I suspected,' he said. 'He's been thrown through a window.'

'. . . You think you're funny?'

Lech shrugged. 'I'm not a medic.'

Shirley looked at young Dog. 'He was like that when we got here.'

'Yeah, right, and who did it to him?'

Ash said, 'Don't look at me. I was standing here? On the *inside*?'

'Maybe someone should call an ambulance?' Devon suggested. 'I mean, I'd do it myself, but I don't plan on getting involved.'

'I have, like, an alibi, because I was talking to my mum? She heard it happen?'

'Who is he, anyway?' Lech asked.

Devon said to the young Dog, 'He's with you?'

'My partner.'

'And you're standing chatting while he's getting thrown through a toilet window? I don't fancy your chances of making the glory wall.'

'Fuck you.' Young Dog looked at Roddy. 'You do this?'

Roddy was simultaneously trying to look like he could have if he'd wanted to, but hadn't wanted to so didn't. 'Why me?'

'Because there's just you and the dyke-looking midget this side. So yeah, I'm looking at you.' He glanced at Shirley. 'Martial arts shit, was it?'

'Seriously? He breaks into a sweat opening a carton of milk.'

Devon said, 'Hang on a minute. Are you Shirley Dander?'

'What's it to you?'

'That'd be a yes.' He glanced at the damage, then back at her. 'I've heard about you. Love your work.'

Young Dog said, 'Shirley Dander?'

'Yeah, but call me "dyke-looking midget" again if you want.'

He stepped back. 'You're all fucking crazy.'

'Now he gets it.'

Old Dog groaned again.

Devon said, 'Someone call an ambulance.'

CC's gun arm twitched. 'What was that?'

'A window,' said Sid. '*Careful*.'

Judd backed away, his confident sheen dulled.

River said, 'Stam? Let's call it a day.'

'He's right, CC. Let's go home.'

'Can't do that, I'm afraid.'

'Yes you can. Easiest thing in the world.'

'Will one of you idiots take that *fucking* gun off this maniac?'

'Still not helping,' said River.

CC's hand steadied, and he levelled the gun at Judd.

River stepped between them. 'Stam? It's over. There's no way you're getting away with this.'

'That was never the plan.'

'Yes, no, good. But let's just put the gun away—'

'Please, CC. Think of the others. Avril. Daisy. Would they want this?'

'They had their moment. This is mine.'

Judd had fumbled his phone into his hand. 'I have an armed response team on call, twenty-four seven.'

CC said, 'And I have a gun. Can you count to three?' River reached out and CC aimed the gun at his face. 'No. No. Get out of the way. Let me do this.'

Sid, steady as a rock, moved closer. 'We can't, CC.'

Judd's voice was a squeak, a dribble. 'Take his fucking *gun* away!'

'I need the pair of you to step aside.'

His gun hand twitched again.

Behind him, someone said, 'CC? Fun's over.'

. . . and what struck her as she headed down the stairs was how suddenly these moments happened – even for a slow horse – the trigger points of a career, like the one in a clothes shop when her target sprouted half a dozen decoys, causing Louisa to lose him, which led to Slough House, and all that followed: the soul-shrivelling inertia, the fog of failure, the blistering effects of being close to Jackson Lamb, so that some nights she had to shower for twenty minutes on getting home; and worst of all, that brief period during which she and Min found happiness to cultivate, which lasted months but was over in a heartbeat, after which she took to blurring her boundaries with drink and strangers, and who knows how long she might have spent exploring that purgatory if not for the diamond she stole on that rooftop, with which she bought herself some peace and quiet, at least for a while, but trigger moments always come round, regular as ogres in storybooks, and here was another one, waiting on the dance floor . . .

Avril watched as Al walked round CC, because only an amateur strikes up conversation with an armed man while standing behind him. Which was precisely what CC was now, because that's what a gun does: turns a loved one into an armed man. Except when it does the other thing it does, which is turn a loved one into a draught excluder. She followed Al and the pair flanked CC. The Brains Trust against the world.

Sid Baker was on the world's team, along with a young man Avril guessed was Service. The pair were shielding Peter Judd, whom she recognised from TV, newspapers, the internet and occasional nightmares. The look on his face suggested he was currently having a nightmare of his own.

'You're here,' CC said, without averting his gaze from the trio in front of him.

His hand, Avril saw, was unsteady. 'You imagined we'd go home?'

'Hope springs eternal.'

Al said, 'This is what Taverner wanted? You're a Manchurian candidate?'

Avril said, 'She told you, didn't she? About what we did.'

'She shouldn't have had to. You should have told me yourselves.'

'We didn't think you'd approve.'

'But I would have understood.'

CC's hand tremored. His colour was high. He spoke to the Service pair. 'River, Sid, I need you to move aside.'

'Can't do that, Stam.'

'Please put the gun down.'

'When I'm done with it.'

'Don't you cretins carry weapons?' Judd said. 'One of you deal with him. Now.'

River gave Sid a sideways glance. 'Having second thoughts?'

'Take his gun away!' Judd shouted.

'Now,' said Al, 'the first problem with that is, taking a loaded gun from anyone is a dangerous business.'

'Just out of interest,' River said.

'The second problem? I don't take orders from pricks.'

'CC, love?' said Avril. 'If you're doing this to protect us, it doesn't matter any more. Really doesn't. The whole world can know about it.'

'But this way you'll be safe,' CC said.

His hand tremored again.

Once her friends had entered the building, Daisy had followed – *they know I'm going to*. Probably part of their plan. Anyway, it was happening.

The door gave onto a corridor, at the far end of which was another door they must have gone through. Approaching it, she peered round: there they were, in a large dark space, along with CC and the young woman they'd left at the service station. Two other men, at one of whom CC was aiming a gun. He doubtless had good reason, but Avril and Al weren't keen.

Backing away, she peered along the corridor. It followed a curve, presumably hugging the dance floor, which meant there'd be access to the far side, allowing her to enter behind the opposing forces – which was what the other men were. Pitchfork had coded this into her system: anyone not on her team was an enemy.

There was no need to check she had her blade. She always had her blade.

The corridor wasn't long, and she moved along it soundlessly. It was funny how the old skills came back.

★

. . . but not bursting onto it because bursting into a room where there's an armed man was a mistake, so she made herself stop, breathe, wait and then push the door open softly, with no light breaking through because the staircase was unlit, and half the group had their backs to her, including the gunman, and looking her way were River and Sid and that pompous arse Peter Judd, and all that was needed was for everyone to keep a cool head and it would be fine, they'd all walk out into the sunshine and laugh about it, enjoy a glass of wine, and she'd tell them about the new job, that she was moving on, but first the present had to be dealt with, meaning the gun, and it was unlikely she'd be able to reach the gunman without triggering a reaction, but the best way of dealing with doubts was to shelve them, so that's what she did – took a deep breath – stepped quietly onto the dark dance floor, inching away the distance between herself and the assembled group, hoping nothing unexpected would intervene . . .

Ash said, 'I'm out of here.'
 'You can't just—'
 She waved her phone at Lech. 'Ambulance?'
 The man on the floor groaned as she stepped round him, and that was a good thing – at least he was alive – though obviously also a bad thing: he'd been thrown through a window. Whatever. With his blood on her trainers, which luckily were machine washable, she headed up the stairs, phone in hand. At the top was a lobby area, and a row of switches on the wall next to a set of double doors.
 With her free hand she slapped all six, and pushed through the doors into the dance hall.

'But this way you'll be safe,' CC said, and suddenly the room was full of light. Something else clicked, this time inside him, and somehow he was falling upright, as if his strings had been tightened. A sentence formed but split into pieces, and he was confetti, scattered piecemeal around the company, settling on their sleeves, on their shoulders, at their feet. The lights went out, but remained on. Whatever he'd been holding he now wasn't, but he couldn't remember what it was, or why he'd needed it, or who mattered.

'He's stroking.'

'I—'

'*He's stroking!*'

River stepped forward as CC dropped like a brick.

The gun went skittering across the floor.

What felt like hundreds of lights went on, and Judd thought: *It's all about keeping your head.*

Like that time a husband came home unexpectedly, and he had to exit through a window in his boxers.

Or any occasion on which he gave evidence before a parliamentary committee.

Or talking to his wife, ever.

Here, it was about not making sudden movements, while all around descended into chaos. '*He's stroking!*' someone said, and the gunman went into a spasm which, with luck, would kill him and everyone else, Judd excepted. For half a second everything stilled, then Cartwright stepped forward and the gunman toppled into his arms, his weapon spinning across the dance floor. *Walk away* – the nearest door – all he had to do was reach it, step through, and leave all this behind him. But his feet were glued in place. One of the two newcomers, an old man, stooped for the gun, the manner in which he did so suggesting he was no stranger to weaponry. Cartwright and the young woman were bent over the gunman; the other woman was on her knees too, saying 'See, see!' as if the others weren't paying attention. *Walk away* – this time he could move, but when he turned a ghost was there, right in front of him; a woman his own age, and he yelped, couldn't help it, and she raised a hand, and his rugby days came flooding back and he did what you do when your opponent is smaller, frailer, weaker: he dropped his shoulder and flattened her while someone shouted, 'Daisy!'

Entering the club, Ash found, was like stepping through a broken mirror – there were lights and action, slotting together in fragments: River Cartwright, holding on to an older man who was having a seizure, and a woman who might be Cartwright's partner, and some old people who God only knew what they were doing, one of them stooping for a gun, and Louisa too, behind the old crew, caught in the middle of something, her posture an unfinished movement, and – nearest Ash – Peter Judd, and yet another old woman he'd just sent sprawling . . . It was true what they said about Slough House, that the place was a nut job's TikTok feed, which, when not boring you rigid, was banging away like a bat in a biscuit tin – the slow horses hadn't been here five minutes and already there'd been someone thrown through a window. She had blood on her trainers. And the old man was pointing the gun at Judd, shouting 'Daisy!'

Not so long ago Ash had never heard of the slow horses: she was still at the Park, a fledgling spook, and the night when it all went wrong hadn't happened. Back then she could have called her mother and told her the truth – that she worked for their country, she kept people safe – but here and now she was on her own, and keeping people safe meant reaching Judd and pulling him out of harm's reach, because the old man wasn't just aiming the gun, he was squeezing the trigger . . .

But you had to be fast to outrun a bullet. You had to be fast indeed.

★

Al shouted 'Daisy!', and Avril looked up to see him levelling the gun just as a woman who'd come out of nowhere launched herself upon him.

If she'd had time to turn her head, Avril would have seen Judd taking flight; she'd have seen Daisy scrambling to her feet.

She'd have seen Ashley Khan taking a headlong dive.

But when Al fired the gun, she had her eyes clenched tight.

. . . but the unexpected happened, because the unexpected always does, and on this occasion it arrived in a storm of light which poleaxed the gunman, sending his weapon Catherine-wheeling across the floor towards the old man to Louisa's left, who scooped it up and aimed it in one motion, and *never jump on an armed man*, that was an instruction learned on the mats at Regent's Park, *never jump on an armed man* because bullets can go anywhere, but she jumped anyway, catching him hip height and spilling him just as he fired, and then she was on top of him, and he wasn't fighting back but she had to be sure he wouldn't start so she punched him quickly in the face, which wasn't where she'd thought she'd ever be – punching a senior citizen – but you don't write your own story, you're propelled by it, and she was levering herself upright when it was her turn to be side-slammed, leaving her on all fours, though the assault was quieter than hers had been, more subtle, and the woman who'd been sent sprawling by Judd moments ago was looking down on her, something dripping in her hand, but she wasn't there long before River was there instead, saying Louisa's name, panic in his voice which didn't seem necessary because panic was for when you didn't know what was happening, for when you were coming adrift, and she felt strangely anchored to the here and now, knowing what her story held in store, it held in store what all stories hold; what it holds in store is an ending.

★

Ash lay staring at the ceiling, which was far away, aware, as she hadn't been a moment ago, of how cold she was, and also how hot; the two states existing side by side, which felt unlikely. She should call her mother – she was bound to have an explanation, or, failing that, an opinion. But as the clamour around her grew, as people knelt and shouted and generally filled the club with the kinds of noise that suggested the evening had taken a bad turn, and as doors slammed and lights went on and off, it became troublingly apparent to her that her phone was nowhere to hand.

I must have dropped it somewhere, she thought, and closed her eyes.

St Leonard's, as has been noted before, puts on a lovely funeral. Then again, it's had practice. Funerals are its speciality, or at any rate, occur with more frequency than other services, which are advertised at distant intervals and cancelled at near notice; and while the doors of this discreet brick building in a quiet corner of Hampstead are always open in the figurative sense – or so the flyers decorating its porch assert – they are, in a more literal manner, generally locked, though directions to less inaccessible places of worship are included among the ephemera on its noticeboards. To the majority of local residents this is simply the way things are, and while it is cheerfully acknowledged that St Len's is the spooks' chapel, the name rarely triggers more than a knowing look and the occasional titbit, delivered as tradecraft – for example, that the plaques on the east wall, memorialising the unflamboyant dead, are tributes to fallen spies. Legend and rumour, of course, and if these particular legends and rumours are true, this barely matters in an age where the difference between the true and the false is held by many to be a matter of opinion.

That afternoon, the day after the rumpus at Nob-Nobs, there was no funeral. The doors were closed. Behind the church, where a small, immaculately tended graveyard could be found, trees were dripping. Unexpected clouds had gathered early over London, calling time on the heatwave, and rain had fallen in its least attractive manner, forswearing squalls and bluster and settling for the mediocrity of the time-server everywhere: steady, uninspired, looking only to get through the next half hour. And each half hour followed the last, and in turn gave way to another.

In the graveyard, on a bench near a matching pair of headstones, sat a bulky man in a raincoat that might have been recycled from a chimp's hammock. He was smoking, or at any rate holding a cigarette, though his thoughts seemed elsewhere. A hat which looked as if it had been buried with a fisherman then dug up by a tramp was keeping his head dry, but his shoes were failing to do the same for his feet: the upper of the left was peeling from the sole, leaving a piece of duct tape poking out. A picture of desolation, in fact, or would have been, had its subject given the impression that he cared.

Sitting there, the man had no way of seeing the car arriving at the front. This was a big black SUV, which, if its eco-fucking swagger didn't get the message across, its motorbike outriders surely did: here came government, and it didn't care who knew it. Diana Taverner didn't always travel with full metal kit, but when she did, she wore it large – this was London Rules: when vulnerable, act like a gorilla with a cluster headache. And if anyone shows concern, take them off at the knees.

Stepping out, wielding an umbrella, she walked alone through St Len's gate and round the side to the back. Lamb was visible immediately, and it struck her that there were probably places on the globe where he might be taken for a figure of worship, like a giant toad in its grotto. Peasants would leave pebbles at his feet, in return for his pearls of wisdom. As she drew nearer, she heard him fart.

Lowering her umbrella, she joined him on the bench without speaking.

After a while, he raised the cigarette to his lips, drained it in a single inhalation, and flicked the stub away. It bounced off

David Cartwright's headstone with a scattering of sparks. As he breathed out smoke, he stared at her feet, shod in black leather, and drier than his own. 'Nice boots.'

'All these years, and I don't believe I've ever heard you comment on anything I've been wearing. Are you developing a footwear fetish?'

'Is that when you get a shoe horn?'

'Yes, that's more you.' She looked around. The tree offered shelter, but there was a steady dripping to her left. Edging away from it would have meant moving closer to Lamb. 'Why risk letting a compliment stand when you can turn it into an off-colour joke?'

He nodded thoughtfully, as if she'd offered an unexpected insight. 'You know,' he said, 'I'm going to miss our little chats.'

'You're leaving us, Jackson? Hanging up your spyglass and code book?' She brushed at her hair, where water had landed. 'Well, that is a nice surprise. But I hope you're planning a swisher farewell do than this. You should get Standish to organise something. Have a whip-round, I'll personally double the takings. That should get you most of half a packet of ten.'

'Which is about what you ponce off me every time we meet. But no, I'm not going anywhere.' He turned to look her in the face. 'You are.'

'If you're going gnomic on me, I'll take one of those cigarettes now.' She waited a beat. 'No? Have it your way. I'll bring my own next time.'

'One of my joes was killed, Diana. And one's at death's door. You think I'll let that slide?'

'Oh, that's why we're here? Yes, of course it is.' She looked around again, confirming they were alone, then said, 'I'm sorry about your losses, they're appalling, but you know what? Shit happens. Sometimes for a reason. The reason here was, I had an outcome in mind, and your crew, not for the first time, stepped in front of it. I'm not accountable for that. But I understand your anger, and trust me, I'll do what I can for the families involved. A death-in-service payment, for example. We won't make difficulties there, despite the, ah, non-curricular nature of your agents' activities. And I'm taking your hint about meeting here, too. St Leonard's.' She nodded towards the headstones. Here was where the Service dead lay, provided they'd died in good standing. Slough House was not good standing. 'I'll pull strings. Have the burial here.'

'You're the reason she needs burying at all, Diana. And creative accounting isn't going to cut it this time. No, you'll pay this bill in full.'

'Do tell.'

'I want you gone.'

She barked a laugh. His gaze didn't falter. Her own broke away, then returned. 'Me, gone? You're forgetting who you're talking to. There's a reason I'm First Desk while you're still working the bins. You're clever, I get that, and you were a legend once. But you did all your fighting in back alleys, while I got my black belt playing chess with menaces in Whitehall dining rooms. So I'll give you a couple of minutes while you get your righteous anger off your chest, and you have my permission to use the biggest swears in your toolbox, but once we're finished I've a meeting with the PM, and what we'll talk about is above your pay grade, but I'll tell you this much. I'll be coming out of that meeting stronger than I went in. So me going, no. That's not on anyone's agenda.'

While she'd been talking Lamb had finagled a cigarette from some recess or other, and he lit it now with a plastic lighter. For a moment it looked as if he might toss this over his shoulder, but he changed his mind. Wreathed in smoke, he said, 'Bold talk from a woman whose idea of a master plan was to use the Thursday Murder Club as a hit squad. So here's a hint from a street fighter. The mad shit never works. That's the reason it's called mad shit. No, what you should have done, once you decided to take a crack at Judd, is arranged to meet him at night by a river, then put a bullet in his head and his body in the water. Instead you went all, what did you call it? – chess with menaces – and here we are.' He took the cigarette from his mouth, studied it, then put it back. 'You had a go at Judd not because he's at his weakest, but because you are. And you fucked up, so guess what? Not only does he still have your dick in his pocket, he's also pissed off at you. So I'd say your future's very much in doubt. Even without me.'

'If you were good at reading futures, you'd have had a long hard look at your own by now and done something about it. Weaning yourself off takeaways and a sixty-a-day habit would be a start. So forgive me if I look elsewhere for career guidance. Besides, are you seriously taking Judd's side? He tried to have you killed once. Or had you forgotten that?'

'Trust me, I hadn't. And nor has it slipped my mind that your own hands weren't clean on that occasion.'

'You think you can do this job with clean hands? You know better. You of all people.' The look she gave him might almost have held pity. 'Because nine times out of ten, you and your kind are the rubber gloves we wear when a dirty job needs doing. And there will always be dirty jobs need doing, no matter who's hosting parties in Number Ten. But let me remind you, nobody made you pick up sticks and play soldiers, and the small print's always been there, right in front of your eyes. You see many spooks going on to careers in the City? Noticed any former joes in line when they're dishing out directorships? No, they don't put up statues to spies and they don't save them seats in the Lords.' She waved a hand. 'This is the best you can hope for. A tidy grave in a sheltered spot. And you knew that when you started, and if your crew didn't that's on you, because you should have told them. So don't come bleating to me about one dead and one at death's door, because that's not a bullet point on my CV, it's a footnote in an appendix. One for the historians. I'll read it when I'm dead.'

'Too long, didn't listen. You finished?'

'Nowhere near. You're a street fighter, and that must have come in handy in your day, but don't confuse the corridors I walk with your Berlin alleys of yesteryear. The shit shovelled over fancy linen in Whitehall is a lot more fucking toxic than anything your KGB oppos dipped their umbrellas in, and I've survived that for longer than you've been past it. So don't think all you need do is issue a few vague threats and I'll crumple like last week's lettuce. Because I'm the one who'll say when I'm ready to go.' As Taverner stood, her arm brushed a low-slung branch, unfurling a curtain of raindrops. 'A lettuce is an edible plant. You get them in salads. Standish'll fill you in.'

'I saw one in a burger once.' He sniffed. 'How long do you think you've got before Judd spills his wagonload of shit? And how do you think the new-broom PM'll react? Stand by you proudly? Or throw you under the first passing train?'

'Judd has a credibility problem, and I'll solve him long before he solves that. Having him blacken my name would be like having Truss call someone unpopular, or Farage call them a cunt. I'll take my chances.' She surveyed the graveyard, perhaps mentally assigning plots to colleagues. 'Because there is nobody I will not flay alive to stay in charge, and you know why? Because I'm not only the best person for the job, I'm the only one who knows how to do it. Who understands that there's no need to justify myself to anyone, because there are times when what I have to do is unjustifiable. That's always been First Desk's lot. No rules, no guidelines, simply objectives. Whether it's Pitchfork way back when or whatever I have to do tomorrow, all that matters is the objective, and the objective is always the same. To stop buses being bombed.' She looked him in the eye. 'Which is what I do, Jackson. And if I have to trample the occasional warm body to do that, so be it. Your people were unlucky, but if they weren't unlucky to start with, they wouldn't have been your people. So let's write this off as a no-score draw, shall we?' She gave a faint smile. 'I run a shop for serious people. You're in charge of a bunch of clowns. So you hurry back to Slough House and pull the blinds down and do your mourning, but don't worry about winding your clocks any more. I think you'll find that's an unnecessary effort, if you catch my drift.'

She was halfway down the path when Lamb called.

'Diana?'

She stopped and waited without turning.

'You were half right. Arranging to meet in a graveyard was a hint.' Once more he flicked a dying cigarette off a headstone. 'Just not the kind you think.'

That was all, and without responding Taverner continued on her way. Once she'd vanished round the side, and the sound of environmental damage had again disturbed the quiet close, Lamb stood, shook himself like an untidy dog and headed into St Leonard's by the side door. Inside, the rainfall seemed more pointed, pattering on the roof like anxious cats. Two candles burned beneath a stained-glass window depicting St Len at his typewriter, a mild blasphemy concerning which there were two schools of thought, neither of which interested Lamb. The candles, though. These were clearly the work of Catherine Standish, who sat on the bench nearest. She was facing the altar, and continued to do so as he made his way down the uneven slabs of the aisle and lowered himself onto the bench with a noise like a dying Li-lo.

For a while there was only the rain's mild percussion and a faint hissing which might have been the candles. Lamb started tapping his fingers against the bench in what was possibly, in his head, a rhythm, but Catherine remained focused on the altar, or whatever lay behind it, or above. He paused. She didn't react. He started again. Same difference.

'Broadsword calling Danny Boy.'

A faint sigh.

'Can you hear the pipes a-calling?'

She said, 'I was thinking, we should spend more time in churches. They're quiet, and you can't smoke.'

He glanced heavenward. 'They have sprinklers?'

'Just don't, that's all.' She raised her gaze towards the rose window. 'We could do with a little stillness. Some mindfulness. You've heard of mindfulness?'

'Didn't that get popular during lockdown, like wild swimming, and going mental?' Lamb looked at his hands, clasped on his lap. One was holding a cigarette, which it hadn't been until just then. 'On the other hand, I don't suppose it takes long. Emptying Ho's head'd be the work of a moment.'

Catherine said, 'I wouldn't worry. It doesn't seem likely that any better-living practices will catch on in Slough House. Not if this morning's anything to go by.'

'You called by the shop?'

She nodded.

'And?'

'They're a mess, what do you think?' She leaned back, closed her eyes. Opened them again. 'Roddy was playing . . . music, I suppose you'd call it. Very loud, very angry music. And Shirley and Lech had had a fight, and I mean an actual fight. There's been damage to office equipment.'

'Who won?'

'Who do you think?'

'Silly me. What about Cartwright?'

'River wasn't there. Not fit for work, remember? And not about to be, either.'

Lamb examined his cigarette, then said, 'Joke's on me. I was planning on putting together a five-a-side squad this year.'

'That's very funny. It's lightened the mood. And I hate to be a wet blanket, but I was looking at the regs. You know, the Service regulations? The book of rules that governs our existence?'

'You want to keep it down a little? You'll offend God.'

'In present company? He won't notice I'm here. And there's a regulation about departmental sizes, about when a section ceases to be deemed large enough to qualify as an independent unit. Do you want to hear how the rest of it goes?'

'No, don't spoil it. I imagine it's something along the lines of forthwith, and cease, and then, ooh, either absorbed into existing departmental structure or something something something triggering mandatory redundancy protocols.'

'Anyone would think you'd studied it recently.'

'It was forced upon my attention. Which reminds me, we're out of bog roll.' He stood, abruptly enough that she flinched. With the cigarette between his lips, he placed himself in front of the metal stand of candleholders, which was as spattered with wax as Nelson was with pigeon shit, but held just the two lone sentries burning bright. 'For Christ's sake, the Park's not going to close us down because we're low on people power. The Park's going to close us down because Taverner's circling her wagons, and anyone not inside pissing out is a legitimate target who, in her words, needn't bother winding their clocks.'

'Your conversation went well, then.'

'I may have told her I expect her resignation on my desk by the morning.'

'I'm not sure it works that way.'

'She wasn't impressed either. Was not impressed at some length, in fact. I thought spies were supposed to be discreet. She could speechify the arse end off a donkey.'

He leaned forward and touched the tip of his cigarette to naked flame.

Catherine said, 'So we have one dead, which may still turn to two dead, and that's not counting Stamoran, who's unlikely to recover from his stroke. All because Taverner tried to have Peter Judd murdered. And it's us who'll be made scapegoats.'

'Yeah. Is it just me or does it seem a bit unfair?'

Lamb stood with his back to her, and smoke ascended to the vaulted ceiling. After a while he moved away, towards the Dead Letter Drop, the array of plaques to those who'd died in their country's service, but whose bodies had never found passage home. It wasn't clear whether he was reading the inscriptions – names and dates; the barest cover stories – or was lost in his own dimension, but at length he reached out and tapped one briefly, then shook his head. He looked back in what might have been guilt, but Catherine didn't seem to be watching. Head bowed, she was leaning forward, crying silently. He slowly returned to her.

'Need a tissue?'

She didn't reply.

'Because I haven't got one. I mean, fucking obviously.'

Half a minute ticked by. Lamb stubbed his cigarette out on the wax-encrusted candle stand.

'Slough House is there to keep the fuck-ups off the streets,' he said. 'But if we could keep them off the streets they wouldn't be fuck-ups. They'd just be office workers.'

Her voice a smeary mess, she said, 'What's your point?'

'That they're too fucking useless to be office workers. Of course they're going to get themselves killed now and then.'

'Oh, that makes me feel better. Thank you for that.'

'Best not to get fond of them. Cats and spooks. They don't live as long as you'd hope.'

'Don't!' Her vehemence seemed to startle Catherine as much as it did Lamb. 'Just don't, okay? Just for once, keep your smart *bloody* comments to yourself. At least until the rest of us have stopped crying.'

After a while, he nodded.

She had found a tissue now, and dabbed her eyes. The church

swam in and out of focus: the flickering candles, the raggedy light, the Stations of the Cross. The altar, with its stern associations of sacrifice and sacrament. There was something soothing about all this, or if not soothing, something, at least, that made it pointless to argue. You just took it, and waited for the next thing. Catherine sat back and let a final sob rack her frame. When she allowed herself to speak once more, her voice was almost steady.

'Do you never ask yourself why, Jackson? Do you never wonder why you keep going, year in, year bloody out?'

He was next to her now, though she hadn't noticed him sitting down.

'Does your heart never break?'

He said, 'If I let that happen, I'd have to walk away. And it's a long time since I've had anywhere to walk to.'

'You were happier when you were fighting a war. When you didn't hate yourself for having come through it alive.'

He looked at her, his face impassive.

'Except you're still there, aren't you? In your head. In your head you're still behind the Wall, and you're still a joe. And you never let your guard down and you never break cover.'

'Only sometimes,' he said. 'In the, what's that phrase? The piss-poor hours of the morning.'

She couldn't help herself. 'Wee small hours.'

'I knew piss was involved.' He gestured towards the Dead Letter Drop. 'If I'd been half the joe some people think, my name'd be up there. I've never been more than a survivor. That's all anyone needs to be, in the long run. Last man standing.' As if illustrating his point, he stood. 'But I'd never scratch someone's name on that wall just to save my own skin. And I never handed anyone a loaded gun I wouldn't have been prepared to use myself.'

Lamb eased out from the bench and approached the candle stand again. There were fresh candles in a box at its base, a collection tin next to it, and after scratching around in his raincoat pocket he produced a crumpled receipt, a button still with thread attached, and a twenty pence piece. After some deliberation, he dropped the coin in the tin. Bending to collect a candle, he held its wick to a flame until it caught, whereupon his face became a shadow show, light and dark flickering in nameless shapes across his features.

He said, 'You know what the real problem is? It's that Taverner's right. She is the best person for the job.'

'The best? She tried to have a man assassinated!'

'That's where she let herself down. Trying's not good enough.' A thin ribbon of black smoke unspooled from his candle's tip. 'Nothing wrong with the intent, mind. You've got a monkey like Judd on your back, you don't feed it bananas. You find a flamethrower.'

'You can't use a flamethrower on something that's on your own . . . Never mind.' Catherine scrumpled the tissue she was holding. Her eyes were red, her face was white. 'It was my fault. I encouraged them. They'd all be at their desks now if I hadn't egged them on.'

'Yeah, and if they'd ever known what they were doing they'd still be at Regent's Park,' said Lamb. 'Outwitting global terrorists while waiting for cocktail hour.' He was studying his candle as if it were lighting his way through a labyrinth. 'If you were all it took to nudge them into another bus crash, they're even more fucking useless than I give them credit for.'

Catherine supposed this counted as comfort.

'Would have helped if you'd kept your trap shut, though.'

She still had damp tissue in her hand, and tucked it into her sleeve. It felt ugly there, as if her wrist suddenly sported a growth, but ugliness was what she needed.

Overhead, on the roof, rain still pattered. This was constancy, but not of the good kind. More like a toothache than a heartbeat.

She said, 'What happens now?'

'Well, Taverner's still the ringmaster. Apparently. She reckons she can swivel the PM any direction she wants, and that Judd's toxic enough that she'll always smell sweet in comparison. And we're a bunch of clowns, and a couple less of us won't make any difference in the long run.'

'You think she's right?'

'About you lot being clowns? Yeah. The rest of it?' He shrugged. 'She's spent so long turning showers of shit into career opportunities, she could give Thames Water lessons. On the other hand, she's walking into the PM's office to discuss a clusterfuck involving Service agents past and present, and a former Home Secretary who's as popular with the current lot as a dose of clap in a convent. So if he fancies a change of the guard, that'll give him all the excuses he needs.'

'You think she'll go.'

Lamb turned to face her, the candle flame bending as it found a draught. 'But that wasn't a farewell speech she made. More like a trailer for forthcoming attractions. She's got something up her sleeve.'

Which didn't bode well, thought Catherine. 'So there's more to come,' she said. 'More grief, pain and . . .' Her voice tailed away.

'Shit-the-bed clusterfucks.'

'What do you plan to do?'

He looked down at the candle, its flame still dancing in a draught, the shadows it cast warping and weaving across his face. His lips moved briefly, or perhaps he was just showing his teeth.

'Jackson?'

'I'm going to burn her fucking house down,' he said.

She had spent so long in hospitals that there was borderline comfort in being in one again. Between these walls, walls like these, life was the supreme priority, but subject to so many other forces that its clinginess was revealed: life was needy, demanding constant attention, and it found this in a rackety combination of the high-tech and the out-of-date, the highly proficient and the undervalued. Here, geography was at the mercy of signage altered so often it resembled fridge magnet poetry, with the names of departments squeezed into spaces not quite large enough. By such means an unintentional hierarchy was established, with longer names appearing in smaller typeface, in different colours. Alongside these were posters offering chaperones and helplines and crayon portraits of nurses; there were ID parades of staff on duty; there were happy thank-you cards and sad thank-you cards arrayed on reception desks. There were the details left behind when emergencies were over: cardigans on the backs of chairs, spectacle cases on bedside cabinets, paperbacks bookmarked at midway points. Frightening smells lingered in the corridors. For what felt like years Sid had lain at the centre of all this, like a well-wrapped fly in a well-meant web. Or perhaps a chrysalis. If she hadn't flown on being released, she had at least managed not to drop to earth.

Why she was here now was less obvious. Her interaction with Charles Stamoran had been brief and from an observer's viewpoint unpromising: he had kidnapped her, dumped her in a motorway service station and then entangled her in an assassination attempt which had resulted in carnage. His own stroke had, at first instance, proved no more successful than his shot at murder, but it would prevail in the long run. Around his bed, the machinery was pessimistic. The numbers were dropping, a countdown in progress, and lift-off seemed an unlikely result.

Avril said, 'Should you even be here?'

'Probably not. Would you rather I went?'

Avril paused, then said, 'That might seem impolite. We can't be sure he's not aware.'

No, but they could really. CC was halfway through the door. If he were still among them, it was only to check his pockets: did he have everything? He was going on a journey.

'Your friends. I'm sorry about your friends.'

Sid nodded. One of them she hadn't known; the other she hadn't known well. But they were part of River's world, and River was hurting. She said, 'I'm sorry too. I know this wasn't your fault.'

'Or CC's. Not really.' Avril paused again. 'Well, no. That can't be true, can it? But it wasn't as much his fault as it was . . .'

She tailed off.

Sid said, 'First Desk. Diana Taverner.'

'Yes.'

'But I'm the one who brought CC her message. So you could say I'm as much to blame.'

'That would be a long road if we started down it.' Avril's gaze didn't leave CC while she spoke. CC, a lump on the bed, held the attention. 'There was something we did, me and the others. It put him in a difficult place. He was trying to shield us. So there's that, too. While you're parcelling blame.'

She was a birdy woman; thin of limb, with a sharp inquisitive face, like a robin's. Smudged with sadness now. CC would die soon, and there would be consequences. No one knew better than Sid that any manner of mischief could be swept under the Park's carpets if it so desired, but the sweeping up could be as brutal as the original accident.

After the clown crash had come chaos. There had been bodies on the ground, CC's among them, and those still upright had pinballed around with more panic than expertise. She remembered Roddy, phone in hand, staring slack-jawed at Louisa, blood pooling around her like a chalk outline; remembered Shirley and Lech folded over Ash, who had caught the bullet meant for someone else. And a line from the Troubles came to her, a civilian's line to a journalist on the street. *It's not the bullet with my name on it that frightens me. It's the one addressed 'to whom it may concern'.*

Judd was gone, and she had the notion he'd been spirited away; that someone had appeared before the Dogs turned up and made him vanish like a card in a trick. Which meant, she supposed, that he'd turn up again, exactly where you didn't expect him to.

As for Al Hawke and Daisy Wessex, they were nowhere. It was possible Avril knew where they'd gone – old joes shared secrets: tell her about it – but if so, the chances of her revealing their hiding place were non-existent. Spies lie, spies betray – it's what they do – but they choose their betrayals carefully.

Without changing the direction of her gaze, Avril said, 'Al's always looked out for Daisy. And she for him.'

'And then some,' Sid said.

'She's not a bad woman.'

'No?'

'She triggers easily.'

'She's a bit stabby with it,' Sid said bluntly.

'She did a long-term undercover stint. In Northern Ireland. During the Troubles.' Avril paused. 'You've heard of Pitchfork?'

Everybody had heard of Pitchfork.

'Is that what it was about? CC blowing the whistle on Pitchfork?'

Avril nodded.

'It's not the best-kept secret,' Sid said.

'He had proof. That the government of the day, the powers that be, knew well what kind of man Pitchfork was. And granted him amnesty anyway, and cover ID, and a pension.'

Government, thought Sid. That was when the games got rough; when government was covering up dark mischief.

CC fluttered briefly, a memory shifting underneath his eyelids.

The rest of them had been taken to the Park, of course – those who hadn't been ferried to hospital – but released in a matter of hours. Which also had the stink of cover-up; Diana Taverner was pulling down a shroud, a stage that would last precisely as long as it took her to decide her next move. Once she'd determined how the investigation should end, she'd allow it to begin. Until then, they were in limbo, gathered round hospital beds, quarrelling in offices, or somewhere off-grid, waiting for the hammer to fall.

Or two hammers. Lamb had joes in morgues and hospital beds. He'd be making someone pay, and using others to collect, and she knew River would be entangled in whatever carnival he was summoning up. No matter what River's status was where the Service was concerned, to Lamb he would always be a slow horse.

She'd said this to him earlier, once the Dogs had released them; in the hospital waiting room, before she'd come to sit with CC. He was waiting for news – they all were – as their colleague lay on the operating table, knives and scalpels flashing above her, doctors striving to stem the flow of blood and preserve life.

'He'll want revenge.'

'Not now. Please.'

'No, this is important. You know what he's like – his joes, his rules. He'll want revenge, and he'll drag you into it.'

'Maybe that's what I want too.'

'But it wasn't their fault. Al and Daisy. They were as much victims—'

'But without bullets in them. Without their throats cut.'

River looked as if he might have suffered one such fate himself: he was whiter than she'd known him, all his grief rising to the surface.

'River, just, please, promise me. Promise me you won't . . .' It wasn't that she couldn't find the words; more that she didn't want the idea to exist in the open. As if, by saying it, she might make it more likely to happen. 'Promise me you won't let Lamb use you. To take revenge, I mean.'

And he had looked at her, but promised her nothing.

Avril's posture stiffened, and Sid returned from her thoughts. Something had changed. Whatever held CC in its grip, unsure whether to drop him or squeeze him tight, was making up its huge, invisible mind.

They waited, all three of them, while it reached its decision.

Her driver silently efficient, or efficiently silent, Diana Taverner watched London slide past: its shopfronts, its kerb flash, the hubbub on its corners. Being in this vehicle rendered her both unseen and high-status, indicating to the pavement-bound that here was an instrument of government, her importance beyond their comprehension, her identity withheld; the tinted windows announcing that here was a story, but declining to tell it. Famously, it was once suggested that anyone over thirty using a bus could be deemed a failure. A more severe metric might be: anyone uncushioned by driver and armoured glass was a has-been, or never was. She was approaching Number Ten, outside which, not long ago, ousted members of government had been watched packing their cars for departure. That was the real nature of failure: no longer being one of the ferried. It wasn't going to happen to her. Her car nosed forward like a fish. It stopped at the gates, and she climbed out without a word.

The madder stories of recent years – the gold-flecked wallpaper, the bring-a-bottle lockdown dos, the incident with the monkey – had been put to bed, but behind the black door was still a warren, the seat of government being an Escher's nest of leftover spaces, where policies were hammered out in box rooms, diplomatic overtures composed in galley kitchens. Taverner had once attended a meeting in a space designated a walk-in closet. Now she received a nod from the officer on duty, and the door opened for her. She knew where she was going but was guided anyway, one of the PM's staff doing the honours. Small talk was not attempted. A door was knocked upon. She was welcomed into the PM's presence.

This did not make her weak at the knees. While it remained true that, viewed through the prism of the recent past, most new prime ministers would impress, it was becoming clearer with each passing day that the current office holder's great electoral advantage had consisted solely of his not being one of his five immediate predecessors, a hand he'd already overplayed. His government had hit the ground runny, like a jelly that hadn't quite set; his most talked about achievement had been the self-completing circle of cutting fuel allowances for the elderly, which would soon enough cut the numbers of elderly requiring fuel, while his much heralded defence of the NHS amounted so far only to his being very much in favour of free spectacles. If transparency had been his watchword in opposition, in government, it seemed, this meant sporting the emperor's new clothes. But at least he hadn't paid for them.

Still, he wasted no time letting her know who he thought was in charge. 'I've read your summary. One dead, three hospitalised, all with Park connections, and your write-up's as illuminating as a twenty-watt bulb. Quote, "an attempt at extorting moneys from the Park has been quashed, and those responsible apprehended". What, precisely, does that mean?'

She said, 'It means, Prime Minister, that one of First Desk's responsibilities is to shield this office from embarrassment.'

'Really? First I've heard of it. And speaking of embarrassment, what's Peter Judd's role? Are you suggesting he was involved in this alleged extortion scheme?'

'Judd is an active mischief-maker, and—'

'I have a twelve-year-old who's an active mischief-maker, but I've never proposed we use state machinery to keep him in line. Are you telling me Judd is an actual bad actor?'

'I'm telling you he has deep-root connections to bad actors.'

'He was a career politician, Diana. That's a job description.'

The chief difficulty, she thought, was his voice. As with most chief difficulties, if it were ever resolved, even satisfactorily, another would rise to take its place, but until then it was a nasal irritation – like a recalcitrant bogey – that made hearing him a chore. No, the PM's voice was not one to deliver good news in. Luckily for them both, nothing he currently had to say was intended to raise her spirits.

'One of those hospitalised was from your Dogs section, yes? I gather he went through a window. That's not a great advert for your Service's ability to police itself.'

'He wasn't there in an official capacity.'

'Let me take a moment while I work out whether that makes it better or worse. No, not getting anywhere.'

She'd had worse meetings. Incoming PMs were always a problem, imagining, having moved into Number Ten, that they were Number One. Talking them down to a more reasonable self-assessment could, depending on the ego involved, prove an uphill struggle – the last half-decade had been Sisyphean. How long it would take the current example to absorb the first rule of political mathematics, by which all whole numbers gravitate towards zero, remained to be seen. On the evidence so far, a few months at most. But long before then, she was going to have to take charge.

He had more to say first, though. 'We have a suspicious, a *violent* death, we have woundings, we have the presence of a formerly significant political figure, and the involvement of Secret Service personnel, including several who were once part of a notorious undercover operation. The sole reason this isn't headline news is the classified nature of such activities, and I am painfully aware, Diana, that despite your elevated position and long experience, your own activities seem to be as far from safeguarding the national well-being as it is possible to get without actually holding a pillow over the nation's face.' It wasn't hard to remember that he'd been a lawyer in his pre-political life, used to summing up a case for the jury. Everything colour-coded, and delivered in paragraphs. 'Now, I need two things from you. The first is a full written report of precisely what occurred last night. The second is your resignation. You can frame it as you like – time for a change, ready for a rest – but it will be on my desk this evening. I cannot afford to have my government, or its officers, embroiled in any situation which reeks of cover-up and corruption.'

'Going well so far,' she said.

'. . . I beg your pardon?'

She gazed round at the over-furnished room, noting an unfaded border of wallpaper around an undistinguished portrait, an indication that a larger picture had been there recently. 'Could you have someone fetch a micro-cassette player? There'll be one in a cupboard.' She rolled her eyes, almost imperceptibly. 'It wouldn't be the first time we've had to rely on last century's technology to get this year's work done. The past has a way of hanging around. Unless it's the kind you can just shift elsewhere and drape a cloth over.'

His lips were a thin straight line. 'What are you talking about, Diana?'

She opened a fist, showing the tiny cassette on her palm.

'You need to listen to this.'

Slough House, like a broken mouth, was full of gaps. Lech felt it, in Louisa's room, where he was methodically tearing in half, then tearing in half again, the printouts of his current research job, littering the floor with scrambled addresses. Shirley felt it, lying under her desk in the room below, for reasons that weren't clear. Roderick Ho felt it, perched amidst his busy screens, self-medicating with energy drinks and pizza; his current assignments included wiping out an invading force of Nazi zombies. The headphones sealing him off from reality pumped angry music into his system, and it fizzed through him, hair to toes.

And Catherine, newly back from St Leonard's, felt it in her eyrie, where she sat at a desk that was for once free of paperwork; a blank space she could control, provided it remained blank, and no extraneous matters materialised.

Left as it was, it should be easy to walk away from. And it wasn't as if she had nowhere to walk to – she had her flat; as quiet as this, but half a world away. It smelled of basil and cut flowers, of polish and scented candles, and even intrusive noises – the *beep-beeping* of a delivery lorry in reverse; the overhead throbbing of aeroplanes circling before descent – felt less an interruption and more a notification that life continued on its even path. Whereas here in Slough House, the constant barrage of sound suggested that the front line, never far away, was getting nearer, and as for the smells . . . Catherine had long come to the conclusion that removing the aroma of stale tobacco would be a three-step process. First you'd have to steam-clean the soft furnishings, then paint the walls, and then knock the building down and scatter the rubble.

There was a crashing sound from downstairs, which could have been anything. She should investigate, but the effort felt beyond her.

The next noise was Lamb, calling her landline.

'I thought you were coming back here,' she said.

'Things to do, people to see. It's not easy being me.'

'I can imagine.' It wasn't that easy being around him. 'If you're calling for an update on your staff—'

'Nah. But get hold of Cartwright.'

'What do you need River for?'

'*Need* him? Christ, don't give him that impression. Tell him I want his keys back. I'll meet him at . . . the hanging gardens. In an hour. The rest of you be there too.' There was a pause while he cleared his lungs out. Either that or a nearby cat was throwing up a frog. 'Not a good idea to be around Slough House right now.'

'Where exactly are the—'

But he was gone.

She cradled the receiver and stared blankly at it. *Not a good idea to be around Slough House*: that could have worked as a motto for any given day these last dozen years. On the other hand, her peaceful sanctuary of a flat with its calming scents and cheerful background noises, its air of being somewhere she could truly be herself, held secret dangers. It was a place where she was left to her own devices, and those devices, when it came down to it, were corkscrews and bottle openers. Left to her own devices, she'd drink. Here – so far – there'd always been something else to do.

At the current moment, this was call River, and round up the slow horses. So, a deep breath later, this was what she did.

The look on the PM's face indicated that he hadn't received many instructions since winning a landslide vote. 'Listen to what, precisely?'

'A recording of a meeting that took place some while ago.' She placed it on his desk. 'It's the reason all this . . . activity came about.'

'It's to do with Pitchfork?'

'Yes.'

He didn't back away, but clearly wanted to. As if she had taken his office for a tree, and was hanging a bag of dog shit on a low branch, like idiots do. 'Then you can't imagine I want to listen to it. It would put me in an impossible position.'

'It's not an operational record, Prime Minister. More an informal aide-mémoire.'

'I have no clue what that means, but I can't see it makes any substantial difference. I've said all I have to say, and this meeting is now over. I'll await your letter. Have a good rest of afternoon, Diana.'

'Don't say I didn't try to warn you.' She put the cassette in her pocket. 'You can think of that as my last act in office. Just as not listening may turn out to be one of the last in yours.'

She didn't quite get as far as the door.

He said, 'The man's been dead for a decade. The operation he was involved in, his . . . other activities, they were done and dusted before I entered Parliament. Besides, it was the party I serve that negotiated the peace agreement that put an end to all that.' He removed his glasses, stared blankly at the lenses as if hoping to identify some flaw, then replaced them. Used to theatrical gestures, she waited patiently. 'Pitchfork was a squalid business, but it is long over. And I may be well versed in theories of collective responsibility, but nothing on that tape can warrant more than an historical apology, and your implication that it might be otherwise is a blatant attempt to safeguard your own position. Which, we've just established, is beyond safeguarding.'

'So you're calling my bluff.'

'If you want to put it like that.'

'A better way would have been to let me walk out of the door,' she said. 'Now, let me reassure you. I'm not suggesting you might be held to account for anything you had no active part in, Prime Minister. Quite the opposite, in fact. Do you mind if I sit while we wait?'

'. . . Wait?'

'While you summon one of those micro-cassette players I mentioned.' Taverner settled herself into a chair, producing from her pocket, as she did so, the tape. 'This thing's not going to play itself.'

When Devon Welles checked in at Holborn late afternoon, he was told he had a visitor. In his office.

The offices were private turf, and visitors – guests – clients – never allowed access to them unaccompanied.

'Why on earth – ?'

The double act who tended reception exchanged miserably puzzled glances. 'We don't know.'

He went upstairs fearing the worst, so wasn't disappointed to find Jackson Lamb behind his desk, studying paperwork he must have hoicked out of a drawer. Without looking up, he twitched his head towards the closed door behind him. 'I'd give that five minutes.'

Devon looked at the door, then back at Lamb. 'That's a cupboard.'

'Needs must. Is this what you charge clients? There's a bill for ninety grand here.'

'It includes VAT.'

'It'd have to include a fucking house.' He tossed the papers to the floor. 'I could start to feel inadequate.'

'On my account? I deserve a medal.' Devon briefly considered challenging Lamb for his office chair, and settled for the visitor's version instead. 'To what do I owe the outrage?'

'Prices you charge, I should let you work that out for yourself.' Lamb was holding a cigarette; it had appeared between the fingers of his left hand while his attention was apparently elsewhere. 'But let's just say I gather you have a vacancy that won't be filled any time soon. Too late for me to throw my hat in the ring?'

Devon said, 'Emma Flyte told me about you. About how edgy you think you are.'

'To be fair, I'm not the only one thinks that.'

'You might be surprised. But okay, I'll go along. One of your crew's dead, another's in intensive care, and you're here, what? Just to make light of that?'

'Where did Judd go afterwards?'

'I got him out.'

'Because he's your client.'

Devon didn't reply.

'And the two oldies, they what? Vanished into thin air?'

Devon blinked. They might as well have done; he hadn't been paying attention. Nor had he spirited Judd away as swiftly as he'd implied, having been momentarily paralysed by the scene on the dance floor: Louisa, her younger colleague; a knife across the throat and a bullet to the chest. The two responsible were nowhere when the ambulance arrived. Spooks of the old school, he'd later gathered, and not being there was something old spooks grew good at. Failing which, they never became old spooks at all.

He said, 'The Dogs took over. The place was locked down. You want to know what happened, read the papers.'

'Which is where I say, there's been nothing in the papers.'

Devon made no response.

'And you say, so nothing happened.'

'It's your world, Lamb. You must be used to it.'

'If it was my world, I'd be the one charging ninety grand for babysitting. And you'd have an ashtray on your desk.' He pushed back suddenly – the chair had wheels – and crashed into the wall. This was punctuation. 'You know what the whole shitshambles was in aid of?'

'Like I said. Your world.'

'Have a stab at this, then. Whose—'

'"Have a stab"? For fuck's sake!'

'Whose shitshambles was it? Or do you think Charles Stamoran just woke with a mad leprechaun singing in his ear? *Why not shoot Peter Judd? Get your name in the papers.*'

'Epic fail on that count.'

'Yeah. What with that and the whole having-a-massive-stroke thing, he must be feeling a bit of a tit.' Lamb put his cigarette in his mouth, rolled it from one side to the other, then withdrew it again. 'You haven't answered my question.'

'You haven't apologised for being here.'

'Think of it as an intervention. If I wasn't here you'd be writing invoices, and some poor bastard'd be looking at bankruptcy.'

'Our clients are mostly corporations. They get what they pay for. And I don't write invoices.'

'First Desk.'

'. . . What?'

'Thought I'd cut to the hunt, given you're busy avoiding the question. Diana Taverner. Used to be your boss, remember?'

'She squeezed Stamoran.'

'And aimed him in Judd's direction.' He tapped the end of his cigarette against his nose. 'I'm failing to detect any surprise here. Though I know how good you guys can be at concealing your responses.'

'"Us guys"?'

'Former Dogs. Lighten up. Speaking of which . . .' He waggled the cigarette.

'You can't smoke in here.'

'I'm not asking permission,' Lamb said. 'I'm asking for a match.'

Devon said, 'Am I shocked Lady Di is behind the attempted hit? No. Does you telling me about it surprise me? Again, no. Because you're clearly after something. So tell me what it is, I'll tell you to fuck off, and then — well. Then you can fuck off.'

'That takes me back. "Lady Di". No one calls her that any more.'

'Can we skip ahead to where you fuck off?'

'You want to be careful. You're starting to remind me of me. How much do you know about your client?'

'I know he pays his bills.'

'I'm sure someone does.' Undaunted by its unlit condition Lamb replaced his cigarette in his mouth, and appeared to inhale deeply. 'Why do you think Taverner wants him black-ribboned?'

'Assuming your retro slang means what I think it does, I have no idea. Above and beyond the obvious.'

'That being?'

'He's Peter Judd.'

'Yeah, that would do it for me. Taverner, though, she's got to tread carefully in case HR find out she's killing people, and make her do an awareness course. Those things go on for days.'

Devon said, 'I'd assume he's got something on Taverner she doesn't want getting out. They've been moving in the same circles so long, they probably breathe each other's secrets.'

'And those aren't even the nastiest circles he swims in. Did you look at his CV before taking him on?'

'I don't do the paperwork.'

'Because it's not what he's got on Taverner that'll interest you. It's what he's done in the past.'

Devon said nothing. Whatever Lamb was about to tell him was the reason Lamb was here, and he needed further prompting like a wolf needs a toothpick.

Lamb said, 'When your pal Emma Flyte was killed, who do you think the shooters were working for?'

THE HANGING GARDENS OF the Barbican hadn't so much been hanged as thrown themselves off balconies. Greenery dangled from railings to the lake below, the surface of which was carpeted with algae so thick that smaller ducks waddled across rather than paddled through it. Walkways overlooked this, and from strategically placed benches a viewer could gaze down on a Ballardian vision made brick. They could film a *Planet of the Apes* here, thought River, without much call for set dressing. You had to concentrate quite hard not to imagine zombies shuffling past.

He said, 'I don't even know why I'm here. I'm not a slow horse any more.'

'You don't have to remind me. I'd planned a cake, a bottle of bubbly.' Lamb shook his head sadly. 'I was gunna set fire to your personnel file, and maybe have a quiet moment, you get my drift.' In case River didn't, he mimed having a quiet moment with his right hand. 'Trust me, I'd have marked the occasion in an appropriate manner.'

'The appropriate manner being your fallback position,' Lech muttered.

They'd been waiting for Lamb for over an hour, and hadn't been making a lot of conversation. Shirley and Lech were still wary of each other following that morning's hostilities, a skirmish occasioned by the former's insistence on keeping all the blinds in the building down 'as a mark of respect', which Lech interpreted as 'so no one looking in will see Shirley doing blow'. Actually, Shirley wasn't doing blow (supply chain malfunction), and nor did Lech think she was (hangover malice), but they hadn't been fighting over blinds either. Grief smothered Slough House like a nurse with a pillow. Even Roddy felt it, cranking his headbanging mixtape to nosebleed levels while flaying swastika-embossed excrescences with what looked like, and possibly was, a glass dildo. Computer games come with age certification; none of them actually say 'mental age of seven', but most should. But a couple of hours ago Roddy had had a phone call, after which the music had abruptly ceased, and he'd begun live-streaming Notting Hill traffic pressure points like a man planning to firebomb a carnival. Lech had noted this, but asking questions would have been tantamount to a gesture of friendship. Besides, he had a wobbly tooth after his difference of opinion with Shirley, and was too busy probing it with his tongue to articulate much.

River had come from the hospital. Sid had been there too, but at CC's bedside. Your grandfather would understand, she'd told him, and River had pretended he agreed. But his grandmother would. Rose, who had spent almost her entire life on the outside of the Service looking in; she'd have understood. And would probably have done the same thing.

When Lamb arrived he'd been clutching a greaseproof package containing either a particularly artisanal kebab or a prop from a horror film. The latter would presumably have been non-edible, but the slow horses were accustomed to Lamb's robust approach to culinary shibboleths. He claimed the bench they'd been congregating on by his usual method – i.e., declining to accept the fact that others were already sitting there – forcing them to scatter. Only Roddy remained in place, headphones loose round his neck, laptop on his lap. As far as anyone could tell, he was still engaged in mapping W3 via its traffic control systems. Say what you like about Roddy, thought River – which, to be fair, was his usual approach – but when he committed to something, he went all in. If he'd made wiser choices as to what those commitments were, he might have averaged out at a speakable human being.

So that left River on his feet, along with Lech, Shirley and Catherine; Shirley leaning against a pillar and Lech staring at the walkway opposite, along which a man was shuffling as slowly as possible without going backwards. He appeared to be wearing hospital garb, though his lower half was shielded from view by the wall, so it might have been a baggy shirt.

River said, 'And what precisely made you shelve your wank-fest? Did my medical clearance come through?'

'Shit, no. You're fuck out of luck there, sonny. They're terrified you'll be a death-in-service payout waiting to happen. And given recent events—'

'Shut up, Jackson.'

' – well, one payment down, another looking likely, the kitty's bare. So no.'

'I said shut up.'

'Yeah, but I'm not your boss any more, remember? So you can't make me.'

River buried his head in his hands. 'For fuck's sake.'

Cramming the remainder of his supper into his mouth, Lamb crumpled the greaseproof paper into a mess the size of a cricket ball. There being no wastebasket handy, he lobbed it in the direction of Catherine, who, to the surprise of the assembled company, caught it neatly, following which, to the surprise of nobody, she tucked it into her handbag for later disposal. Lamb, meanwhile, lit a cigarette with less stage business than usual.

Shirley said, 'So now we all don't know why River's here. What about the rest of us? Or are we not gunna find that out either?'

Her tone was detached, Lech noted; a speak-your-weight

monotone. As if she were coming down. Their recent clash notwithstanding, Lech didn't dislike Shirley; had days when he was quite fond of her, once he'd managed to quell all memory of their more accident-prone outings. Her drug-taking was a problem, as was her tendency to regard any given straw as the last available, but her heart was, if not necessarily in the right place, at least somewhere in that vicinity, like a kitchen utensil not actually lost, but not in its proper drawer. So seeing her now, stuffing leaking out of her, it was as if someone had taken a broomstick to a scarecrow. His heart didn't break, obviously, but he hoped the next person he punched wasn't her. Slough House had taken enough of a beating already.

Lamb was watching the shuffling man now, with the interest a carrion bird might take in a failing woodland creature, and ignored Shirley's input. Instead he said, 'You've seen her?' He was talking to River still.

'Yeah.'

'And?'

'She might pull through.'

'Might,' Lamb repeated. 'Someone's a riverboat gambler.'

'It's Bart's. They're not casting spells and crossing their fingers. She's got a good chance of making it. That's what they . . . reckon.'

Lech said, 'Shirley asked you a question. We all want to hear the answer. Why are we here? I was on my way home.'

Catherine shook her head, perhaps a warning to Lech to tread carefully. But it was River who answered.

'Because he has a plan,' he said.

'Oh, great. Another plan. Last time somebody had one of those, there were two more of us listening to it.'

Lamb said, 'Any more griping, you might find yourself over this wall and in that water. Which, I say water, is ninety per cent goose shit. You'll come out of it smelling like a French deli.'

'Still be an improvement on your coat,' Lech said, or wanted to. He rubbed his cheek instead, feeling familiar knobbly scar tissue under the stubble.

Roddy Ho looked up and around at the assembled company. The look on his face was familiar: he often wore it when making the transition from his screens to the real world. The kind you might see on a zoo animal, when its attention switches from its swing set, its plants, its own feet, and takes in the staring humans. 'Thirty-seven,' he said.

This made sense to Lamb, if no one else. 'Well, that should be a piece of piss,' he said.

Ho nodded, and went back to his screen.

River said, 'Are you teaching him to count now? No, forget it. I don't care what you're doing. I don't even want to be here.'

But he gave no sign of departure.

Lamb said, 'Yeah, sorry to interrupt your crowded schedule of doing sod all.' The man across the way had reached a corner and paused, holding himself upright with one hand on the bricks. 'Any of you had the Met knocking doors down?'

'Nope.'

'Just the Dogs, then. Handpicked by Taverner. Who's painting the walls her own colour.'

'Meaning?'

'Meaning the official story of what went down won't bear any resemblance to the clusterfuck it actually was. Which means she can't just photocopy the paperwork from last time you lot tied your collective balls to a locomotive, but that's her problem. Ours is, we don't know what the official story will be, but you can bet your sorry arses you'll come out of it looking like the sad fuckwits you are. Only actually culpable, rather than just fucking morons.'

'So why aren't we chained up in a basement?' Shirley asked.

'In working hours? You should be so lucky. But from

Taverner's point of view, probably because she's looking at too many loose ends. Principally, Judd.'

'He's got something on her,' she said.

'Something big enough that she wants him dead,' added River.

'To be fair, we've all been there. But yeah, he's her problem. Whatever story she comes up with, she's got to lock it in place before he decides to detonate the firecracker he shoved up her arse last year.'

'Do you know what it is?'

Lamb's gaze rested heavily on River. 'No.'

River said, 'So why hasn't Judd, uh, lit his firecracker already?'

'Either he's biding his time or he's formulating demands.' Lamb tapped a finger against his cigarette, and sparks scattered. 'It was the crumblies did for our two, right?'

'Al Hawke shot Ash. Daisy stabbed Louisa.' River touched his throat. 'But Hawke was aiming for Judd, who'd just shouldered Daisy to the ground. And Daisy probably thought she was saving Hawke, because Louisa jumped him.' He closed his eyes briefly. Then said, 'They were there for the same reason as us, to stop their friend committing murder.'

'Shame any of you bothered. But it doesn't matter who pulled whose trigger, this is Taverner's fuck-up. Anyone else, she'd be toast. But this is Taverner. She could wander into a fairy tale and come back out with hi-def footage of Goldilocks going down on Daddy Bear, so who knows what leverage she's got on Number Ten's latest sock monkey. And if she walks on this, anyone with a clue about what happened last night is in her sights. And you all know how that story ends.'

'So what's the plan?'

'Diplomacy.' He put a cigarette behind his ear, a backup in case the one in his mouth disappointed him. 'We bring our principals together and have them talk through their differences. And reach a conclusion that satisfies all parties.'

'Principals?'

'Taverner and Judd.'

Shirley said, 'What, get them to kiss and make out?'

'Up,' said Catherine.

Lamb said, 'You know me. If I can't bring a little sweetness and light into the world, I go to bed unhappy.'

River and Lech exchanged a look. 'Are you having a stroke too?' River asked.

'You have a better idea?'

'How do you plan to get them together?' Lech said. 'Given that Judd knows Taverner just tried to have him whacked.'

'Yeah, that's where the diplomacy comes in.'

'Sounds like that's where hostage-taking comes in.'

Lamb said, 'Well, you could always decide you're happy with the way things have worked out. Or do you want me to count heads again and come up two short?'

Shirley said, 'When did talking things over solve anything?'

'It's your negative attitude that's holding you back in life, you know. Well, that and being a shortarse with a bad haircut.'

River shook his head, and leaned over the wall to study the water below. Little of it was visible beneath its shroud of algae, though a duck was unzipping a trail behind it, zigzagging slowly from one side to the other.

'You really think Taverner will do a clean-up?' Lech said.

'She'd feed a Girl Guide troop into a sausage machine to get herself off a parking ticket,' said Lamb. 'So yeah. The only thing that'd stop her is knowing she'd be sticking her own head in a mincer.'

'And you think you can talk her down.'

'I may come across as being a little brusque at times, but delicate negotiation's one of my core skills.' He farted, reasonably. 'Alongside people management.'

'So what is it you want us to do?' said River.

'That'd make too long a list. Better stick to the practicalities.'

Lamb looked at Roddy, who was closing his laptop. 'You're sure you've got them all?'

Roddy delivered his trademark pizza-eating grin, though for once his heart didn't seem to be in it. 'Sure.' He paused, as if aware this wasn't up to his usual standards, then added, 'Fight the power.'

Lamb looked at Shirley. 'I hope you're paying attention. Here's someone not afraid to let being a dickhead be his umbrella.' He stood. 'All right, then. No plan can be said to be flawless when it relies on a bunch of workplace accidents like you lot, but you go with what you've got. Never let perfection be the enema of the good, and all that.'

'The enemy,' said Catherine automatically.

'Up your bum.'

'There's a plan?' said River. 'All we've heard is a set of vague intentions.'

'I hate to confuse you with details. It's like trying to explain Denmark to a cat.' He paused. 'That needs work. But you get my drift.' With one hand he removed the burning cigarette from his mouth while with the other he retrieved the fresh one from behind his ear. 'No big worry, though. You'll be driving a car, that's all. Think you can manage?'

'What about me?' said Shirley.

Lamb handed her his smouldering stub. 'You can do something with that. The rest of you, avoid your usual hang-outs. Once Diana's got her ducks in a row, you're target practice. It'll be a novelty for you, actually being useful, but if I have to start from scratch with a new bunch, it'll put me right off my afternoon dump.'

'She's not going to have us killed,' said Catherine. Her voice might have trembled, but she didn't end on a rising inflection.

'Positive attitude. Good. But bear it in mind that if she does decide to do just that, there's less effort involved than there would have been last week. Just saying.' He looked at Ho. 'You're sure you can do this?'

Ho nodded.

'Good.' Lamb looked around at the rest of them, might have been about to add something, but didn't. They watched while he padded along the walkway before disappearing down a stairwell.

Shirley said, 'Fuck am I supposed to do with this?'

Lech took the smoking stub from her fingers, ground it out on the wall, then handed it to Catherine, who snorted, rolled her eyes, and pulled a tissue from her sleeve to wrap it in. That went into her bag, next to the greaseproof wodge. Then everyone looked at Ho, who'd put his headphones over his ears again.

It took him a while to register their interest – with his bins on, it would take him a while to register a Sasquatch – but when he did he pulled them from his head, his expression half wary, half hostile. 'What?'

Catherine said, 'What's Lamb got you doing, Roddy?'

'Why?'

'Because if you don't tell us, we'll feed you to the ducks,' said Shirley.

'Ducks don't scare me.'

'These ducks are quite some distance below.'

'Roddy,' said River. 'Louisa would want you to tell us.'

'She's—'

'Yeah. But if she wasn't.'

Roddy studied the headphones in his hand, as if wondering how they'd got there. Then said, 'Cameras. CCTV.'

'Where?'

Before he could reply, Lech said, 'Notting Hill.'

'You're counting how many CCTV cameras there are in Notting Hill?'

Roddy rolled his eyes: well, *duh*. 'Not counting them, no.'

'Roddy,' said Catherine, with a bark none of them thought

her capable of. 'Why are you accessing CCTV cameras in the region of Notting Hill?'

'To see if I can switch them off.'

'And can you?'

He avoided eyes. 'Course.'

Shirley let out a long breath. 'You should be a verb. To roddy.'

Lech couldn't resist. 'Meaning what?'

'Haven't got that far. Something to do with being a dick.'

River said, 'Meanwhile, back on track, Notting Hill ring any bells?'

'It bangs a few drums,' Shirley muttered.

'Taverner,' said Lech.

'Yeah. It's where Taverner lives.'

'Lamb wants a coverage blackout around Taverner's house,' Catherine spelt out. 'Well, that doesn't sound troubling, does it?'

'Stands to reason, if he's trying to get those two under the same roof, he doesn't want anyone knowing about it,' said Shirley. 'The whole point of a secret meeting is, it's secret.'

'Wouldn't neutral territory be more usual?' said Catherine.

'Yeah, because that worked out nicely last night.'

River said, 'This way, he only has to persuade one of them to be somewhere. The other one's already there.'

Most of them nodded. Roddy went a little cross-eyed.

Catherine said, 'You can make anything sound reasonable eventually. But the fact remains, this is Lamb we're talking about. Taking the reasonable option is not his preferred route.'

'Whereas the rest of us,' said Lech, 'are a proper bunch of regular citizens.'

River said, 'What he said about Judd. That he doesn't know what Judd's got on Taverner. That sound likely to anyone?'

'He can't know everything.'

'But have you ever heard him admit that?'

Shirley said, 'If he knows what it is, what's to stop him pulling the trigger himself?'

'If what Judd's got on Taverner's enough to see her out of her job, it'll be enough to rock the Service as a whole,' said River. 'And I don't think Lamb would do that.'

'No?' Lech wrinkled his nose. The effect was like someone sneezing under a Halloween mask. 'I think he'd set fire to the whole fucking Park if he could get a lighter to work.'

'Not while there are joes in the field,' said River.

'You say stuff like that like it means much,' said Shirley. 'I mean, it does to you, we all get that. But it's the twenty fucking twenties, not nineteen sixty-six. If there was ever honour among spies, it died with James Bond.'

Catherine looked startled. 'James Bond died?'

'Well, yes and no,' said Lech. 'But let's focus. Maybe River's right. Lamb's old school. By which I mean Ofsted should have shut him down by now, but he's not gonna let that change his attitudes. So whatever he says, diplomacy isn't his first resort. Taverner's responsible for the loss of his joes. He won't just ask her nicely not to do it again.'

Catherine said, 'Which is why you ought to think carefully about falling in with whatever he's got in mind. All of you.' She glanced at Roddy, who didn't notice. 'You're hurting. We all are. But so is he. And nobody makes good plans when they're in pain.'

'Lamb, hurting?' said Shirley. 'Is there a whisky shortage?'

'I'm only going to say it one more time. The wisest thing to do is walk away. Before anyone else gets hurt.'

'Yeah, anyone else,' said Shirley. 'That's exactly why we can't walk away. Because we've already lost two.'

'Not two.'

'Not yet,' Shirley muttered.

There was a sudden commotion below, and they turned to look. The man on the walkway opposite, who might have been an escapee from a hospital ward, was leaning over the wall, dropping lumps of what was probably bread into the water. From all sides ducks had appeared, loudly laying claim to the bounty. As ever with such displays, it was impossible to determine whether their benefactor was fond of ducks or enjoyed causing them to squabble.

Catherine shook her head. 'I'm going to find a wastepaper bin,' she said. 'I'm sick of carrying round everyone's rubbish.'

She set off along the walkway. Nobody spoke until she'd turned a corner; three of them because they were watching her, and Roddy because he was absorbed once more in the world as seen from his laptop.

Shirley said, 'I'm not saying she's not on our side. But she's not really a team player, is she?'

'To be fair,' said Lech, 'we're hardly a fucking team.'

'No,' said River. 'But we're all we've got.'

'We're doing this, then?'

'Whatever it is,' said River, 'yeah. We're doing it.'

This was what business as usual looked like, Taverner thought, observing the hub through the glass wall of her office. The boys and girls – because, damn it, who had time to enumerate gender preferences when what mattered was that the boys and girls did their jobs? – the boys and girls were hustling to and fro, and on the screens all around them London was dancing. A surveillance op was under way; they were monitoring a sting on a newly fledged angry-band who'd been making waves on the Dark Web and thought they were about to buy half a dozen automatic weapons from a local gangster. What the angry-band was angry about wasn't entirely clear, but it involved the usual suspects: immigrants, politicians, journalists, the liberal elite, plus, for some reason, people who lived on barges. All in all, it was best they didn't come into possession of weaponry, though judging by the literacy and sophistication of their online muttering, they'd harm themselves more than others if anything more lethal than plastic cutlery fell their way. Besides, an easy win was always welcome. And should the worst happen and the proposed sting go south, well, that would provide a useful distraction from yesterday's events, which were theoretically under wrappers so thick armour-piercing bullets wouldn't penetrate, but were doubtless even now being murmured about in corners. The Park's chief gossip-mongers could give Mumsnet a run for its money. They rarely reached the same levels of savagery, but their commitment to trivia was beyond reproach.

Every so often, one of the junior crew would glance in her direction, anxious for approval; not yet established enough to know that this never arrived before the last i had been dotted, the last t crossed.

She was careful, sipping coffee, not to allow a hint of appreciation to ruffle her face.

The micro-cassette recorder had been some time coming. That was the difficulty with being new in government; you couldn't always put your hand on everything, and didn't know who to ask. Standard piece of office equipment; directions to the fallout shelter: it came to the same thing. She and the PM had spent the interlude doing nothing differently: he glaring into space; she studying the walls with an air of unconcern. When it arrived, the aide delivering it ushered himself from the room as swiftly as if he'd read in the atmosphere an approaching meteor, and didn't want to be near when it landed.

When Taverner inserted the cassette, the PM had bristled.
'Where did that come from, anyway?'
She told him.
'So there's no chain of evidence, no official record of provenance.'
'But it's got a beat and you can dance to it.'
'What?'
She said, 'Best if you just listen.'

Which is what they did. When they reached the end, his face had turned to stone. Without speaking, she clicked the tape off, rewound a short while, and replayed a section.

There's one further matter we need to cover, I think, sir. The question of inflation-proofing the pension arrangement.

She hit the switch again, turning it off. The sudden silence in the room felt out of place, as if it were being piped in from somewhere else.

At last he said, 'And that's it?'

'It's enough to be getting on with.'

She could see him marshalling arguments. She waited.

He said, 'The full details about Pitchfork will hardly come as a revelation. The *Sunday Times* covered the story years ago. It's old news, Diana. It will cause ripples, but hardly a storm.'

'The government of the day pensioned off a known rapist and murderer who'd been an active member of the Provisional IRA for more than a decade. God knows how much blood was on his hands before we turned him. Finding out how much blood was on his hands after we did so – well. It's likely someone could come up with a ballpark figure.'

'All of which, as I've already said, has been the subject of public speculation for years.'

'I'm starting to feel like Sam. Do you want me to play it again? Very well. I'll play it again.'

There's one further matter we need to cover, I think, sir. The question of inflation-proofing the pension arrangement.

'You can't really believe—'

She waited.

'Nobody is going to—'

She waited.

He said, 'It was a long time ago.'

'And you were a young lawyer, already showing great promise. Trusted with matters of state. Destined for greatness.' She made an open-palmed gesture. 'As we can see. The giddy heights.'

'Ancient history,' he said.

'For which there's a surprising appetite these days.'

'Nobody is going to care.'

'Do you really think so?' She stood. 'Because I believe you're wrong. I believe that when the public get to hear a younger version of their prime minister fretting about pension arrangements for a psychopath, there's going to be an uproar. I mean, you weren't cutting his fuel allowance, so there's that, but does that make it worse or better? You're the politician. You decide.'

'I was doing my job.'

'Yes, you might want to give that more thought before you trot it out as a defence. It's famously less effective than you might expect.'

He had removed and folded his spectacles, and clenched them now as if they were a baton, or possibly a buck, he was hoping to pass. 'I thought, and I'm quoting, that one of First Desk's responsibilities is to shield this office from embarrassment.'

'Yes. But if I recall correctly, you relieved me of that position twenty minutes ago. So the stricture no longer applies.'

She might have been imagining it, but his grip appeared to loosen as she spoke. As if he'd just been handed a key, and invited to free himself.

The moment passed; more moments passed. Then she was here in the Park, observing the boys and girls through the glass wall of her office, and Josie was at her door, miming a knock. Taverner nodded, and in she came.

'Mr Nash has been asking for you.'

Mr Nash – Oliver – the chair of Limitations, the Park's oversight committee – was frequently asking for Diana, in moods ranging from petulant to furniture-chewing.

'Did he say what it was about?'

'Apparently there was a shooting last night? An agent-involved shooting?'

Christ, it was like stamping out a forest fire. Every time you quenched a flame, another popped into life. Next thing you knew your shoes were on fire, and it was you who were spreading sparks . . . She said, 'That's strictly on a need-to-know basis.'

'Yes. That's what people are saying.'

Just when it was clear Slough House had to go, here was more evidence that some kind of admin dungeon in which to dump office embarrassments was necessary.

She said, 'People should be reminded that they work for the Secret Service. Emphasis on both those words. If they can't keep a secret, they cease to serve a purpose. Is Oliver in the Park now?'

'He's upstairs, First Desk.'

'I'll speak to him when I have something of value to impart. Let him know. Meanwhile, I'm observing an op. Was there anything else?'

There was nothing else.

Out on the hub, the boys and girls continued their surveillance of a successful sting. Inside her office, Diana Taverner enjoyed the feeling of being First Desk.

Business as usual.

Judd was in his study, looking down on the lawn where, as recently as yesterday, summer had been in its pomp. But rain was pattering down now, there were no window-threatening frisbees in evidence, nor any lightly clad undergraduates wielding them, and while Xanthippe's little – well, not so little – chum's number was still stored in his phone, acting on it was no longer a pressing concern: he hadn't felt a twitch since escaping the nightclub. It was said that a brush with death inflamed an appetite for living, but all he wanted to do was hide under a blanket, and he wasn't ashamed to admit it. Well. He wouldn't have been ashamed, but had no one to admit it to; since Seb's abrupt departure from his service he had no close male associates, and while marriage was held to be the ideal institution in which to share intimacies, it had been years since he'd confided in his wife, and if she'd confided in him in the meantime, he hadn't noticed. So here he was, ill at ease with the world, and what he mostly felt like doing was calling Devon Welles. I mean, Christ. All Welles had done was his job, and it was a pretty lucrative gig at that. It wasn't like they were set to be mates. Always good to share a photo op with a black face, but after that, you started running out of reasons. The man hadn't even attended a proper school.

He had to tip his hat to Taverner, though. He'd have preferred to sit and watch while someone sawed her head off, but fair dos: she'd played him. All this time, he'd thought she'd accommodated herself to their situation – that he pulled strings, and she smiled while he did it – but here was the story: she not only wanted him dead but had laid out the groundwork to make that happen. Nearly worked, too. As it was, the old fool had self-destructed like a set of *Mission: Impossible* instructions, a bomb popping off in his brain at the crucial moment. So instead of Judd lying on the floor it had been Taverner's wind-up assassin who'd hit the bricks, along with two women, both in the mid-to-upper doable range, and one clearly dead at the scene. Actually, when you thought about it, it had all been over right there, so Welles's appearance hardly counted as a rescue – if he'd been doing his job, he'd have been on the scene while the gun was in play. That was an argument for dereliction of duty. Luckily for Welles, Judd's heart wasn't in it right now.

Where his heart was was another question. Clearly, relations with Taverner were beyond breaking point, which left the nuclear option: he could atomise her career by revealing she'd financed an assassination on foreign soil using money from Chinese sources. Where that would leave him was more problematic. Judd was no blackmailer – he had a keen eye for a business opportunity, that was all – but he was facing the blackmailer's dilemma: if he destroyed Taverner, he'd be left holding nothing. As First Desk, she'd been his ace in the hole. As a disgraced former spook, she was just a remaindered memoir awaiting its ghost.

The upside to this was cold comfort. Taverner had recruited an off-the-books pensioner for her dirty work, meaning she was in no position to use Service resources. That levelled the playing field. But the last thing Judd wanted was a level playing field. If everyone played fair, it put him at a disadvantage.

Out in the garden, on a branch at his window level, a squirrel was studying the rain with mild disgust. Its nose twitched, its tail came up, and Judd imagined aiming a shotgun at it and blowing its tiny life into fragments. Make a mess of the garden though. That was the trouble with even the smaller pleasures; they came with consequences attached. Still, he mimed the process, making a gun out of his arm and sighting down it. The squirrel affected not to notice. Bang, he thought. Bang bang, you're dead. It wasn't the squirrel he was thinking about. So when his landline rang at that precise moment his heart skipped, and he had the absurd notion he'd been spotted plotting murder.

He answered anyway.

If the squirrel had turned tables and sighted on Judd during the following several minutes, studying his reactions through the upstairs window, it would have enjoyed a brief catalogue of varying human emotions: fear, suspicion, disbelief, a slight flickering of hope. It's more likely, though, that the squirrel was fixated on its own concerns, these involving its usual daily round of eating, mating, swinging from trees and perhaps the occasional act of slaughter. Either way, by the time Judd had finished his call and crossed to the window again, it was nowhere to be seen.

But. All stories end, just not always where expected, and light can creep out of the darkness through a slit life makes in the curtain, through which noise crawls too, a soft murmuring which is sometimes people and sometimes machines – the machines you see in hospitals, with screens and readouts and declining numbers – replacing what had previously been a void, and before that chaos, a welter of people and sound and movement which had abruptly halted when something slammed into her, something blunt and sharp at the same time, the bluntness a hammer blow robbing her of breath, and the sharpness tearing a hole through her, and it's that hole that's causing trouble now, she knows; it's that hole into which everyone is looking when they gather round her bed, and what they're wondering is whether her life is still leaking out of that hole, or whether it's slowing down now, whether she can hold on to what's left, and keep it inside her, and let it grow until she's herself again . . .

By the time River pulled up outside Peter Judd's house light was leeching from the sky, and the grey canopy that had hung over the capital most of the day was darkening at the rim. Street lights were coming on, though still looked undernourished; within the hour, they would have swollen in strength, and seem like they anchored London to the ground. Here in leafy Barnes, they did so with the help of trees; so many trees, it was as bad as living in the country. River had the feeling that his arrival here, satnav led, had not gone unnoticed; that he was an entry in half a dozen notebooks already, resting on the laps of the self-appointed guardians of the borough. There was nothing Lamb could do about this, unless of course there was, and River had to suppress the image that arrived uninvited of Shirley being sent from house to house, terrifying the residents into surrendering their Neighbourhood Watch records.

'Don't get seen,' had been Lamb's order, unless it was just a suggestion. Magical thinking either way. There were times River thought Lamb, for all his streetsmarts, out of depth in the here and now; more at home in his Berlin alleys or a Marseilles dive, provided both those places were securely located forty years ago.

'I'm to drive him through central London without being seen? The world's most monitored city?'

'Yeah, I've got Ho taking care of the busy bit.'

That was another worry: Roddy being in charge of closing down a section of the city's CCTV. It wasn't so much that Roddy might not be capable of it. It was more that he might like it too much, and take it up as a hobby.

'And Judd's just going to get into my car and let me drive him away?'

Lamb's sigh blasted like the mistral through his phone. 'This is like giving instructions to a cat. You know why I chose you for this bit?'

'No.'

'Me neither. So don't fuck it up.'

The ideal response to this was somewhere out in the ether, and River was still trying to access it when he crossed the river at Hammersmith, Lamb having hung up. Following that, he tried Sid again, and got her voicemail, again. Where she was now, he had no clue. Pulling up at last outside what satnav assured him was Judd's house, light leeching from the sky, he put his phone in his pocket. *You know why I chose you for this bit? Me neither.*

He checked his watch. It was 7:20.

Getting out of the car, he went to ring the bell.

'How's your mouth?'

Lech ran his tongue around his teeth again. He might have been imagining the wobble. He wasn't, though. 'It fucking hurts.'

'Yeah, well. You know why that is?'

He said, 'Okay, okay. You weren't coked up. I shouldn't have said that.'

'I was gunna say because when you feinted left, you might as well have sent an engraved invitation. But I accept your apology. And yes, I will have another of these.'

This being an unspeakable combination of Pernod and black-currant. Sometimes, Shirley drank like she was a sixth-former, aiming at sophistication while heading for oblivion.

They were in a pub on Whitecross Street – where Shirley was familiar enough that service was attentive but avoided eye contact – having arrived without conferring, but definitely needing drinks. Lamb had a plan, and it was even now rolling into motion, but they weren't part of it. When even the slow horses didn't need you, that's when you knew you were surplus.

Their first round, they'd chinked glasses. Louisa. Ash. When you added up the empty spaces, all the desks at Slough House that had seen different riders, you stopped looking for words; you just let the pictures form in your head, then break and drift away like smoke. And while you were waiting for that to happen, you took yourself to the nearest drink, whether it was Pernod and bloody blackcurrant or neat vodka, a slice of lime hanging from the rim like a body slung on a battlement. It wasn't the wisest response to traumatic event, but they weren't saints. Not even Lamb had ever accused them of that, thought Lech, paying for the drinks, looking across the bar, seeing Catherine raising a gin and tonic to her lips.

Ah shit, he thought, and for no special reason checked his watch. It was 7:25.

Thirty-seven.

Just another number.

And if there was one thing Roddy Ho knew *loads* of, it was numbers.

Most of them were putty in his hands. He wasn't one to brag – what you'd get if you Google-Imaged 'the Rodmeister' would be a cross between Steve Rogers and Peter Parker; your boyish, modest, less swaggering superhero – but facts and stats: he could make numbers turn cartwheels, line up in pairs, then lie down and spread their legs. It was one of the less trumpeted aspects of being a king of the keyboard. You didn't hack the unhackable, you didn't soar unsinged over mile-high firewalls like a flame-retardant acrobat, if you couldn't do the maths. So Roddy could juggle three sets of numbers at once; he could pull up square roots with his bare hands, and do long division in his head – well, on his phone anyway, and he was as likely to go round without his phone as he was his head. He could, in a nutshell, add up. The other slow horses, throw a bunch of numbers at them, they'd all be at sixes and sevens. Roddy would catch them, crunch them, and toss them back neatly packaged; a sudoku master, a numerate ninja, forever in his prime.

So what the fuck was going on here, that's what he wanted to know.

The deal was, there were thirty-seven CCTV cameras in the area he'd been tasked with rendering blind. Thirty-five of them were his for the taking – he was three keystrokes away from owning a sizeable chunk of Notting Hill. It was all so super-cool, it wasn't even funny; Roddy might not have the whole world in his hands, but he could pull the plug on a major chunk of real estate while ordering a pizza. Yippee-ki-yay, dumbchuckers. Except two of them – count them: two – two of them remained impervious to his charms. If numbers could be lesbians, he'd just met some.

Closed systems, that was the issue. These cameras, hanging over retail premises and focused on their own pavement aprons, weren't part of larger networks – he only knew they were there because they showed up on other feeds. And chances were they posed no threat, unless you were actually waltzing past on foot, gurning up at the lenses. But Lamb wanted total blackout, which two stray cameras meant this wasn't. Two stray cameras meant that whatever happened might show up on a screen somewhere, and that could be bad news. And if there was one kind of news Roddy knew Lamb didn't like, it was the bad kind.

Roddy checked his watch. It was 7:30.

He could keep banging away at this gate for another half hour, but it wouldn't make a difference – when the hummingbird knows it knows, and dude? The hummingbird knows.

Shut them down by eight. You can do that?

Yeah, he can do that . . .

He had driven west for this final assault, as if being nearer would make a difference, and was parked on a meter off Ladbroke Grove, studying his laptop in the driving seat of his faithful steed, the Rodster roadster; a Ford Kia, that rare beauty. Light was starting to die, and the street music entering its evening phase, its pulse quickening, reaching that sweet spot where it matches the beating of a human heart. On the pavements, Londoners swept past – tourists too – arm in arm or hand in hand, while Roddy sat alone. But that was okay. The kind of cat he was was the kind that walks by itself. And knows where it has to walk, and what it has to do once it's walked there.

Roddy folded his laptop, tucked it under his seat. Sometimes, when something needs doing, it needs doing by hand. Sometimes – hot girl summer or not – you do it by yourself. You didn't have to tell him this.

Dude, the hummingbird knows.

Rows of spirits behind the bar, hanging upside down like it was their natural position. It reminded Avril of – no, she didn't want to think about that. But she thought about it anyway: it reminded Avril of a body she'd seen once, hanging upside down from a pylon. The means by which people were murdered, by which their fellow people murdered them, was a well that would never run dry. Did anyone else in this pub have memories like hers? Thankfully not. Probably.

CC had, but didn't now. CC's memories had been snuffed out when he breathed his last: that was how the world operated, else it would have more than bad air and melting ice caps to worry about. The atmosphere would be choked with unshriven sins and unforgotten nightmares, and half the population would be begging for extreme weather events to wash them away.

She paid for a Scotch, and went to sit at a corner table. A moment later she was joined by Sid Baker, bearing a similar drink.

Avril said, 'You're nowhere near as good at that as you think you are.'

'I scored high at shadowing, in my trainee year. But I've been shot in the head since then.'

'We've all got excuses. The trick is not to trot them out so readily. It gets tiresome.' She raised her glass. 'To CC.'

'CC.'

They drank, then Avril said, 'He had a foolish final act, but don't judge him by that. He was a good friend and he served the country well.'

'Was he shot in the head?'

Avril inclined her own, acknowledging Sid's point.

'Where are Al and Daisy?'

'I don't know.'

'Bullshit. You were a team. A unit. You had procedures and fallbacks and emergency protocols. Not just the ones the Park organised. You'd have had your own, because that's what joes do. They build their own defences because they don't trust anyone else. Not in the long run.'

'You know all about it.'

'I live with someone who does.'

Avril studied her. 'The young man you were with. David Cartwright's grandson?'

She nodded.

'Now there was a man who lived in the secret hours. Is the younger one the same?'

Sid said, 'I don't really think he knows quite how much. But yes.'

'Well, then. Good luck. You're going to need it.'

'Thanks. Do you know Jackson Lamb? He runs Slough House.'

'Can't say I do.'

'He's a bit of a legend.'

Avril said, 'There's never a shortage of legends in the Service. They should open a theme park.'

'Those two women last night were his joes.'

'And he's the vengeful type, is he?'

'Yes,' said Sid. She picked up her glass and sipped from it thoughtfully. 'I don't even think he cares that much about them, but . . . he cares about what they are. What they do. That they shouldn't go unavenged.'

'You mean, he cares more about what he thinks he should care about than whatever it is he should be caring about? Sounds about right for a legend.' She raised her gaze to the ceiling. There was nothing to see except the usual: the craquelure of ages, an unidentifiable stain or two, and, above the bar itself, a montage of postcards from regulars, or escapees. 'I should have just got on a train. Gone home.'

Sid said, 'It wasn't their fault. Al and Daisy. I already told you I think that.'

'And in the grand scheme of things, what does your opinion count?'

'Nothing. That's my point. Lamb won't see it that way, and the others, my friends — they're his joes. It's a stupid, rubbish department and they're supposed to be desk drones, but they're his joes and their friends are dead. Believe me, they'll come for Al and Daisy.'

'Good luck finding them.'

'They won't need luck. They're desk drones, but one of them — he's a dick, but he's kind of a genius, too. When it comes to computers, that is. Al or Daisy so much as pick up a payphone, he'll find a way of tracing them. And Lamb will not let them go.'

Avril found that her glass was empty. One was her limit, though. The Brains Trust had killed a bottle the other day, and she was still feeling that in her eyes, in her organs. The Brains Trust, of course, was no more. She said, 'And you want to stop that happening.'

'Of course I do.'

There's no 'of course' about it, she thought. Spies lie, spies betray. It's what they do. 'How?'

'They give themselves up. Go to the Park. Lamb can't do anything once that happens. He can only take his revenge if they're moving targets, where there's no one to protect them. If they go to the Park, they'll be safe.'

God help her, Avril thought, she means it. She thinks she can devise a happy ending out of this, or prevent a sadder one occurring. She'd been shot in the head; had survived the worst that could happen, so why couldn't everyone else? But whatever her bullet had taught her, it hadn't included that we don't get to choose how things turn out. We only get to play our parts in the story.

She said, 'How do I know you haven't been sent here to tell me just that? That this is what Taverner wants? Or even Lamb, come to that? Whoever he is.'

'You'll have to trust me.'

'God above! Are you serious?'

Sid said, 'The young man I was with, whatever plan Lamb comes up with, it'll involve him. And I do not want him involved. Is that enough of a reason for you?'

'You think you can keep him from harm? I mean, from doing it? If he's that way inclined, you're in for a sorry outcome.'

'I think I can keep him from being used. Or I hope I can.'

Avril said, 'Then you're both in the wrong line of business.' She shook her head, stood and buttoned her coat. 'I don't know where Al and Daisy are. And if I did, I'd warn them to stay hidden.'

'It'll end badly.'

'It'll end. You reach the point where the way it does is irrelevant.' She looked down on Sid, but just barely. 'A word of advice? You can keep your hands clean or you can stay out of the Service. You can't do both.'

'It's not my hands I'm worried about.'

Avril had nothing to say to that. She left the pub, bag in hand, and walked away into the evening.

Judd said, 'This might just be the least wise thing I've done in my life.'

'I wouldn't know about that,' said River. 'I mean, some of the stuff I've heard about—'

'Shut up.'

'Fuck off,' River told him. 'I'm driving the car. I'm not your lackey.'

Judd, staring at his reflection in the rear-view, said, 'You're certainly someone's. But does Lamb have lackeys? Or just fleas?'

'If it weren't for this flea showing up last night, you wouldn't be here now.'

'Yes. I could tell you're a smooth operator by how well your rescue attempt went.'

River tightened his grip on the wheel as a faint dizziness swept across him, a whisper of weakness. *Any physical tremors, spasms, uncontrollable shakes or shivers?* But he didn't have to worry about passing a medical: not any more he didn't. And he wasn't the only slow horse for whom that particular hurdle was no longer a concern.

Judd's eye was still on him, and his own gaze met it briefly. *You're the reason Ash took a bullet in the chest. The reason Louisa had her throat cut.* For half a moment, this threatened to engulf him. He could stop right here, drag Judd from the car and pound him to death on the pavement – this wouldn't merely be justifiable, it would be a public duty. A cracked nose, split lips, broken teeth . . . River clutched the wheel tighter. Louisa had been part of his life for what felt like forever, occupying that special ground where friendship stops a little short of love, and while he'd barely had the chance to get to know Ash, a bond had been waiting for them too. Maybe not a good one – maybe similar to the one he shared with Ho – but a bond nonetheless. *Slow horses.* Which wouldn't happen now, because of this man in the car with him. Rage would lend River energy; grief would hold his coat. Smearing Judd across half a postcode was a better plan than having Jackson broker peace . . . But somewhere underneath his anger, other, steadier voices offered counsel. Louisa wouldn't thank him. Ash: he had no clue. But Sid would rip him a new one. The road shimmered and a car horn sounded. *Come back, now.* He came back.

'Are you fit to drive?' Judd asked.

River didn't trust himself to answer.

Judd sat back, unaware of how close he'd come to a premature ending, but debating his wisdom nevertheless, getting into this car in the first place. It was Devon Welles who had called him, arranging the ride. Taverner, her bolt shot, had apparently offered to play nice.

'You want me to sit down with the woman who tried to have me killed?'

'I don't particularly want you to do anything,' Welles had said. 'But you don't have many options. You can sort the situation out. Or wait for her to try again.'

'"Sort the situation out." What are you, an agony uncle?'

'You're the one with the problem.'

He was sounding less and less like hired help, and in other circumstances Judd would have called him on it. Other circumstances, though, included those in which he hadn't recently been the object of an assassination attempt.

But he was a political animal to the bone. Never let them see your fear. He'd let it show the other night; luckily there'd been no one there, the fool at the wheel and his companions apart. Taverner, though, was a different prospect. Show her weakness and she'd stop snapping at your ankles and start tearing your throat instead. Other people's weaknesses were her weakness. In their presence, she could barely contain herself.

He'd said to Welles, 'I'll talk to her. But you come with me.'

Welles had hesitated. 'I can't.'

'Can't?'

'It's to be just the principals. You and Taverner. With Jackson Lamb as your referee.'

Lamb. Whom he had sent Seb to quieten, once, and had never seen Seb again.

Nor had anyone else.

'I don't like the sound of that.'

Welles said, 'Who would you prefer, the Lord Chancellor? You're holding a stick of dynamite you keep threatening to shove up First Desk's arse. She's fresh off blackmailing a former spook to put a bullet in your brain. It's not like there are legal niceties to be observed.'

'I'd prefer a neutral party to be there.'

'It's a backstreet deal. I'd have thought you were used to those.'

'Remind me whose side you're on?'

'There's an invoice in the post.'

He'd nearly ended the call. But Welles was right: he was used to backstreet deals. And even when he hadn't held the strongest hand at the table, he'd always acted like he had, which made the difference. Taverner's crude attempt on him had given him a sleepless, frightened night, but in the end it had been both those things: crude, and an attempt. Of them both, she had most to fear. Which meant that what he needed to do now was brush his hair, shine his shoes and wear his wickedest smile. This was politics; it was the art of the deal. You showed up with your game face on, or you packed your bags.

To River, now, he said, 'Where precisely are we going?'

'Notting Hill.'

'God. I should have brought the crossword.'

They were idling at a junction; judging by the traffic they'd be thirty minutes in the car yet, easy. The camera above the lights wasn't trained on them, not exactly, but it was watching nonetheless. River noted it without comment. Before they reached their destination, they'd have passed from the monitored world to the unmonitored, courtesy of Roderick Ho. Provided Ho had done his job, that is, though River wasn't too worried. He'd be the last man alive to offer praise to Roddy Ho, who was a prick.

But he was at least a prick who knew what he was doing.

★

What am I doing?

Dude, I am taking inventory.

(He checked his watch. It was 7:45.)

Taking inventory, because the Rodster needs his tools.

So: phone, wallet, keys: check. Laptop – obviously. (When did the Rodmeister go anywhere without his magic carpet? Be like Thor without his hammer, Captain A without his shield.) And then there was the stuff that lived in his car, because having a car was like having an extra cupboard, with wheels, and you never knew when lightning would strike, and you needed a wardrobe change. So there was freshish clothing, plus necessities – shaving gear, hair gel, toothpaste and brush – and let's not forget the old condoms, which were in fact pretty old condoms. He should check the use-by. But anyway, all of that close to hand, plus a certain amount of collateral wastage – pizza boxes, empty crisp packets, energy drink bottles awaiting recyclage, because the Rodster was all about the recyclage; show him a planet, he'd be first in line to save it.

All good so far, but lacking a certain something. Let's move on to the boot.

Blanket, because you never knew when a picnic might be called for, plus a few spare pairs of trainers, because you need the right footwear for the mood. Carrier bag with some other carrier bags tucked inside it, in case he ever needed a carrier bag. 7:46. An old raincoat he wasn't sure where it had come from, and a framed photograph of Scarlett Johansson he'd bought at a street market: forgotten that was there, he should really hang it up. That stuff the Highway Code says you should have, including a hazard triangle and a high-vis jacket.

Spare tyre.

Jack for changing tyre with.

Bingo.

Hustling his manly frame into the jacket, snatching up the wheel jack, Roddy left the HoMobile and took to the streets.

Catherine said, 'Don't be ridiculous.'

'It was a reasonable—'

'Have you any idea what it's like? Day after day? Resisting the temptation?'

'Well, some—'

'Because if I ever slip, it won't be in a pub on Whitecross Street. I'll – I'll fly to the Caribbean. I'll sit on a beach and watch the sun sink into the sea. Drinking something with an umbrella in it.'

Which she wouldn't. If she ever fell, she would splash into a local puddle, drinking whatever was nearest. And then whatever was nearest to that.

But Lech said, 'Catherine, if you ever fly to the Caribbean to fall off the wagon I'll come with you.'

'That won't be necessary.'

Shirley said, 'Yeah, well, I won't.'

'No one asked you to.'

'Too fucking expensive.'

Lech said, 'Were you looking for us?'

She sipped her tonic water: ice and lemon? Please. 'Yes. I thought the nearest pub was a good starting point.'

Though she couldn't deny, it might have been an equally promising finish line. Ice and lemon, please, and a shot of gin to give it heft. There were days and days and days when she never thought of taking a drink. And there were other days when people died, and you were left to carry the weight of that: it would help to be floating when you shouldered it. It would ease the burden.

This is my fault.

Her fault because it was always her fault, whatever *it* was on any given occasion. But her fault, too, because it was actually her fault; her fault for having encouraged the debacle at the nightclub, or at any rate, not having discouraged it. Had she made an objection, enthusiasm would have dwindled, Lech or Shirley or *someone* pointing out that shielding Peter Judd from possible harm was not just outside their remit, it was antithetical to the common good. They could all have been sitting here now – Louisa and Ash too – drinking in the news of Judd's death. And how would Catherine have felt about that? Causing – not hindering – being complicit in – the death of a notorious public figure, versus having Louisa and Ash on either side, warm and breathing? Maybe that would pass for a conundrum to a moral philosopher. To Catherine, it was no choice at all.

But here's a harder question, the alcoholic asked herself. Given the choice, who would you rather had lived; Louisa, whom you've known for years, or Ash, with her whole life ahead of her? Whose mother would you rather write the letter to? The incomplete letter, sitting on her desk at Slough House?

It was not true that she had no answer to this. But it was true that the answer tasted like poison, and when she raised her glass to her mouth, her dull tonic water burned her lip.

Shirley was talking to her. 'Does Lamb want us? Is that why you're here?'

Said with a flicker of hope.

Catherine said, 'No. He doesn't. And let's keep it that way.'

Lech and Shirley exchanged a look. 'What?'

'I know what you're like. What you've always been like, all of you. You're going to be looking for a way to join in.'

'And?' said Shirley.

'And don't. That's all. I don't know what Lamb's got in mind, but whatever it is, you need to keep well clear.'

'He told us what he was doing,' Lech said. 'He's calling a truce.'

'He said he was going to burn her . . . flipping house down. Does that sound like a truce to you?'

'It's a start,' said Shirley.

'One that ends with the neighbourhood in flames.'

'We're here, we're having a drink, we're surplus already,' Lech said. 'We don't need you telling us to keep our heads down.'

'You know where he was before he arrived at the . . . hanging gardens?'

'Lamb? No.'

'He went to see Devon Welles.'

'We met him,' said Shirley.

'He used to be a Dog,' said Lech.

'More than that. He used to be the Dog in charge of Taverner's home security.'

'Ah,' said Lech. 'You think he's actually going to burn down her house?'

'He can barely light a cigarette without someone finding him a lighter,' said Shirley.

'Yes, but that's the thing about Lamb,' said Catherine. 'When he wants a thing done, he can always get someone to do it for him.'

'Which in this case is River and Roddy,' said Lech.

'Yeah,' said Shirley. 'What could go wrong?'

Here's a funny thing: if you put on a high-vis jacket, you became invisible. It was one of those what-d'ye-call-'ems: a parasite, paraglide, para*dox*. Roddy, who had funny bones, could have got a whole set out of this if he had a mind to – he'd watched enough Netflix specials to know how it was done – but right now he had other eggs to fry: two cameras to render inoperative, and it was fast creeping up on eight o'clock. Notting Hill was aflurry with pedestrian life, plus the usual amount of traffic; everywhere you looked there were people in motion, and not one of them paying attention to a neon-jacketed bod hefting a tyre jack, because those very details made him look like a working man, someone on his way to attend to something; one of the unsung heroes of the city, whose daily grind kept London's wheels turning. A closer look would have dispelled that impression, sure – this was Roddy Ho, not some semi-schooled muppet who couldn't get a proper job – but to anyone with their mind on other things, a man in a high-vis jacket, even a *Roddy Ho* in a high-vis jacket, was perinatal, perineal, per*iph*eral to events. Roddy could climb a lamp post unseen, he could smash-and-grab a jeweller's unnoticed, let alone take out a camera. He was the invisible man, without the bandages. He'd even dispensed with the one protecting his tattoo: the hummingbird was ready to fly.

'Are the Village People a thing again?' someone asked in passing.

Roddy checked his watch: 7:55.

The first camera was fixed to the top of a gatepost, there to monitor tradesmen, religious nuts and charity bandits entering the apartment block it belonged to, but which would inevitably catch passing vehicles. Maybe seven feet off the ground, which would have worried lesser mortals, but Roddy was on a mission, and this didn't look any harder than your average slam dunk – he'd never actually played basketball, but college kids played it in the States, so how hard could it be?

His breathing was a trial, though. His heart was beating fast.

He stopped on the pavement, knelt and laid the jack aside while he fiddled with a shoelace, or that's what it would look like to the civilian suckers. Obviously his laces didn't need tying: where are we, dude, 2009? But he needed a moment. The thing about Roddy Ho – one of the things: he was a man of many facets – but one of the things about Roddy, he moved among people who didn't see below the surface. To the slow horses, he was the RodMan, the Rodinator; give him a task, it was good as done. His presence was like money in the bank;

anything they needed, he could provide. King of the keyboard, prince of the city, boss of the boulevards. But in reality, man, he had his moments. He was tender like that. He had a vulnerable side. All confidence on the outside, because he'd never failed yet, but that didn't mean he was arrogant . . . They talked about imposter syndrome, and fact was, Roddy had that in spades – constantly aware there were others out there who'd love to take his place: to walk in his shoes and wear his shades. And that could get you down, brother. Sister, that could wear you out.

Good job he was invisible right now, because if these folk round here could see him, it would break their ordinary hearts.

But the hummingbird knows. And this particular hummingbird knew it had a job to do: for Louisa, for Ash, for all Roddy's fallen. Smash the camera, blind the streets, and let Lamb's plan unfold. What are we waiting for? We are waiting for . . . now.

He grabbed the jack and leaped into the air from a crouching start. Sheer poetry. Didn't quite rhyme, though, in the sense that while his swing of the jack did cause damage, breaking a chunk of sandstone from the gatepost, it didn't make contact with the camera, which remained intact and watchful, its little red eye undimmed. Roddy hit the ground splay-legged, and couldn't prevent an oath escaping as pain shot through both ankles:

'Skywalker on a bike!'

And here's another funny thing: the invisibility that a high-vis jacket bestows only goes so far.

The car had picked up pace, and they were moving at what passed for speed in central London. Judd was mostly watching River Cartwright's reflection, and it was giving little away. But Welles's words were fresh in mind: *Sort the situation out. Or wait for her to try again.* The last thing he needed was to spend the rest of forever looking over his shoulder, so Welles had a point:

he needed to sort this out. So he'd sit here and let Cartwright deliver him to Taverner's place, where he'd enumerate the advantages of the status quo, and while doing that he'd decide whether or not to throw her to the wolves. If she was all regrets and misunderstandings, he'd know she was plotting a second move; if she was icy calm and unapologetic, he'd know she'd altered course. Either way, he'd kick things off with a warning. In olden days, when life crawled by in black and white, he'd have lodged a letter with his solicitor, to be opened in the event of his death; less histrionically, in the here and now, an email detailed enough to fuck Diana over would be dispatched to various parties at 10 p.m., if he didn't cancel it first. That should fetch a little focus.

Meanwhile, it was important to remember that he was Peter fucking Judd, and last night had been an anomaly. The things that happened around him that he wasn't in charge of were things like who was getting coffee, and where was the nearest dry-cleaner's. Stuff the little folk dealt with. So a not insignificant item on today's agenda would be an assurance that when the official history of last night's misadventure was written, sealed in a box-file and buried in a cabinet deep in the bowels of the Park, it would reflect the courage he'd shown under fire. It was important to curate such records sensitively – if he'd wanted history to be an accurate depiction of events, particularly those he was involved in, he wouldn't have led a life in politics. He'd have been, I don't know, a fucking teacher or something.

On the pavements now were unmistakable signs of recent disturbance: people shaking heads, bewildered, laughing. Some damage had been done to a gatepost. A policeman was talking to a group of those selfsame little folk whose career path it was to either smooth Judd's way in life or applaud him from a distance, and then they turned the corner and it was all forgotten. Cartwright said something indistinct, but he was talking to his satnav, and then he was pulling to a halt. Judd had only been here once before – some half-remembered social event; Diana hosted them about as often as pandas mated – but he recognised it well enough: the door an anonymous black, the frontage severe.

He said, 'I just go in, do I?'

'Door's open,' Cartwright said.

He could see that from where he was sitting: a sliver of liminal light around its frame.

Judd undid his seat belt. 'If you're expecting a tip—'

'Don't take sweeties from strangers?' River suggested.

'There's a boy.'

He got out, slipped between two parked cars and stepped onto the pavement. Before he'd got that far, Cartwright was moving on.

The door swung open at his touch, though it felt heavy – reinforced, he guessed. There'd be metal sheeting under the wood. Inside, on the wall to the left, was an alarm panel; a keypad with an LED screen above. It was dead, by the look of it; an inert, lightless box. He closed the door behind him, and crossed to what he remembered was the sitting room, whose own door was open, light spilling from it across the hallway floor. It was a comfortable, spacious room of contrasting gold and red tones, one half dominated by an L-shaped sofa; the other half by Jackson Lamb, slouching in an armchair like King Frog.

Who acknowledged Judd's arrival by uncrossing then recrossing his legs.

'Took your bloody time,' he said.

And that would be good riddance, thought River.

He waited at the next junction and rang Sid, but she didn't pick up. He hoped this meant she was in a dead zone, not that their relationship was. She hadn't been happy when he'd told her he'd been summoned by Lamb, telling him *You're not a slow horse any more*, though she didn't believe that any more than he did.

Face it. He was a slow horse. An increasingly rare breed.

His vision swam, and he had to blink it clear.

Then he called Lech, and could tell from the background noise he was in a pub.

'Yeah, and?'

'And nothing. Just, I've delivered Judd.'

'Great.' Lech sounded flat. 'You were given something to do, you did it. The rest of us applaud you.'

There was a moment's pause while he drained whatever he was drinking.

'Roddy there?'

There was another moment's pause while Lech digested this. 'You want *Roddy*?'

'Yeah, well, no, but—'

'I've got Shirley, I've even got Catherine. Shirley's talking to a girl at the bar, we haven't been introduced yet, but you could talk to her too if you like. But *Roddy*—'

'Jesus, I just want to know he did what he was supposed to do, and I'm not starring in thirty-nine CCTV shows.'

'Thirty-seven.'

'Whatever.'

'Yeah, and why did Lamb want the cameras killed, you given thought to that? Could it be his diplomatic mission wasn't as—'

'So you haven't spoken to Roddy and you don't know whether he did his bit.'

'He said he did.'

'Roddy says a lot of things,' said River, ending the call.

He felt vulnerable of a sudden, here in Notting Hill, along the road from Taverner's house. Killing the local cameras was a mind game; a way of keeping Lamb's three-way summit off the books. Except, of course, it might be more than that. He might have been more than a delivery boy just now.

'I fucking knew that already,' he said out loud. 'Of course I fucking did.'

He'd call the hospital, he thought. Make sure he hadn't missed any news. But even as he had the thought, his phone rang: good, he thought. Sid. But it wasn't.

'It's me, it's Roddy.'

'Yeah, did you—'

'Help me.'

Apparently, when the door is opened on a long-haul flight, anyone standing outside waiting to greet a passenger gets two tons of fart in their face – several hundred people's worth of body odour, bad breath and bellyaches. And if you're a greeter, you have to keep smiling. It's reckoned you need to do this at least twelve times. The first eleven, you're less a greeter than aghast; someone who's just answered the door to their worst nightmare.

Judd thought of making this his opening pleasantry, but decided the subtlety would be lost on Lamb, who didn't attempt to lever himself upright. He did, though, say, 'I'd offer you a drink, but all I can find is white wine.'

'Where is she?' Judd said.

'At the Park. She didn't let you know?' Raising his eyes to a pitiless heaven, Lamb shook his head at God's ill-mannered creation. 'I'd have thought she'd have had someone pick up the phone,' he said, in a grieving tone, 'but you know Diana. She goes through PAs like a centre forward through a hen party. But she's stuck at work. So it's just us.'

Judd said, 'No, I don't think so.' He looked around, decided on the sofa, lowered himself onto it and leaned back, stretching his legs.

Lamb, waiting, adopted an interested expression.

He'd made himself at home, but hadn't removed his coat or shoes, both of which looked like distant early warning signs of requests for small change. The only light he'd turned on – unless it had been switched on already – was the standard lamp by the side of his chair, and he was swamped in the glow it shed, like an illustration from a storybook. The kind which had NOT SUITABLE FOR CHILDREN stickered on its cover.

Judd said, 'There's an alarm pad by the door looking as dead as the PM's voter approval rating. It's been deactivated. She doesn't know you're here, does she?'

'I'd forgotten that about you,' said Lamb, amiably. 'Everyone always goes on about what a corrupt fat lying prick you are. They never mention you can be quite sharp when the mood takes you.'

'I suppose that puts us on a level footing. Though I'm impressed by your security bypass. I'd have thought the house codes were changed daily.'

'Weekly,' said Lamb. He shrugged. 'Or whatever. Not actually sure.'

'But you know a man who is.'

Lamb rummaged for something in his coat pocket, but only a cigarette. 'Don't worry, I'm not gunna light it. Wouldn't want to sully the delicate air.'

'I think that ship's sailed.'

The cigarette went behind Lamb's ear. 'There's a kill code,' he said, 'which can be triggered remotely. It shuts off the alarms and opens the locks. In case of a sausage situation arising.'

'A . . . what?'

'Did I say sausage? I meant hostage,' said Lamb. 'Common error.'

'And that's not changed weekly,' Judd guessed.

'No, that one remains constant.'

'And Devon Welles used to be Taverner's home security expert. Well well well.' His gaze flickered round the room, then returned to Lamb. 'There's a contract I'll be looking at quite closely. Before I sue someone's fucking arse off.'

'Oh, don't be too hard on him. I might have suggested you had no business being on his Christmas list. I mean, even less than for the obvious reasons.'

'What are you on about?'

'That the fat corrupt lying prick bit's public knowledge.' Lamb's fingers strayed to his ear. 'But I told him you were paying the tab of those mercenary fuckers who murdered Emma Flyte.'

Judd stiffened. 'You *what*?'

'I told him—'

'That business in Wales? Bloody cheek! I was the one let Diana know there was a team of hostiles on the loose! I wasn't the one who loosed them.'

'Speaking for myself, I was raised to find it rude to interrupt. But I appreciate that you public schoolboys have your own code of behaviour, like wearing red trousers, and fucking the country up. But yes, to address your complaint, I was lying. Like you just said, that puts us on a level footing. Lucky me.' He reached into his other pocket and this time produced a quarter bottle of Scotch. He unscrewed the top. 'I'd offer you a drink,' he said again. 'But, you know.' He shrugged, and took a swallow.

'So you blackened my name to gain access here—'

'To be fair, blackening your name's not as easy as you make it sound. Given the bar you've set.'

'Now who's interrupting? You blackened my name to gain access, and for what? What kind of . . . *summit* is this supposed to be? Diana's not even here.'

'No, she's observing an op – a gun sale. Well, I say sale. I doubt they're offering discounts.'

'You have a pair of eyes inside the Park?'

Lamb nodded. 'A pair of legs, not so much. But you take what you can get.'

He rescrewed the top on his bottle, and slid it back into his pocket.

Judd said, 'I'm leaving now.'

'Yeah, that would be disappointing. You're supposed to be the saveloy one when it comes to dealmaking.'

'. . . Saveloy? Are we back on the sausage thing?'

'Savvy. Where's Standish when I need her? Why we're doing this without Taverner is, she's who we're here to discuss. You because she tried to knock you off your perch last night. And me, well. Trust me. I have reasons.'

'Trust you? Now there's a big ask.'

'Oh, come on. You know what they say, a friend's just an enemy you haven't pissed off yet.'

'I somehow doubt we're going to be friends, Lamb. And even if we were, you wouldn't be the kind I'd trust.' He stood. 'I'll find some other way to smooth things out with Diana. Letting her know about Welles's little side hustle'll make a good start.'

'Yeah, that kill switch. I should have mentioned, one of the other things hitting it does is, it opens her safe.' Lamb made a clicking noise with his tongue, and mimed a door swinging open. 'I mean, I wasn't there when it happened, but it must have been something like that.'

'I'm not seeing a safe anywhere.'

'Upstairs.'

'And you've robbed her?'

'Now, there you're judging me by your standards. No, I haven't robbed her. Maybe borrowed something, but don't worry. I'll put it back.'

'What are you talking about?'

Again, Lamb's hand dipped into his overcoat pocket, and this time when he withdrew it, it was holding a gun.

'I know what you're thinking,' he said. 'Is it cake?'

He'd lost the tyre jack.

Actually, when you went granular on his current position –

lost, scared, hunted, bruised – might have weed himself a bit – that wasn't the worst that had happened, but still, losing the tyre jack, that was insult to injury. They didn't grow on trees.

Sometimes, it didn't matter who you were, but *sometimes*, it was all you could do not to kick your feet, punch the air and scream blue nasties loud as you could.

Fucking civilians.

Who had outnumbered him by, like, infinity to one.

When he'd hit the pavement – superhero landing, whatever you might have heard to the contrary – when he'd hit the pavement and was amping up for another leap, the first one having calibrated the precise angle of the swing he'd have to make to disconnect the camera from its working life, Roddy had known he'd made an impact. People would be swivelling on their rods to check him out. Invisible one mo; the next, revealed in all his ripped glory. They'd be thinking Batman! Deadpool! Who *was* this tabarded crusader?

'Dick,' someone said.

'Did he just – ?'

'He was trying to smash that camera, man!'

'Is he a fucking terrorist or what?'

Yeah, no, what, thought Roddy. Terrorist? *Me*?

He stood, and nearly folded. His ankles *hurt*, dude.

All around him, life had come to a halt.

What had been groups of people heading in various directions became one amorphous crowd, every element of which wanted to know what Roddy was up to. It was like that giant squid covering half the Pacific floor: it had been lots of different squids, but it just kind of . . . melded. Don't ask him how: he read the internet, man, he didn't write it. But meanwhile here he was, and the crowd was melding, and the crowd was getting angry.

'Did you just break that gatepost?'

'Is anyone calling the cops? Because I will.'

'Look,' said Roddy, Mr Reasonable: good job he was C-O-O-L-cool, and instantly likeable. Because otherwise he might be in trouble. 'Look. This is no big deal, ya feel me? If you all just back away a bit' – because they were starting to crowd him; the crowd was beginning to crowd – 'and let me finish up here, then we're all good.'

'Yeah, I've called the cops,' someone said.

'Okay, so maybe I'll just head off, then.'

'You're going nowhere, mate.'

Roddy was grabbed by the arm.

He was hampered by his personal ethics. Basically, he was a lethal weapon – trained, honed, buffed and polished – and couldn't just, like, squeeze his own trigger in a civilian situation. Someone would get hurt, and the Ho Code didn't allow for that. The Ho Code stated: Christ, he couldn't remember. This guy had an armlock on him; this was no time for pissing around with the small print. Someone else was poking him in the chest. *Where are you from?* he was being asked. *You speak English?* The Code, though. The Ho Code. There was one important element of it had just swum back into mind and it was this: the Code didn't mention a tyre jack.

He thrust it upwards into the chin of the man with the lock on his arm, and the lock broke.

The crowd folded backwards, Roddy lunged forwards, the tyre jack was gone, and adrenalin, it turned out, was good for the ankles: he felt no pain as he ran through his gears and hit sprint mode, breaking free of the mob. Which, like any mob, didn't know how to respond to this, and fed off itself while its chief driver, the one who locked arms, roared in pain and thrashed about. This was outside Roddy's ken, though, because Roddy was all about what was in front of him, not what was behind. There was a corner, and Roddy took it. No shops here: a residential street. Slight incline. He flew up it and reached another corner. He had a car, but fuck knew where it was; he barely knew where his own feet were. He could hear voices still – shouting – baying – but no footsteps, because this was something else mobs did: they remained in place, expressing their anger, looked for whatever was nearest to vent it on.

Another corner, and he took it, realising too late that this was taking him back towards the main drag. He looked behind, and tripped over something – two somethings – his feet – and banged his pretty face on the pavement. He lay panting, expecting hands upon him any moment – to be hauled upright and strung from a street light – but none came. There were lights spinning overhead, and when he blinked they spun the other way, and he recognised them as his own Roddylights. He was Roddyspinning, bright bursts of Roddycolour lighting up the sky, as if Roddyworks were being set off. A car went past as he hauled himself upright, and it slowed, or else his perception altered as it reached him, but it kept moving. So did he. This time, back the way he'd come. There were people, but on the other side of the road, and they didn't appear to care who Roddy was. He put a hand to his head, and it came away wet. Where was he? There were parked cars, and between two of them was enough of a gap that he could lower himself to a crouch and Roddy himself invisible. Just for a while. Just until he was breathing normally, and the hummingbird could fly.

From his pocket he pulled out his phone. Rang the first contact he thought of.

'It's me, it's Roddy,' he said. 'Help me.'

Then he closed his eyes.

Judd said, 'You're not about to shoot me.'

'I get that a lot,' said Lamb. 'People telling me what I'm not about to do. But then, if the people around me knew what they were talking about, they'd have been assigned to a different department. See what I'm saying?'

'I came here in good faith, expecting a reasoned, adult discussion. Now you're waving a gun about. This is insane.'

'I'd have thought you were used to it by now. Guns being waved about, I mean. Or has last night slipped your mind? It hasn't mine. On account of one of my joes being shot, and another being stabbed.'

'That had nothing to do with me!'

'Well, we're going to have to agree you're wrong about that. By the way, sit down? If I do use this, I'd sooner you were stationary.' He waggled the gun. 'I'm not the world's greatest marksman. I could go for a warning shot and end up having your eye out. I'd look a right tit then, wouldn't I?'

Judd stared, but Lamb's expression gave nothing away. The gun might have been cake, come to that. Taverner might be behind the curtain, about to jump out and sing 'Happy Birthday'.

He sank onto the sofa again.

Lamb said, 'Entertain me. You funded Taverner's jolly last year, didn't you? When she went off-book, and had a Moscow hood whacked for committing murder on home soil.'

'I couldn't comment on that.'

'Wasn't looking for a comment so much as a straightforward yes or no.'

'No.'

'Yeah, wrong answer. We both know you did. And it was Chinese money you slipped her, though she didn't know that at the time.'

'Money doesn't actually have a—'

'And you've been holding that over her head ever since, like the sword of Dominic Cummings.'

'I think you mean Damocles.'

'Any two-faced creep with the ethics of a syphilitic stoat will do.' The gun swapped hands. With his right, Lamb caressed the cigarette behind his ear. 'So, she's spent the last year being backed into a corner, with you passing on, what'll we call them, suggestions? Nah, instructions. With you passing on instructions from your Beijing paymasters as to which direction she should be steering the Park. Which, long story short, is why she tried to have you cancelled last night. In fact, if she hadn't relied on a *Dad's Army* dropout with a spark plug where his brain used to be, you wouldn't be here now. Any thoughts?'

'Well, you're a little unfair on Damocles.'

'Probably. I never had the classical education you've based your public persona on.'

'I think I can safely say it would have been wasted on you.' Judd leaned back, and spread his arms out. It would be an overstatement to say he was starting to relax, but he didn't feel the fear he'd felt last night, when it had been Charles Stamoran waving a gun around. This was different – Lamb was a tricky bastard, but one who'd been around long enough that Judd knew he could deal with him. Because if Lamb wasn't in the market for deals, he'd not have survived as long as he had. 'Thoughts, though. Yes. I have a few. But before we get to those, I have to ask. Are you recording this?'

'Re*cord*ing it?'

'Hoping for a confession.'

'I look like a priest? I need a word with my tailor.'

'If I thought for one moment you actually had one, I'd want a word with him myself. I've never made a citizen's arrest. So.' Judd crossed his legs. 'Not a confession, then. I didn't really think so.' He smiled: it looked quite genuine. 'No, I know what you're after.'

'Oh, this'll be good,' said Lamb. 'Tell me what I'm after.'

'Same thing anyone in your position is.'

'One of those chairs you can lean back in till it's nearly horizontal?'

'Recognition.'

'Ah, right. Recognition. Thing is, you've forgotten what it is I do. I'm a spy, Judd. Recognition, it's not the ideal result in my line of work. More of a drawback, if you want to get technical.'

'We both know that's not what I meant.' And here it came, the comfort zone. This was where he lived; he had something to sell and someone to sell it to. 'Recognition can make itself felt in a more practical manner.'

He waited. Truth be told, Judd could barely remember a conversation that hadn't ended the way he wanted it to. People called politics the art of the compromise, but only people who had no fucking clue. Politics was the art of trampling opposition into the dust and convincing them they liked it there. It wasn't that different from sport or sex. Not that he had much time for sport.

Lamb, stroking the cigarette behind his ear as if it were a pet mouse, said, 'What, the way a happy ending can be really specific, in the right sort of massage parlour?'

'Close enough. Let's not say recognition, let's say compensation. Compensation for your long slide out of the mainstream.'

'Not sure the mainstream was ever my paddling pool. But keep talking. That's clearly what you're happiest doing.'

And that was the moment, right there; like the one where the floating voter admits he saw you on a panel show, or the girl tells you she never does that. It was the moment where you knew the deal was done, and you were just haggling over the fine detail.

'Well, I'm not just saying this to get on your good side, but spy or not, I've heard a lot about you down the years. Mostly from Diana. And clearly you've led a useful life and done the Service proud. They'll be telling tales about you long after you're taking up space at St Len's, and you might not be a hero in all of them, but you'll be the one commanding the attention. The one who uses up the oxygen in the room. And I admire that. You know why?' He leaned forward ever so slightly. A lot of what's said is unspoken. You telegraph your meaning with your movement. 'Because there can only be one of them in any given space. See what I mean?'

Lamb said, 'Don't worry. If you go too fast for me, I'll think of some way of slowing you down.'

Judd said, 'Quite. But being a legend's not the same as being the hero, you know? And in the usual stories, it's the hero gets the spoils. What spoils are you enjoying, Lamb, at this stage in your career? Way past your glory days, and still riding a desk on Aldersgate Street? While Diana – well. Take a look around. This furniture didn't come from a fire sale. This postcode, you don't get to live here on the gig economy. No, Diana's like me. She enjoys rewards commensurate, not to her achievements but to her expectations. Because she and I, we're insiders. Always have been. Brought up to it, dined out on it, slept in all of its bedrooms. While you, put simply – are not.'

'Careful. You're in danger of making me feel inadequate.'

'Not inadequate. You're more than up to your role. Because you're one of the engine room lot. You know how it works, and you can make it go, but you don't get to decide the direction of travel because that's not how things are done. The big decisions are made up in the wheelhouse. The only time you get up there is when you're invited. When you're being given a bollocking or maybe an employee-of-the-month plaque. Then they kick you up the arse or pat you on the head, but either way, they send you back to your oily rag.'

'I have to say, you're making me view my career in a whole different light,' said Lamb. 'It's like the snails are dropping from my eyes.'

'. . . Scales?'

'Whichever it is leaves trails of slime. You have much contact with those of us who work below decks?'

'On and off. You met my man Sebastian, didn't you?'

'Briefly.'

'You'd have found common ground if you'd taken the time

to get to know him. But that's hardly relevant now. No, the truth is, like everyone else, I'm more comfortable among my own kind, but that doesn't mean I don't pay attention to what goes on below. Don't get me wrong, I can't do anything to change the way things are. That's not why I went into politics, to make changes for the better for people like you. I went into politics to make sure things stay the same for people like me. But sometimes, in order to keep everything upright, accommodations are made. Which is what we're working towards here.'

'We're working?' said Lamb. 'Because I'm pretty sure I'm off the clock. Apart from anything else, I had a drink five minutes ago. I'm not a slave to the rule book or anything, but drinking during working hours, that's my personal line in the sand.'

'We're working our way towards a positive outcome,' Judd said smoothly. 'One that suits both of us. It's quite simply this. You don't have to be a slave to your pension arrangements. Whatever ceiling you've been looking at, we can raise it. I have contacts who can make that happen. Like you, they're not slaves to the rule book, and they can be very imaginative when it comes to loopholes and tax breaks.' A smile twerked his lips, as if those words conjured up some effective pornography. 'Goodbye Slough House, hello – where? Somewhere sunny? Nice Greek island, with pretty girls – or boys, no judgement – sunning themselves on your balcony? Or would you prefer to head back to Berlin? I'm sure it has corners you'd still feel at home in. And you don't need me to tell you, that city's a cash-in-hand playground.'

Lamb said, 'Well, that's me sorted. What have you got in mind for Diana?'

'Nothing. She took her shot, it didn't work, and she's smart enough to cut her losses. There's a thing about doing the same thing over and over, expecting different results? It's the definition of madness, apparently. Or democracy.' He laughed. 'Diana can keep right on doing what she does, and that'll please people on my side of the fence. It's not like they'll be using her to subvert our sovereignty, if that worries you. Just a little nudge here, a little squeeze there, adjusting our position where necessary. Nothing to threaten the security of the nation. Strengthening our position, in fact. As the great world turns, and the power balance slips eastward, it'll be no small thing to enjoy favoured nation status. That's not going to be a position enjoyed by many. Don't you think?'

'I wouldn't know,' said Lamb. 'Most of the positions I've enjoyed are the normal ones. But aren't you jumping the gun? Pardon the expression.' They both glanced towards what he was holding. 'Diana's hardly top dolly with the new kids on the block. She'll be lucky to last the month, the way she's going.'

'You're assuming the PM's in charge of anything. But all he's managed so far is to piss away the honeymoon. Diana will run so many rings round him, he'll feel like a racetrack. She'll still be First Desk when he's wondering where his majority went, and how come no one gives him free stuff any more. So. Handshake moment. Diana stays in place, which is where my, ah, my *backers* want her to be, we sort out something a little more comfortable for you, and then, well, life goes on. Yes?'

Lamb placed the gun in his lap, scratched his nose, then transferred his cigarette from his ear to his lips, where he sucked on it unlit for a second before removing it and tucking it back where it started. He thought for a moment, and said, 'Not for my joes.'

'I'm sorry?'

'Not for my joes, it doesn't.' Picking up the gun, Lamb shot Judd once, through the chest. Then he produced a surprisingly clean cloth from an inside pocket and wiped the gun with it as he went upstairs. The safe, which was in a wardrobe in the spare bedroom, sat with its door wide open. He put the gun inside, shut the door with his elbow, stuffed the cloth in his pocket, then left the house without touching much.

Before reaching the Underground he passed several traffic cameras, their little red lights – their evil eyes – all grey and shuttered.

He had to wait ten minutes for a tube, but other than that, his journey was a smooth one.

At the other end, he dropped the cloth in the first litter bin he passed.

When River found Roddy, tracing the pin Roddy had dropped, he was crouched between two cars, clutching his phone. Either no one had come across him or no one had cared. River, double-parked, said his name twice through the open window, but Roddy didn't respond. There was nothing for it but to get out and kneel. 'Roddy? It's okay. It's me. River.'

Roddy stared blankly, then nodded.

'Are you okay? There's blood on your face.'

'Fell over.'

'Can you stand?'

Roddy shook his head.

'Well, you're going to have to. Come on.'

A car pulled up behind River's, and sounded its horn.

'Yeah, all right, mate. Bit of an emergency here.'

'Put the fucking drunk in a bag and shift him.'

River rose, walked to the driver's window and bent down. 'He's having a bad day. If you want one too, keep talking.'

The driver wound his window up.

River returned to Roddy and helped him to his feet.

Roddy, shivering, said, 'I was fine. Just laying low for a bit.'

'I know.'

'Thirty-five,' he said. 'I got thirty-five of them.'

'Cameras?'

'Yeah.'

'Good,' said River.

Roddy climbed into the passenger seat, and River walked round, got behind the wheel and set the car in motion.

'Where we going?'

'Pub. Whitecross Street. It's where the others are. Okay?'

Roddy nodded.

They drove for a while, and were crossing Holborn Viaduct before Roddy spoke again. He said, 'We keep getting killed.'

River opened his mouth to reply, then closed it again. They paused at the lights near the old Post Office buildings, and he drummed his fingers on the steering wheel. Roddy was staring straight ahead, the smear of blood on his forehead still wet, so River opened the glove box, found a packet of tissues, and passed it to him. Roddy took it without a word.

The lights changed, and they started moving again, heading towards the others.

. . . and becoming herself again is what's starting to happen, a long slow process, like looking for a car in an enormous car park, no idea of its make or colour, but sure it must be somewhere, and what she needs is a key fob, something she can point and hear a responding *beep*, and maybe it's the power of suggestion or maybe she actually is holding a fob, but anyway *beep* is what she's hearing now, a recurring *beep*, and this must be her car in front of her, its *beep beep* a note of welcome, and she opens its door, she opens its door, she opens her eyes.

When the figure on the bed twitched, there was someone there to see it happen. A nurse, approaching her thirteenth hour on shift. She bent over the bed, close but not too close, and waited to see if the eyes would open. They did.

'And here you are. We've been expecting you back, and here you are.'

'Mum?' said the waking woman.

I**N THE GATHERED DARK** Slough House is less visible than its neighbours, its facade a shade or two greyer, its windows twice as blank. Or that's how it seems to Catherine, who had left the pub once it became good and loud. Roddy and River had arrived, Sid too, and nobody noticed when Catherine slipped off to the bar and kept walking: into the night, along the gummed and littered pavements, across the stressful road, and round the back and through Slough House's door, which, as always, required heavy pushing. Already she can smell Lamb's presence, the damp-dog-in-a-dumpster odour of his coat wafting down the stairs. He's behind his desk, unshod, a drink in front of him, and instead of smoking is shredding an empty cigarette packet, his equivalent of a health kick. He doesn't look at Catherine when she enters.

She says, 'Do I want to know what you've done?'

'No.'

'But you've . . . burned Taverner's house down.'

'I've done what she wanted doing in the first place. But that's the first rule of fairy tales, right? Be careful what you wish for.'

'So much for diplomacy.'

'It's not always a great idea to state your intentions beforehand. It can have the effect of undermining support.'

'So instead, whatever you've done, which I'm sure we'll

discover in due course, you've involved River and Roddy in it.'

'Their choice, Standish.'

'You told them it was just a meeting.'

'Yeah. Spies lie. It's what we do.'

'And when whatever it is you've done bounces back on them?'

'Not going to happen.'

'Oh, it will. One way or the other.' She watches while he raises his glass to his lips and drains it, still without meeting her eye, while in the pub she left ten minutes ago, River and Sid have broken apart from the others, and are sharing words in the corner.

Sid says, 'What did you do?'

'Do? Nothing. I was a driver.'

River mimes holding a steering wheel, aware as he does so that he's evading; that the imaginary car he's driving might be holding true to the road, but that this conversation has already burst a tyre.

He elaborates. 'I collected Peter Judd. Took him to Di Taverner's. Then rescued Roddy, by the way. He was in a state.'

They glance towards the others, and Roddy is clearly still in a state, inasmuch as he is not currently beating his chest or standing on a table. Every so often he rubs his arm, but that's as grandiose as he's getting.

Sid says, 'And what happened at Taverner's? What happened to Judd?'

'I have no idea. I didn't enter the house.' River knows he sounds like he's entering a defence, but it's too late to do anything about that. He says, 'Sid, whatever it is, it's over. And Roddy wiped the local cameras. I might as well not have been there.'

'Sure,' she says, 'if you take away accidental phone footage. Eye witnesses. Passing drones. But the bigger point is, why was

Lamb so keen on killing the cameras if all he was doing was having a chat? And the even bigger point . . .'

He waits.

'I asked you not to. I asked you not to fall in with whatever Lamb had going on.'

'I'm sorry.'

'But you did it anyway.'

'Yes, for Louisa. And Ash.'

'CC died, by the way.'

'Did he? Oh. I mean . . .'

'This whole thing, this world, Spook Street. I don't want to be here any more. I don't want you to be part of it either. It'll kill us.'

'I was driving, it wasn't dangerous—'

'It'll kill *us*.'

'I'm gone, anyway, aren't I?' he says. 'Not a slow horse any more, remember? Failed the medical.'

But Sid just shakes her head, and seems to be looking into a different future. 'When did anything like that stop Lamb getting what he wants?'

He reaches for her hand, but she pulls away and heads back to the others, asking, 'Where did Catherine go?', but no one knows.

She's in Lamb's room, where Lamb is pouring another drink, and as so often has produced a second glass from his desk drawer, rinsed since it last saw action. He places this her side of the desk, and adds a finger of Talisker. Catherine watches without watching; she sees it happen, but pretends she does not. *If you gave in, what would he do? Watch you drink? Or slap it out of your hand?*

She says, 'You got Devon Welles to help you. I thought he was in Emma Flyte's mould.'

'Well, they changed the colour coding.'

'Straight as an arrow is what I meant. How did you get him to fall in with whatever you just did?'

'We've all got buttons. You just have to know which one to press.'

'And you pressed his and used his better nature against him. Because that's what you do.'

Lamb looks thoughtfully into his glass, and says, 'Well, you could say it's his fault for having a better nature to begin with.'

Though right this moment Devon's better nature is swamped by Devon's second thoughts, because noise is starting to happen, and Devon can hear it buzz. He has just received a call from work requesting a status update on Judd — the subject, apparently, of an anonymous call to the Met — and is making a retrospective note about his final call with his former client. *PJ indicated that he would be at home the remainder of the night, and had no need of a security detail.* This will go on Devon's client contact record, and he will go on repeating it until it becomes the truth, or at any rate, obscures what had previously been the truth. As for Lamb's visit to his office, he has already mentioned to the couple on the front desk what that was about: that Lamb was Louisa Guy's former employer; Louisa Guy, whom Devon had offered a job, but who was no longer in a position — Lamb had informed him — to accept it.

Emma, he thinks, would not approve.

Emma, though, will never know.

But Devon himself will be a while forgetting.

Catherine says, 'I had a wasp in my flat the other day.'

'God,' says Lamb, 'I hope this is a metaphor. I bloody love metaphors.'

'And it refused to leave through the open windows, so I rolled up a newspaper and whapped it. Only I didn't whap it as hard as I should have done, so there I was. In my flat with a wasp, except now it was angry instead of just sleepy.'

Lamb raises his glass, studies it, then licks a finger on his free hand and rubs at a mark on the rim. He says, 'That explains your sore arm yesterday morning.'

'I didn't say I had a sore arm.'

'And what this shit is about, your angry wasp story, it's your way of asking whether Taverner is a mess on a windowsill, or is she about to get middle-aged on our arses.'

'Medieval.'

'Yeah? I was worried she'll shower us with leaflets on prostate cancer.' He drinks: a refined sip by his standards, in that he swallows merely half his glass's contents. 'In answer to your question, Taverner currently has more on her mind than who to sting. I didn't use a rolled-up newspaper, and I didn't miss.'

It's certainly true that Taverner has much to occupy her, having arrived home to find two Metropolitan police officers on her doorstep, alerted by an anonymous tip-off to the possibility that a violent event has occurred on the premises; a possibility that recedes as they watch her manage the front door's security system, and reconfigures when they find the body in her sitting room. Within the hour, the three of them – four if you count Judd – have been joined by a travelling circus of concerned professionals, and a jurisdictional tussle is taking place between the Dogs and the Met, a tussle the latter wins partly through force of numbers, but largely because Diana herself takes no part in it. Instead, she sits in her dark garden and smokes a cigarette donated by a young policewoman, and looks – as one of her Dogs notices – almost unnaturally calm. As if she doesn't much care what happens next, he reckons. Funny thing is – he also reckons – this makes her look younger.

While she sits and smokes she is also turning over in her hand a small plastic object the Dog decides is a micro-cassette tape, the kind that sometimes crops up in eighties movies. And when the time comes for a change of location, and Diana Taverner is ushered from her house to a waiting police car, she presumably carries this with her, for all she leaves on the garden table is one cigarette butt, its filter lipstick-kissed. He wonders about tidying this away, before sensibly deciding that it's not his business.

Catherine says, 'So whatever you've done involved force.'

Lamb shrugs. 'You've got to be cruel,' he says.

'To be kind,' Catherine completes.

'What you on about?' He opens his desk drawer with his socked foot – just barely socked; his sock is a holy nightmare – then shuts it again. Opens it, shuts it. He's not looking for anything, Catherine decides; he is merely keeping time to whatever beat occupies his mind.

She says, 'And whatever it is, it'll be causing ructions now.'

Lamb considers this. 'Probably spoilt a few evenings round Westminster way,' he concedes.

Among them that of the prime minister, who has been called from his dining table, swiftly briefed, and is now cloistered with his security minister, Dominic Belwether, who already knows as much or more than the PM, but nevertheless has to listen to him rehearse the following: 'So. We have a former Home Secretary shot dead by a gun belonging to First Desk, in First Desk's home. The gun was found in her safe, which is electronically sealed – not like a burglar could have put his hands on it, even if a burglar could have got into the house, which has a state-of-the-art security system. And we don't even want to mention motive. I presume you've received the same email I did?'

The email which Peter Judd had timed to transmit at 10 p.m., containing details of his dealings with Diana Taverner.

Belwether nods.

'Any truth in it?'

'It's not public knowledge, but insider chat says Judd received backing from Chinese sources,' says Belwether. 'Start-up capital for his public relations firm, and other funds since.'

'State sources?'

'Officially, no. For what that's worth. And whether any of it ever went Taverner's way, we don't know, but it's possible. As for the suggestion that she used such funding to finance an assassination on Russian soil, well. That will require . . . investigation.'

'But your thoughts?'

'There have been rumours.'

'Christ.'

'And then there's last night's events, which we've kept out of the papers, but clearly Taverner knew about. If she didn't in fact orchestrate them.'

The PM says, 'Christ,' again. Then: 'How many people know about that?'

'One fewer now.'

'Yes, thank you, Dominic, levity is what I need. Are we seriously looking at charging First Desk with murder? It would be a bloodbath.'

'We're a long way off a murder charge. But she'll be the focal part of the investigation.'

'And there's no chance we're looking at suicide?'

After all, there have, in recent years, been bodies found in fastened luggage, in shallow graves, in securely knotted bondage, all of which have been determined to be inventively pursued suicides; proof, if proof were needed, that even at the outer reaches of despair, the mind can be curiously resourceful as to how it might find peace.

Belwether, reading his boss's mind, pauses. 'Nothing is off the table yet. I mean, the gun in the safe is a nifty trick for a corpse to pull off. But until it's been established that that was the weapon that killed him . . .'

'The thing is,' the PM says, after a further interval of reflection, 'it would be highly undesirable should an investigation of First Desk's . . . activities reveal anything that might damage our government.'

'This government?' Belwether pauses. 'We haven't done anything yet. Have we?'

Anything wrong, he presumably means.

Instead of answering directly, the PM asks, 'Where is she now?'

'Paddington Green.'

'Do we know if she was carrying . . . anything of interest?'

'Such as?'

The PM says, 'A micro-cassette tape.'

'Not,' says Belwether, 'as far as I'm aware.'

The PM says nothing.

'Of course,' Belwether continues, 'we've not reached the stage where she'll have been asked to surrender articles in her possession.'

'Quite.'

There is a topic being left unaddressed, and Belwether is starting to feel his way around its edges, like a man sizing up a hedge, clippers in hand. To such a man, the existence of an article like a micro-cassette tape, contents unknown, might represent a challenge: is this to be incorporated into the topiary, or clipped away, bagged and dispatched? Soon enough, he feels, the answer will make itself known.

The PM says, 'More immediately, we need someone reliable behind First Desk tomorrow morning. Someone who can pick up the reins without frightening the horses. Any obvious candidates?'

'There's Oliver Nash, he'd do as a locum. Currently chair of Limitations. He knows what's what, but . . .'

'Not one of us?'

'Oh, he's one of us, as far as that goes. He's just not particularly impressive, unless there's an inter-Service pie-eating competition scheduled. Other than that, well. There's always Claude Whelan.'

'Isn't he soiled goods?'

'He was an FUR, yes,' – and here, at the PM's raised eyebrow, Belwether elaborates: 'fuck-up resignation' – 'but that was kept off-book. So he's clean hands as far as the records show.'

'And he'll step up?'

'I'll call him now.' And Belwether stands, apparently about to leave the room and do just that, but once on his feet he hesitates. 'Sir?'

Which is an indication of serious intent: they are on first-name terms, these two.

The PM nods.

Belwether says, 'With regard to the Taverner issue. Are you familiar at all with the term "Waterproof"?'

And their conversation progresses, in an increasingly circumlocutory manner, while back in Slough House Lamb produces a cigarette from the recesses of his coat and slots it between his lips. He pats himself down, as if in imitation of a border guard performing a perfunctory body search, and when this fails to produce satisfaction looks directly at Catherine, who returns his gaze with one of her own: steady but unforthcoming. Lamb sighs, removes the cigarette from his mouth, and holds the end to the bulb of the anglepoise lamp perched on a pile of phone directories next to his desk. Soon, the cigarette begins to smoulder, filling the room with a more than usually unpleasant aroma.

Catherine shakes her head wearily. 'Don't you ever consider those around you?' she asks.

'Constantly,' says Lamb. 'How to make the bastards suffer, mostly.'

'You must be so proud.' She watches, but the process is evidently going to take time, if indeed it ever achieves fruition. 'I spoke to Molly earlier. She has a fan club on the hub.'

'Yeah, I've heard her stand-up routine has them falling off their chairs.'

She pauses. 'All done? No more legless jokes? Fine. She has

her fans, and they keep her in the loop. And apparently Al Hawke and Daisy Wessex are off radar. They might as well have turned to smoke.'

'Well, it's easier for old joes to disappear. They're not welded to their mobile phones.'

'You're not surprised.'

'All old joes have had an exit plan. Flight fund, passports, a destination in mind. Because all old joes know the sky can fall on your head.'

'I thought they were broke.'

'A flight fund's not a nest egg. You use it for one thing only.' He removes the cigarette from the bulb, and examines it. The end has blackened and is giving off smoke, but isn't precisely alight. He takes a drag anyway. His nostrils flare, but the cigarette refuses to go live.

It's a long time since I've had anywhere to walk to, he'd said, but that doesn't mean he has no flight fund. She wonders what life awaits Lamb once he's left this one behind. Beekeeping, beachcombing, barfly?

She says, 'So they're gone.'

'Not yet. They'll be holed up in an attic, waiting for their moment. When the heat dies down.'

It strikes Catherine that there was never much heat to begin with, given the shroud the Park has dropped on events, a thought not dissimilar to one Avril Potts is entertaining in Oxford. Her journey has been circuitous, involving several changes of train; an observer would think her a batty traveller, unsure of her destination, had the erratic route not established beyond doubt that there was no such observer. Alternative forms of surveillance remain possible, but she can do no more than her best. She has walked from the station, along the towpath, aware of the opportunities this offers – a push, a smothered splash, a head held under the water – but has reached the safe house undrowned and unhindered, and is currently observing it from the bus stop opposite. It has been through a minor war; the front door has been mistreated, and is swathed in police bunting, the bee-coloured tape that indicates official interest. But that interest is, for the moment, in abeyance. The door has been padlocked shut, a level of security that would delay Al or Daisy for twenty seconds or so, and as she watches, she sees — she thinks she sees — movement behind the upstairs window. *Once a place of safety is blown, erase it from your mind.* A rule that's second nature to any joe, as is the one about ignoring the rules, because they're what cause the trouble in the first place. With nowhere else to go, this place of safety might well beckon them, Avril thinks. Somewhere to lay their heads until a plan takes shape. The last place they were known to be is the last place they ought to be found, and it is possible that the upstairs movement is a draught teasing the curtain, but still, she will wait before crossing the road and putting the matter beyond doubt, for she would sooner have these last moments of uncertainty than know for sure that she will never see her friends again; know that their joint story has reached its end, and that all that is left to her now is the sense of loss that comes with looking back, the sense of loss that comes with looking forward. A bus pulls up, and the driver looks at her expectantly, but Avril waves it away. The bus departs, and leaves her standing there.

Catherine, too, is on her feet. The air in Lamb's office has grown thick with disappointed tobacco, his cigarette still refusing to catch, though it reeks more pungently with his every attempt to inhale it into life. If spies, unlike books, can be judged by their covers, now would be the perfect time to pass sentence on Jackson Lamb. But she is too tired, too many pages have been turned, and all she wants is to be alone. Besides, she has a letter to write.

At the door, she looks back. 'I may not be here in the morning,' she says.

'Yes you will,' he assures her.

She raises her eyes to heaven. 'And what makes you so certain?'

His cigarette chooses that moment to catch flame, a small orange beacon in a darkening room, and his eyes reflect its glow as he says, 'Because I can read you like a . . .'

She waits until it's clear he won't continue, then says, 'Menu? Billboard? Timetable? What?'

'Book,' says Lamb.

Acknowledgements

My thanks, as always, to publishers on different sides of the Atlantic. If things go to plan, there'll be a list of the Baskerville team a few pages hence, and I'm hugely grateful to all of them, especially Yassine, Anna-Marie, Jade, Jocasta and Sarah. To the Soho crew in the States – Bronwen Hruska, Juliet Grames, Paul Oliver and all their colleagues – renewed gratitude and ongoing friendship. And to my agent, Lizzy Kremer, and her brilliant team, especially Maddalena Cavaciuti, Orli Vogt-Vincent, Georgie Smith and Rachael Sharples, thank you for steering the bus.

Clown Town has its origins in a conversation with Stephen Lovegrove, to whom I'm profoundly grateful. This took place over dinner at the home of Lucy Atkins and John Shaw – thanks to both of them for that and much more, especially the continued feckless skiving with Lucy. And the same to Barbara Trapido, for roundly demolishing the notion that you should never meet your idols.

There's no such place as the Spooks' College, of course, though if there were, it would be fortunate to have Richard Ramage as its librarian. Richard showed me round St Antony's, Oxford, bought me lunch and plied me with music, for all of which I'm in his debt.

Speaking of librarians, they continue to offer glimmers of hope in a world otherwise in danger of surrendering to the dark. Long may their candles burn. Booksellers, too, keep the barbarians at bay, and I'm indebted to the crew at Daunt Books here in Summertown – Elizabeth, Andy, Ulric, Alice, Amie and Daniel – for fighting the good fight, and also to readers everywhere, who make the writing game possible, and to my friends and colleagues in that same game, who make it fun.

To my mum, my siblings, my in-laws, their offspring and their attachments: much love and many thanks, as always.

Finally, but also to start with, this book is for Jo – all my books are for Jo – whose love and support I hope I never take for granted. Our cats have a role to play too, of course. Without Jo, I'd write a lot less. Without Tommy and Scout, I'd write a little more. Readers can decide for themselves who to thank.

MH
Oxford
July 2025

Credits

Mick Herron and John Murray Press would like to thank everyone who helped publish *Clown Town*.

Editorial
Yassine Belkacemi
Zulekhá Afzal
Caroline Westmore

Sales
Megan Schaffer
Kyla Dean
Dominic Smith
Ian Williamson
Jess Harvey
Natasha Weninger-Kong
Kerri Logan
Sinead White
Claudine Sagoe

Publicity
Anna-Marie Fitzgerald

Marketing
Sarah Arratoon
Kate Baguley

Design
Dan Mogford
Sara Mahon

Production
Diana Talyanina

Audio
Ellie Wheeldon

Copy-editor
Hilary Hammond

Proofreader
Ross Dickinson

About the Author

Mick Herron is the #1 *Sunday Times* bestselling author of the Slough House thrillers, which have been published in over twenty-five languages and are the basis of the award-winning TV series *Slow Horses*, starring Gary Oldman as Jackson Lamb. Among his other novels are the Zoë Boehm series, also now adapted for TV starring Emma Thompson and Ruth Wilson, and the standalone novels *The Secret Hours* and *Nobody Walks*. Mick's awards include the Theakston Old Peculier Crime Novel of the Year and the CWA Gold, Steel and Diamond Daggers. A fellow of the Royal Society of Literature, he was born in Newcastle upon Tyne, and now lives in Oxford.